PRAISE FOR THE NOVELS OF ANYA BAST

WICKED ENCHANTMENT

"A superb romantic fantasy . . . Wickedly enchanting."
—*The Best Reviews*

"*Wicked Enchantment* will draw the reader in from the very start and I absolutely can't wait to read the next installment in this great new series." —*The Book Lush*

"I love Anya Bast's books. Her imagination is incredible and her ability to share the worlds she develops is out of this world . . . This book was excellent."
—*Night Owl Romance Reviews*

WITCH FURY

"Full of action, excitement, and sexy fun . . . Another delectable tale that will keep your eyes glued to every word." --*Bitten by Books*

"Hot romance, interesting characters, intriguing demons, and powerful emotions. I didn't want to put it down and now that I've finished this book, I'm ready for the next!"
—*Night Owl Romance Reviews*

WITCH HEART

"[A] fabulous tale . . . The story line is fast-paced from the onset . . . Fans will enjoy the third bewitching blast."

—*Genre Go Round Reviews*

"Smart, dangerous, and sexy as hell, the witches are more than a match for the warlocks and demons who'd like nothing more than to bring hell to earth and enslave mankind. Always an exhilarating read." —*Fresh Fiction*

"*Witch Heart* is a story that will captivate its readers. It will hook you from the first few pages and then take you on a wild ride. It is a fast-paced story but it is also a story that will make you feel emotion. Anya Bast uses words like Monet used paint. It's vibrant. It's alive. Readers will be able to see the story come to life as it just leaps out of the pages." —*Bitten by Books*

WITCH BLOOD

"Any paranormal fan will be guaranteed a Top Pick read. Anya has provided it all in this hot new paranormal series. You get great suspense, vivid characters, and a world that just pops off the pages . . . Not to be missed."

—*Night Owl Romance Reviews*

"Gritty danger and red-hot sensuality make this book and series smoking!" —*Romantic Times*

WITCH FIRE

"Deliciously sexy and intriguingly original."
—Angela Knight, *USA Today* bestselling author

"Sizzling suspense and sexy magic are sure to propel this hot new series onto the charts. Bast is a talent to watch, and her magical world is one to revisit." —*Romantic Times*

"A sensual feast sure to sate even the most finicky of palates. Richly drawn, dynamic characters dictate the direction of this fascinating story. You can't miss with Anya."
—*A Romance Review*

"Fast-paced, edgy suspense . . . The paranormal elements are fresh and original. This reader was immediately drawn into the story from the opening abduction, and obsessively read straight through to the dramatic final altercation. Bravo, Ms. Bast; *Witch Fire* is sure to be a fan favorite."
—*Paranormal Romance Reviews*

"A fabulously written ultimate romance. Anya Bast tells a really passionate story and leaves you wanting more . . . The elemental witch series will be a fantastic read."
—*The Romance Readers Connection*

"A terrific romantic fantasy starring two volatile lead characters . . . The relationship between fire and air [makes] the tale a blast to read." —*The Best Reviews*

Berkley Sensation titles by Anya Bast

WITCH FIRE
WITCH BLOOD
WITCH HEART
WITCH FURY
WICKED ENCHANTMENT
CRUEL ENCHANTMENT

Heat titles by Anya Bast

THE CHOSEN SIN

CRUEL ENCHANTMENT

ANYA BAST

BERKLEY SENSATION, NEW YORK

THE BERKLEY PUBLISHING GROUP
Published by the Penguin Group
Penguin Group (USA) Inc.
375 Hudson Street, New York, New York 10014, USA
Penguin Group (Canada), 90 Eglinton Avenue East, Suite 700, Toronto, Ontario M4P 2Y3, Canada
(a division of Pearson Penguin Canada Inc.)
Penguin Books Ltd., 80 Strand, London WC2R 0RL, England
Penguin Group Ireland, 25 St. Stephen's Green, Dublin 2, Ireland (a division of Penguin Books Ltd.)
Penguin Group (Australia), 250 Camberwell Road, Camberwell, Victoria 3124, Australia
(a division of Pearson Australia Group Pty. Ltd.)
Penguin Books India Pvt. Ltd., 11 Community Centre, Panchsheel Park, New Delhi—110 017, India
Penguin Group (NZ), 67 Apollo Drive, Rosedale, North Shore 0632, New Zealand
(a division of Pearson New Zealand Ltd.)
Penguin Books (South Africa) (Pty.) Ltd., 24 Sturdee Avenue, Rosebank, Johannesburg 2196,
South Africa

Penguin Books Ltd., Registered Offices: 80 Strand, London WC2R 0RL, England

CRUEL ENCHANTMENT

A Berkley Sensation Book / published by arrangement with the author

PRINTING HISTORY
Berkley Sensation mass-market edition / September 2010

Cover design by Rita Frangie.
Cover art by Tony Mauro.
Interior text design by Kristin del Rosario.

For information, address: The Berkley Publishing Group,
a division of Penguin Group (USA) Inc.,
375 Hudson Street, New York, New York 10014.

ISBN: 978-0-425-23637-6

BERKLEY® SENSATION
Berkley Sensation Books are published by The Berkley Publishing Group,
a division of Penguin Group (USA) Inc.,
375 Hudson Street, New York, New York 10014.
BERKLEY® SENSATION and the "B" design are trademarks of Penguin Group (USA) Inc.

PRINTED IN THE UNITED STATES OF AMERICA

10 9 8 7 6 5 4 3 2 1

For my husband. Only you.

ACKNOWLEDGMENTS

Thanks to Reece Notley, Brenda Maxfield, and my awesome agent, Laura Bradford, for doing read throughs and giving their opinions when I needed them.

Many thanks to the Bradford Bunch for always being there to offer suggestions and commiserations. You are an awesome group of ladies!

Thanks, once again, to artist Axel de Roy for creating the interactive map of Piefferburg that can be found on my website, www.anyabast.com.

ONE

EMMALINE *Siobhan Keara Gallagher.*

Clang. Clang. Clang. The shock of hammer to hot iron reverberated up his arm and through his shoulders. As Aeric shaped the hunk of iron into a charmed blade, Emmaline's name beat a staccato rhythm in his mind.

He glanced up at the portrait of Aileen, the one he kept in his forge as a reminder, and his hammer came down harder. It wasn't every night the fire of vengeance burned so hot and so hard in him. Over three hundred and sixty years had passed since the Summer Queen's assassin had murdered his love, Aileen.

Emmaline Siobhan Keara Gallagher.

He'd had plenty of time to move past his loss. Yet his rage burned bright tonight, as if it had happened three days ago instead of three hundred years. It was almost as if the object of his vengeance were close by, or thinking about him. Perhaps, as he'd imagined for so many years, he shared a psychic connection with her.

One born of cruel and violent intention.

He was certain that if the power of his thoughts truly did penetrate her mind, she had nightmares about him. If she ever thought his name, it was with a shudder and a chill.

If Aeric knew what she really looked like, he would envision her face with every downward impact of his hammer. Instead he only brought her essence to mind while forging weapons others would wield to kill, maim, and bring misery. If he could name them all, he would name them *Emmaline*.

It was the least he could do, but he wanted to do so much more. Maybe one day he would get the chance, though odds were against him. He was stuck in Piefferburg while she roamed free outside its barriers. Aileen was far from him, too, lost to the shadowy Netherworld.

He tossed the hammer aside. Sweat trickling down his bare chest and into his belly button, he turned with the red-hot length of charmed iron held in a pair of tongs and dunked it into a tub of cold water, making the iron spit and steam. As he worked the metal, his magick pulled out of him in a long, thin thread, imbuing the weapon with the ability to extract a fae's power and cause illness.

Aeric O'Malley was the Blacksmith, the only fae in the world who could create weapons of charmed iron. His father had once also possessed the same magick, but he'd been badly affected by Watt syndrome at the time of the Great Sweep. These days he wasn't fit for the forge, leaving the family tradition to Aeric.

Making these weapons every night was his ritual, one he had kept secret from all who knew him. His forge was hidden in the back of his apartment, deep at the base of the Black Tower. The former Shadow King, Aodh Críostóir Ruadhán O'Dubhuir, had been the only one who'd known about his illicit work; he'd been the one to set him up in it.

Now the Unseelie had a Shadow Queen instead of a king. She was a good queen, but one who was still finding her footing in the Black Tower. Queen Aislinn might not look kindly on the fact the Blacksmith was still producing weapons that could be used on his own people. Queen Aislinn wasn't as . . . *practical* as her foul biological father had been.

He pulled off his thick gloves and wiped the back of his arm across his sweat-soaked forehead with a groan of fatigue. The iron called to him at all hours of the day and night. Even after he had done his sacred duty riding in the Wild Hunt every night, the forge summoned him before dawn. He spent most nights fulfilling orders for illegal weaponry or sometimes just making it because he had to, because his fae blood called him to do it. As long as his magick held out, he created.

The walls of his iron world glinted silver and deadly with the products of his labor and in the middle of it all hung Aileen's portrait, the one he'd painted with his own hands so he would never forget what she looked like.

So he never forgot.

Despite the heat and grime of the room, her portrait was still pristine, even as old as it was. Angel pale and golden beautiful, she hung on the wall and gazed down at him with eyes of green, green as the grass of the country she'd died in.

His fingers curled, remembering the softness of her skin and how her silky hair had slipped over his palms and mouth. His gaze caught and lingered on the shape of her mouth. Not that he needed to commit the way she looked to memory. He remembered Aileen Arabella Edmé McIlvernock. His fiancée had looked like an angel, walked like one, thought like one . . . and made love like one. Maybe she hadn't been an angel in all ways—no, definitely not—but his memory never snagged on those jagged places. There was no point in remembering the dark, only the light. And there was no forgetting her. He never would.

Nor would he ever forget her murderer.

Emmaline had managed to escape the Great Sweep and probably Watt syndrome, too. He couldn't know for sure; he just suspected. His gut simply told him she was out there in the world somewhere and he lived for the day he would find her. She'd taken his soul apart the day she'd killed Aileen and he'd never been able to put it completely back together again.

It was only fair he should be able to take Emmaline's soul apart in return. Slowly. Piece by bloody piece.

The chances she'd walk through the gates of Piefferburg and into the web of pain that awaited her was infinitesimal, but tonight, as Aeric gazed at the portrait of Aileen, he hoped for a miracle.

Danu help Emmaline if she ever did cross that threshold into Piefferburg.

He'd be waiting.

THE fae checked in, but they never checked out. It was a fae roach motel. Did she really want to cross that threshold and possibly end up a squashed bug? No, of course not. Problem was, she had no choice.

Emmaline Siobhan Keara Gallagher stared at the outer gates of Piefferburg. Was she really ready to take this risk? After all she'd done, all the years and energy she'd committed to the cause, she still shuddered at the thought of going in there for fear she may never come out.

She stared at the hazy warding that guarded the fae from the human world, set a few inches out from a thick, tall brick wall. The wall didn't go all the way around Piefferburg, since the detention compound—*resettlement area* was the more PC term—was enormous and the borders included not only marshlands, where a wall could not be built, but the ocean, too. It was the Phaendir's warding that kept the fae imprisoned, not that thick wall. That was there only for the eye of the humans. An almost organic thing, the warding existed in a subconscious, hive portion of the Phaendir's collective mind—fueled by their breath, thoughts, magick and, most of all, by their very strong belief system.

That warding was unbreakable.

Or so it was thought.

"Emily?"

She jumped, startled. Emmaline turned at the name the Phaendir knew her by, something close enough to her real name to make it comfortable. Well, as comfortable as she could be while undercover in a nest of her mortal enemies. That didn't exactly make every day a picnic.

Schooling her expression and double-checking her glamour—she was paranoid about keeping it in place—she turned with a forced smile. "Brother Gideon, you frightened me."

His thin lips pursed and he smoothed his thinning brown hair over his head, favoring her with a glance that anyone who didn't know him would call nervous. Emmaline, of all people, knew better. Gideon was confident, dangerous. The face he presented to the world was one calculated to make people underestimate him.

Brother Gideon was average in every way possible—medium brown hair, average height and build, unremarkable brown eyes, weak chin, receding hairline. A person walking by him on the street would glance at him and immediately dismiss him as nonthreatening. In reality, Brother Gideon was the most menacing of all the Phaendir, a black mamba in a cave filled with rattlers. While you were busy overlooking and underestimating him, he'd be busy killing you. That's what made him extra dangerous.

It was no secret that Gideon was nursing a crush on her. She'd been carefully fostering that crush for quite some time now, using it as an effective tool. It wasn't a pleasant or easy thing, having a man as vicious as Brother Gideon admiring her. It was, however, a useful thing. Useful to the HFF—Humans for the Freedom of the Fae—an organization to which she'd dedicated her life.

"I'm sorry, Emily," he replied in his very average light tenor of a voice. "I didn't mean to startle you. I just saw you standing out here and wanted to see you off."

A little over a year ago Brother Gideon had attempted a coup. He'd tried to obtain the Book of Bindings before Brother Maddoc, the Archdirector of the Phaendir, could do it. Emmaline was certain it had been a move to take over Maddoc's place. Brother Gideon strove very hard to implement his much bloodier agenda for dealing with the fae and he needed that top spot to put it into action.

Luckily Gideon had been caught and punished by being demoted four places in the Phaendir power structure. But Maddoc should have killed him. During the last year, two of the Phaendir who occupied spots above Gideon had met their ends in freak, horrific accidents. The murders had been brilliantly executed and no one could prove Gideon had anything to do with the deaths. Emmaline had no doubt he was behind them.

Maddoc needed to watch his back.

The prospect of having Gideon leading the Phaendir made her mission more critical. It even made her fingers itch for her old crossbow and it took a hell of a lot for that to happen. If anyone needed a quarrel through the throat, it was Brother Gideon. Maddoc needed killing, too, but he was several shades less threatening.

She forced a smile. "And I'm so glad you did."

"Are you sure you're ready for this?"

"I may be human, but in my heart, I'm Phaendir. I live to serve."

Gideon smiled and she fought the urge to vomit on her hiking boots.

She looked away from him, up at the hazy warding. Gideon thought she was human and a human wouldn't be able to see the warding, so she motioned to the wall. "It's immense and so . . . strong." She made sure she glanced at Gideon with a shy smile as she said the last. "It's a beautiful thing, this place the Phaendir have created to keep us safe." She used the reverent tone of the Worshipful Observer that Gideon believed she was.

Gideon came to stand near her and clasped his thin, pale hands in front of him. "Labrai wills it so." He paused. "As He wills your entry into Piefferburg and your eventual success. You're a woman with a strong, stable character. You're destined to do well."

She wanted to laugh. *A strong, stable character*. Right. Her characters were so layered even she had trouble parsing them. She was a fae HFF member currently undercover as a human Worshipful Observer who was soon going undercover as a member of the *Faemous* TV show crew in order to mine information for the Phaendir while actually working a mission for the HFF.

Yeah. Not confusing at all.

It was an event that would ironically blow *all* her covers, bringing her back to what she really was. A free fae.

As if she wasn't already bewildered enough.

Danu and all the gods, why was she going into Piefferburg of her own free will? She swallowed hard. *The Blacksmith* was in there. She had nightmares about coming face-to-face with him often enough to warrant a prescription for Xanax.

And hell, she was *seeking him out*. He was the only one who could help the HFF at this point. How crazy was that? He wanted to kill her . . . maybe. Probably.

Maybe.

It had been so long—over three hundred and sixty years—since the night she'd killed Aileen Arabella Edmé McIlvernock. She didn't even know if Aeric had survived Watt syndrome, though she hoped he had. If he hadn't survived, and if there was no other fae who could forge a charmed iron key, they were all doomed. She knew Aeric's father also had the talent, but he'd been one of the first fae to come down with Watt syndrome. At the time she'd left Ireland, he'd been very ill and not expected to live.

She wasn't sure about his father, but she felt it in her blood that Aeric O'Malley had survived. She could feel him in there, within the boundaries of Piefferburg. Almost as if he was waiting for her. She shivered. That couldn't be possible, of course; it was only her vivid imagination.

And he wasn't the only one who might be thirsting for her blood. Once upon a time, when she'd been the Summer Queen's greatest weapon in the Seelie war against the Unseelie, she'd burned some bridges. Many, many bridges. There were those in the Black Tower who would love to cross the charred ruins of those very bridges . . . to strangle her.

Danu, she hoped her glamour was strong enough to fool the Blacksmith. If the illusion slipped, if he found out who she really was, her life was as good as gone. If *any* of the Unseelie found out who she was . . .

Or if the Summer Queen found out . . .

Or Lars, the Summer Queen's barely leashed pit bull . . .

Emmaline shuddered. Once she was in Piefferburg, she would have to go to the Rose Tower and check in as part of the *Faemous* film crew. From there she'd have to find a way to get over to the Black Tower to find Aeric.

She shivered. *The Rose*. She wished she didn't have to step foot in it. At least she could avoid the Summer Queen, who likely thought the *Faemous* crew beneath her notice. There was no way she was voluntarily going anywhere near the woman who'd screwed up her life so much and, via Lars, planted nightmares in her subconscious that put the ones she had about the Blacksmith to shame.

Gods, why was she doing this again? Oh, right, because she was the only one who could. *Damn it*.

"Emily? Are you nervous?"

She blinked and glanced at Gideon, pulling herself back from the muck of her thoughts. For a moment, she groped for something plausible to respond with. "Well, a little. I've heard the stories about the goblins." Humans were terrified of goblins, though as a fae she didn't swallow the boogeyman tales. There were other races that were much more terrifying and, honestly, their religion was quite nice. "I saw the bodies of the Phaendir you sent in after the book—"

He waved his hand, not wanting to take that conversational road. He'd sent Phaendir into Piefferburg last year to retrieve the Book of Bindings and the men had returned gnawed upon. "You'll be fine. You're going to the Seelie Court, to the Rose Tower. They're much more hospitable to humans than the Unseelie. No goblins there, only the tamer breed of hobgoblin and a few brownies. They're servants, mostly."

She smiled. "I know I'll be fine. You would never let me come to harm, would you, Brother Gideon?"

He smiled at her and she suppressed another shudder. There was lust in his eyes—a thing no woman wanted directed at her by him. "Never."

"Anyway, like I said, I'm ready to sacrifice my life for the cause of the Phaendir."

Gideon took her hands in his. His skin was papery feeling, dry. On his wrists, she could feel the start of the scars that marked his arms, chest, and back. Brother Gideon flagellated himself every day in the name of Labrai, though Emmaline had long suspected he enjoyed the floggings with his wicked cat-o'-nine tails. "But I am not willing to sacrifice your life, Emily. Not for anything." He blinked watery brown eyes.

"Oh, Gideon," she said in a practiced, slightly breathy voice. "Your piousness is already so attractive and to know you actually care about me as a person is so . . . moving." She didn't melt against him or bat her eyelashes, but she did stare adoringly into his eyes.

"Shh, I understand. I only hope that one day—"

"Brother Gideon? Emily?" It was Archdirector Maddoc's voice coming from behind them.

Gideon gritted his teeth for a moment. His face—just for a heartbeat—made the transformation from medium to monster. Veins stood out in his forehead and neck. His skin went pale and his eyes bulged. He dropped her hands and moved away from her, his natural, unassuming visage back in place in a matter of seconds. Just the glimpse of Gideon's true self was enough to leave Emmaline shaky, a reaction that luckily worked for this particular situation.

The tension in the air between Gideon and Maddoc ratcheted upward. Power struggles within the structure of the group seemed to permeate all their interactions. Then, of course, there was the carefully orchestrated charade she'd been performing for Gideon to make things worse—making Gideon believe she was sleeping with his archenemy.

As undercover HFF, it was her job to throw wrenches into the best of the Phaendir's machines and she was good at her job.

"Are you ready?" asked Brother Maddoc with a warm smile. Brother Maddoc was annoyingly likable, considering he was Phaendir. With him, you got what you saw on the surface. Trouble was, he hated the fae. Not as much as Gideon hated the fae, but enough to want to keep them imprisoned forever.

Her smile flickered. "No."

Maddoc laughed and pulled her against him for a hug. "Don't worry, you're all set up. They're expecting you at the Rose Tower as the newest addition to the *Faemous* crew. Just go in like you're a real anchor and start snooping around for information about the *bosca fadbh*. I don't think I need to impress upon you how important a job this is, Emily."

Except it wasn't her real job.

She knew all about the *bosca fadbh*, and what *she* needed concerning the valuable puzzle box would be found nowhere near the Seelie Court. The fae already had one piece of the box. The second piece, the one the HFF was trying to get, was halfway around the world, off the coast of Atlit, Israel. It just sucked that the only man capable of helping the HFF get that piece was stuck in Piefferburg.

She laid her head on Maddoc's shoulder, an action that made Gideon shuffle his feet and cough as he tried to conceal his irritation and jealousy. "I won't let you down, Brother Maddoc."

"I know." He smiled and kissed her temple. "Now go. They're ready to let you in."

She turned toward the heavy wrought-iron gates that separated Piefferburg and most of the world's fae from the fragile human world. The huge doors opened with a groan and all the heavy protocol that went with the admission of individuals began. On this side of the gate things were monitored by the Phaendir. On the other side of the gate, all deliveries or people passing through were carefully inspected by the fae and all arrivals reported to both towers.

Of course neither side trusted the other. The fae exerted what little control they had by checking to make sure no Phaendir entered—some had tried; all had been brutally killed. The Phaendir, of course, would not allow any fae to leave. Humans could come and go at their own peril. Not many did. Only the very brave and the very stupid dared cross into the land of the fae.

Or the very desperate. That would be her.

Glancing back at Gideon and Maddoc and shooting them

a look of uncertainty she didn't have to feign, she stepped past the gates.

Surely the Blacksmith wouldn't recognize her under her powerful glamour. Surely she would be safe from his wrath. If she could fool all of the Phaendir, she could fool one fae. Even if somehow he did recognize her, hundreds of years had passed since that unfortunate day and her errand was of monumental importance to his people.

Surely this would turn out all right.

TWO

THE scents of lavender and chamomile immediately enveloped her as the heavy gates behind her clanked shut. She held up her hands as two red caps approached her. They didn't carry guns, but they didn't need to. Built like two bald linebackers on steroids, they could snap her in two with minimal effort. Their heads were dyed a bright red, a constant reminder that they needed to kill periodically to survive. In Piefferburg they did that in a controlled setting, in games that echoed the days of gladiators.

She was pretty sure she never wanted to attend.

"My name is Emily Millhouse," she said. "I'm here as an addition to the *Faemous* film crew in the Rose Tower."

She couldn't exactly say, "Hey, y'all, my name is Emmaline Siobhan Keara Gallagher and I'm a three-hundred-and-eighty-year-old pure-blood Seelie Tuatha Dé with abilities in glamour so powerful that I can easily make you think I'm human. Oh, by the way, I'm on your side."

No, as far as these fae were concerned, she was going with the first of her covers. No sense in alarming twitchy magickal trigger fingers. She needed to make sure she could get back out of Piefferburg. The thought of being trapped here forever was enough to bring a touch of bile to the back of her throat.

"Show your identity card," ordered the one on her left with a heavy Scottish accent.

Slowly, she pulled her pack from her shoulder and fished out her wallet from the front pouch. The red cap on her right took her pack and rifled through it, then he patted her down. Once they'd inspected her false I.D., they gave all her things back to her.

As she arranged her wallet, one of the red-skulled power twins spoke. "From this point on, you're on your own. Humans who enter Piefferburg take their safety into their own hands. Do you understand? Human law doesn't apply in here."

She pulled her pack over her shoulders and nodded. "I understand."

"You sure you don't want a car? It's a long walk to the city."

"No, I told them I'd rather walk."

His lips drew back in a smile to reveal pointed teeth. It jarred her a little. Clearly she'd been with humans for too long. "Good luck." He pointed down the dirt road that would lead her into the city. "Stay on the path until you hit Piefferburg City."

Follow the Yellow Brick Road. Man, she hoped there weren't any flying monkeys.

She nodded, hitched her pack higher on her shoulders, and took off. Time to get this show started. Her boots crunched on the dirt as she made her way in. It would be a good few miles, according to the map she'd looked at, before she reached the outskirts of the huge main city.

It was early spring, but it was a warm morning. She would take this time to collect her thoughts and commune with this land that was closest to that of her homeland, Ireland, just from the fact it was occupied by her people.

Piefferburg was a large territory, home to every type of fae imaginable. Sort of like a big, very deadly zoo. These were the Boundary Lands, where the wilding fae lived, the ones that preferred the forest glens, tree groves, freshwater lakes, and treetops. Mostly they kept to themselves, forming their own society apart from the rest. Like the goblins did. Also the water-dwelling fae—the selkies, Untunktahe, kelpie, sirens, and the rest—who mostly resided in the eastern part of Piefferburg, where the ocean met land.

Not far from the gates of Piefferburg was the city. There she would find the Rose and Black Towers and the trooping fae, the work-a-day fae who lived all over Piefferburg, in both the city and the rural areas. The troop idolized the Seelie and the Unseelie for reasons she would never understand. The Seelie Tuatha Dé, especially, were like royalty.

Having avoided the Great Sweep thanks to her ability to cloak her true nature so well, she really only knew these things academically. She'd left Ireland, and the fae world, when she was only twenty years old. Walking through these enchanted woods now, with the pollen dancing through the air, the shimmering lights of nearby wilding fae winking in the foliage, and the low hum and sing of magick in the air around her—it healed her soul. Sprae, the tiniest of her fae brethren, minuscule beings that provided magickal energy to the forest, flocked to her, lighting on her arms, hands, and face. It was like being welcomed home.

Smiling, she took a deep breath of her environment into her lungs and held it there for a long moment. Her mission was critical, but she could take a moment to put aside her fears and relax here, among her kind.

It had been too long. She barely remembered what it was to be fae—what she was under the layers of illusion she'd donned. It was good to be here. She didn't regret a bit not ordering a car to come for her at the gates, even though the walk would not be doing her leg muscles any favors tomorrow morning.

She blinked, glimpsing something down the road that didn't fit with her natural surroundings. Someone striding through the dappled sunlight and pollen-laden air. A man. A large, muscular man walking with purpose toward her. He carried something in his hand, but she couldn't quite make it out.

Her pace slowing, she watched him approach, seeing something intangibly familiar in the way he moved and the broad set of his shoulders. Who was this man? What was he doing way out here? His posture and the way he strode toward her seemed vaguely threatening. Suddenly she wished for a weapon. She usually carried one—old habits died hard—but she hadn't brought any into Piefferburg with her.

He strode on heavy boots and wore black pants and a white poet's shirt that would've made any other man but him look feminine. His long, dusky blond hair was pulled partway back at his nape, free tendrils moving around a face so heartbreakingly beautiful in a savage, brutal way it made her want to cry. Strong, clefted chin; full lips; dark brown eyes. His build peeked out at the collar of the poet's shirt—strong and muscled from hard work—wide shoulders, narrow hips, the fabric of his pants clinging to the thighs of an athlete.

Or of a blacksmith.

The man's identity slammed into her like a freight train, stealing all the rational thought in her head and transforming it into perfect shock. In some faraway part of her brain, she realized she'd halted on the road, bits of floating pollen and sprae caught in her hair, watching the vision approach her. The sight of him arrested her, made her remember him from so many hundreds of years before. He hadn't changed.

Neither had how he made her feel when she looked at him.

"I know you," said Aeric Killian Riordan O'Malley. The words came out harsh, angry, lashed with raw power, just the same way his magnificent body moved. His voice was laced with the remnants of an Irish accent that years in Piefferburg hadn't been able to wash away. "*Emmaline Siobhan Keara Gallagher*. The Summer Queen's assassin. The woman with the crossbow."

Danger. There was danger here. He shouldn't know her. Hell, he shouldn't even *be here*.

How did he know her? *She was glamoured.*

Her feet twitched and she glanced at the forest near her. Her survival center—an exceptionally strong part of herself—screamed *run*. Suddenly she was a mouse to a lion, prey to predator. Her intellect won out and she tamped down the fight-or-flight response, lifting her face to him. Still, the need to lie—to cover her true identity in the face of his brutal wrath—was overwhelming. "I'm not who you think I am."

And that was true enough.

He grabbed her by her collar and shook her like a dog. "I know you."

She yelped. "You don't know me!"

"I do." He bared white teeth in a grimace. "I've been waiting for you. For hundreds of years, *Emmaline Siobhan Keara Gallagher*, I have been dreaming of the day you would reenter my life." By saying her whole name he was reminding her of the power he held over her.

She shook her head. "No, you don't understand. Let me explain—"

"Shut up!"

Her gaze flicked down to his hand. The thing she couldn't make out from a distance was a burlap bag.

She knew what that was for. She'd used one just like it more than once.

Her survival instincts finally cut through the shock. She brought the flat of her hand up, aiming for his nose. She got his chin instead, but it worked. Teeth knocking hard, he grunted and released her, turning away with his hand to his mouth. She was free.

Pressing her advantage, she whirled on the ball of her foot and kicked up high, catching him in the jaw with her hiking boot. He staggered to the side and she set up for another kick, knowing there was no other way to deal with a man of this size. Fists just wouldn't do it. Kicks and hits to tender parts of the anatomy just might.

He blocked her foot and pushed. She staggered to the side, almost landing on her ass in the dirt. He came at her and she whirled to the left, narrowly missing his enraged grasp. She danced away from him, but he was too fast. He grabbed her upper arm and she brought the flat of her palm up again, this time hitting pay dirt. Blood exploded from his nose and he yelped in pain.

Totally intending to hit a man while he was down, she set up for another kick, this one aimed at his kidney. That would send him down for a while. Midway through her turn, he swept her leg out from under her. She went down hard on her side, her breath *oof*ing out of her. He was on her in a second, blood dripping into her face. The burlap bag slammed down over her head and he knotted it at her neck.

A moment of pure panic arrested her breath in her throat. Sharp memories scratched and ripped at her mind.

She exploded in a frenzied attempt to yank it off, but his arms closed around her midsection, pinning her arms to her sides and holding her down on the road. The inside of the bag smelled sweet. She knew what it was—Kass, a Norwegian fae herbal concoction that would knock her out if she breathed enough of it in. It was an old trick, one she'd used herself a time or two.

She held her breath, but he just waited her out. Finally, compelled to take a deep breath, everything went black.

HE still couldn't believe it.

Sinking down onto the floor of his forge, he watched her lying on her side, still unconscious from the Kass.

Long ago, when the days of Piefferburg were still young, he'd befriended Ronan Quinn. Ronan was an Unseelie mage with unique abilities born from his mixed fae and Phaendir parentage. Ronan had put in place a web to trap this woman if she ever set foot on fae ground. The moment her boot had hit the earth past the gates, complete awareness of her presence had flooded Aeric's body and mind—bowing his spine, snapping his head back, and making him bellow until his throat was raw.

Now, on the floor of his forge, she lay with one arm thrown over her head and the other flopping behind her. He'd parked his motorcycle not far down the road from where he'd found her on the road to Piefferburg City. Once he'd collected her, blood streaming from his nose, he'd put her on the back of his bike and driven her through the Boundary Lands and down city side streets to the back of the Black Tower, uncaring who saw him. Apparently no one of consequence had, since he'd yet to have a knock at his door from someone inquiring about the prisoner in his apartment.

Hundreds of years of wishing and here she was in front of him.

He tipped his head to the side, the loose tendrils of his hair falling over his cheek. She was not what he remembered, not at all what he'd ever imagined, with her shoulder-length red hair, bright green eyes, slender stature, innocent face.

Of course she was probably still glamoured, even in unconsciousness. He was not looking at the true Emmaline now, so fragile and slight on the concrete floor. He had to remember that. This was false glamour, the glamour she always wore, the only thing she knew how to be—a fraud.

The Emmaline he remembered was a monster, an assassin. Working for the Summer Queen during the fae wars, she had used her skill with personal glamour to kill more Unseelie nobles than the entire Black Army had managed to slaughter. Slipping into the Unseelie Court, she'd seduced and murdered more than her fair share of men, all the while lusting after him—the Blacksmith. Her crush had been known to him, as it had been known to all.

Back then he'd wanted nothing to do with her. He had his Aileen, his soul mate and perfect match. He was engaged to marry her and would have shared in the time-honored tradition of Joining Vows with her. Never had he imagined the depths of Emmaline's obsession. He'd underestimated her and it had changed his life forever.

He would not underestimate her now. He would not buy into the fragile, innocent guise she wore. Emmaline was going to pay for what she'd done to Aileen—slowly, thoroughly, and mercilessly. Though, he mused as he touched his sore nose, she'd started things off by making him pay. It was sheer luck his nose hadn't been broken. He hadn't seen stars like that in a long time.

She roused, grimacing. Bowing in on herself, she curled into a fetal position, pressing the palm of her hand into her eye socket. He'd used a none-too-gentle herbal concoction to divest her quickly of her consciousness so she wouldn't fight him. She'd be feeling the effects of sickness from the Kass as she woke.

Her red hair curled around her head and narrow shoulders as she writhed, groaning. One green eye popped open, cast about, focused on him, then widened. She scrambled upward and crab-walked back into the wall behind her, staring at him. "You can't do this," she rasped.

His lips parted in a mirthless smile. He sat against a wall, one arm draped over his knee. "I can—and will—do anything I want. Go ahead and scream." He motioned lazily around his forge. "This place is secret and completely soundproofed. The only man who ever knew of this place has gone to dance with the sluagh, so he's not talking. No one will answer your cries for help. It's just you and me, baby."

She raised a hand as if to stave him off. "Aeric, I know you must hate me—"

He raised an eyebrow and that action alone seemed to arrest the breath in her throat. She was frightened of him. Good. She should be. "Hate you? Emmaline, what I feel for you goes far beyond hate. I have nursed a cold, undying passion for your torture and eventual death for the last three hundred and sixty years. I have cultivated it in my heart. Nurtured it. Caressed it. Fed it. It's not *hatred* that I feel for you. It's something much worse."

"But you don't understand what happened the night Aileen died, and you don't know why I'm here now." She shook her head as if trying to get it to stop ringing and put a hand to her temple. It was the Kass; he knew she must have a hell of a headache right now. "You have to listen to me, Aeric. I came to find you because you're the only one who can help. What I have to tell you now goes beyond anything I may have done in the past. My mission is too important. To you. To your people. *Our* people."

Lies. Always with the lies, the illusion, and the deceit.

Rage burned through his veins like acid. Roaring, he lunged to his feet and charged at her. Going down on his knees, he pinned her to the wall with his hands on her upper arms. She tried her best to melt into the concrete wall behind her and turned her face away from his, her hair curtaining her cheek and eye. Her breath came short and shallow. He scented the fear coming off her in waves.

"No," he whispered near her ear. "You will not speak. You killed my soul when you murdered Aileen. You destroyed my future. You *did* kill her, didn't you? You can't deny that."

She swallowed hard and nodded. "I killed her."

"You shot her with one of your fucking trademark assassin crossbow bolts, one with a poisoned tip."

She let out a shuddering sigh. "I did. But—"

"Then there is no misunderstanding here. There are no *buts*. You will pay for your crimes at my hands. Consider it your past catching up with you. Consider it karma. You must have always known that eventually the bill for your sins would come due." His voice was low, silky, dangerous sounding even to his own ears. "You're mine," he murmured near her ear, making her shudder. "Every inch of you. Prepare to suffer."

"You won't hurt me." Her voice shook, revealing her uncertainty about that statement. "You're a good man."

He bared his teeth at her. "Maybe once, long ago, I was a good man. That man died with Aileen."

She shook her head. "No. No, you're still a good man, Aeric. I know you are. You always were and always will be. The essential core of a person never changes."

He leaned in closer and snarled into her face, "Then what does that say about you?"

Her breath hitched in the back of her throat.

He remained that way, intimidating her with his voice, breath, and body. Then, slamming the flat of his hand against the wall by her head and making her jump, he lurched to his feet, spun on his heel, and strode from the room, locking the door behind him.

EMMALINE let out a long, slow breath, her eyes wide. Slumping, she slid down the wall and rested on her side, trying to calm the thumping of her heart. Every single one of her irrational fears had come true.

No, *worse*.

She'd expected that if the Blacksmith recognized her there would be conflict between them. Hundreds of years ago, she had killed his fiancée—but clearly he was not correctly apprised of the circumstances surrounding that death. It was, of course, her own damn fault he wasn't aware of what really happened. She'd tried to protect him and now she was paying the price.

No good deed ever went unpunished.

Shaking, she pushed up and looked around. Immediately her gaze caught on the portrait of the woman in question hanging above the cold forge. Aileen had looked like an angel in real life and his painting had encompassed that same aura of her. Clearly he had kept Aileen as an angel in his heart as well—and Emmaline as the demon who'd killed her.

Which, needless to say, would not bode well for her—or for the objective she'd come here to accomplish.

She closed her eyes, resting her head back against the wall. And the Phaendir—they were probably the least of her worries at the moment, seeing as how she was prisoner to a man who wanted to torture and kill her slowly, but they were still a worry. When she didn't show up at the Seelie Court and report in under her guise as part of the *Faemous* crew, they would be suspicious. The cover she'd cultivated for so many years was now in serious jeopardy and she was in risk of being exposed as a fae and locked in Piefferburg forever.

Of course, the upside was that her life here would apparently be short.

A crazy bubble of laughter escaped from her throat and echoed through the cold, concrete room. She bet this place wasn't always cold, though. It looked like a well-used space, somewhere Aeric still regularly produced charmed iron weaponry. At night it likely glowed with heat and steam, if the glinting iron weapons on the walls were any indication.

She looked around, her misplaced laughter dying. All kinds of weapons surrounded her now—ones she wouldn't hesitate to use to defend herself with. Why hadn't he bothered to restrain her? She'd been an assassin, after all. He must know that she could use those weapons very well.

If she tried to injure him with them, she'd need to be careful. She studied the axes, frowning. After all, if she hurt him too badly, he wouldn't be able to make the key she'd come here for. If she went for his thigh, she might be able to wound him enough to defang him and be able to talk some sense into him.

He really should've restrained her.

Of course, he probably knew she was capable with an ax or knife but still wasn't concerned. She was like a reed stalk compared to his tree trunk. Even with training, the thought that she could wield any kind of weapon against a man of his size and strength was laughable. He'd just snap her in two and throw her away. Weapons weren't even an issue.

How he hated her.

The knowledge burned in her gut like acid, even after all these years. Gods, she'd been in love with him. She'd never burned for a man the way she'd burned for Aeric Killian Riordan O'Malley. He was the most caring, intelligent, attractive man she'd ever known. Even though he was Unseelie and she was true blood, pristine—albeit orphaned and penniless—Seelie, she'd wanted him. But she'd respected his relationship with Aileen and kept her crush—obsession—on the sideline, though she'd always been embarrassed that her adoration had been so apparent.

And she'd never meant to kill Aileen. Oh, Danu, never.

But she had killed her. She could still feel the warm, tacky blood on her hands, even after so many hundreds of years. She could still feel the horror of what she'd done spreading over her and the way she'd chanted *no no no no no no* in her head as she watched the bloodstain spread over the white sheets and the life leak slowly from the woman. She'd wanted to take back the bolt she'd shot.

She knew she'd destroyed Aeric that night, known she was doomed at his hands if she stayed around, no matter the true circumstances of Aileen's death. So she'd run. Not long after, Watt syndrome had hit in earnest and the Phaendir had sprung their hideous trap for the fae. She'd managed to stay out of Aeric's hands.

At least, until now.

A part of her had always been convinced she would avoid a reckoning for that night, but it appeared that—like so very often—she'd been wrong.

THREE

AERIC slammed the bottle of amber liquid onto the table hard enough to shatter and then glowered at it when it didn't. Since he hadn't been able to break Emmaline right off, he needed to see *something* destroyed. He was being soft on her and he had no idea why.

He took a drink from his glass. The rush of pure alcohol burned through his veins and tightened his body. He nearly never drank, but the lure of the whiskey was too strong to ignore tonight. Anyway, it was good liquor. There were some things humans did right and whiskey was one of them. He bought bottles of Jack Daniel's imported from outside Piefferburg even though they were triple the cost of fae-made alcohol. The fae traditionally drank elderberry wine or hard cider. Both spirits were Piefferburg's biggest exports to the outside world, but give him a flask of Jack and he was happy.

Not that he was happy tonight.

He picked up the bottle, rose to his feet, and hurled it against the wall. It smashed into a thousand glittering pieces and leaked amber down to the floor. Satisfied, he grunted and slumped into his chair, throwing his hair back with an angry snap of his head.

Fuck him six ways, he had his greatest enemy locked in his forge. *Goibhniu*, he still couldn't believe it. How stupid could she be to enter Piefferburg? She knew godsdamn well that the fae had a long memory. Apparently she'd been hoping her glamour would protect her against him. And normally it would have. She'd probably never expected the magickal net he'd put in place for her.

Thank Danu and all the gods for Ronan Quinn.

Yet, despite the fact that he'd had graphic fantasies about what to do with her if he ever laid hands on her, he was finding himself flummoxed when faced with her in the flesh. He'd always imagined throttling her on the spot, but he hadn't been able to do it back in the Boundary Lands. She'd looked so fucking innocent standing there in the woods, so *surprised*. He'd ambushed her good, though she'd fought him like the demon she was.

The exact reason why he hadn't crushed her throat right there on the road to Piefferburg City remained elusive. It appeared her death would have to wait until he was ready.

So, for now, he would simply savor his victory . . . and get stumbling drunk.

Aileen. Never had her memory been so sharp as it was tonight. He could still scent the light gardenia of the perfume she'd swipe on her wrists and under her earlobes. His fingers curling in his lap, he could recall the smooth skin of her abdomen and her inner thigh. Her laugh still rang clear in his mind when he called it up, and the way she'd whisper his name in the middle of the night, so full of need, made his cock hard even now.

In the years since her death, he'd been in more than one serious relationship but none of those women had diminished her memory. He'd known Aileen since they'd been in the cradle. Both of them had belonged to the Unseelie Court from birth and had grown up in Ireland, under the Shadow King's rule. Their parents had been friends and he and Aileen had played together as babies, learned to walk together through his parents' garden, and run away from each other's cooties before adolescence had hit.

Back then they'd lived in a small village in Northern Ireland, side by side with humans who didn't know their true nature. Most of the fae had lived in cottages in the woods in that area, while the humans resided in the village itself.

In childhood Aileen had used her looks to get away with all kinds of shit another little girl never would have been able to pull off. He especially remembered the bout of bad behavior she'd displayed when she was about eight. He'd caught her catching and tormenting animals in the woods, projecting her inner pain onto poor defenseless rabbits and birds. The things she'd done to them had been gruesome, but he'd understood that it had been her way—no matter how misguided—of dealing with her traumatic home life.

It was an act that had complemented her magick. She could cause a living thing to bleed internally until it died. That was what made her Unseelie, but it was only part of what she'd done to the animals. Letting them bleed internally hadn't been enough for her. Thinking about it still gave Aeric a stomachache.

He'd helped her through that dark period of her life, helped her through the pain of having an insensitive drunk for a father and a cold, unloving bitch for a mother. It was a time he didn't like to think about, something he'd kept secret from everyone to protect Aileen. Usually he pushed it far from his mind because it tarnished his memory of her, but tonight his emotions were so high they forced him to recall everything.

They'd always shared a special bond, knowing absolutely everything about each other. That bond had deepened when they'd turned sixteen and noticed each other as more than friends. They'd fallen in love—an unbreakable, magickal kind that was rare even to the fae folk. They knew every aspect of each other and shared a unique psychic bond. Essentially, they were soul mates, two halves of one whole.

He would have given his life for hers, if he'd been able.

If Aileen were alive today, they would be married—

soul-bonded, no less—and have a passel of kids, Danu willing. He pressed the flat of his hand to the center of his chest. It physically hurt to think about his loss.

A knock sounded on his door. He shot up from his place, stalked over, and answered it with a snarl, pissed off at being disturbed.

Kieran snarled back. "What's your problem?"

Aeric stepped aside and let the big man through the doorway. Kieran wasn't a blacksmith, but still he had the build of one. "Sorry, man, I'm not in the best of moods."

Kieran entered, clearly riled by the welcome he'd received. Scowling, he glanced around Aeric's apartment, seeing the disarray. His eyes lighted on the smashed whiskey bottle. "Your place looks like shit."

"Thanks for your honesty."

"Anytime."

Aeric couldn't really say it didn't. His apartment was one of the nicer ones in the keep, since he'd always been one of the Shadow King's favorites. His ability to twist charmed iron was the reason why. The place was twice the size of the quarters other Unseelie nobles kept in the Black Tower, airy and open with a high ceiling shot through with heavy wooden beams. The kitchen area stood kitty-corner to the living room. His bed was in the opposite corner, separated by a polished black wood partition. Right now the place was a mess—clothes scattered everywhere, empty takeout boxes on the coffee table, dishes stacked up near the sink. He needed to hire a maid.

Kieran's gaze lingered on the broken whiskey bottle on the floor. His scowl deepened. "Are you all right?"

Aeric smiled and swung an arm wide. "Great, my friend. Never better. Just celebrating."

"Celebrating what?"

There was no way he could tell Kieran about Emmaline. Emmaline had killed Kieran's twin brother during her days as the Summer Queen's assassin. In Aeric's opinion Diarmad Ailbhe Eòin Aimhrea had more than deserved it. Kieran knew it, too. All the same, Kieran would want revenge on her—and revenge was *Aeric's* to take and no one else's.

He lurched to the side and sank into a chair, waving his half-full whiskey glass at him. "I'm celebrating the end of an era and the glimmer of dawn on the horizon. Closure, that's what I'm celebrating. Want a drink?" He tipped his glass to Kieran and then drained it.

Kieran eyed him like Aeric had grown another head and then answered, "Not right now. Gabriel's wondering where you are. Asked me to come find you."

Fuck. The Wild Hunt. He'd totally forgotten.

"I'll be there in a few minutes." He glanced at the floor-to-ceiling fae-woven tapestry depicting the fae wars of the sixteen hundreds that hid the door to his forge. "Just have to take care of something before I leave."

"Are you sure you're okay? You're acting weird."

He stood, sliding his empty glass onto the cluttered coffee table. "Are you worried about me, Kieran?" The man had enough worries of his own, what with carrying the mother of all evil curses. It was really sad when someone like Kieran Aindréas Cairbre Aimhrea was concerned for him.

Kieran grunted and turned away. "I'm just delivering a message, but you know where I am if you ever want a drinking partner, okay?"

"Thanks, man. Tell Gabriel I'll be up in a few."

Once upon a time the membership of the Wild Hunt had been a closely guarded and well-kept mystical secret. They rode every midnight on the backs of stallions that came from the Netherworld and with mystical hounds baying at their sides. The dogs led the way to the souls of the fae who had departed during the night. The Wild Hunt's job was to collect them—a task passed on to them from some higher power they didn't know or understand. The Morrigan, most thought. But last year when the Shadow King had discovered he had a daughter—and subsequently tried to shred her soul in an effort to keep her from attaining the Shadow Throne—all that had been exposed.

Gabriel, the Lord of the Wild Hunt, had been in love with Aislinn Christiana Guinevere Finvarra, the Shadow King's biological daughter, and had moved heaven and earth to save her from the king's wrath. As a last resort to save her life, Gabriel had called on the power of the Wild Hunt. Aeric and the rest of the host had been at Gabriel's side to help. In the process, the host had been revealed. Now all the fae knew who the reapers were.

He showed Kieran out and slammed the door behind him. Leaning one palm up against the dark wood, he bowed his head and closed his eyes against an encroaching headache. Pushing a hand through his hair, he grimaced. All he wanted right now was to crawl into bed, but he had a duty to the hunt. He took his responsibility to the parted souls of Piefferburg seriously.

Only one little loose end to tie up before he left.

Spinning away from the door, he gathered his courage and headed to the tapestry. Flipping the edge to the side, he opened the door to his forge.

He stepped inside the dark room. Immediately he grabbed the upper part of the handle of the weapon whizzing toward his head. Pivoting, he wrenched it from her fingers and slammed Emmaline's slender body against the wall behind him, pulling back a little so he didn't kill her with his weight.

But it had been a bad idea to hold back. Moving faster than he'd anticipated, she twisted to the side, freeing herself, then caught his leg with hers and swept his foot out from under him. Stumbling, he caught himself just in time. A heartbeat before it was too late he saw the leg swipe had only been a distraction and whirled to catch the handle of the ax she was swinging toward him. She grunted in frustration as he stopped it cold, only inches from his thigh.

Goibhniu, that had been close. She'd had a weapon in each hand.

"No," he growled into her face. "Bad girl."

He yanked the charmed iron ax from her and threw it, making it clatter and scrape against the floor as it hit the opposite wall. He pushed away with her upper arm firmly in his grip and led her to the back of the forge like a recalcitrant child.

"Let me go!" she raged, trying to yank her arm away from him.

It was a nice show of spirit, but he was twice her weight and her magick was of the nice, light, Seelie variety—she couldn't kill with it directly. Not that it stopped this woman from killing. For a pure-blooded Seelie Court noblewoman, she was as deadly as they came.

He bared his teeth inches from her face. "Never."

He roughly whipped her around to face him and grabbed a pair of charmed iron cuffs from a nearby worktable.

Her eyes widened. "You wouldn't dare." Her voice echoed in the huge, dark room.

He let out a mirthless laugh and slapped them around her wrists. "You can't even imagine what I would dare. These are to keep you out of trouble and stop you from trying to chop me into little pieces with my own weapons. That was beyond cheeky, woman."

"You don't have to use charmed iron." She gasped as the magick touched her skin and began to do its work. "My skill with glamour isn't any threat to you. This is just plain cruel."

"Get used to cruel." He tipped her chin up, a cold smile playing on his lips. "That's all I have in my heart for you."

Her eyes clouded and she sagged forward, catching herself before she crumpled to the ground. Charmed iron lying against fae skin was very unpleasant. It stripped away all magick, rendering the prisoner naked and vulnerable. It also made the wearer sick if left on the flesh for a long period of time. Eventually that exposure killed the fae. During the wars some had inflicted horrible torture on their enemies by injecting charmed iron under the skin. It was not a good way to die.

"I have a specific reason for using charmed iron on you. I want to see your true face," he growled.

She blanched. For the first time since he'd seen her walking toward him in the Boundary Lands she actually looked frightened. Her guise began to fall away, the charmed iron stripping her ability to mask her appearance.

Her shoulder-length red hair darkened to a deep, rich brown that was nearly black. It became thicker and longer, flowing over her shoulders and curling gently down her back. Her heart-shaped face elongated, the chin and nose becoming sharper and the forehead higher. Her mouth became fuller and a slight cleft formed in her chin. Her green eyes deepened to a dark brown flecked with amber and changed contour, transforming from round and guileless to mysterious and almond shaped.

She remained slender and tall, fragile looking enough to snap between his hands, though that was an illusion. Her eyes never lost that disturbing inner innocence, either. Those were two things he'd been counting on changing. Gods damn her! He wanted the outside of her to match the inside—hard, twisted, brutal, and merciless. Instead she was . . . pretty.

As she slumped defeated against the wall behind her, dissatisfaction clawed in his gut.

Pulling her cuffed hands protectively against her stomach, she gazed up at him through the long, dark curtain of her hair. "Happy now?"

No, he wasn't happy. She wasn't at all what he'd been expecting. Too attractive by half. Too innocent and vulnerable looking. He'd been expecting a bruiser—someone heavy and hard. Someone who appeared capable of killing a blameless woman in cold blood just because she was jealous.

He scowled at her. "No, so I guess I'll just have to find other ways to make you miserable that might content me."

Puffing out a breath of air that stirred her hair, she looked down at her feet. "You're the one person in the whole world best able to make me miserable, Blacksmith. Hit me with your best shot."

"I plan to." He stepped back, not finding the pleasure in the exchange that he wanted. His hands itched for the now broken bottle of whiskey. This woman hadn't been in his forge for twenty-four hours yet and her presence was already driving him to drink.

He rubbed a hand over his chin. "Try that with a weapon again and I'll break it against your body instead of the floor." He indicated the ax, which now lay in two pieces at her feet.

He turned and left the forge, locking the door behind him.

* * *

"YOU stink like whiskey. Kieran told me you've been trying to kill off a bottle all on your own tonight." Gabriel, Lord of the Wild Hunt, wrinkled his nose at him as he came up to the top of the tower. "You never drink. What's going on, Aeric?"

"I don't want to talk about it," he growled, pushing past him and joining the rest of the host.

Melia regarded him closely with her naturally heavy-lidded eyes, her bright red hair shadowing half her face. She was a battle fae, capable of much destruction in times of war. "Ooh, grouchy," she gently taunted in her low, raspy voice.

Aelfdane, her Twyleth Teg mate, sat mounted on a dappled gray beside her, also studying him with a steady, curious gaze. He was Melia's opposite physically—tall, thin, and light of coloring, whereas she was short, curvy, and fiery headed—in more ways than one.

Despite the surface differences, they shared a soul and a brain. They were both thinking the same thing right now—*what the fuck is up with Aeric?* He wasn't about to enlighten them.

Bran, the last member of the Wild Hunt, sat on the roof of the Black Tower, talking softly to his pet crow, Lex. Taliesin and Blix, the sleek black Netherland hounds that appeared every night with the horses to sniff out souls in Piefferburg, lounged happily near him. Bran's magick lay in the realm of nature: he could communicate with animals. One would think he'd live out in the Boundary Lands with the nature fae, but there was a quirk to Bran's power—he could control animals, too, make them maim or kill. That was what made him Unseelie—that ability to spill blood with his magick.

The hunt horses were there. Beyond their regular mounts; there were six of them tonight, to carry the six souls of the fae they would collect. Aeric pulled himself up on a bay with a long, flowing mane and a white star on his forehead. Every night the hunt horses and hounds appeared on the roof of the Black Tower and every morning they deposited the host back on the roof and carried the collected souls back over the rainbow. That was what it looked like, anyway. They rode into the dawn every morning and then winked out of existence, presumably gone back to the Netherworld.

Gabriel mounted the lead horse, Abastor, a huge black without a spot of light anywhere on his muscled body. "So, did you hear the news? A human's gone missing somewhere in the Boundary Lands."

Aeric's hands tightened on the reins. "Really?"

Melia chimed in. "Some woman. She was supposed to be an addition to the *Faemous* crew over at the Rose Tower, but she never made it. My money is on Will the Smith, but it could have been any one of the boogeys out there in the Boundary Lands. The birch ladies can't help everyone in need."

Will the Smith was a man so evil it was said that even the sluagh had rejected him. Spat back out from the Netherworld, he'd been given a second life and the ability to torture or kill anyone he liked—and he liked, very much, to kill all sorts of people. Most humans knew him as the Will o' the Wisp, luring the unsuspecting to their deaths by taking the form of a pleasing light that compelled the viewer to follow. In reality he was a sociopath who also happened to be a fae. His magick was death related, which made him Unseelie, but he was a loner and wanted nothing to do with the Unseelie court. The court wanted nothing to do with him, either.

"It's strange," said Gabriel. "The Boundary Lands have been safe for humans for more than ten years now. Aside from that *Faemous* crew at the Black Tower becoming a goblin dinner some years back, I can't remember the last time a human was attacked out there in the woods."

"No one's looking for her?" Aeric asked.

"The Summer Queen has the Imperial Guard combing the area," Aelfdane answered. "But, strange or not, it does appear a loner dark fae like Will the Smith got her. By now the chance of anyone finding anything but pieces of that woman are slim."

"It's bad public relations for us," Melia added. "Every time a human falls to one of the dark fae, it hurts our possibilities for getting out of here."

Bran gave a scoffing laugh. "Right. You really think we

have any possibility of managing that, short of opening the Book of Bindings, Melia?"

"Maybe. There's the HFF, after all. They're fighting for us."

Bran shook his head. "One small group of humans fighting for fae rights. They're overwhelmed by the ones who want to keep us here and, worse, the majority of people who just don't give a shit."

Melia blew a strand of hair out of her face in a gesture that revealed her frustration with the conversation. "I'm just saying we have a lot of uncontrolled, bloodthirsty fae in here that need to be leashed. Having them run loose isn't helping our image."

The host went on to discuss all the possible monsters that could have picked off an unsuspecting human traveling through the enchanted woods to Piefferburg City. They didn't suspect for a moment that the monster was Aeric.

Interesting. So Emmaline had been posing as a human *Faemous* crew member and had intended to go to the Rose Tower. What was her game? Had she been planning to take up her old job with the Summer Queen? That was the only possible explanation Aeric could come up with. Maybe she'd grown tired of living among the humans or had some other reason for coming to Piefferburg and wanted to secure a place for herself in the Rose.

Apparently he'd botched the return of the deadliest assassin the Summer Queen had ever employed.

All the better he'd waylaid her. Piefferburg was better off.

GIDEON drummed his fingers on his desk and stared out the doorway of his office. Emily hadn't checked in yet from the Rose Tower, according to Brother Maddoc, and he couldn't keep his mind on his work because of it. That lack of focus was telling, since usually nothing kept his head out of the game.

A viscous dribble of blood crept slowly down his wrist, tickling his skin. He wiped at it with a tissue, but not before it marked the papers on his desk with a brown stain. He'd shown his love to Labrai only twenty minutes earlier, using the small room off of his office reserved for his daily self-flagellation. The cat-o'-nine had bit deeply into his flesh today, deeper than usual, because he was so disturbed by Emily's disappearance. One wound still refused to close up.

Brother Maddoc passed the doorway and Gideon bolted from his seat, racing out into the hall. "Have you heard anything yet, brother?"

Archdirector Maddoc turned, the lines of his annoyingly pleasant face etched deeper than usual. "No. I'll be sure to let you know if I have any more news. I must say I'm surprised by this occurrence. Humans have been traveling without trouble to and from Piefferburg City on that road for many years now, ever since the fae began actively courting the sympathy of the humans. It never occurred to me to deny Emily's request to hike to the Rose Tower."

If I had my way, you incompetent, candy-ass weakling, all the fae would have their heads on pikes all along that road and Emily would never have been in danger of anything more than a nightmare.

Gideon scowled and nodded. "I agree. It's more than passing strange."

Except it *was* more than passing strange. On that, as much as he hated it, he agreed with Maddoc. Maybe Emily had just had bad luck and happened upon a rogue fae with an urge to harm her.

Or maybe there was something else odd about this situation. Something odd about Emily.

Gideon's intuition had been niggling all morning and he didn't like it.

No. Emily Millhouse was a wonderful, upstanding, pious Worshipful Observer. Nothing more. Hopefully she was still alive and would contact them soon. He would pray to Labrai that it might be so.

"You're dripping blood on the carpet."

He looked down to see that he was indeed plopping dark brown drops of blood onto the cream carpeting of the hallway. Maddoc wore an expression of distaste.

Gideon used his other hand to close the cuff of his sleeve. "My demonstration of faith was exceptionally vigorous today, my brother."

Maddoc's lips curled in mild revulsion. "Yes," he drawled.

White-hot rage raced through Gideon's veins. In bright flashes, he imagined backhanding Maddoc, jumping on him, and beating that expression off his face until his head was nothing more than bloody pulp and a caved-in skull.

Gideon forced a smile. "All praise Labrai."

"All praise." Maddoc turned and walked away.

Gideon let his expression transform to pure hatred as he stared at his superior's back. He couldn't wait until it was time for Maddoc to suffer all he deserved. He was soft. He'd forgotten the old ways, had grown compassionate and feeble in his dealings with the fae. Labrai would punish him eventually and Gideon would be more than happy to be His tool.

Abruptly Maddoc stopped and turned. Gideon quickly pasted a bland smile on his face. "Brother Cederick has taken ill and has been admitted to the hospital." Maddoc pressed his lips together. "We fear the worst."

"Oh, no." He filled his voice with the sympathy that would be expected of him. "This is the first I've heard of it, though I have noticed he hasn't been in his office lately." His very nice corner office with a view of the gates. The office Gideon would soon be occupying. "What illness has he contracted?"

"A mysterious one that our physicians are at a loss to explain. Tests are being conducted." Maddoc pressed his lips together in that gesture that made Gideon want to smack him. "You're quickly moving up to occupy your former seat, it seems. Our brothers have had very bad luck this past year." Light suspicion threaded his voice, but there was nothing Maddoc could do and he knew it.

Gideon bowed his head, hiding his smile. "I am Labrai's hand, directed where He wills me." When he looked up, Maddoc was gone.

FOUR

HER head humming with a dull ache, Emmaline lifted her head and cracked her eyes open, seeing a warm red glow penetrating the black. She pushed up as best she could with her wrists bound and saw Aeric at his forge.

His hands and forearms were covered in thick leather gloves, but that was almost all he wore. In one hand he held a red-hot length of iron into a fire that burned white hot in the middle of a huge metal table. Shirtless from the waist up, his powerful back and shoulders flexed as he removed the iron from the flames, picked up a hammer, and began to work the piece with strong, ringing clangs.

Molding. Shaping. Bending the ordinarily inflexible metal to his will. That was Aeric Killian Riordan O'Malley. Strong. Fiery. Passionate. He always had been, always would be.

She hated that her body reacted to him. Right now she should fear him, detest him, loathe the very sight of him, but the feelings she had for Aeric were just as strong now as they'd been hundreds of years ago. There was something very, very wrong with her. If she ever got back out of Piefferburg, she was seeking a psychiatrist pronto.

Could she blame him for hating her? He thought she'd ruthlessly killed his soul mate in a fit of jealousy. If she were in his place she would feel the same way. Maybe she would have waited years and years to take her revenge, too. Perhaps she would have dreamed of ways to make the murderer pay for what he'd done.

She wasn't happy to be here, and she would fight tooth and nail to survive this, but she understood his motives.

At least, she understood his motives from his current perspective—from the lie he believed. If he knew what had truly happened the night she'd killed Aileen, she might not be sitting in his forge as a prisoner, wondering if she would live or die.

Here was her dilemma—if she told him the truth, it would alter his view of his soul mate forever and destroy his memory of Aileen. Stupid her, she'd sacrificed a lot to keep that memory pristine.

It might also redeem Emmaline in his eyes.

Ultimately, it was a moot point. He wouldn't believe anything she said. Therefore, she didn't have to grapple with any moral issues about destroying Aeric's memory of the woman he loved so much.

Her, an ex-assassin, grappling with moral issues. That was humorous.

She hadn't been an assassin now for hundreds of years, but the taint of that time of her life had never quite washed clean. And now, confronted with Aeric and having her nose rubbed in all her past sins, her history seemed fresher than ever.

The heavy weight of emotion—regret and shame—settled in her chest. Nothing changed the core truth. She *was* guilty of killing Aileen. Aileen and so many others. Maybe she deserved to be punished by Aeric's hand. Maybe she deserved all of this. Maybe it was karma, like Aeric had said.

Spying a tray by her right foot, she saw that he'd brought her food. A bowl of soup, a sandwich, and a glass of milk.

Her stomach rumbled. At least he wasn't going to starve her to death.

Scooting over, she tried to spoon some of the lukewarm chicken noodle soup into her mouth but succeeded only in dripping it onto the floor.

Aeric spotted her and walked over. In a moment, she was free of the cuffs. Immediately her impulse was to cloak herself in glamour again, but she tamped it down. What was the point? He knew every one of her dirty secrets—and even believed a few that weren't true. There was no sense in hiding from this man.

"Eat," he commanded roughly, throwing the cuffs to the floor with a metallic jangle. He turned back toward his worktable. "But don't expect those cuffs to stay off."

She gathered the bowl in her hands and rested against the wall behind her, spooning up the soup and trying not to eat like a starving animal. When the bowl of soup was gone, she started on the sandwich and only then did the dull ache of hunger in her belly begin to ease.

"Why did you come to Piefferburg?" Aeric asked, his voice low and raspy with anger. He picked up his hammer and walked over to the fire to remove a long piece of metal.

She set the rest of the sandwich back on the plate. "I came to find you."

Clang. Clang. "I'm supposed to believe that?"

"Believe it or don't believe it, it's the truth."

Making a sound of disgust, he threw the hammer down onto the worktable. "You don't know what the truth is, woman. You couldn't find the truth if it stepped out in front of you, big as a barn."

"You don't know anything about the truth, either," she muttered.

He turned toward her with what looked literally like a hot poker in his hand and she stilled. She needed to be careful with this man and that meant she had to watch her mouth better. Ordinarily, her mouth was famous for getting her into trouble. She'd meant what she'd said about believing Aeric was a good man who wouldn't hurt her, but it was still smart to give good yet angry men with hot pokers some respect.

"My best guess is that you're here to get back into good graces with the Summer Queen. I think you want your old job back." He studied her. "Or are you here to kill someone?"

"I don't do that anymore." She ducked her head, feeling shame that she'd ever done it in the first place. "I work on behalf of the HFF now. I'm here on a mission for them, a mission—by the way, that would benefit you greatly. You need to let me go and you need to help me."

"Don't tell me what *I need*, assassin. I know what I need and it's nothing that would benefit you. You're not going anywhere. Your ass is mine now."

"And what do you intend to do to me?" Her voice only shook a little. She was proud of herself.

He set the piece of red-hot iron onto the table and took up the hammer. "I'm weighing my options," he said right before he brought the hammer down on it. "I've been thinking about ways to make you pay for so long that it's hard to settle on just one."

She shivered and pushed the tray away with her foot. "I probably deserve everything you have to dish out."

"No doubt." His hammer clanged down again.

"Although in the last three hundred or so years I may have redeemed myself somewhat. At least, I doubt the sluagh will claim my soul when you kill me."

The sluagh, an army of unforgiven dead, took the souls of all the murdering fae. If Aeric really did kill her, chances were high they'd take him, too.

The hammer stopped in midair and he turned to look at her. "You, redeemed? And just how would that be possible, woman?" His voice was a harsh bark and his brows were drawn together in one severe slash over his beautiful chocolate brown eyes.

Shame on her that she thought his eyes were beautiful. Clearly she was a deeply disturbed person. She needed medication.

"I told you," she barked back. "I've been working for the HFF since it was first created. My ultimate goal is *your* freedom, freedom for the fae. I don't kill for the Summer Queen anymore. I haven't since—" She snapped her mouth closed. Not since she'd killed his fiancée by accident. "Not for hundreds of years. All my time and energy is devoted to breaking the barriers that hold the fae in Piefferburg. I think that when I die Danu and the Morrigan will take mercy on me."

He snorted. "All your killings were ordered by the Summer Queen, so you get a free pass from the Powers That Be." He paused. "All but *one* murder, right?"

Guided by the hounds that came from the Netherworld, the Wild Hunt normally instantly collected the souls of those who murdered in cold blood. It was a swift and accurate punishment that drastically controlled fae-on-fae killings. Though there were exceptions. Those deaths ordered by either royal, Unseelie or Seelie, were exempt, as were deaths dealt during wartime. Sometimes there were random passovers that no one understood. But generally, those fae who murdered other fae were swept up by the Wild Hunt almost right away and taken by the sluagh.

She couldn't explain why she hadn't been swept up after she'd killed Aileen. Perhaps because it had been unintentional. Aileen had simply been in the wrong place at the wrong time. Somewhere she shouldn't have been, doing something she shouldn't have been doing.

"I don't deny I've done many things in my life I'm not proud of, but I've spent a lifetime—many human lifetimes—trying to make amends for those years."

He shook his head. "I don't believe it."

"It doesn't matter if you believe it or not."

"I don't really care how you've spent your life since you killed Aileen. That's all irrelevant to me. The fact that you murdered her is all that matters."

She pushed a shaky hand through her hair. Dying wasn't really on her agenda. She had a mission to accomplish. The question remained: *how could she get herself out of this mess?*

She drew a careful breath and licked her lips. "What if I told you that the HFF knows where a piece of the *bosca fadbh* is and you hold the key—literally—to obtaining it. You know that the fae have already managed to get one piece of the *bosca fadbh* and the Book of Bindings. If you have one more piece, you're that much closer to getting out of here."

"Do you remember the part where I think you're a lying murderer who would sell her own mother for a chance at retaining her miserable life?"

Yeah, that was pretty much what she'd thought he'd say.

"Fine, kill me, then, but you're wasting the best chance you have for freedom."

"But killing you will make my life so much sweeter."

"And then the Wild Hunt will come for you, Aeric, and you will belong to the sluagh."

"It would be worth it."

She raised an eyebrow. "Really? It would be worth it? You'd never get to see Aileen in the Netherworld if you let yourself be taken by the sluagh."

"Aileen is lost to me and always will be. I accepted that a long time ago."

"And have obviously been swimming in bitterness ever since."

He smiled a bright, charming, open smile. The kind of smile that, had he bestowed it on her long ago, would have made her heart do a backflip. "Oh, yes, woman, and I've been saving it all for you."

CÁEL O'Malley had once been strong and vigorous, but age and Watt syndrome had taken their toll. When Aeric entered his father's apartment the formerly mighty man seemed a little more fragile than usual. Aeric dreaded the day the Wild Hunt would come for him. That was the dark side to serving on it—they had to reap their loved ones.

His dad, bent and gray, sat near his living room window. He held a book in his gnarled hands and had a blanket draped across his knees. The sickness made him look about ninety. If he hadn't become ill, he would only appear to be in his early fifties by human standards. Cáel had been one of the lucky ones, though. Not many had survived the sickness.

His father let the book drop into his lap and sat up with a smile of pleasure on his face, but his expression quickly fell. "Jaysus, what's wrong?"

Aeric closed the door behind him and crossed the living room to sit near his dad. The Shadow King had given Cáel a nice apartment in thanks for so many dedicated years of service. Cáel was due every square inch and every stick of wood in the furniture for all the work he'd done. "What makes you think there's something wrong, da?"

Cáel's still sharp eyes narrowed. "You've got that look on your face." He spoke with a thick Irish accent that hadn't seemed to erode even after so many hundreds of years in Piefferburg.

"What look on my face?"

"The one that you always get when you meet a woman you like"—he smacked his lips together—"and you don't know what to do about it."

There were so many things wrong with his father's reply that Aeric didn't even know where to start. "Uh, I met a woman. You got that part right. The rest, not so much."

Cáel cackled and mostly ignored him. "I knew it. And as usual you don't know your arse from your asshole when it comes to wooing her."

Aeric's lips twisted. "What does that even mean, da? And for your information, I know enough not to use the words *arse* or *asshole* when *wooing* a woman. Do you?"

"My wooing days are over. I can use any kind of language I want." He paused and smacked his lips again. "Anyway, your mother never complained."

"Well, Mom was a saint. She had to be a saint to put up with you."

Another cackle. "That's for sure. She was a good woman." A good woman who'd succumbed to Watt syndrome. "Them were good days when she was at my side. Now all I got to look forward to during the day is messing my cacks." Lip smack. "So tell me about her. The woman, not your ma. I can remember every detail about her."

"You got it wrong, da. I don't like this woman and I know

exactly what to do with her." Okay, maybe not. Once he had. Now he wasn't so sure. Before his dad could say anything more, he got up and brought back the chess set. They always played a few games together.

He set the board up while Cáel studied him. "If you say so."

Aeric looked up at him, a chess piece in one hand, and held his gaze steadily. "I say so. And I want *very much* to stop talking about this now."

"Huh. But—"

"Da." Aeric's hand closed around the black queen he held hard enough to hurt. "The reason I have a troubled look on my face *does* have to do with a woman—the woman who killed Aileen. Do you understand now?"

Cáel's face went a shade paler. "The Summer Queen's assassin is here in Piefferburg?"

Aeric nodded. "You can't say a word to anyone, da. *Not a word.*"

"The Unseelie would tear her apart if they knew."

"That's why you can't say anything."

His father's body went rigid. "Are you protecting her?"

"No." Aeric carefully placed the piece on the board, weighing his words before he made a full reply. "Yeah, sort of. I'm protecting her from the rest of the court so I can take my revenge on her at my ease, without interference."

Cáel shook his white head. "Revenge is a bad business. I recommend you get out of it before you do something you regret, something that abrades the fine man you are."

Aeric looked up at his father. "She killed Aileen."

"A very long time ago. You don't know her full story. You don't why she did it, or even if she really did it at all. It's not your place to be her judge, jury, and executioner."

Aeric fought to keep his voice down. "And why not? *She* certainly played judge, jury, and executioner."

"By the Summer Queen's order, she did. Killed men who deserved it. Like Diarmad Ailbhe Eòin Aimhrea, remember him? And Driscoll Manus O'Shaughnessy."

"Why are you defending her? And O'Shaughnessy was Seelie, by the way."

"I remember." Cáel rubbed his lips with his twisted hand, lost in a memory. "Never knew a man who needed killing more than him. The Summer Queen's assassin never took anyone whose death didn't improve the world. You have to admit that. She cleaned up the trash."

Aeric studied the chessboard fiercely, controlling his temper. "She wasn't a godsdamn superhero, da."

"No, she was a teenage girl, Aeric. Just a young thing. I remember."

"You're thinking of her age in contemporary terms. She—"

"No." He shook his head. "She was a teenager by any measure back when she was killing for the queen. I met her once."

Pique momentarily forgotten, he raised his head. "You did?"

He nodded. "Walking the path through the woods one day. She knew who I was, of course, being your father. She was very polite."

"So because she was *polite* you defend her even though she killed Aileen? Aileen was polite, too. Remember her?"

"I do remember her. She was a good woman. If she had lived, maybe she'd be the mother of my grandchildren. I want to see those soon, by the way. I won't be around forever, you know."

"That issue is in the hands of the Powers That Be, da."

Cáel nodded. "*All* issues are. That's why you need to be giving up this idea of revenge against this woman, boyo, before you do something that will change you forever." He paused. "Change you for the worse."

Aeric shook his head and gritted his teeth, but he didn't argue any further because he knew with heaviness in his heart that, indeed, Cáel wouldn't be around forever.

DAVID Sullivan sat in an Internet café in Haifa, Israel, and tapped his fingers on the tabletop while staring at the screen of his laptop. If he stared hard enough maybe an e-mail from the HFF would pop up to ease the niggling fear he had that something horrible had happened to Emmaline.

If he unfocused his eyes, he could see his reflection. His long, reddish blond hair was slipping from the tie at his nape, he needed a shave, and dark circles marked the flesh under his eyes. The reflection showed how worried he was. It had been five days and four nights and no news.

It should have been an in-and-out job. Once she'd connected with the *Faemous* crew in the Rose Tower, it should have been easy for her to slip over to the Unseelie side of Piefferburg Square, find the Blacksmith, and have the key made. It wasn't like a key took a long time to make, right? Even a charmed one.

She should have been out of Piefferburg by now and safe. He should have had an e-mail or phone call from HFF headquarters telling him she was on her way with the key and to get his diving gear ready. Instead all he had was an empty inbox, a quiet cell phone, and a head full of horrific possible scenarios.

Not far away, off the coast of Atlit, Israel, lay Atlit Yam. It was a nine-thousand-year-old village that now lay at the bottom of the Mediterranean Sea. Experts believed a tsunami had done it in, since there was evidence that the people who lived there had fled quickly . . . or had been sucked out to sea.

As interesting as all that was, to David it wasn't the most fascinating thing about the underwater village. More compelling was the box that lay submerged not far from it. Small, yet mysteriously too heavy for divers to lift, it still rested on the bottom of the ocean. Even the use of mechanical means to pull the box free had time and again met with failure . . . as though the box were charmed. And, of course, it was. Luckily, an HFF sympathizer had been on the crew that had discovered the box and contacted them.

The HFF had recognized the writing on the box right away as Old Maejian. A partial translation had yielded a riddle, whose answer revealed that the contents of the box was one of the coveted pieces of the *bosca fadbh*. Well, so they thought, anyway. There wasn't anyone around to tell them if they'd answered the riddle correctly. All they needed was that damned charmed key and they could find out if they were right or not.

Thanks to the influence of the HFF, news of the box hadn't hit the world yet—and therefore, the Phaendir. They'd paid off the humans who'd found the fae artifact. Still, you never knew. The Phaendir gave the term *crafty* a new definition. Then there was always the chance one of the men they'd paid off might be too greedy for his own good and decide to go to the Phaendir for more money. That would earn him the promise of cold, hard cash until he spilled the news—then he'd get a cold, hard blade in the throat. If the Phaendir found out about the box, David could expect company . . . of the killing kind.

Someone set a cup of iced coffee down at his elbow. He looked up, surprised, to find a woman standing beside him. Scratch that—a beautiful woman. Long, thick black hair; dark, almond-shaped eyes; and a slender body encased in a feminine, flowing, orange and pink dress. "You are American, right?" She smiled.

Oh, hell, he hoped she wasn't a prostitute.

He nodded.

She mock-frowned at him. "You are so serious, looking at your computer screen. I thought you must be. Take that coffee on the house. I hope it will cheer you."

After flashing him a stunning smile that almost knocked him right off his stool, she turned and swayed her pretty ass back behind the counter.

David lifted a brow in speculation.

He lifted his glass to her and said, "Thank you," then took a sip of the cool, sweet coffee drink.

She smiled at him again and tossed in a saucy wink to boot.

Hmm-mm.

He dragged his gaze away from the beautiful woman and back to the laptop. Maybe it was time he stopped fretting. Emmaline could take care of herself. He knew that better than most. Anyway, there was nothing he could do for her almost halfway around the world. Emmaline, as much as he hated it, was on her own with this one.

Closing his laptop, he glanced back up at the counter. The woman was gazing at him. He smiled at her and she looked away quickly, a blush coloring her cheeks.

David drained his glass and picked up his laptop. He hesitated near the counter, wanting to go over and talk to her. Shaking his head, he pushed the door open instead. He didn't have time for that now. He was working.

AERIC wasn't sure when the seed of unease that had been present ever since he'd stripped her glamour had begun to sprout and grow unwelcome little tendrils of uncertainty through his brain.

It had something to do with Emmaline's eyes. Mostly it was the way she unflinchingly met his gaze whenever she said something he didn't like—*you won't hurt me*, for example. Or *you're a good man.* Worse still was when she said things like, *you don't know anything about the truth.*

Because he'd always thought he had. At least, until she'd shown up.

Brooding, he sat on his couch and stared at the bottle of whiskey—newly purchased and wholly unbroken—that sat on the little table that held all his alcohol. Usually reserved for guests, the bottles called to him, offering an escape from the hell he'd been plunged into with her arrival.

This was nothing like how he'd imagined it.

She was nothing like how he'd imagined her.

He'd always thought that if this day ever came, it would be easy and satisfying to take his revenge. Now that it had actually occurred, he found himself hesitating, unsure . . . inclined to show mercy.

Mercy. *For Emmaline.*

How many times had he planned her death? How many weapons now hung in his forge that he'd crafted with the intention of using on her? Mercy? He'd thought he'd had none for her.

He fisted his hands and pressed them to his eye sockets, suppressing the urge to lunge across the room for the bottle of whiskey and guzzle the whole fucking thing down in one go. As if he'd seen her only yesterday, an image of Aileen rose up in his mind.

Laughing. Smiling. Twirling in the beautiful blue dress he'd given her. It had matched her eyes and set off her creamy skin. Moments after she'd twirled to show him how the skirt belled, he'd begun stripping it off her. Unhurriedly revealing inch by tantalizing inch of her body, he'd kissed and licked her nude and then made slow love to her under a tree.

He shook his head, trying not to remember the day he'd found her dead, but the images came anyway. Her normally lush skin had been pallid and cold. Her lips thin and blue. The Summer Queen's assassin's signature cross-bolt, fletched blue and white, unmistakable, had protruded from just left of her spine. Emmaline had shot her in the back. Tipped with poison, as soon as the bolt found its mark, it meant death.

She'd been lying on a mound of pine needles looking oddly peaceful, like she'd been sleeping. He'd found her in the morning with dew beading on her dead flesh.

Grief, dark and bitter, rose up from the depths of him. It was like a well that never went dry. Once in a while he tapped it and it flowed into him like toxic sludge, coloring his world a muddy brown.

He pushed to his feet, rage fueling his movements, and stormed into the forge. Emmaline lay where she'd been when he'd left that morning, curled on her side on the floor next to the tray he'd brought her. He reached toward her throat. He would squeeze until no more breath could make it through. Until she was silent and still. It wasn't fair—not right—that she should still live while Aileen was ash.

His fingers closed over the silky skin of that slender, vulnerable column and squeezed. She gasped, her eyes opening wide and her fingers coming up to grip and scratch at his hands. But he was granite and she was feather. She had that much effect. Her legs flailed and her face went pale. In her eyes he saw that she knew this was her end.

He squeezed harder.

Her fingers dug bloody furrows into his wrists. She kicked and twisted, but he only tightened his grip, riding her through until all the fight left her.

You're a good man.

No, he wasn't.

FIVE

SHE went still, the depths of her eyes growing dim, her face bright red. Blood trickled down his wrists, but she'd stopped trying to draw it from him.

He stared down at her, into her big brown eyes and, again, hated what he saw. Their luminous depths reflected his doubt and magnified the fact that he was not a killer—no matter that he'd been sure he could do this if the opportunity arose.

With a roar of anguish, he released her. Coughing, she scrambled back away from him with her hand to her reddened throat until she hit the wall. Then she settled down and panted, watching him with wide, frightened eyes.

He swiped his forearm over his mouth and said in a hoarse voice ravaged with emotion, "You don't deserve to live."

"Maybe not," she wheezed out, then she went into another coughing fit. "I don't know. I've asked myself that same question more than once." Her voice sounded reedy and raspy.

"Stop it!" he yelled.

She held her hand to her throat in a protective gesture. "I know you loved Aileen more than anything. I know her death destroyed you." She stopped and swallowed hard, wincing from pain. "Please believe I didn't kill her out of jealousy. It was an accident that I killed her at all. I didn't mean to do it." She whispered the last sentence, lowering her gaze to the floor.

Aeric wanted to cast away the seed of doubt that she might be telling the truth. He couldn't. If she was lying, she deserved an Oscar.

She looked up at him. "You're a good man, Aeric."

His fists clenched. "I am not. Stop saying that."

"You're not going to kill me."

Silence. Aeric turned his face away from her.

"Yes, you may have fantasized about it, but when it comes to reality, you won't do it. You can't. You don't have it in you."

"Unlike you," he snarled at her, making her jump and press herself backward.

"Unlike me," she said quietly. "You're right."

When he didn't respond, she asked, "If you're not going to kill me, will you let me go?"

"No."

"What are you going to do with me?"

"You're staying here."

The words went unspoken but still hung in the air between them—*but I won't hurt you.*

Optimism flickered over her face and he hated himself. He was betraying Aileen by keeping her murderer alive and giving her hope.

HER throat burned.

She'd thought that had been the end. The look in his eyes and on his face had been so brutal and all consuming. Now she had a sliver of possibility to work with. Perhaps she could leverage it to her advantage. Manipulate this turn of events in her favor.

Leverage. Manipulate.

Sweet Danu, she was beginning to think like the woman she'd been so long ago. She was slipping into old patterns of behavior to survive, small subconscious seeds that triggered in situations when she was in danger. Behavior she'd learned as a child and young adult in order to make it through, to survive, to put food in her belly. With the help of Lars, the Summer Queen had taken all that and used it against her, molded her into a tool to have at her disposal. Forged her into a weapon, just as Aeric did every night.

No, she never wanted to go back to being that woman, *that weapon*.

She watched Aeric turn his head away from her, grief overcoming his features. If only a man would grieve for her that way—love her so much that even hundreds of years after her death he still mourned her.

Aileen didn't deserve it. Emmaline hadn't known then, not until that fateful night, that Aileen hadn't deserved Aeric at all.

"I can't let you go," Aeric ground out in a low, harsh voice, "because I can't let you go back to the Summer Queen."

"The Christians' hell would freeze over before I would go back to her." The angry vehemence in her voice surprised her. Emotion flared through her veins and burned behind her eyes. She took a deep, calming breath through her aching throat.

He blinked at her. "Now, *that* I almost believed. Good acting." He turned and walked out of the forge, returning to dump a blanket and pillow onto the floor near her. Wow, a pillow and blanket. She was making progress. Maybe he felt guilty about nearly strangling her to death.

After he left, she snuggled into the blanket and put her head on the pillow, trying to find a comfortable place on the floor and failing. Cold concrete wasn't anything like comfy and her throat hurt like hell. Plus, there was nothing like almost being murdered in your sleep to keep a girl awake. Time to give up on sleep. Shivering, she sat up and hugged herself, leaning up against the wall behind her.

On the upside, she was further along with Aeric than she'd thought she'd get so soon—and she wasn't sure how she'd gotten there. No matter. She had a sliver of hope that she might live to finish her mission and that was all that mattered. It was more than she could wish for, considering.

She stared into the blackness of the forge and remembered things she wanted to forget. The night she'd killed Aileen, she'd gone to the upper echelons of the Seelie Court to execute one of the worst known torturers of Unseelie, Driscoll Manus O'Shaughnessy, on the Summer Queen's command.

O'Shaughnessy had gone outside the bounds of all fae law, capturing non-human-looking Unseelie fae—goblins, alps, and joint-eaters, among others—in the wars. He'd bring them back to his house, where he had a room set up for such things, and would slowly torture them to the point of death, never allowing them to tip over the edge.

By not killing them he'd avoided the wrath of the Wild Hunt and proven beyond doubt the old adage—there are worse things than death. He would tear off their fingernails, drive nails through their hands and feet, cut off their eyelids, among other fun party tricks, and then abandon them within the bounds of Unseelie land to be found and nursed back to health . . . mostly.

No one really knew why he did it. Maybe he hated the Unseelie so much he felt driven to such unspeakable acts. Maybe he thought he was serving the Summer Queen in some twisted way. Or maybe, as Emmaline believed, he was just a sick fuck who got off on torture. It didn't really matter to the Summer Queen why he was doing it. She only cared that his behavior created tension between the Summer and Shadow Royals at a time when a shaky peace was beginning to come about.

When it became known to the Summer Queen that O'Shaughnessy was the disturbed bastard doing these things, the queen ordered him killed right away. By the time Emmaline had been charged with his assassination, news of his identity had begun to spread through both courts. Since there would be plenty of others ready to kill him, Emmaline was ordered to get to him first, as a show of faith to the Shadow King. It was one death that Emmaline had never been conflicted over doling out.

Emmaline had donned the guise of his hobgoblin servant and let herself into O'Shaughnessy's home in the dead of night, her crossbow and quiver concealed on her body. She'd done her research on the Seelie noble and knew the older man had no wife, no girlfriend, no children. All he had in his enormous home were scads of house hobgoblins, all safely tucked into bed for the night.

She padded silently on plush carpets fit for the Summer Queen, traveling down a corridor toward his bedroom, past the door that she knew led to the room where he did the torturing. Even the air outside of it smelled of foulness—unwashed bodies, sickness, misery, and the very edge of death.

O'Shaughnessy's bedroom was dark, except for the slight light of the moon outside his window. He was in bed, just as she'd presumed. Stepping into the room, she changed to her regular form—not her true form, but the red-haired one she used the most—sought her bow, and nocked a quarrel. Drawing the string back to her ear, she sighted a spot on his back. She was no torturer. She made her kills fast and as terror free as possible—even for scum like Driscoll Manus O'Shaughnessy. Killing a mark while he slept was best for everyone involved. If she got the shot right, the mark never knew what hit him.

She fired.

The body in the bed arched backward and screamed. The scream was feminine, the curve of the body slender and slight. *Wrong*. Cold panic poured into her as she realized what she'd done. It wasn't O'Shaughnessy in that bed; it was a woman.

Her crossbow clattered to the floor and Emmaline rushed to the bedside to take her victim into her arms. The poison was working fast, but the woman was still alive. Her face had a stark look of terror on it.

And, of course, Emmaline recognized her.

No one could mistake the fall of white blond hair, wide green eyes, perfect skin and face for anyone but the most beautiful of the Unseelie noblewomen—Aileen Arabella Edmé McIlvernock. She looked like an angel; everyone said so. Now she looked like an almost dead angel.

Aileen gripped her upper arm hard and said, "Tell Driscoll I love him." And then she died, blood spreading on the bed in a rusty-colored pool. Emmaline had it all over her hands and arms.

Only a moment after Aileen slumped to the mattress, O'Shaughnessy entered the room, talking to Aileen. It made Emmaline's stomach roil. He stopped after traveling three steps into the room, taking in the scene with his hand still on the tie of his bathrobe as though he was about to remove it. His face went white, his eyes wide, and his mouth opened and closed. Then he dropped to his knees, crying out Aileen's name in anguish.

Emmaline stared wide-eyed at the scene, unbelieving that such a coldhearted bastard as O'Shaughnessy could be capable of grief.

A moment later he lunged for Emmaline. And Emmaline lunged for her crossbow.

She was faster.

Swiping up her bow and quiver at the same time, she nocked a quarrel and leveled the weapon at him.

He stopped dead in his tracks and held up his hands. "Wait. I know the Summer Queen sent you, but I have money. We can talk about this."

"Certainly," she answered with the cold-blooded ease she'd cultivated over the years, "but we can only talk in the language my crossbow speaks." *Death.*

Her poisoned bolt caught O'Shaughnessy in the throat. He stopped in the middle of the room, gargled blood as he clawed at the blue-and-white-feathered fletching, then collapsed dead to the fancy, slick black stone floor, blood forming a murky puddle around him.

It had taken Emmaline only moments to assess the situation, moments to understand that she'd royally, incredibly, fucked up. A fuckup so large that it would alter her life forever. Aileen had been having an affair with O'Shaughnessy without Aeric's knowledge, hence her presence in his bed. Even then, Emmaline had worried about how Aeric would take this devastating news.

Because she was a total idiot. Gods, she'd always been an idiot for Aeric.

She considered leaving Aileen in O'Shaughnessy's bed, allowing those who found them to make the obvious conclusion.

Except, they wouldn't.

Everyone had known about Emmaline's crush on the Blacksmith. Anyone who happened upon the scene would think she'd killed Aileen on purpose—that, upon finding Aileen in such a compromising position, there with O'Shaughnessy, Emmaline had taken the opportunity to get her competition out of the way.

Even at her worst, Emmaline would never have done such a thing. Anyway, she'd never thought she'd had a shot with Aeric. Even if Aileen had never been born and he'd been free to be with any woman in the world, she never would have imagined Aeric even looking in her direction.

Since she didn't see an upside to leaving Aileen there, she'd dressed and moved Aileen's body in order to save Aeric pain. It had been hard. Aileen was a slight little thing, but she'd been heavier than she appeared. Emmaline was strong, in shape because of her "job" requirements. With effort, she'd been able to move Aileen's body to the woods before morning. Knowing she'd inconvertibly placed the blame of Aileen's death on her shoulders by doing this, she'd disappeared into the dawn, left fae life, and never looked back.

She'd run away.

It had turned out to be a blessing in disguise because by running away, she'd been liberated. The yoke of service to the Summer Queen had been broken. Lars became only a monster to haunt her nightmares—instead of her reality. Though life had been hard for many years, she'd soared on high-flying wings for a long time, though the guilt of what she'd done had stayed with her forever. Decades later, being cut off from her people had finally started to weigh on her. Instead of flying, she'd floated, entering relationships with humans only to have them grow old and die. Eventually, she'd lost touch with her faeness almost completely.

Then, centuries later, the HFF had been formed. She was one of the founders, along with two other fae who clung together in the sea of humanity. Lillian and Calum were her two greatest friends.

Danu, she sure missed them right now.

THE fact that Gideon's intuition still tingled annoyingly where Emily Millhouse was concerned was only an excuse for the real reason he was breaking into her apartment. He wanted to see what kind of underwear she wore.

The lock was cheap and gave easily. He let himself into the living room and breathed in the faint, lingering scent of her perfume. By the streetlights outside, he could see that the place was furnished more sparsely than he would have imagined. He would have thought floral patterns for Emily, stuffed animals, handmade quilts, and lots of houseplants. Instead the furniture was neutral in color, fairly unremarkable. There were no houseplants, quilts, or stuffed animals.

He stopped at an end table and picked up the copy of Brother Maddoc's book lying there—*The Threat of the Fae in Modern Times*; he scoffed and dropped it back down. Gideon had read it, of course. Maddoc pandered to popular opinion, detailing the great danger the fae posed to humanity while also espousing a wishy-washy, compassionate method of dealing with them. Ugh. Gideon would have put the book straight into the trash can, but he didn't want Emily to know anyone had been in her apartment.

The bookshelves near the television showed a similar taste in reading. Most of the books had been written by the Phaendir or by human scholars of the fae. Scattered among the nonfiction were the classics and a few mystery and romance novels.

The kitchen and bathroom yielded no surprises and nothing suspicious, just as he would have thought. There was only one more room to check; he'd saved the best for last. Moving silently down the short, narrow hallway, he entered her bedroom.

She had a twin-size bed. Good. Not big enough for more than one person. Gideon liked that. Spotting a pretty atomizer on her dresser—an item that looked completely Emily—he picked it up, squirted a little into the air, and inhaled. He closed his eyes, his scar tissue tingling all across his back and down his arms with pleasure. Wallowing in the scent of her, he could imagine himself in that narrow bed with her, her hands stroking down his furrowed back.

Setting the bottle down, he went for the drawers. Opening and closing them, he found sweaters, T-shirts, jeans, and socks. Then, finally, pay dirt. He scooped up a handful of the clothing that Emily had worn so intimately . . . and frowned. Again, this was not what he'd been expecting. He scooped up another handful. Sports bras and cotton briefs. Nothing silky, frilly, lacy. Nothing sexy.

That was odd, since she'd told him once that lingerie was her guilty pleasure. She'd said that buying it was her secret addiction because wearing delicate bras and panties made her feel desirable, even if no man ever saw them. Gideon remembered every single word of that conversation. He'd been expecting to find lots of lovely and expensive things in this drawer. Instead everything was depressingly serviceable and bland. The woman who had chosen these things wanted to feel comfortable, not desirable.

He rifled through the drawer hoping to find something that would tell him that Emily hadn't been lying to him that day. His hand hit something hard, a jewelry box. Holding it up to the light, he could see that it was very old. Gideon was extremely old; he recognized antiques. This silver-plated box was from the early nineteen hundreds and had been well cared for.

Mystified, he walked into the bathroom with it, closed the door, and turned on the light. The bathroom had no windows, so flipping on the light wouldn't draw any unwanted attention. The jewelry inside the box was even older. There were pieces that were clearly from the Victorian era, some much older than that. In fact, the contents of the box were essentially a walk through time, each piece representing a different era of history. Most puzzling, there was a pendant, a pearl in a filigree setting of a type that had been popular with fae nobles in the sixteen hundreds, just before the time of the Great Sweep.

The jewelry and the box itself were worth a fortune. What was it doing in her underwear drawer? For that matter, what was she doing with this stuff in the first place and how had she ever found it all? If he didn't know better, he'd say it was the collection of a long-lived fae woman, mementos collected over her life. But that couldn't be. Emily detested the fae. There was no possible way she would keep the jewelry box of one. The pieces simply had to be antiques she'd acquired somehow. Could they be family heirlooms of some kind?

Of course, that didn't explain the pendant.

He held the filigree and pearl pendant up by its newer chain to the light and wondered.

SIX

WHEN she woke the next morning, a bowl of oatmeal rested on the floor near her head. Wow. First a pillow and blanket. Now oatmeal. She sat up slowly, working the kinks out of her muscles. Two nights sleeping on a concrete floor hadn't done her body any favors.

Her throat hurt even more now than it had before she'd fallen, mentally and physically exhausted, into a fitful sleep. She was certain she had a bunch of bruises shaped like Aeric's fingers ringing her throat, but they'd disappear soon enough. Her heightened healing ability knocked most injuries out in half the time it took other people to heal.

She picked up the oatmeal and began spooning the cooling sludge into her mouth. Movement caught her eye and she realized she wasn't alone. Aeric sat against the opposite wall, looking unrested. Apparently he'd been watching her sleep. Her stomach clenched and she immediately lost her appetite.

"Morning?" It came out as a question because she wasn't sure which Aeric she was getting. Was she getting the enraged Aeric who might lunge across the floor and strangle her at any moment? Or was this the grief-stricken Aeric who was giving up his dreams of vengeance to take the moral high road?

Boy, she hoped it was the latter Aeric. She liked that high road a lot, especially when it kept her alive.

"You said that killing Aileen was an accident."

Her bite of oatmeal went down with an audible gulp. "Did I say that?" Because, hoo boy, she'd never meant to. She set her bowl down.

He nodded. "Last night."

Oh, yes, he meant, *last night after I tried to strangle you and you were begging for your life*. She touched her throat. It was possible she'd let slip a little info. She'd been pretty terrified and hadn't been thinking straight.

Well, she'd see how much she could explain without explaining everything. "It *was* an accident. I knew no one would believe me, since I had that . . . um . . . that—"

"Infatuation with me?"

"Yes, that." Anger suddenly rushed through her veins, making her lash out. "A schoolgirl crush. Something I haven't felt for you in hundreds and hundreds of years."

Aeric only studied her in the half-light, not rising to the rage in her voice.

"I knew no one would believe me because of the crush and because of my . . . occupation. It made it seem like I had killed Aileen out of jealousy. That's why I left Ireland after it happened. I knew that no matter what I said, my reputation would precede any explanation I made. I knew you'd kill me."

"You were right. No *assassin* of the Summer Queen has *schoolgirl* crushes. You were never that innocent."

She crossed her arms over her chest. "Maybe you perceive me that way. I was just trying to survive, Aeric. I was young, impressionable."

"You were a stone-cold killer."

"Yes, I was," she snapped. "I was what the Summer Queen made me. She took me in when I had no one and molded me from the time I was twelve years old."

"Don't blame her. Don't try and play off my sympathy. You made your own choices." His volume ratcheted up a notch and made the hair at the back of her neck stand on end. "I don't have any sympathy for you."

"You're right." He was right; she wasn't just agreeing with him to help him keep his temper in check. "I did make my own choices and they were the wrong ones. I was, however, highly influenced by others. Manipulated. Threatened. Tricked. Even tortured."

And the Summer Queen, via Lars, had taught her how to effectively do all those things to others. Her "education" hadn't stuck with her for long, however. It just wasn't in Emmaline's basic makeup to be that way. She guessed she'd make a sucky Summer Queen.

"Are you trying to make me feel sorry for you? It won't work."

She gave him a slow blink. "I think I know that." She took a deep breath and set her palms on the floor on either side of her. "Look, Aeric, if I had wanted to kill Aileen to get her out of my way, do you really think I would have done it like that? I was an *assassin* to the *Seelie Royal*, the best there was. I knew how to kill people and keep it quiet when the need arose. If I had wanted to kill Aileen and make a move on you, don't you think I would have made her murder look like an accident?" She thumped back against the wall, out of breath and her throat aching.

All expression had left his face. It was like looking at a blank wall.

"It's just logical," she finished, needing some kind of sound to fill up the sudden unnerving silence.

"It's *logical* that you came upon her in the woods and were so filled with murderous rage that you shot her without really thinking about it. Then you panicked and ran."

So that was the scenario he'd been imagining. A crime of passion. Her jealousy had so overwhelmed her that she'd shot Aileen down in a fit of uncontrollable emotion. "You just said I was a stone-cold killer. How much do you think passion or panic entered into my decision making back then?"

He looked away from her, his jaw locking. He still hadn't asked her for the details of Aileen's accidental death and that was a good thing. "You just called yourself a manipulated young woman with a schoolgirl crush. Pick an illusion and stick with it."

Ouch and touché.

"I was both, Aeric. Two sides of the same coin. I learned to kill for the Summer Queen at an early age, and I showed great proclivity for it. Believe me when I say that passion or panic never weighed in my decision making where doling out death was concerned."

He shook his head and gave a laugh that sounded anything but joyful. "You are incredible. You have an answer for everything and I can't believe any of it."

"I can't help you with that, Aeric. The truth is all I have, and that's all I'm telling you. You either believe it or you don't."

"I don't."

She lifted her hands and shrugged her shoulders. "Okay."

They sat together in silence for several long moments, her uneaten oatmeal growing cold and congealing on top. The couple of bites she'd taken sat like little paperweights in her gut.

"You need a shower and a change of clothes," he said finally.

Hope surged through her. There was a toilet here in the forge, but not a shower. That meant the shower was behind that door, in his apartment. If she could get into his place, maybe she could escape him. Granted, she had no idea where she'd go after that, since the Blacksmith had been her destination in the first place, but she'd figure it out after she gained her freedom.

"I would enjoy both."

His answer came as a snarl. "I don't really care—"

"—what I would enjoy. Yes, I get that. Probably you just don't want me stinking up your forge, right?"

He stood. "Come with me. Try anything and I'll nail you to the wall."

Wall. Nailed. Got it.

She struggled to stand on sore legs and hips, then hobbled after him. The bright light of his apartment made her blink and squint. She'd spent the last week in murky darkness.

Once she could see, she assessed her surroundings instantly as a bachelor's apartment. It was a nice place, though there were no windows. Apparently they were underground. The door behind the tapestry was interesting. The forge was a secret. She could guess why. Most charmed iron weapons had been outlawed since the end of the fae wars. She wondered if now she knew too much. Maybe he'd have to kill her after all.

The furniture was the type she would've selected, neutral colors, overstuffed, comfortable. No fussy pieces. No kitsch. Lots of pillows and throw blankets. The floor was wood and covered with colorful area rugs.

It was amazing she noticed the furniture at all under the clutter. Clothes were piled on the couch and chairs. Shoes had been discarded by the end table and the front door and kicked off haphazardly on the floor near a short hallway. The kitchen was a mess of dishes, discarded towels, and abandoned food containers.

Apparently Aeric had never married and likely didn't have a girlfriend. Unless said wife or girlfriend was the messy type. *But of course*. He was married to Aileen in his heart and no other woman would ever measure up.

"The bathroom is over here." He led her past the discarded shoes and down the small hallway. An open doorway led to a large bathroom. A whirlpool tub sat in one corner, clothes draped over the side. It looked like he didn't use it much. A shower stall stood next to it.

Staring at the draped clothes, she wanted to crack wise about things called closets, but her sense of self-preservation kicked in before she opened her mouth.

Turning, she glimpsed herself in the mirror over the bathroom counter. She stopped and stared—arrested. It had been so long since she'd seen herself, *really* seen herself. Centuries had passed. She was no longer the twelve-year-old girl she'd been when she'd taken on glamour permanently. Now she looked to be in her late twenties; age had been kind to her. Long dark hair curled past her shoulders. She had the same whiskey-colored eyes, the same full mouth and slightly crooked nose. The same long face and pointy chin. Yellow and green bruises marked her throat and dark circles stained the flesh under her eyes. *Lovely.*

"Are you all right?" Aeric asked.

She jerked, realizing how she'd been staring, so transfixed. "I'm fine."

He pointed at a towel, washcloth, and toiletries like soap and a toothbrush, all still in their packages on the bathroom counter. "Those are for you to use. I also found you some clothes I think might fit." He leaned up against the counter and crossed his arms over his brawny chest.

"Okay, thanks."

They stared at each other for several moments until dread bloomed in her stomach.

Her jaw worked for a moment as she narrowed her eyes. "You *are* leaving the room, right?"

"Hell, no." She followed his line of sight to a grate in the wall. She never would have even seen it, if he hadn't made her notice it. "You could escape."

She tamped down a flare of total aggravation. Instead she went over to the grate and pointed at it, then herself. "There's no way, *for the love of Danu*, that I could ever fit through there."

"I disagree. You could glamour yourself into a mouse and slip through."

She fisted her hands at her sides, counting to ten. "I can't do that. Glamour is illusion. I can't actually shift into something else. I can't change my actual body mass."

"I'm staying. If you want a bath, you have to do it with me in the room."

"I'm not taking my clothes off in front of you."

"Then I guess you're not getting a bath."

She rolled her eyes. "Even if I got through that incredibly small space, I wouldn't know where I would be going. I'm in the bowels of the Black Tower, as far as I can tell. I would be utterly and hopelessly lost. Remaining here with you, I'm sorry to say, is preferable to getting lost in the heating system and either dying in there or ending up somewhere worse than your forge." Though there weren't many places worse than here, truthfully.

"The deal is that in order for you to get a bath, I stay in here. If you're worried about me being overcome by your nude body and jumping you, don't concern yourself."

Ouch. Though she'd expected nothing less.

"Fine," she replied in a measured voice. "Stay in the room, then, if you're so worried about me escaping, but I think it's stupid and unnecessary."

"Your concern is noted and disposed of."

Great. Just great. Had Aeric been this pigheaded when she'd known him in Ireland?

Dumb question. Considering the candle he'd been holding for Aileen—and his thirst for revenge—pigheaded didn't even begin to describe this man. More like relentlessly driven to get what he wanted.

Glaring at him, she snatched the towel, washcloth, and soap and went into the frosted glass shower stall with it all. No way was she stripping in front of him. She already felt naked without her glamour; she wasn't going to make it official.

She tossed her clothing over the top of the shower stall door and turned on the water, yelping as she regulated it, since she had to pretty much stand in the stream while she did it. Once she had the water the right temperature, she settled into it with a sigh of pleasure, closed her eyes, and tried her best to ignore the fact that an unpredictable man who hated her stood right outside.

HE was having a hard time hating her. That was the problem.

He wished he could. He was trying to hate her as hard as he could, but that sliver of doubt about how Aileen had died had lodged itself in his mind and it didn't appear to be planning to dislodge anytime soon. No matter how hard he tried to remember, or all the years he'd spent waiting for revenge, he couldn't shake it free.

There was something about Emmaline that called to him. He wished he could heat that intangible element up and use his hammer on it, transform it into something he could use to fuel his anger—a weapon. Instead all it did was get in his way, make him change his plans, and, *Goibhniu*, show her mercy.

He hated that he saw innocence in her brown eyes no matter how hard he tried to see guilt. He hated that he couldn't dredge up the strength to kill her for what she'd done, accident or not. He hated that by doing and thinking all of this, he was dishonoring Aileen's memory. Most of all, he hated that he seemed unable to think or do anything else.

No, scratch that; most of all he hated that she looked really good behind that frosted glass.

He turned his face away and cleared his throat, regretting his bright idea to stay in the room. He only noticed her because he was a man, with the normal urges and desires of a man. Emmaline—no matter who she was or what she'd done—was a beautiful woman and his dick noticed it. That was all.

The water shut off and Emmaline pulled the towel from where she'd draped it over the top of the shower wall. A few moments later she emerged with it wrapped around her midsection, the flap tucked in just above one breast, and stepped onto the plush bathroom rug. She'd obviously taken care in trying to cover as much of her body as possible, but she still flashed a nice amount of thigh. Aeric looked away.

Without acknowledging his presence, she crossed to the sink, forcing him to move to the side. He looked on in silence as she brushed her teeth and scrubbed her face clean. He tried not to notice the way the towel clung to her damp curves, especially her ass.

Goibhniu strike him dead.

"Do you have a comb?" she asked, trying to separate the long, damp skeins of her hair with her fingers and wincing.

He fished one out and she set to work.

"Get dressed before you do that," he growled. "You don't need to be standing around in a towel."

She glared at him and set the comb down on the counter. "Only if you turn around and give me some privacy."

There was a bite to her words. Clearly she was attempting to keep her temper in check, probably worried about triggering his temper, but she couldn't quite suppress all of it. It came out in her voice and in dangerous flashes of her eyes. He suspected this was a woman who—in a normal situation—usually always made sure she had the upper hand. She had backbone and a good amount of pride. This situation had to be killing her.

Good.

If he couldn't actually kill her, the very least he could do was make her uneasy. And that, he was pretty sure, was an area in which he'd been excelling.

He smiled and she took a step back, looking suddenly worried. Apparently he needed to work on faking a reassuring smile. Of course, he *had* tried to strangle her; any move he made now probably seemed threatening to her.

"I'll turn my back," he answered. "Okay?" It would be more for him than her, since his slight flicker of attraction for her—no matter that it was completely hormone based—disturbed the fuck out of him.

Her lips parted in surprise and her eyes widened. "Just like that? No battle? No big argument?"

"Just like that." He turned to face the door and the noise of rustling clothing filled the room. It sounded like the fastest clothing change ever. He turned back when he heard the rake of the comb through her hair again.

The clothes really didn't fit her at all. He'd selected his smallest-sized stuff, stuff he couldn't wear. Still, the sweatpants and T-shirt hung off her in an almost comical way.

But at least she was well covered.

"Back to the forge," he barked at her, making her jump. "You can pee in that bathroom, if you need to."

She turned to him, comb in her hand. "Keeping me here is wrong, Aeric. If you only knew what was at stake."

He crossed his arms over his chest. "Is this the HFF thing again?" he drawled, letting his eyelids drift halfway shut. "How you're here undercover for the Phaendir so you can really be undercover for the HFF? How the fate of our people lies in my hands?" He made sure he infused his words with all the mocking he felt.

Suddenly it was like all the air went out of her. "I wish you believed me."

"Do you have proof anything you say is true? Anything at all?"

She chewed her lower lip for a moment. "No."

"Why, out of everyone in the whole world, would they send *you* to *my* door, Emmaline? Whose bloody stroke of brilliance was that?"

"My glamour. I was the only one who could get in and out of Piefferburg with no complications." She gave a harsh laugh. "Guess the joke is on me, huh?"

"Guess so."

She made a frustrated sound and paced the small room. "When the opportunity came, I was perfectly set up to go in. I never imagined that you would have that net set up to identify me as soon as I stepped into Piefferburg. I thought—"

"I see. You thought I would never recognize you under your glamour."

She stopped and stared at him. "Yes, that's what I thought. I meant to check in at the Rose Tower with the *Faemous* crew and then sneak over here to share the situation with you and have you make the key. You were never supposed to know who I really was. I couldn't let our past get in the way of the mission. There's too much at stake, Aeric."

"Illusion under layer of illusion. Lies piled on lies. How I am supposed to know the truth?"

Without warning, she walked over, put her hands on his biceps, and looked up into his eyes. Her touch made him want to run out of the room, but not for the reason he'd prefer. He straightened and pushed back against the counter as far as he could get.

"You don't understand how important this is," she said,

staring into his eyes as if to imprint her words on his brain. "Already the Phaendir will be getting suspicious because I haven't checked in with them. If they start poking around deep enough and discover my identity, I'll never be able to get the key out of here. The fae will lose their best and only shot at recovering another piece of the *bosca fadbh*."

"How did you plan to contact the Phaendir?"

"I have a cell phone in my pack that will let me call outside of Piefferburg."

"Great. Go get it. You can call your HFF buddies and let me talk to them. They'll confirm your story, right?"

The slight glow of hope that had infused her face disappeared, leaving her eyes flat brown. She let go of him and turned away. "No. I can't contact them on that phone. It was only meant to be used to call the Phaendir."

And, conveniently, there was no other way for the fae to contact the outside world.

"So I'm just supposed to take you on faith. *You*."

She cradled her head in her hands. "You weren't supposed to know it was me."

"And that makes me trust you so much more."

She turned to him and held out her hands. "There are bigger things at stake here, Aeric. Bigger than you or me. Bigger than the past." She paused. "Even bigger than Aileen—her death or her memory."

Wrong thing to say.

"Back to the forge," he yelled. *"Now."*

"Wait! I might have something that will convince you I'm telling the truth. I have the model for the key hidden in the lining of my pack. I also have the markings—"

"We're done here. *Move.*"

SEVEN

AERIC rifled through Emmaline's pack until his fingers closed on the thing he sought—the mock key, presumably the model of the item he was supposed to craft from charmed iron and imbue with his magick. It was where she'd said it would be, hidden in the lining along with a paper full of writing in Old Maejian, an ancient fae language he spoke fluently.

He pulled out the mock key and let it lie in his hand. It was large and oddly shaped—like no key he'd ever seen before. A complicated piece.

It was here, just as she'd said it would be. So what did that mean? Why would she be carrying a model for a charmed iron key around with her? It wasn't a common item people needed. Did that mean her far-fetched story about coming to Piefferburg to seek him out was actually true?

And if that story was true, what else was true?

Or was the mock key for some other purpose and she'd simply worked it into a lie to tell him in order to save her ass from the spanking he so wanted to give her?

His hand closed over the object and he sat down against the wall. She lay about four feet away from him, her head on the pillow he'd provided her and the blanket in a knot around her waist. Emmaline constantly tossed in her sleep as if plagued by bad dreams.

When he'd known her back in Ireland, she'd never worn her true form. Back then she'd had long red hair, green eyes, and a pale complexion. She'd been a little shorter and curvier, too. He presumed that she changed forms when she went out to kill for the Summer Queen, using her skill with glamour to get close to her marks so she could slip in her dagger . . . or her signature crossbow bolt with its blue and white fletching.

Emmaline could take any form she wanted—no one was safe from her. That ability, along with her healing ability, had made her an incredibly effective weapon. The Shadow King had both coveted and feared Emmaline Siobhan Keara Gallagher, and it was said that the Summer Queen had mourned the loss of her assassin for centuries when Emmaline had left Ireland.

He watched as she shifted yet again, rolling to her back and grimacing as though in the grip of a nightmare. Her true form was much prettier than the one she'd worn when he knew her, if less perfect. In all the guises he'd ever seen her wear she'd ditched the slightly crooked two front teeth and her subtly bent nose. But, then, Aeric had always found natural beauty to be the most appealing, even if that natural beauty wasn't perfect.

He knew much more about her than he'd let on earlier. He always made it a point to learn as much as he could about his enemies. She'd been born to Seelie noble people, both of exceedingly pure stock. When she'd reached the age of ten, after her abilities in glamour had begun to manifest, her mother and father had died within just months of each other.

Her mother had taken ill and died of pneumonia—the fae were, for all intents and purposes, immortal by human terms, but they still died of illness and from accidents. Her father had died from injuries sustained in a hunting accident. Oddly enough, from an arrow to the chest. Aeric had always wondered about Emmaline's choice of weapon based on that information.

He'd also wondered just how much of a hand the Summer Queen might have had in the deaths of her parents.

At ten, an orphan, Emmaline had been without extended family. She'd had nowhere to go. For two years she'd fought it out on her own, scavenging for food and accepting charity from the local village while grieving the loss of her formally comfortable life—not to mention her parents.

When Emmaline turned twelve, the Summer Queen had stepped in to help her. Of course, help from the Summer Queen never came without a price. Emmaline was right to say that she'd been groomed to be a killer. The Summer Queen had taken a young girl who had been taught she needed to make compromises to survive—and turned her into a monster.

Aeric had assumed that the monster in Emmaline had always been there and the Summer Queen had only pulled it to the surface. But who Emmaline had been then didn't jibe with who she seemed to be now. Maybe Emmaline had never been the monster he'd presumed.

He swallowed hard, clutching the mock key in his hand. Her thick dark hair was spread over the pillow and her long lashes were feathered down against her cheeks. Looking at her this way, in her true form, he just couldn't believe she'd killed Aileen in cold blood.

He sat there until morning, conflict gnawing a hole in his stomach, until she finally woke. When she glimpsed him, her eyes opened a bit wider and her body visibly tightened. "Waking up to have you staring at me is not reassuring."

"When I said I wouldn't kill you, I meant it."

She pushed up to a sitting position, wincing and rolling her shoulders. "Yeah, well, did anyone ever tell you that watching someone sleep is pretty much off the creepy meter? When you do that you compete with Brother Gideon for highest honors."

"Brother Gideon is a Phaendir, of course."

She nodded. "The most dangerous one around. The reason the fae need to find a way out of Piefferburg pronto."

He opened his hand and showed her the key mock-up.

Her eyes narrowed. "You know, going through people's things is pretty damn creepy, too."

"You gave up your right to privacy on the night you killed Aileen, accident or not."

"I told you I had it."

"And you weren't lying." He paused a beat. "For once."

"*Ever*. I haven't lied to you at all, Aeric. Not once."

He fisted the mock key again. "Okay, Miss All-about-the-Truth, tell me *exactly* what happened the night Aileen was killed."

She paled. Licking her lips, she pulled a shaky hand through her hair. "I can't tell you about that night, Aeric. I won't tell you a lie and I don't want you to know the truth."

Damn it. Just when he was starting to think she might not be full of shit.

He moved toward her and she moved away. He knew what he must look like—coldly enraged. Crowding her against the wall, he took her by the upper arms and held her still. "Tell me."

"You won't believe it." Her voice trembled.

"Okay." He gave her a brief flash of teeth. "Then what do you have to lose?"

She licked her lips again in a nervous gesture and he caught himself watching. *Fuck*. "I'm actually worried you *will* believe me. That's the problem." Her eyes shone bright, but not with tears. He wasn't sure this woman had any tears in her. "I'm worried about what the truth will do to you."

He blinked, released her arms, and rocked back on his heels. "Why would you care how I feel? I meant you harm." He paused and then growled. "Hell, I still mean you harm."

She let out a slow, careful breath, studying him.

Realization dawned. "Because your crush on me never ended?" It sounded beyond arrogant, even to him. "Even after all these years? Even now? I thought you said that ended centuries ago."

She cleared her throat and looked downward. "I think *crush* is an unwise word to use."

Her words socked him in the gut. He didn't like where this was going at all. "So what else would you call it?"

"I'm really not sure. Back in Ireland I didn't want you to be hurt, so I took great pains to ease your suffering as much as I could . . . where Aileen's death was concerned. I concealed certain . . . facts." She paused, licked her lips. "I don't want to see you hurt now, either."

"I kidnapped you. I tried to kill you." He could hear the note of amazement in his voice. This was not how he'd seen this conversation going. "Why do you care?"

Her gaze met his, now more angry than nervous. "Yes, I'm aware that I need to see a psychiatrist. I lack good sense."

"An understatement."

"Okay, yes, I need to be medicated. Hospitalized, maybe. Rubber-roomed." She rubbed her face as if she was tired.

"Emmaline—"

"Don't make me tell you."

"You *are* going to tell me, Emmaline. You're going to do it right now and it's going to be the truth."

She sighed and leaned her head back against the wall. "*No.*" She sounded tired, but resolute.

He opened his palm, looking down at the model of the key. It was made of plaster, fragile and highly breakable. It was also something she professed to care a great deal about. He stood and held it out so she could see what he meant to do. "I said I wouldn't hurt you and I keep my word. But I never said I wouldn't hurt this."

She leapt to her feet. "No! Aeric, you can't!"

"All I have to do is drop this to the floor and stamp my boot on it once. Bye-bye, key."

"You wouldn't!"

"Wanna bet? I'm still not convinced you're telling me the truth about this thing. What's to lose?" He moved his hand as if to let it go.

"No! All right, all right! I'll tell you!"

He stopped, closing his fingers around the key and pulling it close to his chest.

She made a sound of frustration and sat back down. "Get comfortable. It's a long story."

He listened, transported back in time to the horror of the fae wars. He listened to how the Summer Queen had commanded Emmaline to kill Driscoll Manus O'Shaughnessy before someone else could get to him, how she'd snuck into his home and into his bedroom. He listened as she told him about how she'd shot the person in the bed from behind, unwilling to make him suffer, thinking it was O'Shaughnessy—and then finding Aileen instead.

She told him about making the decision not to leave the body there and instead transport it to the woods near his home. Then she told him how devastated she'd been at the accidental death. How frightened she'd been of his wrath. How she'd fled that part of Ireland with only the clothes on her back, even leaving her crossbow behind.

By the time she'd finished, his chest and stomach roiled with emotion that couldn't seem to make it up to his brain in any semblance of logical thought. It was just a big black-and-blue bloody mess. He shook his head. "No, she had a friend that was ill. She told me she was spending her nights with her."

It sounded lame when he said it out loud. Had he really believed that?

Of course he had. It was *Aileen*.

Emmaline didn't say anything. She only looked down at her hands, folded in her lap.

"It's impossible," he said softly. Then louder, "You're lying."

She raised her head and smiled. "I knew you wouldn't believe me. The only thing you'd believe was if I told you a story in which I happened upon her in the woods and saw my chance to take out the competition. Or perhaps that I'd just killed her out of spite, planning to run away anyway."

He rubbed his hand over his face. Driscoll Manus O'Shaughnessy and Aileen? No, it simply couldn't be. That fae had been a monster. It had been written into his DNA. And he'd been Seelie to boot. Aileen had been Unseelie to the core and had never enjoyed the company of their flip side brethren.

But the animals in the forest when Aileen was a child . . .

His memory flashed to the horror of that—images he'd pushed out of his mind because he'd been unwilling to mate them with the woman he loved. The blood. The torture. The weapons she'd used. The joy she'd taken in their suffering. He hadn't let his mind go that far down those paths of recollection in a long, long time.

Was it possible? Could her behavior have gone further than animals? Had Aileen been hiding some kind of dark and awful secret from him, leading a shadowy double life of some sort? Maybe O'Shaughnessy and Aileen had found a common dark tie that helped them to foster a relationship. He forced the unpleasant link out of his head.

There were other things, too. Times when Aileen had expressed a desire to seek relationships with other men. Aeric had taken her virginity—as she had taken his. Neither of them had ever been with anyone else. He'd been happy to make the commitment, but Aileen . . . at times he'd thought she wasn't so content.

No. His mind couldn't walk those paths. Not now. Not ever.

"I didn't want you to know because I didn't want to destroy the idea of Aileen that you've been keeping so pristine all these years," said Emmaline in a quiet voice. "I'm sorry."

"Don't be. I would have to believe you for you to ruin her memory."

Her expression settled to stone and her chin lifted. But her eyes flashed with pain for a moment, destroying the image she was trying to project. "Then I'm glad you don't."

He moved closer and her whole body stiffened. "So we've established that you killed Aileen and you're lying about the circumstances to save your pretty ass. We've also established that I'm unable to kill you. The only question that remains is how I should make you pay."

His gaze raked her up and down and his body reacted. His

too big clothing hid her curves, but he'd had enough of a tantalizing glimpse of them during her shower to let his imagination run wild.

The very last thing he should be doing right now was remember the way her body looked behind that frosted glass. It was almost worse than having her naked. The image behind the shower door hinted at lush breasts—an overflowing handful—a narrow waist that flared into a generous, curvy bottom, and shapely legs.

He wanted to find out for sure, using his hands and maybe his tongue, too.

He'd brutally suppressed the urge before, tamping down the attraction he felt for her because it wasn't right. Now, in the violent wake of what Emmaline had told him and his subsequent confusion over whether or not it was true—all that want came rushing back at him. It didn't matter that it was horribly misplaced.

And damned if he could remember why he shouldn't give in to it.

HE was looking at her without anger in his eyes for once.

Okay, maybe there was a little anger in his eyes, but she had the feeling that the anger—for whatever mystical and unbelievable reason—wasn't directed at her, but at himself. And anger wasn't the only thing in his expression right now; there was hunger, too.

And *that* was all for her.

Her heart thudded so fast and so hard she thought it might break her ribs. What the hell? His behavior had changed so quickly she practically had whiplash.

"Aeric?" she whispered. She wasn't even aware his name had slipped past her lips until it was out there. She didn't know what to do with this sudden turn of events . . . although her body sure seemed to know. Her mind was awhirl with confusion, but the rest of her was quite aware that the man she'd wanted and fantasized about for so long was inches away from her . . . and seemed to actually want her back.

"Fuck," he growled, bracing his hand on the wall right near her ear and moving closer to her. "This is not a good thing."

"No." She licked her lips—a nervous habit she'd had since she was a kid, no matter what guise she used. "This is not a good thing for either of us."

His mouth almost brushed hers when he spoke. Her body flared to life, singing to almost painful arousal. Her nipples leapt to hard little points and she ached between her thighs. This man seemed to either terrify her, piss her off, or plunge her straight into animalistic heat.

His voice was a low growl, laced with anger. "I should chain you to my bed in charmed iron and take my revenge that way."

She closed her eyes, her breath shuddering out of her. "I wouldn't object."

His eyes narrowed like a hunter's sighting prey—and, boy, was she ever. Wounded, limping prey at that. She had no chance. "Don't you have any shame?" he asked in a low, harsh voice.

"Not where you're concerned. I never have."

He eased her against him and dropped his mouth to her throat. Goose bumps erupted all over her skin. He nipped her flesh and then licked the small hurt. As though he wanted to punish her, but couldn't make himself do it. "I fucking hate that I want you."

She sucked in a breath. He wanted her? When the hell had that happened? "Ditto," she replied in a shaky voice.

"You killed someone I loved."

She shivered at the grief and torture in his voice and wished for the millionth time she could turn back the hands of time and change the events of that night. "Yes, I did. I wish I could go back and relive that night, not kill her."

Tell Driscoll I love him.

Aeric could never know what Aileen had said that night. She would never tell him. It would serve no purpose.

"You can't." He bit her again, this time hard enough to bring her to the edge of pain right before a sweet rush of pleasure. She yelped and then melted against him. "I should handcuff you and fuck you like I've been imagining. Satisfy this urge I have for you and then be done with it."

"I wouldn't stop you." Her cheeks burned even as she uttered the words. She was not a weak woman, never had been, but Aeric Killian Riordan O'Malley was her Achilles' heel. He always had been and, apparently, he always would be. Her fingers found purchase in his broad shoulders and she hung on for dear life. She wanted anything he cared to give her, any little stroke of his hand. *Pathetic*. She'd wanted him for so long and, it was true, she had no shame.

She just wanted him to touch her.

"Get up."

EIGHT

SHE rose on shaky legs.

If she'd been a smarter woman, she would be fighting him. If she were a stronger woman, she'd be screaming her head off right now. Instead, her knees went weak and her breathing went shallow and excited when he pressed her against the wall and molded his large, warm body to hers.

He didn't ask, he just took. Lifting the hem of the jersey she wore, he freed her breasts, baring her to him from the waist up. His gaze swept over her and her nipples tightened as if he'd stroked them. His gaze caught and held for a moment on the scars that marked her stomach and thighs, then skated over them.

She'd forgotten the scars, forgotten she wasn't hiding them with glamour. She tried to force the jersey down, but he wouldn't let her.

He covered a breast with his big hand and her nipple tightened against his palm. "Why do you have to be so fucking gorgeous?" he asked, rasping his hand over her sensitive nipple until her breath caught.

Gorgeous? Surprise jolted through her. She wasn't gorgeous. The Summer Queen had always called her gangly and plain. An ugly child who would never become a swan. She'd bought all that when she was a kid, though now she knew the queen had been manipulating her by tearing down her fragile adolescent self-esteem. Still, Emmaline knew her looks were average—not gorgeous.

Lifting her hands above her head, he pinned them to the wall behind her and stared hard at her. "I want to fuck you, Emmaline. Long and hard. I want to fuck you all night just to satisfy my craving for you. Doesn't that scare you?"

"Scare me?" she echoed dumbly. She was having trouble breathing. The slow, sweet ache between her thighs had intensified with his words. She wanted his hand there, his cock. Every inch of her cried out to be touched by him.

Holding her wrists in one huge hand, he used his other hand to stroke down her extended arm, over one breast, all the way to the waistband of her sweatpants, which were so big on her that they hung on her hips, threatening to fall at the slightest brush of his hand. His fingers glided over the skin of her hip bone and she shivered.

"You love this, don't you?" He sounded amazed.

"You won't hurt me."

His jaw locked. "Hurting you is not on my agenda." He stroked one of her nipples until her knees went weak. "I want to watch you come. I want to touch you. I want my cock inside you." He paused and his voice got lower, rougher. "But don't make the mistake of thinking I'm a good man, Emmaline."

He lowered his mouth to one of her nipples and sucked the rigid peak into his mouth. Her breath hissed out of her and her back arched. The effect was that she pushed into him, offering herself to him. Freeing her wrists, he cupped the other breast in his work-calloused hand and brushed his thumb back and forth across her nipple, making a moan struggle up from her throat.

He worked the nipple in his mouth with his tongue, flicking the tip and alternately scraping his teeth over it.

Pleasure coursed through her, centering between her thighs. Her clit felt huge and ultrasensitive. One stroke of his hand between her thighs and she would come. She would quake and shiver and moan his name like some silly virgin in the hands of a sexual master—and all he was doing was touching her breasts.

God, she hated this. If she had any backbone—any pride, like he'd said—she'd push him away instead of rubbing up against him like a cat in heat, desperate for more contact from this man *who hated her*.

The far-too-large-for-her sweatpants, which she constantly had to yank up, finally fell down, puddling around her ankles and leaving her totally nude and vulnerable. His breath caught as he realized what had happened and he stilled. Then he made a low, guttural sound at the back of his throat. A sound of desire and of need.

Roughly, he forced her thighs apart and his hand between them. His fingers slicked over her, finding her hot and wet. She shuddered when he found her entrance. Two big, broad fingers pushed deep inside her, forcing her muscles to stretch and filling her up. He thrust hard and fast. No slow easing of the way. No gentleness. This was raw. This was a total possession of the most intimate part of her body.

The cry of surprise she gave ended in a moan. Her knees weak, she clung to his shoulders, holding herself up as he rocked her against the wall with every inward thrust. The pleasure pouring into her body, along with a healthy dollop of total shock, cleared her brain of all thoughts. Soon she was nothing but animalistic sexual need.

He buried his face in her hair, the fabric of his shirt rasping against her bare breasts and her sensitive nipples. The angle of his hand changed a little, his fingertips dragging over some spot deep inside her that felt so good it brought her right up against the threshold of an orgasm.

"Come for me," he murmured near her ear. "I want to feel you come, Emmaline."

Her climax crashed over her. Pleasure racked her body in wave after wave that made her bones feel like butter. Moans tore from her throat, making it sore. Her sex milked his thrusting fingers as it washed through her, stealing her thought and almost her ability to stand. She squeezed her eyes shut and dug her fingernails into his shoulders hard enough to draw blood, in part to keep her balance, in part to punish him for doing this to her.

Panting as the last of the orgasm shivered through her, she opened her eyes and sagged back against the wall.

He stared at her, a feral look on his already savage face. His gaze took her whole body in, his fists clenching at his sides. She knew what she must look like, nipples hard and red from his mouth, legs parted, sex swollen and needy, the fair skin of her chest, stomach, and thighs reddened from the rough brush of his clothing, her eyelids heavy with sexual satisfaction and lust. The way he looked at her, it was like he was trying to stop himself from dragging his pants down, pushing her thighs apart, and fucking her right here and now.

It was a battle she hoped he would lose. She would take this man any way he wanted to come to her, even though a part of her hated him for doing this, for making her feel so helpless and so fucking weak. He raised his gaze to hers and saw the accusation in her eyes.

Swearing under his breath, he turned her roughly to face the wall—maybe so he didn't have to look at her—and pressed her against it. It was cold and rough against her bare skin and her erect nipples. She heard the sound of the zipper of his jeans being lowered, the rustle of fabric. He kicked her feet apart, angled her hips so her rear thrust out. Then he was there behind her, his body heat and the press of his cock against the vulnerable flesh of her sex.

Nothing.

The wide and rock-hard shaft of his cock nestled flush against her opening, the head butting up against her swollen clit.

But he did nothing.

A part of her thrilled, hoped he would stop, that he would have the strength to say no to this when she just simply didn't. A part of her died, hoping he would reposition himself, sink deep inside her, and ride them both to heaven and back.

He moved a little, hands on her hips, and then stopped. A vituperative stream of Old Maejian tore from his lips. He moved his pelvis away from hers, his hand slipping down over her abdomen, sliding between her thighs from the front.

With a sob of pure need, she ground herself against his fingers. He petted her aching sex, stroked her clit until she came apart again. He was gone before it was over, leaving her to slump down the wall to the floor, still shuddering under the tail end of the power of her second climax.

Fists clenched at his sides, he watched her shiver and quake on the floor, caught in the throes of the pleasure he'd given her. Breasts still bare, clothing in piles around her, she was sure she was quite a sight.

When she finally could, she looked up at him. He'd already buttoned his jeans. What she saw on his face made her cover her breasts and curl into herself. Anger and lust all rolled into one, his expression was brutal.

She pushed into a sitting position. "What are you thinking?" The words came out before she'd thought them through—typical. She wasn't sure wanted to know the answer to that question.

His expression darkened. "I'm thinking about all the different ways I want to fuck you and how I can stop myself from doing it." Then he turned and left the forge.

She watched him leave the room and then slumped down again in relief. This was crazy and out of control and it needed to end now. She could not do this.

She needed to find her willpower where this man was concerned.

This may have been a one-time thing, some sort of strange temporary blip in the universe. Maybe it would never happen again. After all, *unpredictable* and *volatile* were terms that Aeric owned. But if it did happen again, she had to be ready. She couldn't give in to him like some pathetic doormat happily ready to wear the marks of his boots.

She needed to find her self-respect and soon. She needed to make it stronger than her desire for that man.

It was a matter of survival. Her heart couldn't take him touching her without caring for her, too. She couldn't endure his hands on her, his cock inside her, while he wore an expression like he'd just been wearing. She didn't want anger and hatred from him.

It would kill her more effectively than any of the weapons hanging around her.

Thinking about what had just happened, she fisted her hands, her rage building to a fine trembling in her limbs. How dare he take advantage of her like that? At the moment she couldn't decide who she disliked more—herself or him.

"I can't believe you've only been here two weeks and you've already hooked up with a woman. I want that kind of luck." Calum's huge voice boomed through the hotel suite.

Calum, one of David's closest friends—and Emmaline's—had come in from the States that morning to act as another pair of eyes and ears during Emmaline's strange absence. Calum's arrival demonstrated that the HFF was becoming concerned, too.

David was glad that he was here for more reasons than one.

He'd gone back to the coffee shop to take advantage of the Internet and the beautiful woman who'd given him the free drink who had been working at the counter. She'd given off every signal known to man of a woman smitten, yet shy. His resolve to stay on task had weakened and he'd struck up a conversation with her. Turned out the conversation had serious legs. David liked her. A lot.

David gave himself a final check in the mirror hanging on the wall of his posh hotel suite. The HFF was funded by a few mysterious and deep-pocketed individuals. They only gave their operatives the best. "You'll be able to tell if she's linked to the Phaendir in any way, won't you?"

Calum nodded, shifting his enormous body on the couch.

"If she's got the stink of the Phaendir on her, I'll smell it. If she's fae, I'll know it. When she gets here, I'll check her out."

Calum was trooping fae, not enough Tuatha Dé blood to make him Seelie and no dark magick to make him Unseelie. Calum was just Calum—a geek who also happened to be fae. He was a fae scholar, who sometimes worked in the archives of the old fae tomes the HFF kept in Ireland. Calum was the one who'd deciphered the Old Maejian on the box and who had made the mock key that Emmaline had carried into Piefferburg for the Blacksmith. His magick was light and harmless—the only thing he could do was sense other fae and the Phaendir—and anyone who had the stink of the Phaendir on them. It was how he'd avoided the Great Sweep.

"If I give you a thumbs-up, you'll know she's all right," Calum finished. "No fae, no ties to the Phaendir."

At this point, it would break David's heart if Kiya turned out dirty in some way. Maybe he was being overly cautious. Of course, in times like these, playing for stakes this high, there wasn't any such thing as overly cautious.

David was smitten with her. Probably a little more than he should be, since he was leaving soon and she would remain almost halfway around the goddamn world. He couldn't seem to help it, though.

Her name was Kiya and she was an Egyptian immigrant who had come from a rich family and attended boarding school in the U.K. as she grew up. Now estranged from her parents for reasons she wouldn't discuss, she lived and worked in Haifa while contemplating what she would do with the rest of her life.

He'd wooed her for a couple days, turning on his charm at the counter while she laughed and filled orders. After all, apparently he had time to kill. Why not make the best of it? Finally she'd accepted a dinner invitation. Now he was in his hotel room with Calum, waiting for her to arrive.

Calum rose from the couch and clapped him on the back. It hurt. Calum was a big guy with a heavy beard, a mustache, and a bald head. What he lacked in hair on his head, he made up for in muscle. "Don't look so worried. I'm sure Kiya's fine. No sense in you sitting around here in the hotel room twiddling your thumbs while we wait for Emmaline. If you have a hot woman, you might as well get out there and spend some time with her. I haven't seen you date anyone since the divorce."

Someone knocked on the hotel room door.

"Ah, it's the hot woman," Calum said with a wink.

David let her in. She was dressed in a filmy blue and white dress and her hair was pinned up against the warm weather, dark, loose tendrils falling around her slender neck. He had a sudden urge to lean in and nibble on that expanse of coffee-and-cream-colored skin. God, she was beautiful.

She looked surprised to see Calum. "Hello."

Calum reached out to shake her hand and she took it. "Hi, I'm a colleague of David's," he said with a smile. "Here in town on business. Nice to meet you."

She favored him with a dazzling smile. "Very nice to meet you. I hope you enjoy your stay in our city, Calum."

Calum broke the handshake and gave the thumbs-up signal with a knowing wink at David. "You two have fun tonight."

David let out the breath he'd been holding. Of course she was clean.

"You don't want to come along, Calum?" Kiya asked. "We have room at our table for one more."

"No, thanks. I feel worse than a whore with—" He bit off his sentence and cleared his throat. "I mean I'm pretty jet-lagged."

"Oh. All right, well, I hope you get some rest, then."

David put his hand on Kiya's waist—a thing he was more than happy to do—and led her out the door. "Don't wait up for me, Calum," David called over his shoulder.

"Wouldn't dream of it."

Making small talk, they traveled the not very pretty, but oddly compelling, streets of Haifa to a nearby Ashkenazi restaurant, where they settled down to an amazing array of sweet and salty dishes flavored with aromatic spices.

"So, what business brings you and Calum to Haifa?" Kiya asked. "I asked you before, but you never really did answer my question."

Yeah, no kidding. Time for some creative white-lying.

"I'm here because I'm an archaeologist and a diver. I intend to explore the ruins of Atlit Yam. Calum is a scholar. He's studying some of the artifacts that have been found around the site."

"Oh." She leaned forward, her eyes sparkling with interest. "How exciting."

"I'm looking forward to it."

"How long will you be in Israel?"

"My time here is open-ended. I'm not really sure when I'll go back to the States. Depends on when we get clearance to dive and what we find down there." Clearance wasn't in their program, of course. They just needed that fucking key.

She glanced at his ring hand. "So you have no wife back in the States who is anxiously awaiting your return?"

He looked down at his hand. There was still a thin white mark from his wedding band. *Ah.* He'd only recently taken it off, though his marriage had ended three years earlier. The question convinced him that she was interested in him. It seemed designed to make sure he wasn't concealing a marriage, by forcing him to answer this question directly.

He reached across the table and covered her hand with his. "I wouldn't have asked you to dinner tonight if I were married. I am not that kind of man."

Her whole body eased. "That's good."

"I was married once," he said. "I'm divorced now."

She swallowed her bite of food and set her fork to the side. "I would say I'm sorry it didn't work out, but I'm not. If it had worked out you wouldn't be having dinner with me." She gave him a shy smile.

He laughed. "Well, I was more interested in the marriage than she was."

Her dark eyes danced. "Not interested in a relationship with you? I find that hard to imagine. I find you very compelling."

"Very *compelling*?" He laughed again. "Should I be flattered or . . . ?"

"You are handsome, intelligent, and interesting. Those qualities all combine to make you compelling."

"Ah, okay, then. I'll be flattered."

"Your ex-wife—what was her name?"

"Emmaline."

"How unique."

"An interesting name for an interesting woman." He tipped his wineglass at her and then took a drink. He wouldn't reveal the fact that Emmaline was fae, of course. Only a handful of humans knew that little tidbit, all of them trusted HFF. He set his glass down. "But that chapter of my life is now closed."

Because he didn't want it getting in the way of any new chapters.

His relationship with Emmaline had been short and disastrous. Emmaline was a long-lived fae and had been in and out of many relationships over her lifetime, but there had always been someone who'd retained a shadowy claim on her emotions. Some nameless man from her past. David had hated him. Because of that intangible tether—that untouchable competitor—she'd never fully invested herself in their relationship, and that missing part of her had destroyed their marriage in record time.

He'd never really known the real Emmaline. Hell, she'd never even shown him her true appearance, the one she was born with. He'd never pressed the issue, since he'd fallen in love with her heart and her mind, not her packaging.

David still cared very much for Emmaline, but they were better off as just friends and colleagues. They had always worked well together at the HFF. Once upon a time they'd been partners. That was how they'd grown so close.

Years ago she'd told him about the Blacksmith. Before she'd entered Piefferburg, she'd called David and told him how worried she was about this mission because of that man. But her skill in glamour was so strong that she could make the Phaendir believe she was human, so surely she could slip past the Blacksmith without him realizing her true identity.

Although she'd been nervous, she'd believed that, and so had David. He'd reassured her that was the case.

But what if they'd been wrong?

Something had fucked up. It didn't take a genius to understand that. He knew Emmaline could handle herself, but if anyone hurt her—that fucking blacksmith, for example—fae trapped in Piefferburg or not, David would find a way to hurt him back.

There were other enemies inside Piefferburg, too. Emmaline had made more than her fair share of them in the Unseelie Court. David knew her past could catch up with her. If it ever did, it would wallop the piss out of her.

"Well," Kiya said, "selfishly, I hope you're staying here for a while."

He smiled. "I'm all yours."

She leaned into him, sliding her hand into his. "Music to my ears."

AERIC couldn't look at any one piece of furniture in his apartment without thinking about how Emmaline would look sprawled on it naked. The couch was an especially bad thing because he could so easily envision her bent over the arm of it, lovely ass raised and thighs parted as he took her in long, driving strokes from behind.

The shower wasn't much better because all he could think about was Emmaline in it, warm water running down her body and her tight pink nipples peeking through white soapsuds. He envisioned himself slipping into the shower with her, pinning her face-first against the tile wall, and easing his cock deep inside her from behind. Hell, it almost drove him to take baths, and he never did that, not since the shower had been invented.

It was like a sickness, this sudden and overwhelming sexual need for a woman he should hate. He guessed a psychiatrist would have a field day plumbing the depths of that one.

The way he saw it, he had two options. He could give in to his driving need to nail this woman, put her in his bed for a night of screwing each other's brains out, and hope that excised the demon that was riding him so hard. Or he could go back on his vow to keep her and let her go. But then what? Would she go back to the Summer Queen and take up her old life as an assassin?

He turned over a charmed iron knife he'd made as he sat at his kitchen table. It was an elaborate piece, the grip carved into the shape of a dragon. The handle was the body; the top the sleek, scaled tail. The mouth was the hilt from which the blade protruded like a tongue that could cut a man to bloody ribbons. A part of his fae gift was the ability to carve iron like it was wood and this was one of the pieces he'd created by hand, one of the pieces he was most proud of.

He flipped the knife onto the tabletop. It spun to a stop, tip pointing at him. He'd come down hard on Emmaline for her work as an assassin, yet he had no room to cast stones. No room at all. His handiwork during the wars had killed far, far more fae than Emmaline had. His weapons had rendered fae magickless, sucked their life force away while they'd languished in prisons. His weapons had killed and maimed thousands.

He was a hypocrite to judge her.

The only difference between them was that her kills had been up close and personal. It was his weapons, created by his magickal hands but wielded by others, that had claimed his victims. And that was really no difference at all when you got down to essentials.

Back then he'd been fighting for the survival of his people. The Seelie had taken it upon themselves to try to exterminate all the Unseelie they could, and the Unseelie had retaliated in kind. Just as the goblins had decided to exterminate the red caps, the sirens had declared war on the selkie, and the Hu Hsien had decided to off the phookas. The fae race wars of the sixteen hundreds. It had been utter chaos and had ultimately outed them to the humans.

But just as he'd thought he'd been helping his people to survive, so had Emmaline. They'd simply been on opposite sides.

He remembered how hot it had made Aileen when he'd crafted all the charmed weapons that the Unseelie had used in battle. She used to sit in his forge and tease him by playfully flashing her thighs and bending over so he got glimpses of her breasts. Finally he would end up taking her on his workbench. Her orgasms always seemed more intense when surrounded by weaponry—things that caused pain.

That was not a good thing for him to think of now, yet it was only one of many memories that had been floating through the gentle clouds of goodness that he'd surrounded Aileen with over the last three centuries. There were things about her he'd suppressed that might fit into a scenario in which she'd been sleeping with O'Shaughnessy, a man whom, appropriately, the Unseelie had called the Butcher.

The Butcher, the Blacksmith. The Candlestick Maker? Aeric wondered who else Aileen might have been sleeping with. He hated that he doubted her fidelity now, after all these years—though he'd doubted back then, hadn't he? It was only after her death that he'd elevated her to the status of angel and washed over all the bad in his memory with rosy hues of happiness.

That's what people always did after people died, right? All the bad became good. The dead became saints. In Aeric's case, he'd perhaps made his relationship with Aileen into the one he wanted, rather than the one it had actually been.

He pinched the bridge of his nose between his finger and thumb. *Fuck.* It was true that you had to be careful what you asked for in case you got it. He'd been praying to Goibhniu that Emmaline would eventually be caught in his trap. Here she was, caught in his trap. With her had come an emotional earthquake. His reality might not be the one he'd always assumed. Aileen might not have been the woman he'd believed her to be.

Emmaline, too.

He stood and went to the forge, glancing at Emmaline, who lay sleeping on the floor, before he went to the painting of Aileen. The image he'd painted of her had been created with hands of love and through eyes of adoration. It was not a true image. Even if Emmaline was lying about Aileen being in bed with O'Shaughnessy, it still wasn't a true image. It was time he came to terms with that.

When he turned away from the painting, Emmaline was awake. She was sitting with the blanket around her waist, his too large sweatshirt making her look like a marshmallow. He knew exactly what she looked like under that marshmallow and he wanted to pull that stupid jersey off her. Wanted her naked on the floor, moaning for him, thighs spread and his cock buried to the hilt inside her. The look on her face told him she didn't want the same thing. Not today.

"How dare you, you fucking bastard!" Emmaline yelled at him. She'd pulled her knees up protectively against her chest and wrapped her arms around her legs. "How dare you come to me like that, take advantage of me that way? You asshole!"

His lips twisted. "This is kind of a delayed reaction, don't you think, sweetness? I seem to remember moaning, sighing, rubbing up against me, grinding your—"

"Shut up!" Her face flushed.

"Two orgasms with my hands on you, fingers *inside* you, coming apart in my arms, begging for my—"

She leapt to her feet. "Stop it! I may have been caught up in the moment, but I've had time to cool down and think. What you did was wrong."

"I'm glad you finally see me for who I am." Her whole body was shaking with anger. "But I don't think I need to point out that you wanted it."

"You took advantage of me, of the situation."

"Oh, sweetness, I could have gone further. I was holding back." He walked to her and got in her face. His voice was low and harsh. "If I had given in to my urge, I would have fucked you senseless right up against this wall, Emmaline. You would have come with my cock inside you, over and over, moaned till your throat was raw, and you would have begged me for more."

"You're an arrogant bastard."

"Tell me something I don't know," he snarled.

"You're an arrogant bastard and you know I want you." She

paused and her eyes narrowed speculatively. "But you want me, too. That's quite the quandary for you, isn't it? Wanting the woman who killed your true love. That must be rough."

He tipped his head to the side. "Now who's being arrogant?" He wanted to kiss her. *Fuck.* He backed away a little.

"Answer me." Her voice and gaze were like steel, a lot like her backbone.

"Yeah, I want to fuck you. I want you bad, Emmaline, and I know damn well you killed my soul mate." He shrugged like it was nothing. "I'll deal."

A muscle in her cheek twitched and she looked away from him. She swallowed hard. "I know you don't believe me, but I'm sorry. I regretted Aileen's death that night and have regretted it every night since. She was an innocent woman and I killed her. Those are the facts. Even if she was having an affair with O'Shaughnessy; it wasn't like she was helping him do what he was doing. She was blameless."

"Emmaline—"

She held up a hand to stop his words. "You can say a lot about me, and you would have the right to say it all, but most of the people I killed under the Summer Queen's command were people guilty of heinous crimes." She stopped, drew a deep breath. "Not Aileen. Killing her rocked my world. It changed my life forever."

"I'm not sure how innocent Aileen truly was." The words hurt to say. They pulled from the heart of him like a bloody string.

"What? What do you mean?"

"I don't want to talk about it."

She closed her mouth and regarded him with knit brows, clearly dying to know what he'd meant. It was something he could barely consider right now, let alone voice aloud.

"Did the Summer Queen ever order you to kill me?" He needed to change the subject. "It would seem logical if she did, since I was the only supplier of charmed iron weapons to the Unseelie." They'd done devastating damage to her Imperial Guard. He was sure he'd been high on her list of people to take out, but Emmaline had never made a move on him.

"She did." She kept her eyes carefully averted. Her shoulders rounded a little. "I refused."

He cocked his head to the side. "Why?"

"The Summer Queen said my refusal was because I was in love with you." She pressed her lips together. "I was never in love with you, Aeric. I was too young back then to know what love was. I was infatuated, obsessed, but never in love."

"So, was your infatuation the reason you refused?"

"I never would've been able to kill you."

"Was the Summer Queen angry?" Dumb question. No one denied the Summer Queen and expected to live.

"Yes." Her shoulders rounded a little more and she still wouldn't look at him. "She punished me for it. She locked me in charmed iron for nearly three weeks. Charmed iron that you had made, of course. That was the point. She gave me to L—" Her throat worked like it was dry. "I almost died."

"Who'd she give you to?"

She shook her head, but didn't answer.

"How old were you?"

She made a face, apparently searching her memory. "I was sixteen."

"I'm glad you didn't kill me." He paused. "Although after the events of the last week and a half I bet you aren't."

She laughed and finally raised her gaze to his. "I still contend that you are a good man."

"You're crazy."

"I'm a good judge of character. Sorry I can't say the same for you."

He pushed a hand through his hair and stalked to the door of the forge. Throwing it open, he said, "You're free."

"Free?" she echoed behind him, as if she couldn't believe it.

She pushed to her feet and exited into his apartment. Making sure the door to his forge was closed and the tapestry was covering it, he went to the front door of his apartment and opened that one, too. *"Free."*

Emmaline stood in the middle of his living room, looking

at the door and back at him as though the exit were booby-trapped in some way.

"No tricks, Emmaline. I want you out of here before I do something I'll regret."

Her eyes flashed with anger, her jaw locking. "You're not the only one who would regret it, Aeric."

"Good. We actually agree on something. Look, I don't know if you've been lying or telling me the truth. All I know is that I have enough doubt in my mind that I can't hold you here anymore. So, if you've been lying, great job. You're accomplished beyond belief."

"Aeric—"

"Just go. Get out. Go back to the Summer Queen if that's what you want to do. Do whatever you want."

She plopped down on the couch and crossed her arms over her chest. "I'm not going anywhere."

He stared at her. "What? Why? Get the fuck *out*, I said."

She shook her head and crossed her legs, getting comfortable. "You're forgetting a very important thing. The thing I came here for."

Of course. "The key."

She nodded. "I told you that I came to Piefferburg to seek you out, Aeric. I need that key made. Nothing else matters."

"I need you out of my sight, Emmaline. That's what matters to me."

"Not as much as I need you out of my sight. However, like I said, the mission of the HFF is bigger than us both." She shrugged. "Hey, look at it as motivation. Make me the key and I'll be out of your hair. The faster you do it, the faster I'm gone."

He swore and slammed the door shut.

Nine

"OKAY, wait a minute. You have *Emmaline Siobhan Keara Gallagher* in your apartment right now? The Summer Queen's assassin during the wars—*the one I learned about in history class*? That one?"

"Yes, that one."

Looking a little stunned, Aislinn, the Shadow Queen, Unseelie Royal of the Black Tower, curled her feet under her on the couch in her plush white-and-rose living room. She wore a pair of loose jersey pajama pants and a sweatshirt and seemed thankful to be out of the constrictive, elaborate black and silver gown she'd worn all day at court.

The tattoo of the Shadow Amulet was visible under the collar of her sweatshirt. It made Aislinn impervious to death; its wearer was literally immortal—unless the royal suffered a wound grievous enough to kill outright or the sluagh pulled the royal's soul from his or her body. The former had been the fate of the Shadow King who preceded her. The amulet was an actual physical object, but it only became so at death. When passed to the new recipient, it sank into the body, leaving the tattoo behind. It also imbued the wearer with powerful magicks, making the royal the strongest fae in the court.

Aislinn was also a necromancer, able to call souls from the Netherworld and control them. With that power came the ability to control the sluagh, the army of unforgiven dead. Aislinn was more powerful than any of them, even the Summer Queen. Luckily she also had a strong conscience and high morals to temper all that power.

Aeric was one of a handful of her advisers and close friends. The year before, he'd helped Gabriel Cionaodh Marcus Mac Braire save her from the dark clutches of her biological father, the former Shadow King. He'd wanted not only to kill her, but to obliterate her very soul because Aislinn had been not only the heir to his throne, but also a necromancer—with the ability to cross over the threshold of the Netherworld at will after she died and haunt her murderer for all eternity. Because Aeric, along with Gabriel and several others, had risked his life to save her, that had earned him a special place in her regard—although that hadn't been the reason he'd done it. He'd done it because it had been the right thing to do.

You're a good man.

"Um," said Aislinn, "I need details."

He shook Emmaline's voice out of his head and told Aislinn the whole story from the start. By the time he'd finished telling her everything, she was sprawled on the couch with a half-full mug of tea on the coffee table in front of her and he'd drained two glasses of whiskey to the dregs.

"Wow," said Aislinn once he'd finished. "I can see why you're having trouble believing her about the key. Your history with her is a little tangled."

"Yes." He leaned forward, cupping the short, chunky crystal glass between his hands. "And getting more tangled by the minute." Especially if he couldn't get her out of his apartment before he gave in to his desire to fuck her.

She took a measured sip of her tea and he settled back into his chair to await her opinion—on both the key and the fact that he'd kidnapped, imprisoned, threatened, and tried to kill Emmaline. These were things the fair and levelheaded Aislinn wouldn't like at all, no matter the circumstances.

"You fear that the key she wants you to create is for some nefarious purpose?" she asked. "You think she may be lying about the HFF and the charmed box?"

"I don't know if I can trust her or not."

"Hmm . . . yes. Yet, I think the possibility that she's telling the truth outweighs the risk if she's lying. If the key she wants you to make really might lead us to another piece of the *bosca fadbh*, that's an opportunity we can't blow off."

"Yes, I see what you're saying."

Aislinn set her mug on the table, folded her hands in her lap, and leveled her gaze at him. "I think you're just going to have to take a chance on this woman, Aeric."

That was what he'd been afraid she'd say.

"You'll have to stay close to her, watch her carefully, but go ahead and make the key."

He nodded even though he hated this. "All right."

"I would like to meet her. Can you bring her to me?"

"Of course."

She licked her lower lip and appeared thoughtful. "I think we should keep her presence here hushed."

"So do I. She'll have more enemies than just me. They'll interfere."

"The only people I want to tell are my closest advisers."

That was himself, Gabriel Mac Braire, Ronan Quinn and Bella Mac Lyr, Niall Quinn, the rest of the Wild Hunt, Kieran Aimhrea, and a handful of others.

"Kieran can't know she's here."

She looked thoughtful for a moment, then nodded. "You're right. I don't like keeping him out of the loop, but yes. Skip Kieran with this information."

"Thanks. I don't want to have to crack his skull. He's a friend."

"I know that this woman is clouded in mystery and that you don't want to believe what she's told you about the events of the night your fiancée was killed, but I feel you should give this woman the benefit of the doubt. It says a lot to me that you kidnapped, imprisoned, and tried to kill her, yet when you offered her freedom, she turned it down in order to fulfill her HFF mission."

His lips twisted. "If she really is on an HFF mission."

She shrugged a shoulder. "Well, her story checks out. The day she arrived, the Seelie Court was expecting a new member of the *Faemous* crew that never showed up. So she's not lying about that, at least."

Aeric grunted, unwilling to give Emmaline an inch.

Aislinn bit her lower lip, studying him. "Look, Aeric," she said finally, "I know this is hard for you. I know it's dredging up emotions you never wanted to deal with—or maybe changing the image of the woman you've been maintaining for so long. However, you need to make a decision if you're going to get through this. You either need to get Emmaline out of your space and your life immediately and forget this ever happened, or you need to accept that Emmaline may be innocent of the dark intent you always believed of her, forgive her, and let the past go."

Let the past go.

The idea of letting the past go made a weight lift from his shoulders. Just let it go. All of it. Let all his doubt about Aileen's fidelity go. Stop wondering if she'd been an accomplice in Driscoll Manus O'Shaughnessy's torture of Unseelie. He wanted to let that go because he couldn't stop imagining Aileen at O'Shaughnessy's side, helping him do what he'd done, excited by it. Aeric couldn't help imagining his angelic Aileen and O'Shaughnessy fucking in that stinking room of pain in O'Shaughnessy's house, both their bodies slicked with the blood of those they'd just tortured.

If he let it go, let *her* go, he'd be letting the good memories go with the bad . . . but maybe that was the way it had to be. Maybe it was time.

If he did let all it go, he'd be giving Emmaline a clean slate. And forgiveness? That was a thing easier said than done.

* * *

"TELL me more about this key." He turned the model over in his hand. It seemed simple enough to make. Too simple to have anything to do with the *bosca fadbh.* There had to be more to it. The file with the pictures of the box, a sheet with the translations, and a detailed representation of what the final key should look like lay spread on the coffee table in front of him.

He leaned forward, poring over them.

Yeah, it wasn't going to be simple at all.

Emmaline had taken the seat farthest away from him in his living room. She tended to do that—stay as far away from him as possible at all times. That suited him just fine.

"Like I told you back when you didn't believe me, the piece is in a charmed box at the bottom of the ocean. It was found mostly buried in sand near the ruins of an ancient village called Atlit Yam. We're guessing the box is as old as the village, which means it's been down there for nine thousand years. It's in amazing shape, of course, because it's a fae artifact and charmed to be so. The box is small but cannot be lifted or moved by any means that've been tried. The markings on the box say that only a charmed iron key will open it. We figure, make the key, send a diver down to open the box, and get the piece."

"You hope."

"Of course. The pieces of the *bosca fadbh* were scattered for a reason. Once the relationship between the Phaendir and the fae hit the skids someone decided the *bosca fadbh* needed to be scattered to the four corners of the earth. The pieces weren't meant to be found by anyone but those with the direst reason to take the risk of handling them. There's no telling if the box has any magickal booby traps. We're just hoping this works."

He studied the mock key, brow furrowed. "Who will open the box?"

"An HFF member, a diver named David Sullivan. He's already there, waiting for me to deliver the key."

Aeric looked up at her sharply. "A human?"

"Yes, David is human."

He shook his head. "This guy, whoever he is, won't be able to open the box, not even with a charmed key."

"That guy, *whoever he is*, is my ex-husband. The only man in my entire life I thought was good enough to marry. Trust me, he's more than capable."

"He's *human*," Aeric snapped. She'd been married? He didn't like that for some reason. Made something unpleasant prickle at the back of his neck. "I thought you had someone who could read Old Maejian."

She bristled and sat up straighter. "We do."

"Well, your crack translator fucked up. The Old Maejian markings on the box say only a fae can open it."

She slumped back down. "Damn it. There are only three fae in the whole organization and I'm the only diver. David taught me."

"Then I guess it's you, cupcake." He stared at the model, studying it closer. "Also, this key is going to be tricky to make."

"It is? Why?"

"Come over here and I'll show you."

She hesitated, probably for as long as he'd hesitated to ask her. Finally she came over and sat beside him. Immediately she was too close. "Okay, I'm looking."

He dropped the mock key on the table—an inaccurate representation of the final key—and held up one of the photographs of the box. He pointed to a series of markings on the bottom front. "Right here. Those are the schematics for the key. I'm *fluent* in Old Maejian"—he gave a withering glance—"obviously better at the language than your so-called translator. Does the man drink much?"

Her expression went stormy. "Calum does good work for the HFF, Aeric."

He grunted. "But does the man drink? 'Cause looks to me, he does. *A lot.*"

She glared at him and he had his answer.

"Anyway, those marks tell me the shape, size, and density

of the key. The mock-up doesn't tell me any of that. It's a fucking complicated piece of work. I can't just make a mold from the mock-up, pour hot iron into it, wait for it to harden, and knock it out. I'm going to have to carve this sucker by hand."

"You can carve . . . iron?"

"I'm the only fae who can."

"Good thing I came to you, then."

"Honey, you never *came* to me. I dragged you kicking and screaming to me."

"No doubt," she muttered.

"Also, I'm going to have to add in extra-special fucking faery magick, according to the translation you brought me. All that's going to take time."

"That's something we don't have." She chewed her lower lip. "How much time?"

He shrugged a shoulder. "Won't know until I start. At least a week if I'm working on it nonstop. I'll be at the mercy of my magick. Once it's gone for the day, once I'm too tired, it's gone. Gotta wait until I recharge. The Energizer Bunny, I'm not."

"This is not good."

"Yeah, well, I don't like the idea of being stuck with you for another week, either."

She bolted from the couch, biting her thumbnail. "No, I mean, this is *really* not good."

"Why? The box isn't going anywhere."

"The longer we wait, the greater the chance the Phaendir will find out about the discovery of an ancient fae artifact at Atlit Yam. If that happens, they'll seriously muck things up." She whirled to face him. "And we've wasted two weeks already."

"Calm down. Even if they find out, the piece will be as unobtainable to them as it is to us."

"Yeah, they'd need you."

"No Phaendir would ever set foot in Piefferburg now, not after the way the goblins dealt with the last bunch that came in."

She shook her head as if she pitied him. It ratcheted his blood pressure. "Don't be naïve. If the Phaendir want you, they'll get you."

"Maybe," he barked at her, "but they still wouldn't get the fucking key, now would they?"

She stared at him for a moment. "Anyone ever tell you your accent gets more pronounced when you're pissed?" Without waiting for a response, she started to pace. "They might not need a key. Their magick is powerful when they use it in a concerted effort—like the hive mind magick they use to keep the warding up around Piefferburg. There's no telling what they might be able to do with that box." She came to a halt, her brow furrowing. "Plus, David will be in danger. They'll send the brothers over there to take him out."

Why did he get so annoyed every time she talked about this guy? Especially when she talked about him like she cared. "Yeah, well, David better be able to watch his back," he growled.

"He can, but I still worry about him. Listen, I need to contact the Phaendir. They're going to be wondering what happened to me." She pulled the cell out of her pocket and looked down at it, saying nothing. Dread sat in the line of her chin and in her eyes.

"How are you going to explain where you've been for the last two weeks?"

She blew noisily, moving a tendril of hair out of her face. "I've been thinking about that. I suppose I could go over to the Rose, meet up with the *Faemous* crew, and concoct some story about where I've been. Honestly, though, I don't want to set foot in the Seelie Court. I don't want to go anywhere near the Summer Queen if I can help it, even in heavy glamour."

"You were ready to come to me glamoured. I guess that means you fear the Summer Queen more than me."

She looked up at him. "Yeah, I do. She scares me witless, even now."

"Okay, so what excuse are you going to feed the Phaendir for not showing?"

"I'm going to tell them the truth."

"What?"

"A modified version of the truth, anyway." She pushed buttons. "Okay. Here goes, um . . . everything."

Aeric watched as her former glamour overcame her features. In a moment, she was Emily Millhouse, Worshipful Observer and personal assistant to the Archdirector of the Phaendir. She met his eyes once, then turned away. "Brother Maddoc?" Even her voice had changed.

Pause.

"No, no, I'm okay." Her voice shook a little as if she were frightened but putting up a brave front. "No, really. I'm fine. I'm mean, no worse for the wear, anyway." Shaky laugh. "I've had an exciting couple of weeks."

The voice on the other end was barely audible, but Aeric heard it become more strident.

"What happened to me? Let me tell you. . . ."

She mostly did tell him the truth. In her version of the story she'd been kidnapped on the road to the city by a rogue Unseelie and taken to the Black Tower. There she'd been saved from the wretch's evil clutches by the new Shadow Queen. Sensing her misfortune to be actually a turn in her favor, she'd lingered, exploiting her chance to get into the Shadow Queen's graces. Her plan was working, Emmaline-as-Emily said, because she was on to some hot information about the *bosca fadbh*. She needed more time to mine it.

Aeric's jaw locked as he watched her, a muscle ticking in his neck. She was good. She was *really* good. Using just the right voice inflections, she projected an image of a sheltered, gentle woman who was in over her head, yet committed—no, *passionate*—about her cause and who would risk all to accomplish her goal. Goibhniu, she almost had him convinced by the end of the phone call.

She clicked the off button and turned toward him. "That went as well as I think it could have. Brother Maddoc didn't sound suspicious, but with him . . . well, you wouldn't know he was suspicious until blood was oozing out your ears." She grinned. "I have no oozing blood, so I guess everything's okay."

"You did that very well."

"Thank you."

"It wasn't a compliment."

She sighed. "This is what I do. I'm *good* at it, Aeric."

"Good at lying, yeah. I see you do this and it makes me doubt everything all over again."

She shrugged. "Okay. I don't know what to say to that. I'm just doing my job with the best of intentions."

He leaned forward. "Take that glamour off. I want to see you."

She complied without argument. *Amazing*. He studied her—from her small, bare feet to the top of her dark head and everywhere in between.

She shifted from foot to foot and glanced around the room while she did it. "Why don't you just take a picture?"

Only if you were naked, princess. "You look tired. It's late and I'm tired, too. You take the bed and I'll crash on the couch."

"No—"

"Take the fucking bed, Emmaline. I'm a four-hundred-year-old male fae. Old habits die hard. The woman always gets the most comfortable place to sleep."

"Hmm . . . wish you would have been clinging to that polite notion before you made me sleep on a concrete floor for two weeks."

He rubbed his chin. "Yeah, well, that was different. Let's start over." The words pulled painfully from him because he still wasn't sure about giving her this benefit-of-the-doubt thing. He also didn't vocalize the words *for now*, though they were there.

They were definitely there.

TEN

SOMEONE kicked the door in at around three in the morning.

Aeric bolted from the couch with a battle roar and a readiness that he hadn't known he still possessed. A dark figure pushed right past him and went to the bed. Emmaline screamed and the sound was abruptly cut off.

He jumped over the couch and raced to the bed, but before he got there, the intruder *oof*ed and flew backward, dragging the nightstand with him. The lamp crashed to the floor. Emmaline leapt from the bed and kicked high and hard into the side of the man's face, but the huge man barely seemed to feel it and he was on her again. Emmaline yelped and crashed to the mattress under the other man's body.

Aeric yanked the fae male off her, spun him around, and caught him hard in the jaw with his fist.

The big male bellowed and tripped backward. *Man*, his hand hurt. Whoever he was, he had a hard face. Aeric popped him again, while the man was teetering from the first. The intruder grunted, staggered backward, and sprawled on his ass.

Aeric picked the lamp up and turned it on. It was a miracle it still worked. The intruder stared up at him with blood streaming from his nose and over his lips. "Kieran, what the fuck!"

Kieran pushed to his feet and pointed at Emmaline, who was on her feet next to the bed and in a fighting position. "Do you know who she is?"

"I know who she used to be," spat Aeric. His blood was up, way up. "The former assassin of the Summer Queen. Our enemy."

Kieran roared and lunged for her. Aeric bodychecked him up against the wall, making the whole apartment shake. They struggled, but Aeric held him firm, trying not to hurt him and trying to keep Emmaline from getting hurt, too.

My, how times had changed.

"She killed my brother." Kieran's voice was a low, dangerous growl. His brows were knit together and his lids half lowered. Murder sat in the lines of his body. "She shot him in the chest with one of her poisonous crossbow bolts."

Fuck. How had Kieran found out about her presence here?

Aeric fisted Kieran's shirt at his shoulders and rocked him back against the wall to reinforce the fact that he had him pinned there. "Your brother was an asshole, a murdering waste of fae flesh. How many times have you said that yourself? And how many innocent Seelie did Diarmad kill in the war? How many noncombatant troop? Record numbers. How many did Diarmad kill and *enjoy* it, Kieran? She was just doing her job for her side in the fight, man. Give it up. It was a long time ago and it was during a time of war."

Kieran's gaze fixed on him. "How can you defend her? She murdered Aileen."

"Sometimes things aren't what they seem," Emmaline answered.

Kieran pointed at her. "*You* don't speak. The only thing *you* need to do is die."

"Whoa, Kieran. Take it down a notch," Aeric growled. "She's right about things not being what they seem."

"Some things might not be, but *this* is." Kieran pushed

against him with a roar, trying to get past him to Emmaline. Aeric dug his heels in and pressed his elbow to Kieran's throat. Aeric was one of the physically strongest males in the Black Tower, but Kieran was a big guy, too—maybe one of the only ones who could give Aeric a good fight. He really didn't want to find out for sure.

"Emmaline is working for the HFF, *for us*. We need to leave her alone." Aeric reached down one-handed to the side of the bed and came up with a charmed iron short sword. He set the blade to Kieran's throat. "Let it go for the greater good. If I can let it go, you can, too." He pushed the issue with the sharp edge of the blade a little. "Right?"

Kieran pressed against him one last time, then went still, glaring at Emmaline as though he hoped his gaze could shoot a lightning bolt across the room at her.

Emmaline said nothing and made no sudden moves. Her hand hovered at her throat as if to protect it. That was probably a subconscious, involuntary reaction to being attacked. Guilt pricked in Aeric. He'd probably created that one.

Aeric held out a hand. "Are we all good here?"

"I'm not the only one who is going to want to see her suffer." Kieran's gaze never moved from her.

"I'm aware," Aeric answered. "Believe me. I wanted the same thing at first." He looked over at Emmaline. "But now they're going to have to come through me to get to her. No one touches her. No one."

No one but him, it seemed, and in a decidedly nonviolent way.

Kieran finally tore his gaze from her to look at him. "You're asking for trouble."

"Yeah, so what's new?"

"You're asking for half the Unseelie Court to come down on your head."

Aeric could ask him to keep her presence quiet, but Kieran wouldn't agree. Kieran's stake in the information was too personal. "Bring 'em on. They get to her over my dead body."

"You're a crazy fuck. That's exactly what might happen."

He threw up his hands. "Again, tell me something I don't know."

Kieran swore under his breath and crossed to the door. "I won't touch her because you asked me not to, Aeric, but others will want a piece of her." He turned before he left and shot Emmaline a cold glare. "You just wasted your life for a bit of Seelie garbage." Then he was gone.

Emmaline slumped as if fear and tension had been the only things holding her upright.

Aeric slammed the bolt home on the inside of his door. He was going to make some charmed iron pieces for it to make fucking sure no one got through.

"Are you okay?" he asked, crossing the room to her.

She shook her head. "No, I'm not okay, not at all. He was right, Aeric. I'm putting you in danger by staying here. I need to leave, go somewhere else . . . not the Rose, but I'll find somewhere. It'll be okay—"

"Hey." He caught her by the upper arms and forced her to look up at him, although she only did so for about a half second. "Stop."

"No." She licked her lips, an action he was fast recognizing as something she did when she was nervous. "I've put you in danger. I knew that if my cover was blown and the Unseelie found out I was here, they'd come looking for me. The fae have long memories. I have my glamour." She tried to push past him. "I can fend for myself."

He tightened his grip and she stilled, refusing to look at him. "Yeah, like you fended for yourself with me? I saw right through your glamour. Forced you to give it up."

That made her look up. "You're the only one *ever* to be able to do that."

"If I can do it, so can someone else. Remember, you're not with the humans anymore. You're with your own kind. We're not as harmless."

"I don't really need to be reminded of that, considering."

"You're staying here, got it? I brought you here and I can keep you here."

"My ass is yours?"

"You fucking better believe it."

"I thought you wanted me out of here so bad, Aeric. What happened?"

He released her and stepped back. "I can't discount the possibility that your story about the piece of the *bosca fadbh* is true. If you're really working for the HFF it's important you stay safe."

"So you've gone from wanting to kill me to wanting to protect me."

His lips twisted. "How's that for a change?"

She cleared her throat and gave him a shaky smile. "Yeah."

"You can stay here. I'll reinforce the door with charmed iron pieces. When you leave my apartment, you'll do it glamoured. You'll be fine."

"I'm not worried about me."

"Aww, isn't that fucking sweet. I can take care of myself, Emmaline."

She frowned at him. "You swear a lot."

"Yes, a recent occurrence, much like my sudden binge drinking and bouts of unpredictable violence. I developed a few bad habits when you arrived."

"Swearing, fighting, and drinking. I'm a great influence."

There were worse influences, like the one that made him want her so much. The one that made his dick hard when he watched her move or caught the scent of her hair and skin. Yeah, that one was a lot worse. No way was he telling her about that one.

Hell, he was having a hard enough time not *showing* her.

She moved away from him before he could tell her to go back to sleep, sending up a wave of the scent of the shampoo she used, whatever that wicked stuff was that she kept in her backpack. "I need a drink, myself." She looked a little wobbly on her feet.

"Okay, let's both have one. I don't think either of us is getting back to sleep for a while after that interruption."

Of course he could think of better ways to pass the time.

He went for the whiskey.

"What's this?" she asked, holding up an ancient bottle of golden liquid that had no label.

"Aged apple liquor. You probably knew it as Amber Sip. Fae-made."

"Amber Sip." She uncorked it and sniffed. "Wow, I haven't had this stuff since before the wars."

He grabbed a couple of glasses and took the bottle from her. "Then let's kill the bottle."

Some time later Emmaline swirled the liquor in the bottom of her glass. She'd had more than one and apparently she'd never win any drinking contests. She glanced up at him with exhausted, heavy-lidded eyes, her dark hair framing her face in a way that made him want to brush it back, cup her cheeks in his hands, lean in, and . . .

"You think I'm gorgeous?" She drained the glass. "You said that . . . the, uh, other day. You know, in the forge." She looked away from him.

He unlocked his jaw long enough to answer. "Yeah, I think you're gorgeous. Don't you ever look in a mirror when you're not glamoured?"

She frowned and stared into her empty glass as though wondering where her drink had gone. "No, actually. That day you let me have a shower was the first time I'd seen myself in hundreds of years."

"Wow. No offense, but that's a little fucked up."

She looked up at him and blinked. "Yes, it is. I guess . . . I never really liked myself all that much. You know, because of that whole assassin thing."

He held the bottle up to her with raised eyebrows and she held out her glass for more.

"That whole assassin thing, yeah." Every muscle in his body tightened and he forced himself to relax. "We've all done things in the past we're not proud of."

"Some more than others." She drew a breath and then gave him a dazzling smile. "So, I'm looking okay, then?"

A corner of his mouth hitched upward. He slammed back the rest of his drink before answering, since he needed it. He was about to tell a woman who had been a sworn enemy only weeks ago that he thought she was pretty. "More than okay. Like I said, gorgeous."

She smiled a little, but her eyes were sad. "So, tell me about Piefferburg. I read all I can about this place, but nothing's like a firsthand account. By not living here, I've missed a huge chunk of fae history."

He snorted. "It's not history yet. Seems like current events to me."

"With your help, soon it might be history."

"By the fae timeline Piefferburg is just a blip. We were here long before humanity stopped swinging from the branches and we'll be here long after they disappear."

She swirled the rest of her drink in her glass. "And so will the Phaendir."

He sighed. "Yeah. Those bastards are like cockroaches. Not even a nuclear blast could get rid of them."

She finished her glass and settled back into the cushions. "So, tell me. How did they trap you here, Aeric?"

He set his glass aside and started in. He told her about how the Phaendir had hunted them down like dogs and trapped them all over the world with the help of the humans. He told her about the ship stuffed to bursting with fae who were either sick with Watt syndrome, trussed up in charmed iron—that had been created by him, originally, and commandeered for that purpose—or both. There had been hardly any food, almost no clean drinking water. Disease had been rampant. So many died on the trip that the sharks followed in their wake, waiting to be fed. Of course, the fae weren't the last to travel the ocean to the New World under such conditions. *Hardly*.

He told her about Piefferburg's earliest days, how cold it was and how there was so little food and no shelter. He told her how they'd built the city from nothing but grass and trees and how all of them had seethed in anger over their treatment. That common bond drew all the fae races together, ending the pettiness of the wars and uniting them in a common purpose.

If any good had come out of Piefferburg, it was that.

Eventually, though, the fire of their indignation had been lost in simply surviving—maintaining an economy that could support all of Piefferburg's inhabitants.

Now that righteous fire was back, sparked by the Phaendir and the way they'd barged into their city the previous year in an attempt to gain the Book of Bindings and kill their new Shadow Queen. These days Piefferburg seethed again. The fae wanted blood.

Hopefully they would get it.

When he was done, he looked over and found Emmaline asleep. The empty glass had rolled out of her fingers and onto the cushion. Her face rested comfortably on one of the throw pillows, her long dark hair tucked behind her ear. Her breathing came deep and easy, almost as if having someone try to kill her happened every day.

Although—he frowned—these days it sort of did.

She really was beautiful, as much as he hated to admit it. Not beautiful in the perfect, ethereal way that Aileen had been beautiful. Emmaline's attractiveness was a different kind. Natural. Unique. Compelling. Interesting.

He eased his hand to her chin and turned her face toward his. Emmaline Siobhan Keara Gallagher. How had she landed in his life this way? He wished she hadn't. Wished he didn't find her as compelling or as interesting as he did.

He wished he found her guilty.

It would have made things so much easier if he'd just been able to stick with his original plan. But reality was whatever it was, no matter if you liked it. He was a fan of seeing the truth in events and in people, no matter if the truth was complicated and the lie was a comforting old friend.

So, new plan.

He set the empty glass on the coffee table and gently scooped her into his arms. She mumbled a little in her sleep and put her arms around his neck, nuzzling his throat like he was a lover. Every nerve in his body leapt to life. He closed his eyes for a moment and gritted his teeth, gaining a handle on that annoying, misplaced superattraction he had to her. He could fuck any woman in Piefferburg, but not this one.

Not Emmaline. He needed to resist.

She weighed more than she looked, but it was still no problem to get her over to the bed and lay her down. She snuggled into the pillow and blankets with a sleepy-sounding murmur. He covered her before he had a chance to skirt her body with his gaze and imagine what she'd look like if she was nude. He already knew, right? He'd already touched her, made her come. His fingers itched to do it again—to peel off all her clothes and stroke down her soft skin.

He swore under his breath and turned away from her. Maybe he should sneak out and fuck one of the women in the Black Tower, one he knew would welcome an early morning visit with no strings attached. His hands fisted. Yeah, but that woman wouldn't be the one he really wanted—she wouldn't be Emmaline. No woman had tempted him this much since Aileen.

The irony of that was not lost on him.

Yet, there was that truth thing again, slapping him in the face with its inconveniences. He wanted to say *fuck the truth* . . . but he couldn't.

"AISLINN?" Aeric stepped into the room and motioned to Emmaline to join him. "Emmaline is here to see you."

Emmaline stepped from the corridor and into the Shadow Queen's quarters.

The Shadow Queen turned from her desk and Emmaline caught her breath. Out of sheer instinct, she dipped low into a curtsy. She dropped her glamour, too, now that the door was shut behind her.

Man, she hadn't made that curtsy move in a long time . . . and never to the Unseelie Royal. The Summer Queen had always demanded that she dress for the occasion when she entered her throne room, but Emmaline hadn't packed any finery, figuring she could buy it within the borders of Piefferburg. Now she wore a pair of faded jeans and a black sweater. Not fit for a queen to see.

"Emmaline Siobhan Keara Gallagher, please rise. I don't

stand on court protocol the way the Summer Queen does."

She rose, but still couldn't quite catch her breath in the face of the queen. As was the tradition for both the royals, the Shadow Queen was dressed in traditional garb. She wore a huge, elaborate gown in hues of peach and white. Folds of fabric draped over a hoopskirt and cascaded to the floor, forming a train. The bodice was tight, pressing her breasts to overflowing at the top. The collar formed a fan around the back of her neck. Her hair, a silver blond, was pinned on her head with glittering diamonds, curling tendrils falling around her face.

The Shadow Queen motioned to a figure near her. "Please meet my husband, Gabriel, the Shadow King."

Emmaline's gaze cut to the man. He was devastatingly good-looking, dressed from head to toe in black. His long hair, the same hue, pretty much melted into his clothing. He bowed to her. "Nice to meet you, Emmaline. We know you by reputation already, of course."

She dropped her gaze at those words. "Those days are far behind me."

"They might be far behind you," Gabriel answered, "but the Unseelie remember. You have many enemies in this court, Emmaline."

Her lips twisted. "I am aware."

Gods, he was handsome with all that long black hair. He was an incubus, according to Aeric. They were always devastating. It was part of their weapon—a way to get women to have sex with them. They exuded pheromones, too. Emmaline blinked to get herself out of her stare.

Aeric was far more compelling. The two men didn't have the same kind of attractiveness. Gabriel was classically good-looking, smooth, while Aeric was all brute strength, pure male.

"Aeric told us about what Kieran did last night," the queen added. "According to the way Unseelie law is constructed, I can't punish him. If he wants to take revenge against you for his brother's death, he's within his rights. Just like I can't punish Aeric for what he did, though he knows I'm not happy with him over it."

She inclined her head. "I understand."

"But you are within your rights to defend yourself as well."

"I did defend myself." Emmaline looked up and smiled at her. "And, believe me, if Kieran tries it again, I will do my best to kick his ass."

The Shadow Queen moved to a large chair in the middle of the room with heavy swishes of fabric and sat down. "Aeric tells me you're with the HFF, working undercover among the Phaendir."

"For many years now."

"That's why I asked you here. I want to find out anything we can about them. I figured you'd be willing to share."

She inclined her head. "Of course. In fact, that's one of the reasons I came here."

"You came seeking the Blacksmith to make a key."

"It didn't quite work out that way, but—"

Aeric cleared his throat. "She would have sought me out, if I hadn't—"

The Shadow Queen raised an eyebrow. "Abducted, imprisoned, and threatened her?"

"You forgot tried to kill her," Gabriel added with a dark look on his face for Aeric.

Emmaline didn't like where this was going. "I killed someone he loved. Most men would have drawn and quartered me before having all the details. It's a credit to Aeric that he backed off when he started to have doubts about the circumstances."

"Amazing," murmured Gabriel. "You're willing to forgive him?"

"Like I said, I killed someone he loved. It was an accident, but the facts remain. Had I not been an assassin, Aeric's fiancée would be alive today. Like the queen said, he was within his rights to seek revenge."

"Please, take a seat," said the Queen. "Do you want anything to eat or drink?"

"No, thanks." She and Aeric sat down in the sitting area in front of the queen and Gabriel came to stand near his wife.

"Okay," said Queen Aislinn. "Tell us about the Phaendir. Tell us why they're so worried about the fae."

She laughed. "They're scared shitless of us." She covered her mouth, horror pulsing through her veins. "*Danu*, I'm sorry! I didn't mean to—"

Queen Aislinn smiled. "Emmaline, I wasn't always a queen. A little over a year ago I was just a member of the Seelie Court. I even swore sometimes. Don't let the gown fool you. If I didn't have to wear it, I'd be in jeans and a sweater, just like you."

Emmaline relaxed. "Well, anyway, they're frightened of us. The thought of the warding breaking and all the fae escaping, it's like their version of Armageddon except we're the hellfire and damnation." She paused. "You have to understand that they think what they're doing is right. They believe they're protecting humanity from a scourge of evil."

"Yes," said Gabriel dryly. "So we've gathered."

"There's one man, named Brother Gideon. His full name is Gideon P. Amberdoyle. I've been watching him. I've been involved with the Phaendir for a long time and he's the most dangerous of them, in my opinion. He's pious. He *believes*, you know? That makes him trouble for the fae. He wants to see all of us exterminated from the face of the earth so that the Phaendir, alone, are considered the most unique, the chosen ones. Gods on earth. He believes his mission has been given to him by Labrai."

"But he's not in charge."

She shook her head. "Not yet. Archdirector Maddoc still holds the reins, but Gideon is working on it. If he ever attains power, we all better watch out. He staged a minor coup within the power structure of the Phaendir last year, your majesty. He's the one who sent the rogue brothers into Piefferburg to make that desperate effort to get the Book of Bindings and almost killed you in the process."

"It was him?" Gabriel growled the words. Suddenly he didn't seem like just a good-looking man anymore. Handsome, smooth. Now he seemed as dangerous as the sharp edge of a sword. "Why did he take such a risk?" His voice was deceptively quiet. The menace in it made her shiver.

If Brother Gideon ever came face-to-face with Gabriel, he would die for endangering Aislinn. That was clear enough.

"Two reasons," Emmaline answered. "First, he wants Brother Maddoc's spot. He wants more than anything to have ultimate power in the Phaendir in order to execute his agenda for the fae. Second, he wants me."

"What?" The query exploded from Aeric.

She looked over at him. "I've been posing as Brother Maddoc's assistant for the last two years. As soon as I came into the Phaendir, I saw the dynamic between Maddoc and Gideon and understood Gideon was a man I needed to watch. As a woman, I knew the best way to get close to him was to invite his regard. So I studied him, understood what best would float his boat, and became that."

"So what . . . *floats his boat*?" Aeric growled.

She smiled and fluttered her lashes. "A demure and pious woman . . . with the heart of a slut. He requires careful handling. I flirt with him subtly, promising without outright saying that while I might be an angel on the outside, I'd be a hellcat in bed."

"Did it work?" Something dark flittered through his eyes.

She shuddered at the thought. "I will never let it go all the way. There are things I won't do, not even for the HFF. I'm just manipulating him for information, that's all. He's an evil bastard. I don't feel bad about leading him on, not for a moment."

"Some habits are hard to break," said Aeric, his eyelids half lowered.

She flinched as though he'd hit her. "Maybe my morals are a little flexible, but at least my immoral behavior is serving a good purpose these days."

ELEVEN

WITH one hand clutching the ancient pendant he'd found in Emily's apartment, Brother Gideon knelt in worshipful sufferance, the lash of his beloved cat-o'-nine-tails digging into the scarred flesh of his back.

Every time he did this he was amazed he had blood left to bleed, amazed the cat could get through his thickened flesh. Yet blood trickled down his back and arms, dribbled over the necklace in his hand, and dripped to the floor. He possessed a never-ending supply for Labrai, it seemed. Sharp, sweet agony tingled through his body with every lash he delivered.

Emily had contacted Brother Maddoc. She was all right, *safe* in the Black Tower—if one could actually be safe in such a place—and had been taken under the wing of the Shadow Queen herself. It was an apparently fortuitous change of circumstance, according to Brother Maddoc.

Gideon's hand tightened on the necklace. He wasn't as confident. It stank to him. All of it.

Labrai curse it all! He wanted to *believe* in Emily Millhouse. It had been so long since he'd had a woman to believe in. Not since his mother had died. No other woman had been worth the time or the trouble. All of them were worthless, using men to their advantage, lying, cheating.

Not Emily.

He plied a particularly vicious stroke of the lash to his back. His spine arched and he choked back a cry of pain. He needed that pain to help him see clearly. Just like he needed to believe Emily was just Emily. There had to be an explanation for the necklace. This flicker of suspicion he had was just some remnant from his past dealings with the women in his life. A mirage to keep him from finding happiness. Something sent by Labrai to test his faith.

That had to be it.

Right?

Trembling, his fingers clumsy with agony and uncharacteristic uncertainty, he washed the leather tails of the cat in the room's small sink and hung it on its peg. Then he cleaned himself up as best as he could, trying not to recall all the times it had been Emily's gentle hands that had wiped his blood away and applied the antiseptic.

After he dressed and went back to his desk, he laid the pendant down and stared at it. Dark brown blood spattered the piece of jewelry whose origins were so clouded in mystery. What was it? A family heirloom? A memento kept from some encounter with a rogue fae? A purchase Emily had made for some reason? Maybe she collected old jewelry. Maybe having a fae piece was important to her because of the symbolism—Emily hated the fae as much as he did.

Yet how could she afford such an expensive antique on her salary? He'd seen her apartment. There was no hidden fortune there.

Maybe it was time he looked into her background a little more closely, just to put his mind at ease. With a sigh of resignation, he reached for the phone. He knew just who to call.

One of the lesser brothers entered his office with his daily afternoon tea. He was a short blond man; his name was Bowen, Gideon thought. He put the phone back in its cradle, happy for the interruption. The man kept his gaze averted—as was proper—and set the tray with the teapot and cup down on a clear space on his desk.

"Brother," said Gideon with a nod of his head. "May Labrai walk beside you through all things."

"Brother, praise Him who sustains us through this turmoil," Maybe-Bowen answered, bowing his head and backing out the door.

Still staring at the necklace, Gideon poured himself a cup and took a sip. The tea was far more bitter than usual. He choked down his mouthful and set the cup on its saucer, frowning at it. He was going to complain.

Looking at the phone with an equally bitter glance, he picked up the pile of papers sitting next to the blood-spattered necklace and glanced through them, composing a list of things to do for the afternoon.

His windpipe tightened and he coughed in an effort to relieve the pressure. Clearing his throat, he looked back at the papers.

An invisible vise closed around his neck, cutting off his air supply. The papers flew up into the air as he put his hands to his throat and toppled off his chair. Moaning, he collapsed to the floor. Pain slammed through his body, making the world go white and black alternately.

Poison.

The tea had been poisoned.

Footsteps pounded to his side, making the floor shake. Brother Maddoc's worried face entered his field of vision, his mouth opening and closing as he spoke, but Gideon couldn't hear a word. Gideon lurched to his knees, hand out toward Maddoc as if in supplication, then his vision narrowed to a pinprick.

Gideon pitched forward onto his face.

Then even the pinprick disappeared.

AS they left the Shadow Queen's receiving room and entered the corridor Aeric touched his jeans pocket, verifying for the fifth time in an hour that the rough-hewn chunk of iron and his sheathed charmed iron knife were still in there. He'd already made the first incisions into what would become the key. They'd been fucking hard to make; he didn't want to have to do it again. Carving it was going to be a bitch.

He followed Emmaline down the corridor toward his apartment. Even with her glamour on, her body remained the same and, damn, her jeans looked good on her. So did her sweater. Her shoes, too. To him, it was all just frosting he wanted to lick off so he could take a big bite of the cake underneath.

That meant she needed to get the fuck out of his life. For good.

And soon.

Damn key.

Kolbjorn Einar Soren Halvorson came out of nowhere, barreling down the corridor like a white Satan from the Christians' hell. His long colorless hair streamed around his massive body; his pale blue eyes were alight with rage. Aeric was a big guy, but Kolbjorn was a monster. His arms and chest were ripped like a champion bodybuilder's and he had murder on his pockmarked face.

Aeric knew what that massive, pissed-off Scandinavian fae wanted—Emmaline's head on a platter for killing his father. *Damn Kieran to the Netherworld and back!*

Aeric was ready to fight, but Emmaline—fully awake for this attack—was ready faster than he was. She assessed the situation, leapt into the air right before Kolbjorn collided with her, and caught him in his colossal throat with the flat of her boot.

Kolbjorn gagged and fell to the floor.

"Stay down," she ordered in a low voice while in a battle stance. Kolbjorn writhed on the floor at her feet, choking.

Aeric stared down in surprise. "I can't believe you just did that."

She glanced at him and then stomped her boot into Kolbjorn's chest when he tried to roll to the side. *"Don't move."*

"He's one of the strongest Unseelie in the Black Tower, Emmaline, and you just laid him out."

Kolbjorn undulated like a snake and leapt to his feet before Aeric even finished his sentence, pushing Emmaline back.

Apparently he'd spoken too soon. He hated when he did that.

Kolbjorn's pale blue eyes fixed on Emmaline. His thin gray lips parted and he flexed his huge arms. "I can see through you. I can see right through to the heart of you *and I remember*. You killed my father, you Seelie bitch." Kolbjorn was one of the few fae who could see through glamour. Emmaline wasn't fooling this one with her guise.

That wasn't Kolbjorn's only magickical skill, either. The other he'd inherited from his father in a diluted form. Emmaline had taken out Kolbjorn's father early in the war . . . because Kolbjorn's father was capable of doling out death in huge numbers.

And so was Kolbjorn.

Magick prickled through the air, raising the hair on the back of his neck. Aeric groped at his side for the charmed iron weapon he didn't have. *Fuck*. All he had on him was his little carving knife, hardly good in a fight. Kolbjorn could kill pretty damn easy with his magick and Aeric knew he couldn't reason him out of murder the way he'd talked Kieran out of it. "Emmaline, we need to get out of here. Now."

She stood on the balls of her feet, looking fierce. "I can take him."

"No." He grabbed her upper arm and yanked her back. "You can't take this guy, Emmaline. Neither can I. His magick is too powerful."

She glanced at him and her eyes widened, seeing the truth of his statement on his face. Together they whirled and ran down the corridor. Behind them Kolbjorn ramped up a nice, big bolt of lightning to send at them.

Fucking lightning. They couldn't fight that.

They turned the corner just as Kolbjorn let fly. The magick

hit the corner they'd only just veered around, sending electrified chunks of sleek black marble and dust everywhere. The boom echoed through the Black Tower and made the floor beneath them shake. Aislinn wasn't going to be too happy about the damage to her tower. But if Aeric had anything to say, there would be more damage. This bastard wasn't getting Emmaline—not over Aeric's dead body.

"I will get you, assassin, and I will make you pay!" Kolbjorn roared behind them.

"Only if you catch us first," Emmaline threw back over her shoulder just before a bolt of lightning nearly caught her heels. She yelped and shut up.

"You can't run from me!"

Except they could. Kolbjorn was at a disadvantage because he was so big. They moved faster than he did. Kolbjorn also had to stop to draw enough power for his lightning bolts. That gave him and Emmaline an edge.

They raced through a common area, scattering surprised fae as they went. Aeric yanked her through a door and down a winding stone staircase, one of four that existed in the tower. They pounded down the stairs as fast as they could without tripping and rolling down them. That would be accomplishing Kolbjorn's goal for him.

Somewhere above them, over the sound of their labored breathing and the pounding of their shoes, came Kolbjorn's roar of displeasure.

"We need a door to the outside," said Emmaline. *"Now."*

"Two more flights and we'll have one." He wished for one of those nifty secret passageways that Melia knew about. Finally they were at the foot of the stairs. He pushed the heavy wooden door open. It let them into an alley at the foot of the tower.

They weren't far from Goblin Town. Overcrowded and confusing, it would be a great place to lose Kolbjorn. "This way." He yanked her along after him.

The narrow old streets of the *ceantar dubh* were spotted here and there with Unseelie fae and those troop who loved the Unseelie. They all got out of the way as he and Emmaline barreled past. This part of town mirrored the area at the base of the Rose Tower, though it was a little less hoity-toity. Though there were few expensive jewelry and dress shops, there was still a lot of commerce—just commerce of a different nature, a little darker. They dodged shoppers on the sidewalk and cars on the cobblestone streets as he led her straight across the *ceantar dubh* to Goblin Town.

They came out of an alley and smack into the heart of it.

"Oh, sweet Danu," Emmaline breathed beside him. It made him remember that even though she was fae, she was still just a visitor here. This was her first look at one of the more unique parts of the city.

Goblin Town was thronged with . . . well, goblins. Tall, thin, and gray in color, they looked deceptively breakable. Instead, they were some of the most bloodthirsty and threatening of the fae races. Luckily, they also lived by a strict code of conduct and were content to let the other races live as they wished, so long as everyone let them live as they wished.

Most of the fae races had fertility problems, keeping their numbers low. Not so the goblins. Females walked down the streets in droves, one spindly arm hooked through a shopping basket and a goblin baby tied to their hollow chests with brightly colored fabric. The babies sent up thin, alien cries once in a while to mix in with the conversations of passersby, all conducted in the guttural goblin language Alahambri.

Because the goblin population had outstripped the area allotted for Goblin Town when Piefferburg had been created, stores and homes sat packed cheek by jowl, rising into the air through construction add-ons in teetering, towering, reaching extensions. The streets were dirtier here than in the rest of Piefferburg, owing to a combination of overpopulation and a simple difference in culture.

And there were many differences in goblin culture. That was why they required—desired—their own little part of the city. It was a boon the rest of the races had been happy to grant. For example, most of the other races didn't have the same culinary preferences the goblins did. The marketplace was an area in Goblin Town best avoided by outsiders.

Just over the roofs of the unstable, narrow buildings, Aeric could see the golden dome of the Temple of Orna, the primary goddess of the goblins. A hell of a lot of damage had been done to that beautiful place when the Phaendir had dared abduct the Unseelie Royal last year.

"It's incredible," murmured Emmaline, coming to a stunned stop at the mouth of the alley.

He yanked her forward, casting a look over his shoulder. "Sorry we don't have time to sightsee." She was shivering. "You're cold."

"Well, yeah. It is cold out here."

It *was* cold. He just hadn't noticed. It was still early spring and the days went from warm to cool in the blink of an eye. "Okay, come on, we'll get you a coat." A shop would be as good a place as any to wait out Kolbjorn.

"We're not going to be able to go back to the Black Tower, are we? Too many Unseelie want to kick my ass."

Aeric shook his head. "But I think I know where we can go."

But fuck if they weren't going to have to stay together. Goibhniu help him.

He led her into one of the many goblin clothing stores, the little bell at the top of the door chiming their arrival. Emmaline was tall and thin, not unlike a goblin. They could probably find something to fit her.

The crowded shop swallowed them up. Racks of clothing, piles of shoe boxes—there was hardly any room to walk.

A goblin female greeted them, her thin lips pulled back in the grimace that passed for a smile in this species. Curiosity regarding their presence shone in her large green eyes. Not many outsiders shopped in Goblin Town. In Alahambri she asked if they needed help. The shopkeeper probably spoke English and both New and Old Maejian, but goblins liked to force the rest of the races to speak their tongue.

While Emmaline stared, Aeric slipped into Alahambri

easily, explaining they needed to find a coat that would fit a fae of Emmaline's size.

The woman went into the back and returned with a dark blue silk jacket with an image of the fat, squat goddess Orna embroidered on the lapel. It was a beautiful jacket, but, more importantly, it would keep her warm. He pulled out his wallet, paid the woman, and they cautiously headed out of the shop.

. . . Only to have a lightning bolt hit the concrete of the sidewalk about a foot from where they stood. Emmaline yelped and stepped backward, a hand to her leg.

No time. They bolted, running down the street toward the temple. "Are you okay?" he yelled over at her.

"What a dumb question," she fired back angrily as their feet pounded the pavement.

He wished for a charmed iron weapon of some sort, something more than just his little carving knife, so he could turn and fight. But even if he had one, he couldn't deflect lightning bolts. He'd still be shit out of luck.

Parked on a side street near a café, he spotted a motorcycle he recognized. *Bran*. He was in Goblin Town often, buying up the animals in the marketplace and setting them free in the Boundary Lands. He dragged Emmaline to it.

"What the hell are you doing?" she asked, casting a nervous glance over her shoulder.

He sought the extra key he knew would be under the seat. "I know who owns this." He scanned the café but didn't see Bran anywhere. He was probably at the market doing the animal goodness that only Bran could do. "He's a friend."

"He's not going to mind you stealing his motorcycle?"

"Uh"—he grinned—"yeah, he'll mind." Shoving the key into the ignition, he turned it and the bike started with a roar then settled into a kittenish purr. It wasn't his baby, but it would have to do. "Get on."

She hesitated, but then Kolbjorn came around the corner and she threw herself onto the back of the bike. She'd barely grabbed his torso before he took off, making her yelp in surprise and clutch at his chest. They sped down the street, scattering bits of paper and other refuse in their wake and leaving a disgruntled Kolbjorn eating their exhaust fumes.

HOT blood made its way down Emmaline's calf and dripped off her foot. Her leg throbbed with hot pain and made her light-headed. Still, she tried to concentrate on the sights around them. Piefferburg was an amazing place. Not somewhere she wanted to get stuck in forever, but a cool place to visit.

She'd seen pictures of the city, of course—the odd mix of old and new architecture, the cobblestone streets and Piefferburg Square. The Boundary Lands were less photographed and they were beautiful. Lush, filled to bursting with flowers that should not be growing so early in the season. The air that met her nose was fragrant and too warm for early spring. This was a place of magick—literally.

The woods had never been this alive in Ireland, this condensed with sprae. Being who she was, she'd always been aware of the various nature fae, but back then they hadn't been allowed to really let loose with their magick. Back then the most magick she'd noticed in the forest had been a shadow out of the corner of her eye, or maybe a sparkle that shouldn't have been in the foliage. Here, ironically, the nature fae were free to do their thing and their magick made everything beautiful.

If the humans weren't so stupidly afraid, they could enjoy this, too.

It seemed like they drove many miles, an hour out of Piefferburg City for sure. There they went off-road and followed a small, overgrown path into the woods. She clung to Aeric, her arms around his tree trunk of a torso, her hands barely able to link on the other side.

Finally they came to a stop at a small cottage that was overgrown with weeds. "This place belongs to the birch ladies," he said, shutting the engine off. "Normally I would let them know we were here, but I don't want to endanger them if Kolbjorn tries to hunt us down. They won't mind if we use this place, though. The birch ladies help travelers in need, especially female travelers."

"The nature fae already know we're here," she answered, her voice sounding breathless. "I'm sure a birch lady will be arriving shortly."

"It's possible. The small ones might let them know." He paused. "Uh, Emmaline, you can let go of me now."

"Sorry." She'd rested her head on the back of his broad shoulder. He was so warm. She unwound her arms and dismounted. Putting pressure on her leg made her yelp. Damn, it was worse than she'd thought. She limped a few steps then sank to the ground.

"What's wrong?" His gaze skated over her body, froze on the blood soaking the bottom of her pant leg. "What the fuck, Emmaline? Why didn't you tell me you were hurt this bad?" He sounded enraged.

"We needed to put distance between ourselves and Kolbjorn. No time to stop. It happened when we left the shop in Goblin Town, the lightning bolt. I was running on adrenaline, didn't feel any pain until you found the cycle. I figured getting on the back and getting out of the city was preferable to fainting at that time." She touched her head. "*Oh.* Might be a good idea now, though."

Danu, she *was* going to faint. Oh, hell, fainting would be so embarrassing. Especially after the way she'd kicked that fae's butt back at the Black Tower for a whole minute and a half. She'd been feeling so badass, too.

His hands cupped her shin, making her wince. Her skin was laid open in a wide gash from her ankle to her knee, speckled with tiny bits of pavement. When Kolbjorn had exploded the sidewalk near them in front of the shop, she'd caught some shrapnel.

He lifted her in one smooth move and she blacked out for a moment. When she came to, he was laying her on a bed covered with a thick multicolored eiderdown. The inside of the cottage was chilly and small but clean. He muttered at her under his breath as she weaved in and out of consciousness.

When she could, she glanced around. There was a small kitchen, a fireplace, and couple of rocking chairs. The place looked idyllic. "Where are we again?"

"A safe place. The birch ladies keep these little houses all over the Boundary Lands. Just relax, okay?"

"How did you find this place?"

He bared his teeth at her. "Because I'm a special snowflake. Now chill out, be quiet, and stop asking questions."

She chilled out. Chilled out so much that she passed out.

Searing pain made her come screaming to awareness sometime later.

"Drink this." He pushed a cup at her. "Fuck, I was hoping you'd stay unconscious while I did this."

There was an obvious question that needed to be asked in response to that, but she was pretty sure she didn't want to hear the answer. She gripped the cup in shaky hands and looked down. He'd stripped her jeans off. They lay in a bloody—cut to ribbons?—heap on the floor near the bed. She wore only her white cotton panties. Normally that would have seriously pissed her off, but the gash stole all her righteous indignation.

She examined the wound and heard a tiny sound. A moment later she realized the tiny sound had come from her.

He followed her gaze to the slash in her shin. "Yeah, it's bad. It's kind of a miracle the bone didn't snap, but luckily it's just a flesh wound. Some of the sidewalk from Goblin Town sliced you open. I cleaned it out really good while you were out, but you need stitches." He jerked his head at the cup. "Drink."

"*You're* giving me stitches?"

He gave her a withering look. "Yes, *I'm* giving you stitches. One of the birch ladies is here helping, if it makes you feel any better. She has some healing ability. Okay?"

She nodded.

"Drink."

She drank down the bitter, warm liquid and after only a moment, she knew no more.

TWELVE

AERIC scooped the empty cup from the floor and set it by the sink in the small kitchen of the cottage, then he leaned on the counter for a moment. The birch lady, Aurora, had helped Emmaline's wound to heal, though it would still hurt when she woke. She'd be walking with a limp for a while; though Emmaline's beefed-up healing ability would help. She'd have a scar, too. No way around it. A nice moon-shaped one from where the bit of concrete had kissed her flesh.

The wound had been worse than he'd told her. She'd lost a lot of blood by the time they'd made it to the cottage. It was a minor miracle she'd been able to stay upright on the bike. She was damn lucky that Aurora had been able to help because he wasn't sure he would have been able to do it on his own. Aurora had left some clothes and clean sheets, too.

He poked around the cabinets until he found some soup and heated it up on the stove. He wasn't going to think about the fact that he was nursing Emmaline back to health, that he was actually *worried* about her. A wave of cold fear had gone through him when he'd seen all that blood and the magnitude of the wound.

Fuck. He needed a drink.

No, actually, he needed a *shrink.*

Emmaline moaned from the bed and he turned from where he stood at the stove. She roused and pushed the blankets off her legs. The drink the birch lady had given her would work on pain, she'd said, and make Emmaline a little groggy.

"I need to p—" Her gaze caught his and she frowned, falling silent.

Oh, hell.

Rolling his eyes, he set the spoon on the stovetop, turned the heat down, and went to her. "Come on, I'll help you get to the bathroom."

"Thank you." She was slurring her words just a little. "For everything."

"You're nuts to be thanking me for anything after what I did."

"Yeah, well, it's no real secret that I'm probably certifiable."

"Join the club."

She hooked her arm over his shoulder and put weight on her good foot. Slowly, he helped her across the room to the doorway of the bathroom.

"If you want to distill my help down to its purest element, everything I'm doing is for the HFF and the fae of Piefferburg."

She shook her head. "Nope. Not this." She motioned at the cottage. "Not cleaning or dressing my wound. Not helping me to the bathroom. Not—"

"I hate to point it out, but it's still all for the key. You need to stay alive, remember? You're the only one who can get it out of here. You're the only one in the HFF who can open the box."

"Yeah, you're right." She looked so disappointed he almost wanted to call his words back.

Suddenly he felt like the lying bastard he was. Sure, what

he was doing was for the mission, but he was also doing it because he cared about her welfare. Hell, he even liked her. Respected her, too. He didn't like to see her hurt. He just couldn't seem to be able to tell her that.

They made it to the bathroom and she braced herself on the counter. "I'm okay from here."

"Are you sure?"

She shot him a look. "That drink thing you gave me knocked me for a loop, but I'm not so far gone I want an audience while I tinkle."

He held up his hands and backed through the doorway. "Just as much, I don't want to watch you tinkle. There's soup when you're ready."

"Oh, thank Danu, I'm starving."

He closed the door and turned away.

A few minutes later, he heard a crash. He raced to the door and put a hand on the doorknob, ready to yank it open. "Emmaline?"

"I'm okay! I'm okay! Wait." The door opened and she stood there on one foot. "See, I'm fine. Wow, what was in that drink? Whatever it was, I want the recipe."

He helped her to the table, where he'd set a couple of places, and poured them both soup.

"So I wonder who in the Black Tower *doesn't* want to kill me," she said between mouthfuls. "Think there's anyone?"

He grinned. "I'm sure there are a few."

"I'd lay a bet on that one," she muttered.

"Yeah, well, you have a rep and it's not a good one. You made your bed, you know?" He slurped up some soup.

"I'm not proud of it, but I was good at my job."

"And look at all the great benefits you got," he shot back.

"Yes, no dental, just death threats."

"Soon you'll be out of here and you won't have to worry about it anymore."

She gave a small, unamused-sounding laugh. "Yeah, until the warding around Piefferburg is broken. Then I'll have to go into the Fae Protection Program." She frowned. "Except there isn't one."

"If that happens and the fae know you played an important role, you'll get a pass for all the things you did back in Ireland for the Summer Queen."

"Must suck that you've fallen into the job of helping your worst enemy keep her soul attached to her body, huh?"

He took a careful sip of soup and set his spoon down. "You are no longer my enemy. I believe that you killed Aileen by accident and I forgive you."

She stared at him with her spoonful of soup raised halfway to her lips. Her face had gone white and her eyes were wide.

"Eat your soup." He sat back in his chair with a tired groan.

"Sorry." She blinked. "I think that drink is making me hear things."

"You heard right."

"I thought you'd never believe I killed Aileen by accident because you'd never accept that she was having an affair with O'Shaughnessy. *I* couldn't even believe that, Aeric."

"There are things no one knew about Aileen." He shifted in his seat and swallowed hard. "Things that might explain a pairing like that, between her and O'Shaughnessy. There might have been a good reason they were together."

Emmaline kept staring.

"Stop that."

"I'm sorry." She ate the mouthful of soup and laid her spoon aside. "I'm just surprised."

"Denial is a powerful thing." He pushed a hand through his hair. "Fuck, I don't want to talk about this."

"And so we won't." She looked at the empty, cold fireplace and shivered.

Taking the hint, he went over to the basket of twigs beside it. In a couple of minutes a growing blaze was eating its way through the kindling he'd set up. He threw a log on and turned back to find Emmaline making her way slowly back to the bed. "The birch lady said the drink would make you drowsy."

"I think I'm drowsy from running from Kolbjorn. Well,

and from bleeding. I did a lot of that." She reached the bed, sat down, and glanced around the room. "Sleep in the bed with me tonight, Aeric. I promise I won't jump you." She yawned. "I'm too tired."

He glanced at the two chairs in the small sitting area in front of the fire and at the wood floor. There was no comfortable place to sleep besides the bed. Yes, he could sleep in the bed with her; it was big enough. The problem was that he wasn't sure *he* wouldn't jump *her*.

He pulled out the key-in-progress, the paper with the schematics, and his carving knife from his pocket and sat down in one of the chairs near the fire. "I'll think about it."

That seemed to satisfy her. As he started to work, she lay down, pulled the covers over her, and was fast asleep in only a few minutes.

He stayed up to work on the key into the early morning hours. The gentle glow licked over the carpet in front of the hearth and bathed Emmaline's sleeping form. Finally, when he couldn't see the key well enough anymore to risk not messing up the close, careful carving, he stood and stretched. Leaving the key and knife on the table near the chair, he stepped over the small pile of metal shavings and decided not to sleep on the floor.

The floor didn't seem all that appealing when Emmaline was in the bed.

He glanced at the door of the cottage. There was just one more thing he needed to do before he slept.

SHE woke up tangled in him. In his scent. In the heat of his body. In the strength of his arms. For a moment, longing coursed through her so sweet and so strong that she almost melted against him. Then she remembered the vow she'd made and disentangled herself from him.

Danu, she'd even managed to slide her uninjured leg between his thighs.

She scooted as far from him as she could and turned over, coming face-to-face with a wooden crutch. Lifting her head from the pillow a little, she reached out and touched it. Apparently he'd hewn it sometime in the night from a piece of wood. Either that or the crutch faeries had visited her, which in Piefferburg was certainly possible, but unlikely.

She tried to get out of bed, but a strong arm reached out, grabbed her, and pulled her back against him. She yelped and struggled, but once she hit his chest she melted in spite of herself. He was asleep and had no idea what he'd done.

It couldn't hurt just to enjoy it for a few moments, could it? Anyway, he was holding her so tight, it wasn't like she had a choice.

Groaning low in his sleep, he nuzzled the nape of her neck. Her body flared to exquisite, almost painful, arousal. Oh, hell, she couldn't do this. If it was any other man, she could resist, but not Aeric. This man was her kryptonite.

She tried to move his massive arm off her, with no results at all. It was like trying to move a boulder. "Aeric?" she whispered. Then a little louder, "Hey, Aeric?"

His deep and even breathing arrested and his body tensed. *Awake*. But he still didn't release her.

"Uh, Aeric? You grabbed me and pulled me against you like this. I didn't—"

He moved so he was hovering over her, looking down into her face. Now he had her almost pinned beneath him . . . on the bed.

Oh, no.

She shimmied out from under him as fast as she could and slid off the bed, using the crutch for support. "I need to, uh—" She jerked her head toward the bathroom and then headed there at a fast limp.

Once inside she leaned the crutch against the wall and rested her palms on the bathroom counter, taking a moment to catch her breath.

Strong, she chastised herself. She needed to stay strong.

Aeric was the one man who possessed the ability to completely demolish her heart. Under other circumstances she would allow herself to give in to . . . well, whatever it was that was happening between them—mutual lust, she guessed.

But she had deeper feelings for Aeric and she couldn't let her body lead her into a relationship with him—no matter how temporary—because she knew her heart would get involved, too. Then her heart would break and it would take a hundred years for her to put all the shattered pieces back together again.

It was just better not to walk down that path in the first place.

Turning on the tap—how was it there was working plumbing way out here?—she splashed her face with cold water. Raising her head, she looked at her reflection in the mirror.

"Oh, my goddess," she muttered. "I look like hell."

Taking her time because of her wounded leg, she took a bath. After she'd brushed her hair and teeth, she exited. By then the scent of coffee filled the cottage, a fire roared in the hearth, chasing away the morning chill, and Aeric sat in a chair whittling away at the key. The scene was sort of cozy and domestic. It made her heart hurt a little, watching him sit there and work, knowing she could look but not touch.

He would never be hers.

Her heart squeezed. She'd known it back then and she knew it now. Delusion wasn't something she engaged in much, but the truth really sucked sometimes.

"Thanks for the crutch," she said.

He looked up from his work. "No problem. You won't need it long. The healing the birch lady did on you, along with your own natural ability, will speed things up."

"My leg feels better already." Ah, this was nice; they were both pretending that superawkward moment in the bed had never happened. Just like they'd pretended that whole thing in the forge with the nakedness and the multiple orgasms had never happened. Good.

"I should have the key finished within a couple days." He turned back to his work. "Then you can get the hell out of this place and not have to worry about Unseelie with scores to settle."

The news should have cheered her, but it didn't. "Great." She moved to get herself some coffee.

* * *

"I want to know everything about you." Kiya leaned toward David and smiled, her dark hair shadowing half her face. They sat under a tree at a local park, watching the kids play on a swing set. "I want to know where you were born and how you grew up. I want to know your favorite color, your favorite movies, and what kind of music you listen to. Everything."

He laughed. "I want to know all that about you, too."

"Okay, then let's make it a game. I'll ask you a question, then you ask me a question. We can switch off and learn more about each other."

"Sounds like fun." He caught her nape and pulled her toward him for a kiss. Their lips meshed and he drank in the delicious soft flavor of her before she backed away, smiling.

David was in love.

God, how did a man fall in love this fast?

Wait, that was a dumb thing to wonder. He'd fallen in love this fast with Emmaline. In just a little over twenty-four hours of being in her company he'd been head over heels and ready to propose marriage, which he'd done only a scant three months later.

A couple of his buddies in the HFF had said it was because he was fae-struck. They meant he was one of the humans who were instantly enamored of anything fae just because it was fae. Admittedly, there were two types of person drawn to the HFF. Those who were staunchly behind fae rights and the fae-struck.

He was firmly in the first camp.

He'd fallen in love with Emmaline for many different reasons, none of them her looks, since he'd never known what she truly looked like. He'd loved her intelligence and her self-deprecating sense of humor. He'd found her interesting, charming, and easy to talk to. He'd also been drawn to her vulnerability, how even though she'd had so many years to figure it out, she still didn't know who she was. That bothered Emmaline and made her a touch insecure. He'd even loved her insecurity.

David knew that the identity problem had been caused by the fact that she'd had to leave her people when she was still young. She'd spent the vast majority of her life as a freak among humans.

It was all the Blacksmith's fault. Every bit of it.

The Blacksmith was the reason she'd run and had been forced to give up all ties to her heritage. Unfortunately, David had always believed that it was the Blacksmith who had possessed a part of her heart all these years, too. He was the reason Emmaline had never been able to give herself to him completely while they were married.

And now Emmaline was with that dick. Guised or not, it was risky. David worried about her more every day that passed without word.

Though Kiya was doing her best to keep him distracted. That was good, since there was nothing David could do for Emmaline.

"David?"

He jerked in surprise and looked at Kiya.

She frowned, her lovely, perfect brow creasing. "You were a million miles away. What are you thinking about?"

The sound of the children playing on the swing set seemed to grow louder for a moment as he sought an answer that wouldn't hurt her feelings. He guessed *I was thinking of my ex-wife* wasn't something most women wanted to hear when on a date. He didn't want Kiya to think he was still hung up on Emmaline romantically, because he wasn't. Not really.

Maybe just a little.

"I'm worried about a friend, that's all." He flashed a smile. "Someone back in the States."

"Oh. Anything I can do to help?"

He shook his head. "No. This friend is in a tight spot, I think, but she's all alone on this one."

She stared at the children for a few moments. "If you want to talk about it, I'm here."

No. He didn't want to talk about Emmaline. He didn't want her ruling his head anymore and especially not his heart. He didn't want to be worried about her and he didn't want her coming between him and a beautiful, caring woman he could easily bring home to his mother . . . if his mother didn't live all the way in Kansas.

David turned to Kiya and eased the plastic cup filled with tea that she was drinking out of her hands and set it on the grass. She looked a little surprised as he leaned into her and cupped her cheek, gently laying his lips on hers.

She sighed against his mouth and kissed him back.

Emmaline had broken his heart and ruined him for other women for a long time. He couldn't allow her that kind of power over him anymore. It was time he embraced the possibilities of his future.

Kiya was such a possibility.

She was vibrant, intelligent, and beautiful. He could spend hours just talking to her. Her hand fit really well in his, and she had a huge heart that he wanted to spend decades exploring the depths of.

If this went further than just a brief affair, they would make it work somehow. If it was meant to be, it would be. But no longer would he allow the ghost of Emmaline's love to dictate his future, just as Emmaline should never have allowed the ghost of her love for Aeric Killian Riordan O'Malley to rule her marriage to another man.

He would not make the same mistakes she had. He would not remain emotionally committed to a woman he could never be with . . . one who didn't want to be with him.

Kiya set her forehead to his and smiled so beautifully his breath caught. "I'll go first. What was your childhood like?"

EMMALINE stood watching Aeric whittle at the key and sighed. The tails of his black linen shirt were untucked from his jeans and his feet were bare. Damn, he was beautiful. She was so stupid to carry such strong emotional ties to a man she could never have. A man who didn't want her in any way but a sexual one.

Hells, even if Aeric wanted her in more than a sexual way,

it wasn't like she was staying here. She shuddered. No way was she getting trapped in Piefferburg if she could help it. Just the thought made her feel claustrophobic.

He set the key and the knife aside. Pushing both his hands through his hair, he groaned.

"Are you all right?"

He glanced at her. "It takes all my concentration to carve this thing. The ones who designed the key and the box never meant for it to be easy. My magick is tapped for now, so I'll have to continue tomorrow. This may take longer than I thought."

Doom clouded her stomach black for a moment. She worried about David over in Israel, but she knew Aeric could only work as fast as he was able.

"It was us, the fae," she answered. "That's who we think hid the parts of the *bosca fadbh*. Long ago." She levered herself down into the chair opposite him. Her injury was much better, but not yet totally healed. "After the fae and the Phaendir had their falling-out."

Once upon a time the fae and the Phaendir had been friends and allies. Something had happened to cause a rift and eventually make them become enemies. Most thought it had been the rise of Labrai and the Phaendir religion that had caused the wedge.

In order to deny the Phaendir the power of the Book of Bindings, the fae had hidden the book and the pieces of the *bosca fadbh*, the key that opened the back of the book, where the strongest spells were kept, all over the planet. That was what was thought, anyway. Most of the records from that time were destroyed and not even fae lived for a millennium.

There were some fae who could delve deep into the line of maternal and paternal memory, traveling back in time and viewing the memories of an individual's ancestors. All the information the fae had about this subject came from those with that ability, but it was tricky to find the fae with the right memories to search.

Aeric leaned back in his chair, looking exhausted. "You look worried."

She chewed her lip. "I am."

"About David, huh?"

She nodded.

"Tell me about him."

She looked up at him. "David? Why do you want to know about him?"

"He's your ex-husband, right? The only man you ever married? You said that before."

"Yes. We were married for just a few years. We weren't right for each other, but he's still a close friend of mine. I care very much about him. He's a good man, intelligent, and very into doing the right thing. He's dedicated his life to the goal of fae rights."

"Even the goblins? Even the Unseelie? Even Will the Smith, the boggarts, and the alps? The fae aren't all the shining Seelie or the harmless troop, after all. A lot of us are monsters."

"David would point out that the fae and the humans lived side by side for eons without incident before Piefferburg, so why not now?"

Aeric bared his teeth for a moment. "Because the fae never had an ax to grind with the humans before Piefferburg. We're a proud people with a long memory. Humans shouldn't assume we won't hurt them if we get out of here."

Anger surged through her veins in a hot white flash. "It's the Phaendir who deserve the ire of the fae, not humanity."

"Tell that to the goblins."

"We will, if we're ever able to break the warding."

"It's naïve of you to think they'll listen. I never pegged you, of all people, for naïve."

"Look, do you want out of Piefferburg or not?"

He gave her a withering look. "I wouldn't be breaking my magick against this key if I didn't."

"Then what's your problem?"

"*Woman.*" He closed his eyes and gritted his teeth for a moment. "You always mix everything up in my head. From day one you did that. I want out of Piefferburg, but the humans can expect repercussions if we get free." His expression turned savage. "The Phaendir can expect death."

"The fae were here before the humans. They have just as much right to live free as everyone else."

"At least we can agree on that."

"Once those walls break, it will be open season on Phaendir. The fae will go after them, not the regular joes. I feel confident the goblins and other Unseelie races won't hurt the humans if they're reasoned with."

He snorted. "Good luck with that." He stared hard at her. "Why do you talk about the fae in terms of them instead of us? Why do you identify with the humans?"

She shifted in her seat and looked away from him. "Because I don't really remember what it is to be fae, Aeric, if you really must know."

He nodded. "How does it feel to finally get that mask off?"

She looked at him, held his gaze for a long heartbeat. "Good. It feels really good."

He smiled and her heart broke a little. "You look better without it."

"Better . . . natural?"

"Oh, yeah. I love the way you look." He studied her with heavily lidded eyes. Her mouth went dry at the expression he wore, as if he was thinking about all the different ways he wanted her in that bed over there.

A sound in the distance caught her ear and made it twitch. "Do you hear that?"

He listened for a heartbeat and then rose, going to the door and opening it.

"Sounds like a drum," she said, pushing up and hobbling over to him, using her crutch.

"That's no drum like you know. That sounds like a bodhrán or two."

"Bough-rawn?"

He nodded and grinned at her. "Yeah, bodhrán. You really are out of touch with your people."

She frowned at him.

He grinned. "Come on, kitten, we're going to find the source of that sound."

"What about Kolbjorn?"

"He's got no idea we're out here in the Boundary Lands. Even if he did, he wouldn't have the first clue where to look. No one short of one of the royals could find us out here, unless they were blessed by Danu herself."

She peered out the door and into the twilight thick woods, the sound of the music growing louder. The tribal beat called to her, igniting her fae blood. She wanted to go. "If you say so."

"I say so. Let's go dance." He glanced at her leg. "Or hop, as the case may be."

It wasn't hard to find the celebration since it wasn't far away. The musicians had set up in a clearing in the woods, lights from the sprae twinkling around them and the lush sentient foliage pulling back to provide them more room. Even as she watched, vines sprouted with blossoms and grew around her, unfurling their petals to the world and releasing their perfume into the air.

On one edge of the clearing stood five members of a band, four men and one woman. Scots fae, Emmaline judged. The Scottish fae were of a smaller number than the Irish, having fared less well for some reason with Watt syndrome, though their customs and traditions were rich and touched all the fae. It was from the Scottish that the tradition of the Unseelie and Seelie courts had come originally, though court culture was a blend of all the fae cultures now. These musicians were not of either court; they were nature fae of some sort. Or so Emmaline presumed.

All four of the men were shirtless, wearing only well-loved kilts in the ancient way around their waists and all of them in knee-high leather boots. Tattoos writhed over their muscled chests and down their arms—two men on bodhrán, one on a huge drum, and the other on a set of bagpipes. The woman, also dressed in a tartan of the same color, was barefoot and with leaves and twigs wound artfully through her long brown hair. She also played drums.

The music they played was like magick, the beat of the drums, the bodhrán, and the bagpipes singing through her blood and waking parts of her psyche she'd thought dead. The beat pounded through the earth at her feet, through her legs. If she imagined it hard enough, the music healed her wounds—more than just one of them.

In the clearing, in front and around the musicians, the birch ladies danced. In flowing gowns of white or earth tones, the fabric moved around their forms as they swirled and leapt in the moonlight, catching sometimes on the forms of their consorts—strong men dressed in tones of black, brown, and green. All of them appeared to be a natural part of their verdant surroundings, which they were. These were the fae of the wild places; they helped sustained the forests of the earth. The rest of the world had suffered the loss of their presence greatly.

Humankind could never fully understand just how much damage they'd done when they'd banished all the magick from their world. They wondered why nature turned against them so often, why crops failed, why there were so many hurricanes, floods, and earthquakes. They wondered why buildings crumbled sometimes for no good reason. By imprisoning the fae, they'd destroyed the ecosystem of their world. The hardships they endured now were their karma.

One of the birch ladies stepped toward them. Reddish blond hair curled past her shoulders, decorated with small twigs twisted through its length. Her thick hair framed a heart-shaped face and a full mouth. In the moonlight her luminous skin seemed to glow. She was barefoot and her long, bare arms were streaked with dirt, but, oddly, it seemed to suit her—making her even lovelier than she already was. Emmaline recognized her as the one who'd healed her at the cottage.

"Aurora," Aeric greeted her. "We heard the music and decided to check it out."

Aurora smiled. "Good. Music and dance will help Emmaline to heal."

"Thank you for treating my injury," said Emmaline.

"Any friend of Aeric's is a friend of mine." She inclined her head. "I was happy to help and, anyway, you're someone very important to the future of the fae. I could hardly let you suffer."

Emmaline gave Aeric a pointed look.

Aeric raised his hands. "I didn't say a word."

Aurora laughed. "That was only my intuition speaking, nothing else. I don't know specifics. I only know that you're trying to do something very big for us, something that could affect our future in a major way."

"Yeah, well," Emmaline answered. "I'm going to give it my best shot, anyway."

"That's all anyone can ever ask. Now, please enjoy the music." Aurora nodded at them both and then melted back into the merry celebration.

Emmaline leaned on her crutch and watched everyone dance with the chaotic loveliness of the music pulsing around her.

"So, wanna?" Aeric asked with a jerk of his head at the dancers.

"Wanna what?" She wrinkled her face at him. "Dance? I can't dance. If you haven't noticed, I'm on a crutch over here."

He rolled his eyes. Stepping up to her, he pulled her in close to his chest, urging her to put her feet on his. Then he took the crutch from her grasp and tossed it aside. Holding her close, pretty much holding her up, he began to dance.

Her breath arrested in her throat. A memory of dancing with her father once this way assaulted her brain for a moment. However, this was different. Much, much different. After all, she was not feeling particularly daughterly in Aeric's arms.

Not at all.

The scent of him, leather and man, teased her. The heat of his body and the bunch and flex of his muscles as he moved. His arms, so strong, supporting her. All of it combined to make her head spin and her libido flare to life. She could tell herself all day long that sleeping with Aeric was the worst possible thing she could do, but there was no convincing her body of that. Just the press of him against her made her knees feel weak and fantasies whirl uncontrolled through her mind.

She didn't really know what to do with her head, or her eyes, for that matter. He was taller than she was, but he was looking down at her as they danced. The pace they danced at was slower than the music out of necessity. It was intimate—too intimate.

"It's okay if you lay your head on my chest," he said, his voice rumbling through her as he spoke. "I won't hold it against you."

Swallowing hard, she did it. The warmth of his body radiated through his shirt and warmed her cheek. After a moment she gave in to the powerful urge to close her eyes.

He held her and danced until the moon was high in the sky and partially covered with clouds. Soon only the small, glittering lights of the sprae lit the clearing. Someone brought out bottles of elderberry wine and apple liquor, a few baskets of cheese and fruit. Someone else lit a fire.

Later on all the birch ladies and their men ended up sitting or reclining on lush foliage, talking while the musicians played on in the background. Aeric and Emmaline sat nearby, under a huge tree. The power of the woods unfurled upward from the magick-soaked ground, bathing them in rich power and sweet scent. It made Emmaline feel almost drunk, though she'd hadn't consumed a sip of alcohol.

"So you'll be the one to bring the key to David," said Aeric. They were sitting on the side of the fire farthest from the Scottish fae band, whose playing was becoming more chaotic in direct correlation to the amount of elderberry wine they consumed. "How do you plan to work that out with the Phaendir?"

She drew a finger through the grass near the basket of food they were munching from. "I have that set up. I told Maddoc that the stress of the mission would require me to take a small vacation when I returned and I planned to visit my mother for a week. I'll have to be careful they're not watching me, but as soon as I check in with the Phaendir, I'll be off to Israel."

"Off to David the diver." There was a dark note in his voice that didn't fit.

She looked at Aeric cautiously, trying to figure it out. "Yeah. David lives for diving. We used to take our vacations in all the places where the diving was good. He always wanted me to go with him." She chuckled. "But I far preferred to lie on the beach with a good book."

"Why didn't it work out between you?" He popped a grape into his mouth and chewed.

Her smile faded. "I wasn't the right woman for him. He deserves someone who can offer all of herself."

"So you never loved him."

"No. I did love him. I loved him very much. I just didn't—"

"Love him enough?"

"It wasn't the kind of match either of us wanted." She paused, drew a breath. "Well, not the match I wanted, anyway. We both wanted soul-deep, crazy love. We didn't have that. Instead of a raging thunderstorm, our love was more like—"

"A light rain?"

"Stop." She pushed his shoulder and laughed. "We just didn't have what it takes."

"You've been with a lot of men, though, right? All human?"

"Well, yeah. I haven't been a nun, Aeric. You might be surprised at how few men I've been with over the centuries, though. I've been picky."

"But none of the relationships worked out for the long term."

She opened her mouth, then closed it, wanting to argue with him. She couldn't. "I've yet to the find the love of my life, if that's what you're asking."

"That's because you need a *fae* man, not a human."

"Why would you say that?"

He shrugged a shoulder and popped another grape into his

mouth. "You need a man who will truly understand you. A human will never be able to do that. Humans love the fae, fear the fae, or hate the fae, but they will never *understand* the fae."

It was true that she felt good here, in this clearing with her people. The beat of the drums and the sound of the bagpipes did more than make her want to dance, they ignited a part of her heritage, a part of herself she'd been forced to make dormant since she'd left Ireland so long ago.

"Maybe, but the problem with that is threefold. One, it's not like there's an ocean of eligible fae men beyond the walls of Piefferburg. Two, there are fae men here in Piefferburg, but I'm not staying. Three, all the fae men in here want to kill me anyway."

He grinned. "But then you win them over, bend them to your will, and compel them to take you dancing."

"Something like that."

"Emmaline Siobhan Keara Gallagher." The words boomed out from behind her in a bass voice.

Every muscle in her body tightened and she gripped her crutch, ready to bring it up into the speaker's gut. Aeric also visibly went on guard.

"*Emmaline Siobhan Keara Gallagher*. I remember you." The words were spoken with a thick Scottish burr. The speaker had never had his accent washed out the way she and Aeric had. Her Irish accent was completely gone, and Aeric's was but a mere whisper of what it had been once upon a time.

And she knew that voice.

Aeric hopped up and got into the man's face. "Listen—"

"Wait." She looked up. *"Graeme?"*

"My wee lass has gone and got herself all grown up." He grinned. "Pretty as ever." He raised a brow. "And not even wearing that stinking glamour."

"Graeme!" She struggled to her feet with the help of the crutch and threw herself into his arms. "I can't believe it. It's been so long. How did you know who I was?"

"Ah." He jerked his head at Aurora. "She thought I might know you from the old days. Thought you could use a friend." That last was accompanied by a pointed look at Aeric.

She laughed, totally shocked at seeing him after all these years. "I was so worried about you. I thought maybe Watt syndrome got you."

"The Watt's never touched me, lass." He touched her cheek. "And I was worried about you *long* before that."

The joy that had made her heart feel so light turned into a black cloud as she remembered. Her smile faded. "I survived it, Graeme."

He smiled. "So I see."

She turned to Aeric, who looked more than a little perplexed by the whole exchange. "Aeric Killian Riordan O'Malley, please meet Graeme Alaisdair Mackenzie."

Graeme grabbed Aeric's unwilling hand and shook it. "The Blacksmith. I know you, too." Then he leaned in close to her ear and murmured, "Why hasn't he killed you?"

"Long story," she murmured back. Then to Aeric she said, "Graeme helped me after my parents died and I was all alone. He's one of the few people who ever saw me without my glamour."

"I'm sure he did," Aeric muttered.

Graeme grimaced. "Please. She was but a small girl back then. I had no designs on her." He gave her an exaggerated leer. "Though maybe now I do."

Emmaline laughed. Then she threw herself into his arms again and gave him a long hug. "It's so nice to see you, Graeme. So nice to see a friendly face."

Graeme jerked a thumb at Aeric. "And this one? He's not a friendly face? Do I need to do something about him, then?" Graeme was a big man, burly in the way some of the Scottish wildings could be. His magick lay in the realm of the trees, oaks, in particular. He was built like one, but she doubted he would be a match for Aeric in a fight.

Aeric emitted something that sounded a lot like a growl.

"Hey," Emmaline said, putting up a hand. "There's too much testosterone all of a sudden. I didn't mean Aeric. I meant the fifty-two thousand Unseelie fae in Piefferburg who want to see me strung up."

Graeme laughed, a big, booming sound. "Well, you did

offend quite a few of them. Go on over to the Rose Tower; you're a rock star over there."

Aeric bristled. "Over my dead body."

"Mine, too." She shivered. "No, thanks. If I ever see the Summer Queen again, it will be too soon."

"Where are you staying, lass? Can I help you with anything?"

Aeric cut in. "She's staying with me and we don't need any help. Emmaline, it's time to go."

Emmaline frowned at Aeric. "What is your problem, Aeric? I would like to stay and talk to my friend. He's the only one I have here, after all."

"What am I, then?" He pulled her, stumbling, to the side and held her up so she didn't fall. He whispered near her ear, "Make no mistake; *I* am the only person you can trust right now, Emmaline. I don't like that he knows who you are. I don't like the vibe I get from him. Now let's get the fuck out of here."

Her jaw locked and her eyes narrowed. If she didn't know better, she would have said he sounded jealous. "You're being completely un—hey!" He'd lifted her over his shoulder in one smooth motion; her crutch dangled from one hand and her fist pounded on his back. "Let me down. Gods damn it, Aeric. I can hurt you, you know! I'm a trained—*oof*!" He jiggled her on his shoulder to make her stop talking.

Aeric stopped in front of the Scotsman. "Sorry, Graeme, we've got to be going."

He walked the whole way back to the cottage like that, despite her protests. "You don't have to be jealous of Graeme," she groused at him when he finally set her on her feet inside the building.

"Jealous? Who said anything about jealousy?"

"You sounded pretty jealous to me back there, Aeric." Her face reddened. "Not that I think you want me or anything, just jealous in a general . . . 'all women are mine, I am man' kind of way."

He raised an eyebrow. "I have an 'all women are mine, I am man' kind of way?"

She puffed out a breath in frustration. "Most men like you do. You know, because you're men. Manly . . . uh, men. You have a caveman urge to claim all women as your own, even the ones you don't really like." She was making this worse. She should shut up.

"Manly men." He walked over to her. "Urge to claim all women? For your information, I am very much a *one* woman kind of man. I see a woman I want and nothing stands in my way of claiming her. *Her*. Singular."

Her mouth went dry.

"When I want a woman, she is mine. No other man stands in my way, and I find no other man a threat. Therefore"—he tipped her chin up with his finger—"no jealousy. No reason for it. Get it?" His voice was slow, like warm honey, and his eyes were heavy lidded. He added something low in Old Maejian that she didn't understand.

Oh, Danu.

She swallowed hard and backed away from him a little. He was making her heart pound. Once upon a time she would have given anything to be the one woman he wanted, the one he wouldn't let anyone stop him from taking. That time didn't seem long ago at all. In fact, she could recall it quite easily. . . .

"Okay. Well, anyway, Graeme's gay." She cleared her throat. "So, you know, uh, just for your information. That was my point." That point seemed really superfluous right now.

He reached out and pulled her flush up against him. Lowering his mouth to her ear, he whispered, "Good for Graeme."

She dropped her crutch.

THIRTEEN

HE moved her backward, toward the bed.

"Aeric? What are you doing?"

"Taking what I want." He pushed her gently backward, spilling her onto the mattress. He came down over her, arms on either side of her, almost so she couldn't get away.

Not that she wanted to.

Annoyance sparked all the same. "Who says *I* want *you*?" Danu, the words came out heavy and just a little slurred. She was such a bad liar for an ex-assassin. "You have such a high opinion of yourself."

He nuzzled her throat, just under her ear, and gooseflesh rose all over her body. "If you don't want this, tell me to stop, Emmaline. It's simple." He bit her gently, his teeth rasping over the skin where her shoulder met her neck. The sensation registered much farther down. "Do you want me to stop?"

The only response she had for him was a whimper.

He slid his knee between her thighs and forced them apart.

The hard, wide length of his cock rubbed against her sex through the fabric of their clothing. Her breath hitched and her body seemed to catch fire.

"You want me to fuck you, don't you, Emmaline?" His teeth caught her earlobe and dragged across it, making her shiver.

Her fingers fisted in the material of his shirt. "You want it, too."

He cupped her rear, pushing her against him so she could feel the evidence of his arousal. "Yeah, I want it." He stared down at her, his mouth only inches from hers. "It's a bad idea, considering our history."

"Undoubtedly."

He dropped his head an inch lower and brushed his lips over hers. Her breath caught and her whole body went rigid, then melted past the point of no return. "You know it and I know it. Still, we can't seem to stop wanting it anyway," he murmured. "Maybe we should just do it."

Not waiting for her response, he dragged his mouth over hers. He groaned and forced her lips to part, not tempting or tasting or asking—but demanding. She opened her mouth to allow him in and his tongue slid past her lips and mated with hers, hot and addictive. His tongue stroked against hers, languorous and slow. Over and over. Warm. Wet.

His kiss wiped all the thought from her mind and made pleasure skitter up her spine and radiate through her body. A growling sound that seemed part ecstasy, part torture curled from his throat and made her shiver.

He'd made her come, but he'd never kissed her. And, oh, his kiss was better than any orgasm. This man kissed like other men made love, his teeth nipping occasionally at her lower lip and making her shiver, his tongue sliding into her mouth in slow, long strokes that drove all the rational thought from her mind and turned her into a melting mess.

"I fucking *need* you, need to touch you," he growled, breaking the kiss. His fingers found the hem of her shirt and had it over her head in a moment. He touched one of the long white scars on her stomach and thighs and looked up at her. "What are these from?"

"I don't remember."

"Don't remember, or don't want to remember?"

Danu, she did not want to talk about this right now. "What's the difference?" She pulled him down on top of her and sealed her mouth to his.

Soon, the rest of her clothing was gone and she was bare beneath him while he was still dressed.

That had a familiar feel, gave him all the power and made her vulnerable.

As usual.

"Aeric," she breathed, her eyes coming open as she grappled for a hold on her sense of self-preservation. "Wait. I can't do this."

He stopped, moving his head so he could look down at her. His hair shadowed his face and his eyelids were heavy with lust. "Why?"

Because you're going to break my heart.

"Because—"

He lowered his head and kissed her again, his tongue dipping into her mouth with long, slow, possessive sweeps that made her moan in the back of her throat and forget exactly what she'd been saying a moment ago.

Her fingers sought his shirt and freed it from his jeans, then made quick work of the buttons. Her palms ran over the powerful expanse of his chest and his broad shoulders, running over his biceps and the flexing muscles of his back. He was a magnificent man, the kind that made a woman feel totally feminine and protected—even if they were fae ex-assassins who could take care of themselves.

She touched the button and zipper of his jeans, undid them, and slid her hand inside. He shuddered and murmured her name as she took him in her hand and stroked. He was huge—long and wide—silk-over-iron beautiful.

"Fuck, Emmaline." He pulled her hand away. "I want you too much. You're going to make me lose control."

"Do it. Lose control, Aeric. I want you to."

Not answering her, he moved down, careful of her wound, pushing the blankets aside as he went. Her nipples and skin pebbled in the cool morning air. His hand skated her abdomen, stroked the smooth skin of her inner thigh until she moaned, then touched her somewhere even more sensitive.

His gaze held hers as he slipped his fingers between her folds and slid deep inside her. Her back arched and she closed her eyes, a low moan dragging itself up from her throat. Using her moisture as a lubricant, he petted her blossoming clit until her breath came faster. Knowing just how she liked to be touched there, he skated her right up to the edge of a climax and held her there, on the edge of ultimate pleasure.

Then he dropped his mouth to her.

The sight of his head between her thighs and his tongue lapping at her so lazily nearly did her in. Her fingers fisted in the blankets as he forced her thighs to part wider for him and he drank her in, his tongue and lips nibbling and licking at the most sensitive part of her body.

Hips bucking and a guttural moan ripping its way from her throat, she came against his mouth. He held on to her, laving her clit while she orgasmed, extending it and making it stronger.

When it stuttered to a halt, she reached for him, but he shook his head. "I can't without hurting you." He looked at her leg.

She grabbed his jeans and yanked him to her. "Do it slow and gentle, if you have to. I need to feel you inside me."

He growled against her lips. "I can't do it slow and gentle. I want you hard and fast. I want you up against a wall, over the side of a couch. I want your thighs spread and my cock inside you thrusting deep. I've been thinking about it too much. I've wanted you for too long." He shook his head. "There's no slow and gentle. Not right now."

She shuddered at his words, her body reigniting. Reaching into his jeans, she stroked him again from tip to base, making him swear under his breath. "Take them off," she whispered against his lips.

"No." He pulled away from her. "You touch me with your hand or your mouth and it will push me too far. I'll hurt you. I don't want to do that."

"You did once. You didn't seem to have a problem hurting me then."

"I know." He shook his head. "Not anymore. Things are different now." He stood at the side of the bed, pushed a hand through his hair. He stood there shirtless, his unbuttoned jeans hanging low and revealing the lean jut of his hips. Her fingers itched to touch him. That fantasy was not to be fulfilled.

Perhaps it was for the better, even though it hurt.

She pulled the blankets over herself. "You're killing me, Aeric."

He lay down beside her and groaned. "Yeah, well, dealing with you is no picnic, either, sweetheart."

THE next morning someone knocked on the door. When Aeric answered it, Emmaline could see an entire line of the Summer Queen's Imperial Guard in full rose-and-gold regalia glinting in the morning sunlight.

Emmaline bolted to her feet, using her crutch. She barely noticed the pain it caused her leg. "No." She backed up away from the door, ice-cold panic racing through her veins. *"No!"* She glanced around the cottage, hoping a back door would magickally appear. It didn't.

Aurora stood in their midst. She spread her hands. "Please forgive us. When the royals come looking for someone, we can't deny them."

One of the guards stepped forward. "Emmaline Siobhan Keara Gallagher, you are to come with us immediately, by order of Her Majesty Caoilainn Elspeth Muirgheal, the Summer Queen of the Rose Tower and ruler of the Seelie Tuatha Dé Danann."

"No." Emmaline backed away even farther, right into the solid wall of the cottage. "No way am I going to see the Summer Queen. *No.*"

The head of the guard entered the cottage, baring his teeth

at her. "You don't have a choice. Your queen has summoned you." He jerked his head at Aeric. "Aeric Killian Riordan O'Malley. He comes along, too."

"Fuck, no. She's not my queen," Aeric growled, watching more men enter the small building. "Emmaline's not going, either. The Summer Queen isn't her ruler anymore."

Technically, Caoilainn Elspeth Muirgheal would always be her queen. No matter how much time had passed, no matter that she'd been living among the humans. Emmaline was Seelie. Her blood was of a pure line of Seelie Tuatha Dé Danann and her magick was white, harmless. Therefore, she was every inch the Summer Queen's subject.

That didn't change the fact that she was *not* going to see her royal. Not now, not ever.

She put one of the chairs between herself and the guard. "What does she want with me?" *How does she even know I'm here?* That question went unspoken.

"The Summer Queen does not favor us with such information. She said to bring you and so we will."

"Yeah, I don't think so, buddy," said Aeric a half second before chaos exploded in the cottage. He attacked the guard nearest him.

The captain set his sights on Emmaline. Keeping her eyes on him, she moved around the chair, going into fight mode. That was going to be difficult with her injury. Even if she hadn't been wounded, their chances weren't great against at least twenty of the Summer Queen's best. She threw her crutch away, forcing herself to put weight on her leg. Pain shot up her shin and thigh, but she could do it.

On the balls of her feet, she gripped the back of the chair and readied herself for the moment the captain would make his move. The captain lunged and Emmaline yelled out of the pure agony of having to make the motion, bringing the chair up and hitting the man in the abdomen with it. He made an *oof*ing sound and staggered backward, the weight of his rose and gold armor toppling him to the floor.

She staggered but caught herself right before she also collapsed. Near her Aeric was kicking ass.

But now all the guards were pouring into the cottage. There were too many. No way would she and Aeric fight their way out. Still, it was clear they were of the same mind—they were going down swinging.

She and Aeric found themselves back-to-back in the middle of the small sitting area, both on the balls of their feet and ready to engage the guards. One of the shorter men lunged toward her and she whirled to the side, kicking up high with her good leg, catching him in the throat. He went down holding his neck, turning red, and making choking sounds. She didn't feel her injury anymore. Adrenaline and pure terror had numbed it.

Lars.

Just the thought.

Aeric met her eyes in a soundless communication—*are you all right?* Then two of the guards went for him and he was back in the thick of the battle again, leaving her on her own.

Emmaline went for the soft places—the throat, eyes, and their unprotected knees. Using every bit of her training, she kicked and punched at the men who were trying to restrain her. She had an advantage because, clearly, they had orders not to hurt her. Whereas she had no problem hurting them. She knew the Imperial Guard; they were just like she'd been so long ago—if the Summer Queen had told them to kill her, she'd be dead right now.

Aeric knocked one of the guards into the chair with a bellow of pure rage. Both guard and chair went down, the chair smashing into splintered bits and the guard going still on the floor.

Four jumped him at once, throwing him down and leaping on top of him. Two of the guards grabbed Emmaline by the upper arms and pushed her face-first against the wall. She struggled, kicking and yelling, but they had a good grip on her. They wrenched her arms behind her, pinning her hands to the small of her back. She heard the distinctive clink of charmed iron and the cool metal closed around her wrists.

That horrid sensation of her magick being stripped away

colored over her in a wash of sickly green, tearing away her glamour and making her sag against the wall. They pulled her roughly away and pushed her toward the door. Blood gushed down her shin from her reopened wound, making her feel nauseous.

On the floor, Aeric was motionless and silent. "What did you do to him?" she yelled.

"He's okay," one of the men answered, giving her a push past Aeric's body. "He's just too much trouble conscious. Now move."

They'd ridden horses to the Boundary Lands, a wise choice considering the lack of roads. They slung Aeric's big body over one of the mounts and put her on another. The motorcycle stayed at the cottage.

Aurora watched with tears in her eyes as the Imperial Guard took them away. The birch ladies helped people. It was what they lived for. They especially helped women find their way. This had to be a bitter defeat for her. She looked devastated.

Emmaline glanced at Aeric, teetering precariously on the back of the poor overburdened horse they'd inflicted his bulk upon. The partially carved key was likely in his pocket. Not the safest place for it, but there was nothing she could do about that.

They rode for a long time, out of the woods and into what looked like suburbs, but not like human burbs. Here the houses were all different sizes and shapes to fit their respective fae families; they didn't all look like they'd been stamped from a similar cookie cutter. There were different-shaped yards for each home, all containing different sorts of plants. This was where the troop lived, all the fae who were not a part of either court and weren't nature fae, either.

Eventually they hit the city again and everyone stared as they passed by. By early afternoon they reached the Rose Tower, a tall expanse of gleaming rose quartz. Outside a group of humans stood with camera equipment and microphones. She recognized them. This was the crew of *Faemous* she'd been supposedly going to join.

"Do you have a statement to make about these prisoners?" Brian Bentley, one of the *Faemous* commentators, said, holding a mic to the captain's face.

The captain, who had a nice bruise blooming on his cheek from Emmaline's fist, pushed the mic away and growled an obscenity at the reporter.

Bentley, undaunted, thrust the mic toward her. "What's your name? Why are you under arrest? Who is this man with you? Do you have anything to say for yourself?"

The captain pushed Bentley away from her horse and hauled her down off it. For once Emmaline was grateful for the captain and for the loss of her glamour. If Brother Gideon or Brother Maddoc was watching the twenty-four-hour, never-ending *Faemous* show they wouldn't recognize her. Her cover was dangerously close to being blown right now and she did not like it one bit. If her cover was blown, the fae could kiss the next piece of the *bosca fadbh* good-bye.

And she'd be locked in here with the Summer Queen forever.

They marched her through the huge double doors of the Rose Tower and down the gilt-and-rose-marble corridors to—Emmaline was certain—the throne room. Emmaline didn't march; she limped. Dried blood caked her shin and shoe. On either side of her, richly dressed Seelie nobles, men and women, watched her pass and murmured among themselves.

Ugh. The flashbacks were rampant.

The Seelie never changed. They loved their clothes, balls, and shallow little lives. She would be a hero here if they found out who she was. There would be applause, smiles, shouts of approval for all the kills she'd made back during the wars. As it was, there were only sly, curious glances and whispering. Emmaline was grateful for that, grateful beyond belief for her anonymity.

Another heavy set of double doors opened and the Imperial Guard escorted her into a huge throne room. Whereas the Shadow Queen received her guests in a small, officelike setting, this room was the polar opposite. A fresco of the Cath Maige Tuired, depicting the Sídhe taking over Ireland from the Firbolg, spread over the arched ceiling above her head and continued down the rose quartz walls. Pillars dotted the cavernous, echoing chamber. They were the only other things marking the space besides the large self-important throne that Caoilainn Elspeth Muirgheal's ass currently occupied.

The Summer Queen doesn't hold any power over me now. Emmaline hoped that if she repeated it often enough in her head it might make it true.

The queen's skirts dripped over the edge of the throne and onto the stairs leading up to it like a pool of molten ruby. Diamonds glittered at her ears, around her throat, and on her carefully manicured fingers. Her long pale blond hair was twisted onto the top of her head and pinned there with even more diamonds. She was young-appearing, beautiful, timeless in her chilly, powerful elegance. She hadn't changed at all.

Emmaline didn't curtsy and it wasn't because she was injured. She stood, head held high, gaze centered on the woman on the throne. Her expression said: *I will not bow to you. Not anymore.*

The Summer Queen met her eyes in cool challenge. *"Kneel."*

The queen's voice of power washed through her, bending her knees involuntarily. Emmaline went down on her knees with a cry of pain, the throne room going icy as a result of the Summer Queen's flash of temper.

In that moment the last three hundred plus years washed away. Once again she was the young, unsure woman she'd been, eager for any crumb of approval from the frosty woman who was her royal . . . and the only reason Emmaline lived. The only reason Lars didn't have dominion over her.

Then she came back to herself, remembering that she was no longer the person she'd once been. She'd lived among the humans, made a life for herself, had gained confidence and had survived on her own, without this woman's help.

In the time she'd been away from the Summer Queen Emmaline had grown up, grown wise, come to understand that this woman was probably responsible for her parents' deaths.

That perhaps the queen had set her up from the start—manipulating her life to make sure the fae girl with the powerful glamour and the handy healing ability could be molded into a weapon.

Emmaline straightened, feeling cold, slow anger pour through her body. "What do you want from me?"

The Seelie Royal raised an eyebrow. "Is that any way to address your queen?"

Near her, the guards dropped Aeric onto his stomach. He roused a little and groaned.

"You stopped being my queen when I left Ireland," Emmaline answered in an even voice.

The temperature in the room dropped several degrees with the rise of the Summer Queen's anger. "Leave us!" she barked at the guards. All of them bowed deeply and left the room, closing the heavy door behind them.

"How did you find me?" Emmaline asked. "How did you—" She made a sound of frustration, turning her head away and closing her eyes for a moment on a rush of emotion. "How did you know I even entered Piefferburg?"

The queen gave a short laugh and glanced at Aeric, who had rolled to his back and was struggling to open his eyes. "Do you think *he* was the only one wishing and wanting and *waiting* for you to enter this place? I knew the moment you crossed past the wardings of Piefferburg, but he got to you first. Then you were trapped in the Black Tower and beyond my reach. I had to arrange to have you run out of the Black before I could pluck you for my own use."

What? Her mind fumbled for a moment, putting it all together. "You mean you arranged to have Kolbjorn come after me? To run me out of the Black? Did you . . . pay him?"

She laughed again. "No, I didn't have to pay him. All I had to do was have a few words dropped into certain ears over in the Black. You have so many enemies over there; it was only a question of time before someone went after you. Kieran Aindréas Cairbre Aimhrea was *most* interested to hear about it. It seems his oh-so-powerful friends kept him in the dark with that pertinent little piece of information."

Next to her on the floor, Aeric groaned. "Kieran could have killed her, you bitch."

The Summer Queen's eyes narrowed and Emmaline braced herself to be spanked by her magick, but the queen only lifted her chin and addressed Emmaline, as though Aeric were but a half-dead bug on the shiny marble. "I'm surprised, but grateful, that the Blacksmith didn't get the job done . . . killing you, that is. I'm mystified as to why he didn't. I thought you'd be lost to me forever, Emmaline, once he got his hands on you."

Aeric pushed up from the floor carefully, his dusky blond hair shadowing his face. "Why don't you just come out with it, *Caoilainn*? You want your assassin back."

The Summer Queen's hands tightened on her throne and the temperature dropped again. Emmaline was going to want a coat soon. "The Unseelie never give me the respect I deserve. If I knew it wouldn't spark a war between the Black and Rose I would put you down right now, Blacksmith."

Aeric raised his head and studied her through his hair. "Do that and the Shadow Queen will put *you* down."

The queen laughed. "Aislinn? I knew her when she was a baby. She's ignorant and untried."

"She's young, but powerful. Don't underestimate her. I am claimed by the Unseelie as a subject and Emmaline is under Queen Aislinn's protection. You can't do anything to either of us."

"I have no interest in you, Unseelie. You're just along for the ride, though I would like to know what made you go from Emmaline's killer to her protector." The Summer Queen turned her viperlike attention back to Emmaline. "Why are you here in Piefferburg, my dear? Certainly you didn't come just to catch up on old times."

She didn't want to tell the Summer Queen about the key or the piece of the *bosca fadbh*. Her jaw locked and she looked down at the floor, trying to come up with some kind of plausible story. She'd never, ever thought she'd come face-to-face with the Summer Queen with the weight of her true identity on her.

"Oh, come now. We have no secrets between us, Emmaline. I was like a mother to you at one time. I still have your crossbow, you know. Would you like to see it? Hold it, perhaps? I'm sure the wood misses the feel of your expert hands."

Emmaline flinched as if the queen had hit her.

"We're done here," Aeric rasped in anger. "You can't hold us without pissing off the Shadow Queen, so let us go."

"Wrong," the queen barked. "*You* can leave, Blacksmith. I'm keeping my former assassin until she sees the error of her ways. She is mine, *body and soul*, and it's my right to hold her."

FOURTEEN

AERIC studied the Summer Queen from the hem of her heavy gown to the top of her diamond-encrusted hairdo. Being one of the older fae, he knew a lot about Caoilainn Elspeth Muirgheal. Already ancient at the time of his birth, she'd been queen since long before he was born, but his father often talked about the dark times before she'd taken command of the Seelie. Amazingly, she was a bringer of the light to the Seelie Tuatha Dé after a period of sadistic violence when her father had ruled.

But blatant brutality had been traded for other problems.

She was an egoist, not so much ruling her court as creating her own personal adoration society. She fed her people lies about the Unseelie, creating fear and loathing where it wasn't necessary. She kept her court weak magickally, most thought because she feared someone might challenge her rule.

He also knew that although the Seelie as a whole were fairly harmless, the Seelie queen was not. She was infamous for ordering executions for even minor offenses; the floor Aeric stood on had seen quite a few bloody heads rolling across it. Her magick was not to be underestimated, either. She might be the ruler of fluffy bunny white magick users, but she was not one herself. The Summer Ring she wore, like the Shadow Amulet, gave her enough magick to be the ultimate defender of the Seelie Court. She could toast someone on the spot if they pissed her off enough, and she hated disrespect.

One would be wise to be cautious in her presence, speaking to her with the utmost deference and reverence.

"You will not touch her, you fucking coldhearted bitch."

Aeric had never been cautious, deferent, or reverent.

The temperature in the room dropped below freezing for a moment and the Summer Queen rose from her throne. Her words echoed throughout the chamber, laced with angry magick that roughed their skin with the sensation of burlap. "You need to learn the meaning of the word *circumspect*, Blacksmith. It's something you are required to be when you are in the presence of one of your betters."

"Admit you killed her parents." He pointed at Emmaline, who was studying the floor. "Admit you engineered everything when she was young and vulnerable in order to create the perfect assassin for your use. *Admit it!*"

Emmaline's head snapped up and her gaze locked with his. Her eyes were wide and her lips parted in surprise. Yeah, he'd figured that part out all on his own; it had just taken him a few centuries to get there.

"Guards!" the Summer Queen yelled.

The Imperial Guard slammed the double doors open and marched into the throne room, their boots stomping on the marble and their rose and gold armor clanging.

"Admit it!" Aeric roared, advancing on the Summer Queen. The guards grabbed his upper arms and hauled him backward. He bellowed at them and fought his way free, only to have several more grab him.

"Subject of the Unseelie Court or not, you are under arrest, Blacksmith. If the Shadow Queen wants you back, she's going to have to pay for it." She waved her hand. "Get them both out of my sight. Emmaline, Lars has missed you. He can't wait to see you again."

Emmaline went stock-still and paper pale at the mention of that name. Her reaction made a strong wave of protectiveness surge through him, made him fight the guards as hard as he could.

The guards yanked him back toward a door partially concealed in the throne room wall. He watched with rage simmering in his veins as they manhandled Emmaline out of the room. She'd appeared in shock when confronted with the Summer Queen, almost pushed over the edge psychologically. Now she was angry, pulling and pushing at the iron-strong hands of the guards as they dragged them both out of the throne room through a door that let out an odor of old blood and unwashed bodies as soon as it was opened.

The dungeons.

Just like the dungeons in the Black Tower, these were dank and filled with misery. It appeared even the shining ones couldn't escape all the ugliness of life.

They tossed him into a small cell with a concrete floor, piss bucket, and heap of moldy straw. Emmaline went into an identical one beside him. The fact that they weren't completely separated was the only upside to this ordeal.

He collapsed to the floor when they pushed him inside, his palms and almost his nose finding the gritty floor. "Are you all right?" he asked as he pushed up and looked over at her. She was sitting on the floor, one hand splayed behind her and her head bowed, hair concealing her face.

"The key." Her voice was rough with emotion.

"I have it." He moved closer to her. "*Emmaline*, are you all right?"

It took her a moment to look at him. Her eyes weren't quite focused. "I'm fine."

She wasn't, of course. Seeing the Summer Queen again had thrown her. That name, *Lars*, had been like a kick to her abdomen. He licked his lips and looked around the cell for some way to escape. He wanted to punch something—*someone*, maybe someone named Lars. "How's your injury?"

"Messed up again."

"We'll get out of here. Don't worry."

She shook her head and looked up at him with a film of despair over her eyes. *What was wrong with her?* She needed to snap out of it. "She wants me back, Aeric. You'll get out of here. I won't."

There was a note of helplessness in her voice. Emmaline Siobhan Keara Gallagher was not helpless. She was a fighter, a survivor. Had seeing the Summer Queen flipped her backward in time, back to when she'd been under the Seelie Royal's thumb? What sort of trauma had she received at the Summer Queen's hands that would cause that kind of reaction?

He gripped the bars that separated them so hard his knuckles went white. "You fucking stop that right now. You have to get out of here, Emmaline. The mission. The key. *The key*. Don't you remember?"

The haze cleared from her eyes and they locked on his with a ferocity that he recognized. "The key. You're right." Her expression hardened. "I need to make it through this."

"Fuck, yeah, you do. The Shadow Queen will bargain for us. We'll both get out."

She shook her head. "The Shadow Queen can bargain for you, not me."

"You can bargain for your release with the promise of the piece. She'll let you go if you agree to give it to her once you get it."

"No." The word was a lash of anger. Her expression turned vicious for a moment. "She can't know about the piece, let alone possess it, Aeric. She can't be allowed that much power. The piece needs to go to the Shadow Queen. I see that very clearly, having met her. The Shadow Queen lacks the . . . insanity of the Summer Queen."

"Why does the Summer Queen want you back so badly?"

"I was the perfect assassin. I could take on the appearance of anyone, I was strong, I healed fast, and I wasn't much trouble." She grinned. "I'm much more trouble now that a few centuries have passed. The Summer Queen just doesn't realize it yet."

"She really fucked you up, didn't she?"

Emmaline's grin faded and her eyes went out of focus again. "It wasn't easy back then."

His voice was a low growl. "What did she do to you?"

Her face took on that haze again, but she blinked and came back to herself almost right away. "I didn't realize until years afterward that she'd murdered my parents and arranged for the conditions that pressed me into her service. Back then I really thought they'd died by accident. I was just a kid. I didn't put it all together until later on."

"She *did* kill your parents. I'm sure of it."

"Yes." The word sounded heavy with a grief he wasn't sure she'd ever truly allowed herself to process.

"What else did she do, besides make sure you starved for a couple years?"

"I was ten when they died. Yes, you're right, I starved for two years, though not all the time. I wasn't totally alone. Graeme helped me sometimes."

"Not enough," he rasped in anger.

"After I'd had a good taste of the world as an orphan, that's when the Summer Queen took me in. It was nice at first. I was warm and there was food, regular baths, safety. She made it clear it wasn't for free. I was expected to work for my keep. She gave me crossbows and I trained with professionals. I learned how to use a knife, how to fight. When I turned fourteen, that's when my first order to kill came." Her fingers curled tight around the bars. "I resisted."

"And what happened?"

She touched her abdomen in what seemed like an unconscious gesture and Aeric remembered the scars he'd seen there and on her upper thighs. His body tightened.

"What happened?" His voice was a low, enraged lash in the fetid air.

She jerked herself out of her stare and looked at him. "At that point, I trusted them." She blinked. "They broke it, my trust."

"How?"

"They took away my security, my comfort." She looked away from him. "They showed me what life would be like if I disobeyed."

His hands tightened on the bars. *"How?"*

"I don't want to talk about it."

"Emmaline, you can trust me." He touched her fingers and she grabbed on to them through the bars as if he could save her.

Drawing a ragged breath, she forced the words out in a rush. "Forced nudity, solitary confinement, making me wear a black hood for as long as I could go without food or water." She pressed her lips together, trembling, while he mentally kicked his ass a hundred different ways for forcing her into the burlap sack. No wonder she'd gone berserk. "I don't want to talk specifics. The bottom line is that they broke me down and built me back up the way they wanted me. By that time only the killer they'd trained me to be was left. It suited them."

"You keep saying *they*, Emmaline. Who besides the Summer Queen did these things?" He was pretty sure he knew the answer.

"Lars. It was always Lars. The Summer Queen never got her hands dirty; she only gave orders." Her hand went to her stomach again.

His gaze flicked downward. "What about the scars? Did Lars make those?"

She nodded.

He was going to kill this man. Tear his limbs off. Some of those scars were in very intimate places and *she'd been a child. "How?"*

Emmaline had a faraway look on her face. It took her several moments to answer. "Knives," she whispered.

"Look at me."

She continued to stare off into the distance.

"Look at me, Emmaline."

Blinking slowly, she turned her head toward him and her eyes focused on his face. "Sorry. I haven't thought about that in a long time. I blocked it out."

Aeric gripped the bars and fought his temper. He'd always had a bad temper, but right now it was boiling. He wanted to find the Summer Queen and rip her apart with his bare hands.

He wanted to strap Lars down and deliver that bastard's karma fiftyfold.

He took a deep breath, knowing he needed to at least seem calm for Emmaline's sake. "Hey, Emmaline, it's okay. That was a long time ago. It's over and it will never happen again." He spoke the last words with icy vehemence. He needed to get her out of here before the Summer Queen made him eat his words.

It *had* been a long time ago, but what had happened to Emmaline had cut deep and left emotional scars. Those scars hadn't healed; she'd only slapped some psychic Band-Aids over them. Seeing the Summer Queen again had ripped those Band-Aids off and she was bleeding.

He wouldn't be able to handle it if they hauled Emmaline away to fuck her up, bring her back to the same emotional state she'd been in when she'd worked for the queen. He'd go nuts if that happened and he was stuck in here unable to help her. He wasn't sure how much magick the Summer Queen had—but despite being Seelie some of it was dark. It was possible she could use magick to strip away some of Emmaline's free will, just as she'd done when Emmaline was a child.

He had to get Emmaline out of here. Now.

"Funny. Feels like it happened yesterday." She gave him a smile that didn't reach her eyes. "I never should have come into Piefferburg. It's brought up junk that I buried a long time ago. I should have laid it all out to the HFF and we could have tried to arrange for someone else to come. It would have been hard, but maybe we could have managed it."

He motioned to her. "Come here."

She scooted over to the bars as close as she could get to him. Sighing, she laid her head against them and closed her eyes. He stroked her hair, wishing he could take her into his arms, regretting he'd ever doubted her story and hating himself for thinking she'd come to Piefferburg to go back to the Summer Queen.

He settled for resting his head against hers on the other side of the bars and closing his eyes, images of retribution against the Summer Queen and Lars dancing through his head.

THE next morning Aeric woke sore and stiff, having fallen asleep slumped on the floor next to Emmaline. He blinked, groggy, realizing the sound of the opening cell door had woken him.

A rose-and-gold-bedecked guard stood in the threshold. "Get up. The Summer Queen has ordered your release."

"And Emmaline?"

"She stays."

Emmaline roused beside him, her eyes coming open blearily.

He rubbed his eye with the heel of his palm, chasing one fuck of a headache. "No, I won't leave without her."

The guard looked at him as if blue snakes had suddenly sprouted from his head.

"What?" Emmaline pushed into a sitting position. "No, Aeric. That's crazy. Go. Get out of here!"

He shook his head. "Nope. Not without you, cupcake."

She pushed to her feet, gesturing in frustration. "Aeric, you can't help me anyway! You're locked in a cell! Look, you're amazing for wanting to stay with me, but you can't do me any good in here. *Are you hearing me?* Take this chance."

"Make your decision, Blacksmith," said the guard. "I won't stand here all day."

You can't do me any good in here. Are you hearing me? Yeah, he heard her. Maybe he could do her some good beyond these walls. Maybe she was hoping he could.

She needed hope.

But, damn it, *no*. He couldn't leave her alone, not in her current mental state.

She stared at him, brows knit and jaws locked. Then she limped to the bars and curled her fingers around them. "Come here," she ordered.

He pushed up and went to her, wrapping his fingers as best he could around hers. "Yes, cupcake?" he drawled.

Her eyelid twitched. Ah, he was annoying her. There was the Emmaline he'd come to know and admire. "You want to get me out of here, right?"

"Of course."

"Then go be my hero, Aeric. *Go.*"

He hesitated, but it was going to be painful leaving her here, not knowing what the Summer Queen had in store for her.

"Aeric, go," Emmaline pleaded softly. "Please."

He slid his fingers through to touch her cheek. "I'm getting you out, Emmaline. No matter what I have to do. Do you understand? Are *you* hearing *me* this time?"

Fear flashed in her eyes. She was worried he'd use the piece of the *bosca fadbh* to bargain for her, and she had reason to be worried. "Don't tell her—" She glanced at the guard. "Don't, Aeric. I'll find a way to get free on my own. Don't do it."

"No promises. You can't stay in here. I saw just how much damage she did to you yesterday and that means you need to get the fuck out of here before she does more." He pulled away from her.

She tried to grab him as he backed away. "Don't do it, Aeric. Do you hear me? Don't!"

He walked away from her, toward the guard. He could still hear her yelling at him clear down the corridor. She was strong, that woman, for not taking the easy way out of this mess.

He hoped she could stay strong for a little longer.

WRAPPED in charmed iron, Emmaline knelt at the Summer Queen's feet. She parted her lips and forced out a strong voice despite her weakening from the effect of iron against her skin. "I won't go back to working for you."

"Who said you have a choice?"

Magick flared along Emmaline's skin, soft and seductive, coaxing her to let down her guard and allow it past so it could have its way with her will. The lucky thing for her was that she was older now—much. And she was more experienced. In the years since she'd left Ireland, she may not have fully dealt with the atrocities of her childhood, but she had found her inner strength in other ways. She was no longer the vulnerable, starving child she'd been, willing to give up her soul for even the ghostliest illusion of a mother figure.

"I have a choice and my choice is to remain free."

The magick grew heavier, less like silk and more like sandpaper. She squeezed her eyes shut, her body going tense. It would get worse and worse, more painful. She remembered.

The bitch wasn't getting her this time.

"Emmaline, give in to me. This way is much easier than the gentling."

That's what she'd called the stripping of Emmaline's will back when she was a child. The forced nudity, the sack, the weeks of confinement. *Gentling*.

Emmaline didn't respond. She only kept her head bowed and endured the rasp of the Summer Queen's magick along her body, denying it entry into her mind. The fact that the wound on her shin throbbed didn't help, nor did her incredible fatigue. It took all her concentration to reject the queen's power.

"Perhaps you'd like to see an old friend, then?"

Oh, gods, please, no. Not Lars. *Pleasepleaseplease.*

There was a rustling of fabric and the sound of booted footfalls on the floor. Then an object was placed on the marble floor in front of her.

Her crossbow.

"I had it preserved using magick. It's as pristine today as the day you left it on my throne. Do you want to touch it? It's almost as if I can feel it yearning for your fingers on its wood, Emmaline. The weapon always did seem a little sentient, didn't it?"

It did. And, Danu, it was a beautiful weapon even by today's standards. The Summer Queen had spared no expense having it made, since it had, by default, represented her as queen. The stock was of polished oak. She could remember the way the wood had warmed in her hand and she could see the slightly worn areas where her fingers had fit. Normally a crossbow's string was difficult to pull back, but not this one—this one had been charmed to make it easy, allowing her to get off shot after shot when she needed to.

The weapon really did seem to call out for her to touch it. A part of her felt compelled to pick it up, hold it, and make it hers again. In an odd way, this crossbow was a part of her. Yet the weapon also repulsed her because it represented that horrific part of her life.

But the real reason she didn't touch it was because the Summer Queen wanted her to.

The queen sighed as if sorely put out. "Fine. I can see this is nothing like the old days." The displeasure in her voice kissed Emmaline's skin with ice. "But don't think I don't know what you have nightmares about, Emmaline. Don't think I don't know where your weak spots are. I know very well indeed. Lars!"

Emmaline began to shake as soon as his name hit the air. *Lars.* Oh, she remembered him like it was yesterday. Her body remembered it, too, clenching up and shivering—like a beaten dog, that was how the queen had always described her reaction to him.

Heavy black boots hit the floor in front of her nose. She closed her eyes against the still-familiar scent of him. Just a little like the freshly turned earth he worked in, coupled with a faint trace of evergreen and a dash of old blood. She'd hoped that Watt's had gotten him, but here he was, her worst nightmare made flesh.

Swallowing hard and centering all her willpower, she looked up. He hadn't changed at all, maybe he was just a little older. Light blond hair cut short, fine form dressed in hunting leathers. Beautiful. Looking at him, you'd never expect the monster that lived behind those pale blue eyes.

He smiled, showing perfect teeth. "I've been waiting a long time for you to come back to me, Emmaline."

Her gaze dropped to his hand. He held a knife.

FIFTEEN

BACK in the Shadow Queen's receiving room, Aeric paced back and forth while Aislinn, Gabriel, and Niall Quinn watched. "What did you give the bitch to get me back?" His body trembled with a fine, cold rage. Aislinn had bargained for him, and he'd had to leave Emmaline behind.

Aislinn had petitioned the Seelie Court for another audience, this time so Aeric could meet with the Summer Queen, but they were being stonewalled. The Summer Queen knew what he wanted, of course, and didn't want to hear what he had to say. That left Emmaline over there in her evil clutches, subject to whatever torture she planned to dish out. He felt powerless, ineffectual, *fucking impotent*. It was pissing him off so much he'd punched a hole in his apartment wall.

Aislinn didn't even blink at his language. "The cauldron."

Aeric swore for a full minute. The cauldron was rare and very special. It had the power to give those who drank from it powerful visions, usually of a dark nature, visions that would help the drinker through his or her personal demons. More than that, it was a piece of Unseelie history—a piece they'd just lost to the Seelie.

"You're worth it," said Gabriel. "You're the Blacksmith and part of the Wild Hunt. The Summer Queen knows all that and she squeezed Aislinn hard because of it."

And Emmaline was still over there in her bloodless grip.

"She wouldn't negotiate with me at all for Emmaline," Aislinn continued, "and I had no way to force her to make a deal since Emmaline is Seelie."

"Yeah, the bitch has a serious hard-on for her."

"I noticed that. She's very"—Aislinn pressed her lips together as if searching for the right word—"proprietary where Emmaline is concerned."

That was the correct term. To the Summer Queen, Emmaline was nothing more than a valuable arrow in her quiver, or an expensive and deadly sword to keep sheathed at her side. He was only afraid that the queen was attempting to resharpen that sword even as they stood here talking.

"I'm going over there. If the bitch won't see me voluntarily, I'll force the issue." He stalked toward the door, but Gabriel and Niall got up and stood in front of it. "Get out of my way."

"No," stated Gabriel with a hint of violence in his voice.

"Are you crazy?" Niall growled at him. "You're just going to barge in there with your hot temper and your potty mouth again? We just got you out, Aeric, and the Unseelie Court is running out of priceless relics to trade for your mangy hide."

"Get out of my way," Aeric growled again.

Gabriel stepped closer to him, folding his arms across his chest. "You can try to make us."

Goibhniu, he didn't have time for this. "We can give her the section of the *bosca fadbh* Emmaline's going after. It's a bargaining chip that will work."

The room went quiet.

Aeric turned to the Shadow Queen. "We have to get Emmaline out of there. You don't understand just how much trauma the Summer Queen caused twisting her into an assassin. Now she's over there right now, trying to twist her again. Emmaline can't take it."

Aislinn appeared to be choosing her words carefully. "We don't know how the Summer Queen feels about the wards of Piefferburg being torn down, Aeric. I am not totally convinced she wants them gone. She's a big deal in here, the celebrated focal point of the Seelie. Out there, among the humans, she wouldn't be. When—*if*—it comes time for her to give up what she's holding for the greater good . . . well, I'm not sure she won't fight."

"She's already got the first piece," Gabriel added. "That's bad enough. She shouldn't have two."

Aeric whirled to face the two men. "Are you all insane? If we don't get Emmaline out of there, there won't be a second piece to fight over."

"We're just saying that we need to find another way to free Emmaline," said Aislinn patiently.

"How?"

No one had an answer.

He stared hard at Aislinn, a woman he counted as a friend as well as his queen, and pointed at Gabriel. "He moved the very *Netherworld* to save you. Why does Emmaline deserve less?"

No one had an answer for that, either.

"You know," said Niall into the suddenly quiet room, "I realize we have to help this woman because of the key, but has it struck anyone else how ironic this is? I'm one of the only ones in this room old enough to remember the wars—and I *do* remember. I recall very clearly what a scourge Emmaline Siobhan Keara Gallagher was."

Aeric swung his gaze around to meet Niall's and put all his rage into it. Niall didn't take the hint.

"And by the way," Niall continued blithely on, "have you forgotten that this is the woman who killed Aileen? Now you're all hell-bent on preventing her from being *traumatized*? I remember a day when you would have ripped this woman bloody with your bare hands. Aeric, what the *fuck* is going on with you?"

"None of your business, mage," Aeric barked.

"I'm afraid it is my business, *Blacksmith*."

"Stop wasting my time, all of you." He made a sound of frustration and pushed past Gabriel. "I'm going over there right now. To stop me, you'll have to fight me," he growled into Niall's face. "Good luck with that."

"I could kick your ass with magick, big guy," countered Niall with a cool gaze. "You know that as well as I do."

Aeric practically pressed his nose to the mage's in challenge. "Then either do it or stand aside."

Niall's jaw locked and Gabriel swore loudly in Old Maejian, but neither man made a move to stop him.

Aeric pushed past him, stormed out of the room, and was gone.

THE Seelie Court fops all had their panties in an excited twist and the *Faemous* film crew did their best to waylay Aeric as he stormed down the corridors of the Rose Tower toward the throne room. The Unseelie never came here unless on official business for the Shadow Royal and they never just stomped in and started cracking Imperial Guard heads together.

He could hear the sound of boots, the clang of rose and gold armor, and the creak of leather behind him now. Reinforcements. He needed to get to the Seelie Queen before they got to him. He broke into a run.

Two guards stood at the double doors of the throne room. "Halt!" they yelled.

Not a chance.

He ducked the swinging blade of one and pivoted, catching the man in the gut and slamming him back against the wall. Gripping him at the edge of his armor, he yanked the stunned guard to the side, into the second. They collapsed in a heap.

Aeric pushed through the doors so hard they slammed into the walls on the other side. The Seelie Queen sat on her throne, almost as if she'd been waiting for him.

"Another piece of the *bosca fadbh*!" he yelled. The Imperial Guards stormed through the door and jumped on him. He fought them off as he bellowed, "It's yours if you let Emmaline go!"

"Guards, stop," came the queen's icy voice.

The guards ceased trying to wrestle him to the floor and backed away from him.

"What would you know of the *bosca fadbh*, Blacksmith?"

Aeric straightened and walked closer to her. "Outside Piefferburg, Emmaline works for the HFF. They know where the next piece of the *bosca fadbh* is, but they need something from me in order to get it. Once they have the piece, they intend to bring it back into Piefferburg. If you let Emmaline leave with me right now, we'll let you keep it."

She drummed her fingers on her throne and said nothing for several long moments, as though weighing the juiciness of his offer against the worth of her former assassin. Every heartbeat made Aeric grow tenser.

"Emmaline can't be worth more than a piece of the *bosca fadbh*," Aeric said. Maybe he was trying to convince himself of that fact, since now he wasn't so sure.

"It's a good offer. I won't deny it. Had I known earlier, things might have turned out differently. However, I'm afraid I have some bad news about Emmaline."

Aeric took a step forward, his fists clenching. "What?"

"She was mine to do with as I pleased. Mine to—"

"What the fuck did you do to her?" he roared, stalking toward her.

She flicked her wrist and the guards were on him in a moment, holding him back from doing her bodily harm. She sighed. "Fine, if you want her that much, you can have what's left."

SIXTEEN

GIDEON woke to white.

White ceiling, white walls, white floor, white upholstered chairs. White everything, broken only by shiny, metallic medical equipment. Blessed Labrai Hospital. The one on the Phaendir campus in Protection City, Carolina, that catered to the unique physiological makeup of the druids.

His world was soft, hazy. He felt like he was floating. Drugs. They must have him on something. He reached over and touched the IV that was attached to his arm.

"Don't move around too much," said a nurse, leaning over him. She patted his arm and smiled into his face. "You've been out for several days. I'm glad to see you came back to us. We thought we might have lost you there, Brother Gideon."

She shuffled away and he closed his eyes. Labrai help him, he felt like he'd missed death by a breath for real.

He hadn't known what to expect when he'd ordered it, but that was *not* what he'd been going for. Someone was going to be in trouble for this one.

"They told me you were awake," said Brother Maddoc, entering the room dressed in an expensive blue suit. "I came right over."

Gideon moved his head with a difficulty he didn't have to fake to look up at Maddoc standing at his bedside. "What happened?" he croaked. "The last thing I remember is drinking my tea." He fought through the drug-induced haze that gripped him. This conversation was important.

Maddoc's usually open face clouded. "Yes, your tea was accidentally poisoned, it seems."

He blinked and tried to sit up, only to fall back weakly against the pillows. "Accidentally? How does tea become *accidentally* poisoned?"

"When the kitchen help making the tea mistakes the cubed rat poison for sugar. The worker has claimed responsibility for the mix-up and has been punished."

"Rat poison in the kitchen? Near the sugar? *Cubed rat poison?*" Gideon succeeded in pushing into a sitting position, wincing at the soreness of his body. "How is that possible?"

"It was a freak accident, a series of unfortunate and highly improbable events."

"I'm aware of the meaning of the term *freak accident*, Maddoc," Gideon snarled.

"You should be."

"Yes, I should be." Gideon stared up at him meaningfully, infusing his voice with just enough suspicion. "There have been quite a few freak accidents lately, haven't there?"

Maddoc's jaw tightened. "There have. One might almost think they weren't accidents." There was a hard note of suspicion in his voice.

"Are you accusing me of something? Right now? While I lie here in the hospital having narrowly escaped death?"

"You have been the one to benefit the most from this string of unfortunate mishaps. I need not point out your use of the words *narrowly escaped.* Miraculously, you're the only brother to have survived his respective . . . *accident.*"

Gideon sputtered. "Are you suggesting that I somehow poisoned *myself*?"

"Or arranged for the poisoning, all the better to make you look innocent of clearing your passage through the hierarchy through *murder*, Brother Gideon. Here you lie, an innocent victim just like all the rest. Thank Labrai you made it through." The note of sarcasm in Maddoc's voice wasn't lost on Gideon.

"How dare you."

Brother Maddoc's face went red, then purple. "How dare you, Gideon!" he bellowed. "I should have executed you last year instead of showing mercy."

No doubt.

"Hey!" said the nurse, rushing into the room. "No, Brother Maddoc. Stop that," she scolded, waving a finger in his face. "As much as you are respected around here, I cannot have you upsetting my patients!" She touched Gideon's arm and while the nurse's face was turned toward Maddoc, Gideon cracked a smile that made Maddoc go even redder. "This man has just woken up from a coma. Now, please, go. The doctor is coming in to examine Brother Gideon shortly, anyway."

Maddoc stared down at Gideon for a heartbeat, smoke practically wafting from his ears like in some cartoon. "Fine, I'll leave." Maddoc pointed at him. "But you haven't heard the last of this, Brother Gideon." Threat delivered, he turned and walked out of the room.

Gideon stared hard at his retreating form. Brother Maddoc hadn't heard the last of this, either, and he wasn't going to like the next part. Not at all.

"How are you feeling?" the nurse asked with a friendly smile.

Gideon wiped all traces of murderous rage off his face and smiled back. "Happy to be alive."

She laughed. "I can imagine."

He scooted down into his pillows and did his best to look pitiful. "Could you do me a favor"—he glanced at her name tag—"Nurse Teresa?"

"Of course."

"I really need my cell phone. Can you get it for me? It's

probably still in the top drawer of my desk in my office over in HQ. The recharging cord should be there with it. I'll need that, too."

She nodded and winked. "I'd be happy to do that for you. Sit tight and I'll be back with it. The doctor will be here in a few minutes."

Gideon relaxed and closed his eyes. Everything was going exactly to plan. He just had to make a couple of phone calls to make sure they *kept* going that way. He smiled.

EMMALINE blinked and a strange, opulently furnished room came into view. Noticing right away that she wasn't cuffed, she pushed into a sitting position. Her head pounded and her stomach burned. Someone had bandaged her wounds and dressed her in a very feminine light nightgown that reached her toes.

She blinked and glanced around, seeing nothing familiar. Where the hell was she?

Didn't matter. She hopped from the bed and limped toward the door on bare feet. If she had a chance to escape, she was damn well going to take it.

A strong hand captured her upper arm. "Where do you—*gugh*!"

She'd brought her elbow back hard into the man's unprotected abdomen. She whirled, arms at the ready to do more damage, and saw immediately that it was Aeric.

"Oh, Danu." She touched his shoulder. He was bent over, holding his gut. "I'm sorry."

"No problem." He straightened, wincing. "My fault for sneaking up on you." He pointed at the bed. "Back to bed."

There was something very nice about Aeric ordering her to bed. Still . . . "I feel okay, Aeric, really."

"Back to bed."

She jumped at the lash of anger in his voice, but she knew it was because he was worried about her. She limped back the way she'd come, thankful she could lie down again. Weakness from standing had entered her limbs and her head and stomach ached.

"Where am I?"

"You're in the Black Tower. The queen has issued an edict. Any Unseelie who attacks you does it on pain of death. You should be safe here."

"Kolbjorn?"

"Restrained. The Shadow Queen wasn't pleased about the damage he did to Goblin Town. That's all stuff the Black Tower will have to pay for. He's being punished."

She nodded. "Okay, I trust the Shadow Queen." Oddly, she did. Seemed like she shouldn't trust any fae royal after what she'd been through, but she understood Aislinn's history. Aislinn was a good woman, for all that she was the leader of monsters. "But I feel okay, Aeric, really."

His expression went rigid. "You haven't asked how long you've been here."

"Oh, hell. How long?"

"You've been mostly in and out of it for the last week, Emmaline. We kept you drugged while you healed up the damage done to you. You were broken when the Summer Queen gave you back to me." He watched her tuck herself in. "So, you might feel okay now, but that doesn't mean the way they brought you to me isn't still fresh in my mind." His eyes seemed to go dark and his body tensed. "They fucked you up bad, before I was able to get you out."

She averted her gaze, staring straight ahead. "I don't remember much. She showed me my crossbow—*Danu*, it was like new," she breathed. "Then . . . Lars. After that, I don't remember."

"Lars?" His voice was sharp. "Was he the one who hurt you?"

She gave a rough laugh. "The queen calls it *gentling*. There's nothing gentle about it."

"Lars is going to die." His voice was the coldest and most determined she'd ever heard it. It was a simple statement and he meant it. Lars's death was on his To Do list. It was on hers, too.

"I like that idea."

"You were conscious when they handed you over. You really don't remember anything?"

She shivered. "No. My mind used to shut down. It was a survival thing. Maybe I did it again."

He studied her, saying nothing.

She settled back into the pillows and closed her eyes. Her body was far weaker than she'd first presumed and she wasn't sure she wanted to know what the Summer Queen had ordered Lars to do to her. All she knew was that her stomach hurt badly. "Before you go off on a hunt for Lars, which, by the way, is a *fantastic* idea, have you finished the key?"

"Soon. It's almost done. You just concentrate on healing and don't worry about the key."

She opened her eyes and gave him a weak smile. "Thank you for getting me out."

"You won't thank me when you find out what I traded for you."

Danu, she hadn't even been thinking about that. She sat up. "You didn't. Please, Aeric, tell me you didn't."

He stared stonily at her.

She pushed the blankets away and bounded from the bed. Her shin gave only the slightest protest. It was mostly healed, apparently. Her head pounded out a staccato rhythm and her stomach burned, but it was no match for her anger. "The piece wasn't yours to bargain with!"

Her knees folded and he caught her. She pushed at him, cursing a blue streak, but he only held her close to his body. "I understand why you didn't want me to give the piece to her. Aislinn explained." He spoke close to her ear. "I just couldn't leave you in the Rose for the time it would've taken to devise an alternate way to get you out. Not now. Not now that I know about your past."

She sagged against him, feeling defeated. But what was done, was done. "Don't you understand yet what a danger the Seelie Queen could be to the freedom of the fae?"

He sat her on the bed and then sank down beside her.

"One bridge at a time." He cupped her cheek. "All I care about right now is that you're out of there."

Was Aeric really cupping her cheek, gazing into her eyes and professing that he cared about her well-being? She blinked. Nope, not dreaming. This was even better than the sexual interludes they'd had. There was emotion here. Emotion of the nonviolent kind, even. Amazing.

He lowered his mouth and pressed his lips to hers, his mouth slanting across hers. His tongue eased inside her mouth with long, slow sweeps. His arms came around her, warm and strong, bracketing her in an embrace she never wanted to leave. With a deep groan, he pulled her flush up against him, so close she was sure he could feel the stupidly crazy beat of her heart.

He dragged his lips across hers once in a while, nibbling at her lower lip before sliding his tongue back within. His kiss was like the finest wine or the most potent drug. It made her forget her pains and aches, almost made her forget how to think. She just wanted—needed—more. Her body was aware of his kiss in the most sensitive way—her nipples hard, her sex warm.

Carefully he lowered her backward into the pillows, still kissing her. When he finally pulled back, his eyes were dark and his body taut. His expression could only be described as hungry. He wasn't the only one.

"Rest now," he rasped at her, pulling away.

"Rest? Are you crazy? You kiss me like that and then tell me to rest? It's like taunting a starving lion with a steak and then telling it to go to sleep."

"You're injured and if we continue this I'll push too far."

"Would that be so bad?"

"Yes." He turned away. "I'll send up some food. I'm setting guards I can trust at the door, too. Insurance against any fae who wants to break the queen's edict."

"You're leaving?"

"I have to." His voice was low and rough. "At least for a little while. I'll be back."

He walked toward the door and her gaze caught on an object she'd hoped she'd never see again. "My crossbow," she breathed.

He stopped and turned to her. "Wow, you really don't remember, do you?"

"Remember what?"

"The Summer Queen tried to send your crossbow with you. I told her to shove it up her royal ass, but you stopped me and asked me to take it. Have you changed your mind? Hell, I'll burn it for you if you want."

She stared at the polished wood for a long time before answering. "No. There's a reason I asked you to take it. It's time I faced my past. I need to stop letting it scare and control me. Leave it."

"Whatever you need, Emmaline."

SEVENTEEN

AERIC shut the door behind him, nodded to the two guards standing watch outside, and then headed for the stairs. His hands were shaking in relief. He'd been so afraid she wouldn't make it through. Then, when it had become apparent that she would pull through, he'd worried that after they'd weaned her off the drugs she might wake up different, permanently changed for the worse.

Emmaline was the strongest person he'd ever met. He'd gone from hatred to unadulterated admiration.

He rounded a corner and came face-to-face with Niall. "Hey, I've been looking for you all week," Niall said.

"Been a little busy," he growled. Niall wasn't the person he most wanted to see right now.

"Look, I'm sorry for how hard I came down on you before you went over to the Rose for Emmaline. I can tell that you've developed some pretty strong feelings for her."

"And you don't get it. Yeah, I remember this conversation."

"You risked your life for her by storming into the Rose,

and, man, that's a story that's going to be told for the next hundred years. Then I saw how you carried her back here, what kind of shape she was in. You disappeared behind a door with her and didn't leave her side until you healed her."

Aeric fidgeted. "Is there a point to this conversation?"

"My point is that I see you've come to care deeply for a woman who isn't Aileen. I remember you two." Niall shook his head. "I didn't think it was possible for you *ever* to love a woman other than her." He pressed his lips together. "Your choice is a little strange—"

"Who says I'm *in love* with Emmaline? That's a little strong."

"Okay, maybe, but you can't deny that your actions would lead the observer to think *love*."

"Point?" Aeric barked.

"My point is that I'm old and I remember. I remember how fucking infatuated you were with Aileen, how you couldn't see *anything or anyone* but her. You couldn't even see she was sleeping with another man while she whispered sweet nothings in your ear."

Aeric went very still. "How do you know about that?"

"I'm probably the only one who does, and I only know it by purest chance."

"Tell me."

"I saw them together once, walking in the woods. They were very deep in the forest, all alone. Holding hands and laughing." He paused for a moment and looked like he was debating whether or not he should continue. "They looked like they were in love."

"Why didn't you tell me?"

Niall laughed. "Fuck that. You would have killed the messenger. I kept that little secret to myself. I wouldn't have mentioned it at all if it weren't for Emmaline. If Aileen had been with any other man in those woods that night, I would've forgotten the whole thing long ago." He drew a breath. "But she was with a Seelie, one that Emmaline offed—"

"Driscoll Manus O'Shaughnessy."

Niall's eyebrows raised into his dark hairline. "You know."

"All but one very significant part of everything you just told me, yes."

"I'm sorry to be the bearer, man. You're not going to kill me, are you?" Niall glanced down at Aeric's hands.

Aeric forced himself to unclench his fists. "No."

"I still don't understand what you see in the Summer Queen's assassin."

"She's not the Summer Queen's assassin anymore. She's just Emmaline." Aeric pushed past Niall and continued on his way.

Once in his apartment, he went straight into his forge and stood at the foot of Aileen's portrait. Walking hand in hand in the deep forest. Laughing at one another's comments. Looking like they were in love. Because they had been, of course. O'Shaughnessy had offered Aileen what she'd needed. Things that Aeric never would have been able to give her.

He reached up and took the portrait down, turning its face toward the wall.

"Good-bye, Aileen."

AFTER Aeric left, Emmaline pushed from the bed and crossed the room, approaching her old crossbow as if it were a poisonous snake that might lash out at any false move. Finally she reached it and, swallowing hard, picked it up.

Touching it made the last three hundred–plus years disappear in a heartbeat. Suddenly she was back in Ireland, in the polished halls of the Seelie Court hidden under the hills with her crossbow and quiver slung across her back. The weight of the crossbow felt good in her hands, the wood rubbed smooth where she'd always held it. Her finger brushed the trigger and she remembered the way it felt to aim and release, the backlash of the weapon against her shoulder, the sound of the bolt slicing through the air to find its target.

She remembered the rest of it, too. The way the light would evaporate from her mark's eyes as he died, the sound of the bolt finding flesh, the thump of the body falling. She remembered the cold timbre of the Summer Queen's voice as she ordered death after death.

And Emmaline had obeyed her.

Emmaline set the crossbow down and backed away from it.

GLIMPSING *the man she wanted through the trees, she flipped back the edge of her cloak, readied her crossbow against her shoulder, and sighted his back. The bolt was already nocked; she'd been stalking him all morning.*

His name was Aydan Corrigan Mac Gearailt. She didn't know what he was guilty of, but it was probably excessive killing of Seelie in the war. Generally, those were the ones the queen sent her after—the ones capable of mass murder through magick—in an effort to even up the odds between the courts.

When it came to killing, the Unseelie had a pretty big advantage.

It didn't matter what he was guilty of. Mac Gearailt was her task, and once the queen chose a task for her, she thought of nothing but completing it—delivering death. Guilt or innocence meant nothing. Getting it done. That's what she'd been made for.

She drew back the string, keeping the Unseelie in her sights while she hid behind a clump of trees. This one had magick enough to crush bones with his glance, and that meant she really didn't want him looking her way.

He stopped, went still.

Her whole body went rigid, her breathing puffing white in the cold air of the woods in twilight. She shifted her weight and a branch cracked, sounding as loud as cannon fire in the quiet forest.

Mac Gearailt turned, magick gathering.

But it wasn't Mac Gearailt when he turned; it was Lars.

He smiled, showing sharpened metallic teeth. Then he was there, behind her. She turned and he was to the side of her, blocking her way. She whirled and he was in front of her. Disappearing. Reappearing. Too fast for her to track.

She dropped her crossbow to the ground and he leapt, his knifelike teeth ripping a bloody chunk of meat from her shoulder.

She came awake with a scream and with shakes racking her body. Aeric stared at her in the murky half-light of the room, his face an inch from hers. His hands were grasping her shoulders as if he'd shaken her out of a nightmare.

His face looked tense, lined with worry and exhaustion. "Are you okay? You were screaming in your sleep." He pulled her close and she melted against him.

A second later she realized she'd molded herself to his body and backed away. "Yeah." Except she was still shaking. She curled her arms over her chest and licked her lips. "Just a bad dream."

His lips curled into a sardonic half smile. "Gee, can't understand why you'd have those. Want to tell me about it?"

"No." The word snapped out of her like a bullet. She drew a deep breath and closed her eyes for a moment, steadying herself. "But thanks for the offer."

"What do you need?"

"A shower, a change of clothes, a good stiff drink."

"Luckily I can provide all of those." He pointed toward a shadowed doorway. "Bathroom is in there. A change of clothing has already been placed on the counter. I'll order us some dinner, okay? It'll be here when you get out."

"Wow, you really seem to want to fatten me up," she complained gently as she stood. "You sent that huge meal before I fell to sleep and now dinner."

He caught her wrist before she could move away. "I want you to keep your strength up so you can heal."

She stopped and gave him a shaky smile. "Be careful. Someone listening might think you care about me for more than just my ability to procure the piece of the *bosca fadbh*."

He didn't drop her wrist or refute her words. He held her gaze steadily, a muscle working in his jaw.

Her heart thudded and the playful smile she wore faded.

Clearing her throat, she finished, “Anyway, I’m healing up fine. I feel much better than I did this morning.”

“You’ll have more scars, according to the doctor.”

She gave a bitter laugh. “Won’t be the first set.” She pulled away from him and went in to take a shower.

When she came back out, scrubbed clean, dressed in a pair of jeans and a sweater and feeling refreshed, it was to a dinner laid out for two.

“Nice,” she said, walking over on bare feet, her damp hair loose around her shoulders. “Salmon with roasted veggies and potatoes.”

“How’s your stomach?” Aeric asked, lounging in a nearby chair.

Despite her bravado, she’d been appalled when she’d unwound the bandage around her midsection. Lars had always focused on her stomach for some reason. She shook the memories out of her head. “Better. Just a couple more marks to add to the loveliness of my person.” She touched her midsection and gave a small laugh. “I think they add character.”

Aeric rose and walked over to her. He splayed his hand over her abdomen and her breath caught. The warmth of his palm bled through the fabric of her sweater, but it was no match for the warmth in his eyes. “Nothing they could ever do to you could make you less attractive.”

Then he went down on his knees, pushed the hem of her sweater up and laid his lips to her fresh bandage, and slowly kissed every one of her older scars that showed.

Her insides turned to jelly at the tender touch of his lips to her skin and the symbolism behind it. He dragged his mouth across her belly button and his warm breath whispered over her skin, raising goose bumps along her arms and legs.

His fingers found the button and zipper of her jeans and undid them. Slowly he eased them down over her hips and pulled them off, leaving her in only her cotton panties and sweater. Then her panties were gone, too. Still moving slowly, he slipped them down her legs and off, his hand trailing in their wake.

He pulled her hips to his face and his tongue snaked out to

lap her clit. Her head fell back on a moan and her hands tightened in his hair. Ripples of pleasure echoed through her veins. Oh, Danu, yes, she wanted this.

She sank down onto her knees on the rug beneath them so she could look him in the eyes. They were dark, the pupils dilated from his arousal. His face wore that hungry expression she liked so much when it was directed at her.

He lifted her sweater up and over her head, letting it drop to the floor. She wore no bra. Now she was nude and he was still fully dressed, a thing that needed to be remedied. Holding his gaze, she reached out and tugged the hem of his black T-shirt up. He let her pull it over his head, leaving that delicious, muscular expanse of his chest bare to her eyes and to her hands.

Slowly she caressed his warm skin, moving from the swell of his biceps down his nipples and over the hard ridges of his abs, all the way to the button of his jeans. His hand moved to cover hers and she was on her back in a flash, her hands reached over her head and pinned gently to the floor. His jean-covered knee forced her thighs to part and rasped against her sensitive sex, making her shudder in need.

He didn't move. He only stared down at her, as though seeing her for the first time. Her nipples hardened in the cool air of the room and from the sharp arousal building in her belly. His chest lightly rubbed against her breasts as he moved, making her sex clench with need.

"So now do you believe me about everything?" Her voice came out a little breathless from the pounding of her heart. "That I never intended to go back to work for the Summer Queen, that my intentions where the key is concerned are good? That I'm not a liar?" She swallowed. "About anything."

"Yes, I believe you." He paused. "About everything."

"And it only took being threatened by the Summer Queen and almost dying to make that happen."

"Let me make it up to you." He lowered his head and kissed her under her ear. Her eyes fluttered closed and she melted.

"I might let you," she murmured with a small smile. "Maybe."

"I want you. I need you, Emmaline." He moved to her mouth and nipped her lower lip gently. She shivered with pleasure.

"So, take me," she murmured. "I'm yours if you would just stop treating me like a breakable doll."

"Are you sure you want this? Are you healed enough to handle it?" he growled near her ear. "It's going to be hard and rough at first. I warned you. I want you too much for it to be any other way. At least . . . for the first time."

Danu, help her . . . *the first time*. "I'm healed enough and . . ." She licked her lips. "I want this."

His eyes seemed to go a shade darker.

He let her wrists go and she put her hand to the button of his jeans again. This time he didn't stop her when she undid it, along with the zipper. Reaching within, she found his wide, hard length and stroked him. He closed his eyes and groaned. He was as hard as a rock, so hard she wondered if it hurt.

"Turn over and raise your hips," he gritted out through a locked jaw. "*Now.*"

She rolled to her stomach, which gave only a twinge of protest that quickly became lost in a flood of desire. He didn't wait for her to position herself. Looping a hand under her, he lifted her rear to fit against his hard cock, forcing her up onto her knees with her thighs spread.

He pushed his jeans down just enough to get his cock free and set the head to her slick opening. "Are you ready?"

"Yeah," she breathed, bracing her palms on the floor.

He pushed the crown inside, widening her muscles and making her moan. Inch by inch, he worked all the way inside her, all the way to the root. She clawed the floor, her spine arching. Danu, he was huge, just like the rest of him. He completely dominated her, possessing every inch.

Sliding a hand between her thighs from the front, he found her slick folds and rubbed his fingers through them, playing around the area where his cock was sunk so deeply inside her. She squirmed beneath him, moaning, her blood on fire. Gathering moisture, he found her clit, already swollen and sensitive, and petted her there.

"Come for me, Emmaline," he growled, giving her a couple of long, fast thrusts that made her see stars.

She did. It washed over her body so completely her knees went weak and her fingers scrabbled at the floor. The muscles of her sex pulsed and rippled around his length, making him groan her name. He continued to stroke her right through the nearly painful sensitivity of postorgasm, until the first one stuttered out and then flared again. Another took her, pleasure racking her body until her throat felt hoarse from moaning.

Then he gripped her hips, pulled her back up to her knees, and started to thrust. Fast. Hard. Deep. All consuming.

Emmaline gasped and held on, understanding why he'd pushed her to come so fast. He'd needed her extra wet. Rough sex? Sweet Danu, this was it.

The sound of their bodies coming together filled the air, accompanied by their labored breathing. The inward and outward thrust dragged the head of his cock over her G-spot every time and soon she was climaxing again, her fingers scratching for a hold in the rug she lay on.

He swore low and groaned her name, his cock jumping deep inside her.

They collapsed together on the rug, tangled in each other, his cock still buried inside her. They were both breathing heavily and covered with perspiration. Her body ached, but it was the good kind of ache, the kind that came with great sex.

"Oh, Danu," she whispered, trying to catch her breath.

He kissed the top of her head and pulled her against him, his cock slipping free of her body. "I told you it would be that way." He caressed her breasts, petting her nipples until she sighed. "I'm sorry."

"Sorry?" She laughed. "I came three times."

He rolled her to her back and kissed her. "You deserve better. You deserve to be put into a bed, touched slowly and softly, licked and kissed—savored. Not taken like an animal on the floor."

She shivered. "It all sounds good to me, Aeric."

He nuzzled her throat and his erection poked her stomach. "Fuck, Emmaline, I want you again."

She gave a satisfied-sounding, throaty laugh. "How is it possible that you even can?"

He nipped her lower lip. "It's a little extra gift I have. Most women don't seem to mind." His voice had a teasing lilt.

"Oh, I didn't say I minded." She spread her thighs and pushed up at him, finding the head of his cock and forcing it to slip inside her. Pushing her hips upward, he sank into her again. She closed her eyes and her teeth sank into her lower lip. It felt right having him inside her.

"I'll have more control this time," he murmured, nibbling at the place where her neck met her shoulder. He drew out and thrust back in so slowly she felt every single last inch of him from tip to root.

She gasped from the ripples of pleasure invading every part of her body. "I like it when you have control." Swallowing hard, she added, "And when you don't."

He took her slowly this time, in long, measured thrusts. All the while he looked down at her, their gazes melded. Emotion threaded between them, making tendrils of warmth curl through her stomach and giving her a hope she'd abandoned hundreds of years ago. A hope she should crush under the boot heel of reality, yet she couldn't.

She just couldn't.

She wanted to nurture that spark of deep emotion that lay between them now. She wanted a fire. She wanted Aeric.

He came again, her name spilling from his lips.

EIGHTEEN

EMMALINE sat on a chair with a sheet wound around her nude body, trying to salvage what was left of their now cold dinner. She had a bowl of fruit on her lap and nibbled grapes and strawberries while across from her Aeric sat in only his jeans, his chest and feet bare. He was working on the key with his head lowered in fierce concentration, the muscles of his chest flexing with his movement and his long, dark blond hair escaping from the knot at his nape.

It was quite a nice sight. All in all, she couldn't complain.

He had forbidden her any clothes, which was fine by her, all the easier to acquiesce if he wanted to make love to her again. She was ready to engage in that particular activity all night long if she could.

Despite the recent ordeal she'd undergone, a sense of almost kittenish bliss had overcome her. Maybe it was simply the afterglow of really great sex. Most likely it was the result of having Aeric's attention so totally centered on her—positive attention this time. That was a nice change.

Aeric was the sort of man who could make a woman feel

like she was the most cherished person on the face of the earth. Under his furious and dangerous protection, no woman would ever fear. When he focused his attention on her, she was the center of the universe and nothing evil could ever touch her again.

That was how she felt this night.

Of course, there was the flip side of that coin, a side she was more than familiar with—one never wanted to be the object of Aeric's ire. It was still like being the center of the universe, a universe of hurt. She knew that to be true since she'd so recently been the focus of his wrath.

"Your forge. It's secret, isn't it?" She glanced at the old-fashioned tapestry—a huge rug that the fae were famous for weaving—that hid the doorway.

He halted in his work and glanced up at her. Perspiration shone on his forehead, revealing the mental effort it took to weave magick into the key. "The Shadow King, Aodh Críostóir Ruadhán O'Dubhuir, he commissioned it for me. He wanted me to continue making weapons for him on the sly, in addition to using the public forge in another part of the Black Tower for making charmed iron restraints and swords for the Shadow Guard."

"Aislinn wouldn't like it if she found out, would she?"

"I don't know." He grinned. "Don't aim to find out, either."

"Bad boy."

"Making these weapons is in my blood. I won't give the forge up."

"I can understand that, I guess."

His gaze went to the crossbow. "Are you all right with that in here?"

She stared at it for a moment before she answered. "I'm making my peace with it, with the things I did in my past. I pretended it wasn't there for so long and now all that history has been dredged up. It feels like a wound in me. I can't erase what happened so acceptance is my best option, I think. So, yeah, I'm all right with that in here. In a way, maybe the Summer Queen did me a favor by giving it back to me."

He gave a cold laugh. "Yeah, that bitch never does anyone but herself favors."

"That's why she shouldn't have that piece, Aeric." Her voice had gone stony. She might feel all warm, sated, and kittenish, but the business of the key was deadly serious to her. After all, she was risking her life—multiple times—for it.

His hands faltered on the key. "You know where I stand on that issue," he said without looking up. "Your well-being is more important than which royal gets the piece. Don't worry, when the time comes, if the Summer Queen shows any reluctance at turning it over for the greater good—"

"There will be a war. A war between the courts like there was in Ireland. It might spill over into the fae races and then we'll have an ordeal like the one that did us in during the sixteen hundreds."

He looked up at her. "We? Usually you say *you* when referring to the fae."

Her lips twisted. "I guess I'm making progress."

He returned to his work. "I think we've learned from our mistakes. In any case, the Summer Queen can't stand against all of Piefferburg. Goibhniu, even her own court would turn against her if she'd tried to prevent us from tearing down the warding."

Emmaline was doubtful. She chewed her lower lip. "Maybe. There are some who probably don't want the walls to fall, though. Even if it's a small number, they might stand with the Summer Queen." She shook her head. "Damn it. I'm telling you, this has the makings of another war."

"Hey." He looked up at her. "Let's just get through this, okay? I'll finish the key; you get the piece and bring it back here. Hell, we have no idea where the third piece even is. It's too early to be thinking about fae wars and walls falling down."

Someone knocked on the door. Aeric laid the key and knife aside and answered it. Apparently he didn't mind that she was dressed in only a sheet, making it clear that they'd been doing more in the room than just resting, but it made her uncomfortable—especially when she saw who it was standing outside in the hallway.

Kieran.

Emmaline stood, her body going taut with battle readiness. Damn it, a sheet wasn't the best thing to fight in and doing it naked was not appealing at all.

"Kieran." Aeric blocked his way into the room. "Back off, man. Okay?"

"Don't worry. I'm not going to hurt her."

"Swear on the eyes of Danu?"

The warrior nodded. "I swear."

Kieran entered the room, giving them both a once-over and a sneer.

"Why?" Emmaline asked sharply.

Kieran's dark eyes found and held her gaze. "Why what?" he snapped.

"Why haven't you leapt over the couch and tried to kill me yet?" She clutched the sheet around her like it was armor. Her teeth were gritted. Fighting was the last thing she wanted to do right now.

She remembered his twin brother, Diarmad Ailbhe Eòin Aimhrea. He'd been big, a warrior like Kieran. Broad shoulders, all muscles, same dark and brooding countenance. He'd been a nasty fuck. Diarmad had not just killed Seelie in the war; he'd ripped them apart and bathed in their blood. Not even women and children had been exempt from his cruelty.

She'd taken him in the chest, the heart, actually, one snowy night deep in the fae woods of Ireland. He'd come upon a family of brownies and was busy pulling them limb from limb. Blood had splashed bright red on the blanket of snow. Brownies were a gentle race, trooping fae. They had been completely vulnerable to that asshole. The memory still boiled her blood.

Approaching quietly—unable to help most of the family at that point—she'd nocked a bolt in her crossbow and said his name. Diarmad had turned and she'd let fly. Clean. Easy. He died in the snow near his latest victim, the young daughter of the brownie family he'd been slaughtering.

Of all the kills she'd made back then, she didn't regret that one. Not that she was about to admit that to Kieran.

Kieran bared his teeth at her. "The Shadow Queen has issued an edict that none of us are to touch you. I obey my queen at all cost."

"Unlike Diarmad?" The question slipped out in challenge and she instantly regretted it. Where, exactly, was her common sense? And why couldn't she ever marshal her mouth?

"My brother was not a good man. I've suffered, believe me, for his sins." His voice lowered to a dangerous growl. "But he was still my brother. My twin. And you killed him."

"That does leave us in a bad place, doesn't it? I guess we'll never be having tea and crumpets."

"Emmaline, don't goad him," Aeric said.

"I'm just trying to understand why Kieran wants me dead so much. His brother was a monster. Diarmad killed innocent Seelie and trooping fae just because he could, just because the Wild Hunt wouldn't come for him because it was wartime. Yes, I killed your twin brother, Kieran, but he deserved it. If I hadn't killed him, how many more innocents would have died at his hands? I know that you did not share his brutality. What did *you* think of your twin's actions back then? Or did it not matter to you since he was killing Seelie and members of the so-called less-than-fae races?"

"I was connected to him psychically. He nearly made me go insane. I almost killed him myself," Kieran snarled at her. "Are you content that you made me admit that?"

She drew a careful breath. "No, of course not."

"I heard what the Seelie queen did to you. I think you have been punished for your past. I've also been told about the key." He paused and took a breath, as though summoning courage. "I came here to offer you peace."

She blinked. Wow, that was a surprise. "Thank you."

"Not friendship, just peace. If the Shadow Queen ever lifts her edict, I still won't come after you." He paused, then growled, "But no *tea and crumpets*."

"Okay, I can live with that." A smile flickered over her

mouth. "One less enemy in the Unseelie Court. That leaves . . . what? . . . only, like, a couple hundred left. Awesome."

"Two less, apparently," Kieran replied with a pointed look at her sheet. "You and Aeric have obviously become . . . close."

Emmaline's cheeks heated.

"Do you want to come in for a drink or something?" Aeric asked him.

"No. Like I said, I'm ready to offer her peace, not have a drink with her." He turned away, his eyelids half lowered in an expression of dislike. "Good luck bringing the piece back."

"Thank you."

He left and Emmaline stood staring at the door. "That was unexpected."

Aeric shrugged and walked to her. "No. I knew he'd come to his senses eventually. Kieran is a good man. He loved his brother, but the things Diarmad did back then nearly killed him. He tried to get him to stop. He couldn't stand feeling the pleasure that Diarmad got out of the murders, having to live through every one as if it was he, himself, committing them."

"The psychic link?"

"Yes."

"So when I killed Diarmad, Kieran knew it, felt it. It was like I killed him."

"Yes."

She chewed her lower lip. "So is that what Kieran meant when he said he'd been punished for his brother's sins?"

"Having to experience all of his brother's kills and his death was definitely punishment, but that's not what he meant. The family of one of the Seelie Diarmad killed paid to have a curse placed on both the brothers."

"What sort of curse?"

"Since Diarmad showed no love for those he killed, he and Kieran were cursed to never be able to feel it for themselves. If Kieran ever falls in love, he's destined to die a slow, horrible death and be claimed by the sluagh. Any woman he falls in love with will share his fate."

"That's pretty harsh. Who laid the curse?"

"Priss. She's known as the Piefferburg witch now."

"The Piefferburg witch? She's still alive, then. Won't she lift it?"

"She says she can't. Once a curse is created and spelled upon the cursed, that's that. There's no reversing it. Kieran is damned."

"It's too bad we can't talk to Calum." She looked thoughtful. "Did you know that there are all kinds of fae texts left over in Ireland? The HFF had a hell of a time locating them and then getting them somewhere safe, somewhere the Phaendir couldn't locate and destroy them."

"We figured. It's not like the Phaendir and their human roundup posses allowed us our sacred books and historical documents. I'm glad to hear they're safe."

"I'm the only fae living outside Piefferburg. There aren't many of us, but we're around—the ones who escaped the Great Sweep. Three, including myself, work for the HFF. Calum is the oldest of us and, besides being a jovial drunk, he is the one with the greatest knowledge of the old texts. He spends most of his life examining those books and translating them from Old Maejian. He's looking for clues about the whereabouts of the third piece even now."

"Yes, even though his Old Maejian sucks. Does this have something to do with Kieran the Damned? Because you lost me."

"I don't buy that there's no way to dissolve the curse. Calum *loves* stories about the cursed and in every one that Calum ever told me there was some magickal antidote."

Aeric grinned. "True love's first kiss breaks the spell?"

"Sorry, no. Usually it involves a lot of blood. When I get out of here, maybe I'll ask Calum about it. I think the Piefferburg witch is holding out on Kieran."

"She's not the kind of woman you push."

"No. I know that. I've heard the stories. Still, I think there might be a way to untwist the curse. It wouldn't be easy and it certainly wouldn't be painless, but I do think it's possible."

"Find a way, do that, and Kieran might just decide he wants to have tea and crumpets with you after all."

She grinned. "Maybe I can redeem myself one miracle at a time."

He pulled her to him and kissed the top of her head. "Count one already."

Laying her head against his chest, she closed her eyes and inhaled the scent of his skin, enjoying the heat of his body and the steady thump of his heart. His arms came around her and she wallowed in all that was Aeric. Never in all her life would she have predicted she would share an embrace like this with him, and it was better than anything she'd ever imagined.

"Is there anything else you want to tell me about the night you accidentally killed Aileen?"

"What do you mean?" She looked up at him.

He hooked a tendril of hair behind her ear. "Like the Piefferburg witch, I think you might be holding out. So, anything else you want to tell me, Emmaline?"

The mood shattered, she turned away from him. She pressed a palm to her eye socket, remembering what Aileen had said: *Tell Driscoll I love him.* "Do I *want* to tell you anything more about that night? No, Aeric, I don't."

"So there is something," he said wonderingly. "It was only a suspicion."

"Just leave it alone, please."

He turned her to face him and forced her to look up at him. "You cared about me back then, right? Enough to try and cover up the evidence of her affair. Do you care about me now?"

Tears pricked her eyes. "I don't sleep with men I don't care about."

"If you care about me, you'll tell me everything about that night that you can remember, so I can find some closure."

"That I can remember? Aeric, I've replayed it so many times in my head it's burned into my brain. And I don't want to tell you this because I care about you."

"Emmaline, tell me."

"No."

"Tell me."

"No. I'm too afraid."

"Afraid? Afraid of what?"

"I'm afraid you'll think I'm making it up, just so I can get closer to you."

"I'm done thinking you're a liar." He dragged her up against his chest and kissed her breathless. "And, baby, you can't get any closer to me than you already are."

"I've sacrificed a lot to protect your memory of Aileen," she whispered.

"That false memory almost killed you. You should be wishing it gone forever. Anyway, that memory is already destroyed. Gone. Just like her portrait in my forge."

"I don't want to hurt you, Aeric."

"I already know the truth. Nothing you could tell me would be any worse than what I've already heard. I think she was in love with O'Shaughnessy."

She didn't say anything for a moment. If he already believed Aileen had been in love with him, there wasn't much point in not telling him the rest. "Okay." She backed away from him. "I'll tell you this. After I do, we'll have no more secrets between us."

"That's what I want."

She drew a careful breath. "As Aileen lay dying in my arms, she told me to tell O'Shaughnessy she loved him."

Aeric closed his eyes for a long moment, saying nothing. "Ah, there's closure."

"I'm sorry, Aeric."

He opened his eyes and shook his head. "Maybe she was with me because we were expected to be together, because our parents had always planned it that way."

"O'Shaughnessy was dark, twisted. I don't understand—"

"I do. Aileen had a darkness inside her, too. I thought I'd helped her banish it." He gave a rough laugh. "I was so naïve, so . . . arrogant to think I could do that. It was deep inside her, that twistedness. Apparently she found a match in O'Shaughnessy. He gave her what I couldn't."

She went cold with surprise at the implication. After drawing a careful breath, she said, "Then I'm glad you couldn't give her what she wanted."

"No, I couldn't." He grabbed her by the wrist and pulled her up slowly against his body. "But I might have what you want." His mouth came down on hers.

Her body warmed and melted at the press of him. His lips eased slowly over hers with a thoroughness that made her think of bare skin, the tangle of limbs, and soft sighs of pleasure. The touch of his lips on hers seemed to drop her IQ, too. That was the only way she could explain the fog her mind settled into.

He pulled the sheet away from her body and drew her back toward the bed. She couldn't think of a single reason to protest. His body slid like hard silk along hers, coming down over her and pinning her in place. His jean-clad knee slid between her thighs and his palm skated slowly from her knee to her rear, where he cupped and settled her against him until her bare sex rubbed against his groin.

Emmaline shuddered with pleasurable anticipation. His hand pressed hers down against the mattress as he hovered over her, kissing her deeply and thoroughly, seeming to promise that was the way he'd make love to her, too.

He eased a hand between her thighs and stroked her there. Pleasure ignited and caught fire at the touch of his fingers on her and inside her. He petted her clit and watched her expression as she melted into sexual need.

"Come inside me," she whispered.

"Not yet. I love to watch you come," he murmured. "I love being in total control of myself while I watch you come undone beneath me."

That answer, along with the look on his face, nearly did make her come undone.

He eased a finger deep inside her and then added another, thrusting as steadily and slowly as she wanted his cock. Dropping his head to her breast, he sucked one nipple into his hot mouth and then the other. He knew just how to touch her, where, and how to use just the right amount of pressure to drive her crazy.

She moaned his name, her back arching as an orgasm played with her body. He stroked her clit just right, raising his head so he could watch her when she shattered. Gripping fistfuls of sheet and blanket, she cried out as the pleasure crashed into her.

When the waves were ebbing away, he reached down and undid the button and zipper of his jeans. She put her hand over his, rising from the bed and pushing him down onto it.

"My turn to be in control," she murmured, freeing his cock.

Lust flared darkly in his eyes as she lowered her mouth to him. She slid the smooth head between her lips and pushed his length in as far as she could take him. He groaned and his head fell back into the pillows. His Adam's apple bobbed as he swallowed hard.

She nibbled and licked her way up and down him, discovering all the sensitive places that made him groan her name. It made her feel powerful, rendering such a strong man helpless this way. Giving him a sly look, she ran the underside of her tongue over the smooth crown and used the tip to lick the especially responsive place just along the bottom edge. Aeric made a strangled sound and she forced herself not to smile. She was feeling pretty pleased with herself.

Suddenly she was on her back with him above her. By the time she'd let out a yelp of surprise, it was all over. He hovered over her, his eyes heavy lidded and a predatory expression of sexual need on his face.

Maybe she hadn't rendered him as helpless as she'd thought.

He roughly kneed her thighs apart and settled between them. Positioning her sex against him, he slid the tip of his cock inside her and her breath caught. Inch by slow inch, he eased the rest within. Her teeth sank into her lower lip as he rolled his hips, thrusting slow and easy, over and over. She felt every ridge and vein of him intimately, had never felt so filled—so totally possessed by any man.

"Baby," he breathed into the curve of her throat, "fuck, you feel so good. Like hot silk." He hooked her leg over his hips and braced her against the mattress to drive deep inside her.

Their gazes collided and held. Being eye to eye while he was buried so deep inside her made the moment intensely intimate. He leaned forward a little and kissed her, the roll of her hips meeting his thrusts in a perfect rhythm. His mouth rubbed slowly over hers, making her shiver. He parted her lips and brushed her tongue with his.

Taking her wrists in his, he pinned her to the mattress and lowered his mouth to one nipple and then the other, sucking and gently nipping them until she squirmed beneath him. His hips rolled and he thrust faster and harder, making the bed move against the floor. The sound of their bodies coming together and their mingled breathing and soft moans filled the room.

She shattered, the muscles of her sex milking his pistoning length and forcing his climax. He groaned her name and came deep inside her, his cock jumping several times with the force of it.

He collapsed on her and then rolled to the side. Pulling her against him, his hands lazily played over her, stroking her breasts and between her thighs. She stretched like a cat and let her hands play, too, roaming over his fine body as though she could gain nourishment from touching him.

She couldn't believe she was here in bed with Aeric in postcoital bliss. The last few weeks had been almost too much to comprehend. Few weeks. The key was almost finished. Heaviness invaded her bliss.

Soon she would be leaving Piefferburg.

Danu willing, she'd be back to deliver the piece of the *bosca fadbh*, but then she'd be gone after that task was finished. She would have no opportunity to develop this . . . whatever this was with Aeric. And, anyway, *whatever* this was was just sex, right?

She might fall in love with Aeric. Hell, she already was in love with him. She'd never really stopped loving him, not ever. But it was different for Aeric. After all, she'd killed Aileen. Even if it had been an accident; even if Aileen had been cheating on Aeric when it had happened; even if Aileen had been doing the unthinkable at O'Shaughnessy's side—Emmaline had still killed her. How could he ever get past that?

There was no chance this relationship with Aeric was going anywhere past the bedroom. She would take what she could get from him, though. If it was just sex, so be it. She would soak up every moment of it and keep the experience locked away in a special part of her heart to be cherished on some cold, lonely night in the future.

So be it.

NINETEEN

HE was falling in love with her.

Aeric stared across the table at Emmaline, going icy still for a moment at the realization. Out of all the women in the world to fall in love with, did it have to be this one?

Laughing at something Melia said, Emmaline took a bite of her apple cake. They were having dinner with some of the Unseelie fae in the Black Tower who didn't want to kill her. When she laughed, which, granted, wasn't often, she did it with her whole body. With tiny lines creasing the corners of her eyes and unafraid of being heard. He couldn't even tell that just days ago she'd been recovering from a trauma that would have broken most other people.

Yes, it had to be this one.

Aeric had been with many women over his lifetime, though no one could rightly call him a womanizer. When he entered into a relationship with a woman it was because he was interested in all aspects of her, not just because he wanted her for sex. He could count all the one-night stands he'd ever had on one hand. For such a long-lived male fae, it was an abnormally low number. Gabriel would need all the fingers and toes of everyone in the Black Tower to count his.

Emmaline was by far the most interesting woman he'd ever known. There were still facets of her that seemed mysterious and completely unknowable. He wanted to know them all and, gods, he wanted to make her laugh more often.

He wanted to take the shadows out of her eyes that entered whenever the Summer Queen was mentioned. He wanted to erase the hurt of her childhood, give her her parents back, slay all her dragons. Right now he wanted to get her out of here and spend some time with her alone, listen to the sound of her voice, and maybe eventually feel the slide of his skin against hers.

Yeah, he never did anything halfway. He never felt anything in a lukewarm way, either. When he hated, *he hated.* When he wanted revenge, *he wanted revenge.*

And when he loved, *he loved.* He did it with everything he was, throwing himself into it completely.

It was nice to see her having fun tonight. His friends were being good to her. All in all, he guessed most of the Unseelie who didn't have a blood score to settle with her would be accepting of her past. After all, the majority of the Unseelie in the Black Tower were able to kill or maim with their magick. They were well acquainted with death and the various ways to cause it. Ultimately, Emmaline probably had more in common with the Unseelie than she did with the people of her birthright.

She and Aelfdane cleared the table and Melia brought out coffee. They went to sit in the living room of Aelfdane and Melia's comfortable apartment to drink it and talk. Bran's crow settled onto his shoulder and seemed to fall asleep. It was that kind of a get-together—very relaxed.

"This is such a nice, normal evening." Emmaline sighed and sank into an armchair. "I can't remember the last time I had one."

"We're happy to have you here," answered Gabriel.

"It's extra nice none of you want to kill me," she replied, taking a sip of her drink.

"Nope, we don't want to kill you. Just give you dessert and coffee," said Melia.

"Yummy coffee, too."

Bran stroked the feathers of the crow and glanced at Emmaline. "So, tell us about what it's like to live among humans." He'd been remarkably understanding about Aeric stealing his bike off the street in Goblin Town.

"Humans?" She sipped her coffee, weighing her answer. "They're complicated. Not much different from the fae."

"Less dangerous," chimed in Aelfdane.

"They're plenty dangerous. You don't need magick to be a menace. After all, look what they did to us."

"The Phaendir did this to us."

"They instigated it, they directed it, and they control it. But they never would have been able to pull it off without the help and cooperation of the humans."

"It's a perspective shared by many of the fae in Piefferburg, especially in the outlying areas, in Sharp Teeth, particularly. If the warding ever breaks, there are some humans who should watch out," said Bran.

"Yeah. Aeric and I have had this conversation before. That can't happen. If the fae target the humans with blood vengeance, the fae will find themselves squashed flatter than they are now."

"No. The fae have magick to call," Aelfdane replied. "Humans have nothing."

"One fae has magick to call, but as a group the fae are disorganized and the humans outnumber us—what? five thousand to one, maybe? Not very good odds."

"The fae are tribal, you're right about that. It's always been that way. Ever since the time when the Phaendir and the fae were allies, back as far as we keep records." Gabriel paused and then finished, "At least the records that survived the Great Sweep."

Emmaline met Aeric's eyes across the room, sharing a secret between them for a moment. Then she told them about Calum and the fae archives that he protected and studied.

They spoke about history, the world outside Piefferburg,

and fae politics up until it was almost time for Aeric, Aelfdane, Melia, and Bran to join the Wild Hunt. Then they said their good-byes and went for a walk in Piefferburg Square before he had to meet the rest of the Furious Host.

The evening was warm and the sky clear, sprinkled with stars. The Black Tower reached straight up into that diamond scatter. They walked close to each other, in a companionable silence, until they reached the statue of Jules Piefferburg in the center. It was dressed in a lady's gown and a fancy hat with a plume. To top it off, someone had stuck a curly blond wig on the statue's head.

Emmaline laughed and shook her head.

Aeric looked up at it, admiring the vandal's handiwork. No one liked to touch the statue of the human founder and architect of Piefferburg because it was made of one hundred percent charmed iron. "We have to get our kicks somehow."

"Did you make this statue?"

He sobered, remembering. "Yes. They held my da and threatened to kill him if I didn't."

"The Phaendir?"

Aeric nodded. "They took him into custody. He was very ill with Watt's then, very weak. I made the stupid statue."

"Bastards."

He said nothing, staring up at the hunk of metal. At least it provided the imprisoned fae with a laugh once in a while. They couldn't take it down because it was made of charmed iron, but they pelted the statue with rotten food almost every day.

"I like being here," murmured Emmaline. "I know that it's a prison and I know that all the rest of the fae want out, but . . . it's not as bad as I thought it would be."

Aeric let out a laugh. "What are you talking about? You've been kidnapped twice, three people have tried to kill you, and you've been tortured by another. Emmaline, this place hasn't exactly been heaven for you."

"I know. I know that, but my people are here, my roots."

"Judging by the time you've had in Piefferburg, I'll go out on a limb and say your people are assholes. Myself included."

She flicked a smile at him. "It just feels good to be around the fae, that's all I'm saying, not necessarily the ones who want to kidnap, kill, or torture me. The rest of them. That dinner we had tonight was the best time I've had in so long I can't even remember. It's good to be with people who know what I am, where I come from, who share a common bond. I haven't had that for so long."

"Yes. I see what you're saying." He turned away from the statue, looking toward the Rose Tower. It made him think of the Summer Queen. He closed his eyes against a rush of anger, then pulled Emmaline against him. "You need to meet my father," he murmured into her hair and then kissed the crown of her head.

Her arms came around him. "I do?"

"Yes. He's the only family I have left. I want you to meet him."

She said nothing.

He pushed her away far enough so he could see her face. "Do you want to meet him?"

"Yes! Yes, I do. I'm just surprised you asked." She smiled. "Hey, tonight was sort of like a date, wasn't it?"

"Yeah, I guess it was." He leaned forward and kissed her softly and slowly. "Wanna come up to my place for a quick drink before I have to meet the hunt?"

She made a low purrlike sound in her throat that heated his blood. "I want more than just a drink from you."

CÁEL O'Malley seemed a lot like an elderly human man. His hair had gone gray and his back was stooped. His fingers were gnarled and his knuckles knobby. One could tell by just a glance that Cáel had once been as tall and as strong as his son, maybe even more so, but his brush with death had stripped all that away. By all accounts, Cáel O'Malley had come as close as one could to meeting the Wild Hunt without actually doing it.

But he was still a strong man. The expression he wore on his face and the light in his eyes told you that right away. Emmaline saw Aeric had inherited much from his father.

He lived in an apartment in the upper tier of the Black Tower. That was where she and Aeric met him the next day after Aeric had depleted his ability to work on the key.

"Ah, I remember you!" Cáel reached out his knotted hand to her and she took it. "Met you on the road to the village one day, I did. A long time ago. Back when you were doing things you shouldn't for the Summer Queen."

"You have a good memory."

He squinted at her and patted the seat beside him on the couch. "Do you remember meeting me?"

"I remember." She glanced at Aeric. "You were his father, so I remember it well. It made an impression at the time."

Cáel jerked his head at his son, who had taken a nearby chair. "This one made you out to be an enemy, but here you are sitting beside me now. What changed?"

"Lots of stuff, da. I finally put the past in context."

Cáel cracked a smile filled with bad teeth, but it was beautiful nonetheless. "I told you, son, everything is perspective. I'm glad you finally got some." He patted Emmaline's hand and she glowed with happiness. Against all odds, Cáel liked her.

"Yeah, da," Aeric said, meeting Emmaline's gaze. "Me, too."

"He doesn't bring many women to meet me," said Cáel with a cackle. "Must mean you're special."

Aeric covered her hand with his. "She is." He paused. "But don't get your hopes up too much, da. She's not planning to stay in Piefferburg."

The flare of happiness that had sparked in Emmaline's chest died with a little gasp. *That's right, one should never get one's hopes up.*

STANDING in Aeric's living room, she reached out and touched the polished wood of her bow.

"Emmaline?"

She jumped, startled, pulling her hand back from the crossbow like it was a blazing fire.

Aeric's warm, broad hands closed around her shoulders. "I'm sorry."

"It's okay."

He remained that way, staring down at her old weapon with her for several moments. "Let's go out and shoot it."

"What?" She gave a surprised laugh.

"Yeah. I've done all I can do on the key today. My magick is drained to the dregs on that stupid thing. Let's take it out to the Boundary Lands and shoot it."

She studied the weapon with a mixture of longing and apprehension. "Why?"

"Because you didn't want me to get rid of it."

She gave him a weird look over her shoulder. "What does that have to do with going out to shoot it?"

He turned her to face him and tipped her chin up to force her gaze to meet his. "It means, Emmaline, that you might be a little afraid of this weapon, but you want, somewhere deep inside you, to accept it back into your life."

She shook her head. "No—"

"Not the killing, obviously. I mean the object itself. It represents a part of your personal history, a tumultuous part, but maybe accepting this weapon into your present means that you can forgive yourself for the past. It's a symbol."

"I don't deserve forgiveness." She turned to look at the crossbow. Carefully, she picked it up and held it. This time she didn't want to put it down again, so maybe, even though she didn't deserve forgiveness, some part of her wanted it.

"You do." He paused. "Everyone does."

She stared down at the weapon in her hands and hesitated before answering, "All right. Let's go."

A few minutes later she had the bow strapped to her back and they were on the back of Aeric's cycle, headed out of Piefferburg City and toward the woods.

He parked the bike at the start of one of the many paths leading into the Boundary Lands and hid it with foliage. Then they walked a distance in and found a tree—a target for her to shoot at.

Aeric settled back against another tree and folded his

arms over his chest, watching her. His body was relaxed, but his eyes were keen and sparked with interest.

"This," she said, holding the bow out. "*This* is the weapon that killed Aileen."

He nodded. "I'm aware."

"And you want me to accept it back into my life?"

"In actuality, *you* were the weapon that killed Aileen. I've accepted you, haven't I? That crossbow is nothing but a tool." He paused, looking hard at her. "I want what's best for you, Emmaline."

She selected one of the steel-tipped quarrels from her quiver. Swallowing hard, she nocked the bolt into the bow. It slid home with a soft sound that she remembered all too well. She closed her eyes for a moment against a rush of emotion.

"Emmaline?"

Her eyes popped open. "I'm okay."

"Try to hit that leaf up there, the light purple one."

She looked up into the fae-magicked tree, seeing the leaf he was talking about. Without even really thinking about it, she lifted the bow, sighted, and let fly. Her body remembered. Her mind and eyes and fingers remembered. Instinctually. The bolt sliced clean through the purple leaf and embedded itself high in a tree trunk beyond it.

Aeric let out a low whistle of appreciation, looking at the perfect hole. "You didn't even rip it from the tree."

"Yeah," she replied in a shaky voice. She lowered the weapon to her side. "It's a good crossbow."

"And you obviously haven't lost your touch."

She looked down at the bow. "I guess not. Not sure if that's a good thing or not."

"How's it feel to shoot it again?"

"Um." She looked down at the bow, considering it. "As long as I'm not shooting at people, it feels pretty nice."

"It's a good weapon for you, something you're familiar with, and obviously a thing you have some talent with. You should carry it. It would be an excellent defense against the Summer Queen and the Phaendir." He paused, his eyes narrowing. "And Lars."

"Carry it? Aeric, it's not exactly pocket-size."

"No, a handgun it isn't, but it's still a pretty damn effective weapon. You can use glamour to hide it when you leave here."

She shook her head. "Aeric, I don't know."

He walked over to her. "Please do it for me. It kills me to know I can't protect you once you leave this place. If I know you're carrying a weapon like this one, I'll feel better."

The concern on his face and in his voice made her mouth go dry. She glanced down at the crossbow again. "Yeah, okay. If you want me to carry it, I will."

"Good." He tipped her chin up and kissed her, his tongue stealing in to part her lips.

Soon her crossbow was forgotten.

EMMALINE stood, wrapped in a warm blanket, looking up at the tapestry that concealed the door to his forge. It was a chilly morning. A fire burned merrily in the fireplace against the bite and she held a cup of coffee in her hand.

The tapestry was beautiful in a chaotic and savage way. It depicted one of the scenes from the fae wars. A murder of crows flew in the sky, fighting on the side of those wildings who'd taken part in the battle. She remembered that. The wildings like Bran, those who had the ability to communicate with animals, had enlisted their help. It was one of the ways in which the fae had revealed themselves to the human world.

War. It had awakened all their passions, pushed them past their inhibitions, and caused them to engage in all kinds of risky and self-destructive behavior. She never wanted to see that happen again.

When she'd woken that morning, Aeric had been beside her, his arms around her so tight and protective that she'd never wanted to leave them. Then he'd rolled over her, kissed her slow, and slid between her thighs without a word.

Aeric was a man who never asked, he just took what he wanted. And he wanted her, insatiably. Single-minded in his purpose, he was relentless in pursuing his desires. He'd made love to her thoroughly, silently. She'd come twice, shuddering and sighing out her pleasure against his mouth.

He'd held her close afterward, nuzzling her throat. Finally, they'd risen to meet the day. Aeric had taken up his work with the key. She'd made coffee and roamed his apartment.

Footsteps sounded behind her. She turned to see Aeric standing near the bed. There were dark shadows playing over his face and he gripped the carving knife loosely in one hand. "It's done."

The blissful, content sensation that had warmed her only a moment earlier transformed to icy, jagged spikes of emotion that made her knees turn to butter for a second.

She should have been happy.

She should have been *ecstatic* that her mission was now back on course and she could accomplish her objective.

She should have been excited about finally leaving Piefferburg, the Summer Queen, and Lars—not to mention the Unseelie Court, where everyone wanted to cut off her head and parade around with it on a pike.

But it also meant she'd be leaving Aeric.

She swallowed hard and tried to smile. "That's great."

He dropped his knife on the coffee table and walked toward her. He looked tired, as he always did after expending the magick, energy, and concentration it took to create the key. "I was very careful and took my time. Going from the translations on the outside of the box, I have confidence that this key will work."

"Unless there's some booby trap we're not aware of, I'm sure it will."

His steps faltered. "Don't say that."

"It's a possibility, Aeric."

"Yeah, I know. One I'm trying not to think about." He reached her and opened his hand. The key lay there, shiny and warmed from his skin.

She picked it up and held it to the light. It looked like any other key might look that had been crafted from iron. Unattractive. Unassuming. It hardly looked like the key—literally—to unlocking part of the path to freedom for all the fae. It didn't look anything like the powerful object it was.

Her fist closed around it and she shuddered from the sensation of the charmed iron against her skin. She'd have to wrap it in fabric to carry it for any length of time. "Thank you."

He cupped her cheek and kissed her deeply. There was sadness in the touch of his lips against hers.

She set her forehead against his. "I guess that means it's time for me to leave," she said on a heavy sigh. "I'll go get my things."

TWENTY

IT didn't take long for her to be ready to go. She would have liked to linger, but she couldn't justify it, not when she had the key. Not when David was waiting for her. Not when he might already be in danger.

Anyway, she'd be back. She'd see Aeric again.

For a little while, at least.

After they traveled through the city, they parked Aeric's motorcycle at the edge of downtown Piefferburg, where the city abruptly gave way to the territory of the wildings. The road that led through the Boundary Lands and eventually to the gates of Piefferburg began here. The one he'd abducted her from over three weeks earlier. She had to walk it alone, the same way she'd come in.

Her crossbow was strapped to her back. She'd conceal it with glamour once she got close to the gates, just as she would her appearance.

"There's no guarantee that we'll ever locate the third piece of the *bosca fadbh*." Aeric walked next to her. His boots crunched fallen leaves and gravel.

"No."

"So there's no guarantee that the walls of Piefferburg will ever be broken."

"No." She stopped walking. "Aeric, where are you going with this?"

He stopped and looked up at the sky for a moment. It was a nice blue, broken by a few wispy clouds. Sunlight dappled through the tangled ceiling of tree branches above them. He turned and met her gaze. "It wouldn't be fair of me to ask you to stay."

"What?" Her heart thumped crazily in her chest. "I have to go. The key—"

"I mean when you come back with the piece. It wouldn't be fair of me to ask you to stay then, since it would be like asking you to put yourself in prison voluntarily."

"Aeric," she breathed. Ambushed. She'd been totally and completely ambushed by this. He wanted her to stay with him?

"Just think about it. You said yourself that you like it here despite everything." He walked to her and pulled her into his arms. His mouth came down on hers softly at first and then grew hungrier and hungrier. "Goibhniu, I'm going to miss you."

She tried to smile. "Funny, the last time we stood on this road, you couldn't stand the sight of me."

"That was then."

"This is now." Her slight smile faded. "Yes, I know. I have to go, Aeric."

"I know."

She pulled away from him and started down the road on her own.

"Come back to me."

She stopped and turned around. "What?"

He closed the distance between them and pulled her against him again. Burying his nose in her hair, he inhaled like it was the last time he'd ever catch her scent. "Come back to me, Emmaline."

"I will. I have to." She laughed. "The piece, remember?"

He held her away from him so he could look into her eyes. "Be careful, all right? Watch for anything suspicious. The Phaendir are tricky. Just make sure you come back to me."

She reached up and cupped his face. "I promise I'll be careful, Aeric. This is what I do. I've been swimming with these sharks for years now. I know how to avoid getting bitten."

He leaned in and gave her a lingering kiss. She savored it, stretching it out for as long as she could. After Aeric broke the kiss, she turned away and cleared her throat, trying to get a handle on her emotions.

She started down the road she'd come in on, looking back once to see Aeric standing silently, dust motes making a halo around his already fading figure.

EMMALINE made it out the other side of the gates in full glamour and with the key—wrapped in fabric to keep it away from her skin—secured safely in her bra. It was the only place she could think to put it where she wouldn't be searched . . . if the Phaendir even searched her, which was doubtful. They trusted her and as long as no one had delved too deeply into her cover story, she'd be okay.

If they had delved deeply, well, then all bets were off. She had her crossbow, at least. Its weight was surprisingly reassuring over her shoulder. Like an old friend who had her back.

In the distance, she could see Brother Gideon striding toward her. *Oh, hell.* Of course, she should have known he'd come to greet her. The Phaendir guarding the gate would have called to tell him who was coming through. She'd so successfully put the ruse that she was working for the Phaendir out of her head during her time with Aeric that she'd forgotten that little point. Brother Maddoc would be close on Gideon's heels.

Luckily she'd remembered to don her Emily Millhouse suit. It had felt strange to cover her true appearance. As strange as it had felt when Aeric had first forced her to wear her true self.

She summoned her courage and forced a smile. "Brother Gideon. It's so good to see you again."

He embraced her. The sensation of oil slicking through her aura made her shudder. He backed away and pushed a hand through his thinning brown hair. "Your stay was more extended than we'd originally presumed."

"It was." She gave him a shy smile. "But I gathered some good information."

He took her by the upper arm and began to guide her toward the Phaendir headquarters. "Come. Let's not talk here. Brother Maddoc is waiting for us and I'm sure you can't wait to get as far from Piefferburg as possible."

They began to walk. "Oh, yes. It's even more frightening in there than I could have ever imagined."

"I'm sure," he murmured. He walked for several moments, saying nothing. Finally, he said, "I'm surprised that such a fragile, pious flower as yourself could spend three weeks in the Shadow Court with all those . . . animals."

She almost missed a step. It *was* a stretch to think that Emily could. He was suspicious of her. "Oh, Gideon." She stopped and turned toward him, taking his hands in hers. "It was awful. I can't believe I made it through. I—I—" She threw herself against him, sobbing against his shoulder. She had to be careful he didn't put his arms around her and feel the crossbow. She could glamour it away from the eyes, but it was still a physical object on her person.

Gideon stiffened for a moment, in shock, and then patted her shoulder. "There, there. You did an exceptional job. We're all so proud of you."

She sobbed harder for a moment, sniffled, and looked at him. "I wasn't sure I was going to make it through a couple of times." That wasn't even a lie. "Being around all those monsters." She swallowed hard and made a show of steeling herself. "But I knew how important my mission was so I stuck it out. I stayed strong."

"Admirable of you."

"It was the hardest thing I've ever done."

He looked at her for a long moment, his watery brown eyes warm and soft. They were of the same height, which meant they were looking into each other's eyes right now. Far more intimate than she wanted to be.

Just as Gideon had clearly decided this was "a moment" and was leaning in a little for a kiss, she collapsed weeping onto his shoulder.

"Oh, poor Emily. It's all right." He patted her shoulder, his other arm snaking around her waist. She had a moment of panic. Gideon looked so very harmless . . . right up until the moment he gutted someone. "You should have a reward for your service. Jewelry, perhaps."

She left off on a loud sniffle and raised her head. "Jewelry?" How random a comment was that?

"Don't you like jewelry, Emily?"

She blinked. Emily Millhouse wore nothing but a watch. She didn't even have her ears pierced.

"How about *antique* jewelry? Do you collect it?" His eyes were glittering dangerously.

Her blood went cold. She kept a box of jewelry she'd collected over the years in her underwear drawer. The signature piece was a pendant that had been her mother's. She'd been wearing it the day she'd run away after killing Aileen. Had this toad broken into her apartment and gone through her *underwear drawer*? Undiluted rage was quick to follow on the heels of panic that he might have uncovered her true identity.

Gideon's cell phone rang, interrupting the exchange. "Yes, we're on our way," Gideon snapped and then closed the phone.

"Brother Maddoc?"

"Who else? Let's go in and have a cup of tea. You can tell everything to me and Brother Maddoc and we can discuss a reward for you later."

She sniffled loudly and pulled away from him. Frowning, she studied him. "Are you all right, Gideon? You look like you've been ill."

"I have. I'm better now, though. Don't worry about me."

They began to walk down the wide paved road that led away from the gates of Piefferburg and to Phaendir headquarters. Normally only trucks traveled it, either delivering goods to Piefferburg or taking them out. Every truck was thoroughly inspected, of course. Other than vehicles, only the occasional stray human traveled past Phaendir headquarters and came up to the gates.

On one side of the road was the old Church of Labrai, the first one founded on American soil, with its large graveyard where all the Phaendir were buried. Above it circled about twenty black vultures. They had a roost here, the biggest in the country. Bird-watchers came from miles around to see them. That the vultures circled a graveyard full of dead Phaendir was fitting on two counts, since the vultures and the Phaendir both liked to pick at the dead.

Phaendir headquarters dominated the opposite side of the road. Rising seven stories—a sacred number in their religion—and constructed in a U shape, it housed almost the entire order of Phaendir. A few were stationed here and there around the world, but most of them needed to remain in close proximity to each other, in order to sustain the magicked portion of their minds that kept the warding up. Very rarely did they venture out into the world beyond. They were too afraid they'd be negatively affected by the outside. In nearby Protection City, their houses were side by side; they shopped at the same stores; they worshipped in the same churches.

She and Gideon entered the building and passed several of the brothers. Each of them watched her curiously as she walked by. She wasn't sure if it was because they knew where she'd been or because she was a woman. There weren't very many women here. Only the few who worked at HQ and the occasional female Worshipful Observer, who were a little like Phaendir groupies. Most Phaendir didn't marry.

They passed through the echoing foyer and climbed a steep set of stairs to the top floor. At the end of a long corridor lay Brother Maddoc's office. She knew it well, of course; she was his personal assistant. They passed through the small outer chamber where she normally worked. A trim brunette—the temp—smiled at her as she passed. The woman had a shine to her eyes that was typical of a Worshipful Observer, one that Emmaline had practiced for hours in front of a mirror to achieve before she'd come to work undercover.

Archdirector Maddoc was waiting for them, excitement clear on his rather handsome face. That was one more reason for Gideon to hate him, of course. Maddoc was more attractive than he was. It was a fact she subtly taunted Gideon with every chance she could. The more discord she could sow, the better.

"Maddoc," she cried and rushed to him. Laying her head against Maddoc's broad shoulder, she glimpsed Gideon standing in the doorway, gnashing his teeth.

Maddoc kissed her temple, his hands on her shoulders. They hadn't slept together, though she was aware Maddoc wanted her. All of headquarters presumed they were working "overtime" together, Gideon included.

"I'm so glad you're back," Maddoc purred into her ear.

"Me, too," she said, pulling away. Having learned a while back to cry on command, she wiped a teardrop away.

He went to the small tea stand set up behind his wide, heavy desk and poured her a steaming cup. She took it gratefully and sat down in one of the huge leather chairs, careful to sit forward because of her crossbow. Maddoc didn't offer Gideon any. He was still on the outs with the Phaendir for what he'd tried to pull last year with the Book of Bindings, but the cold glance with which Maddoc favored Gideon made her wonder if something else was afoot.

"Now," said Maddoc, settling behind his desk with his own cup of tea, "tell us everything."

She would tell them a pack of nice lies, hope they didn't suspect, and then be out of here. She'd arrange for some time off after she'd done this for them—to "recuperate." First thing she'd do when she had a chance would be to contact the HFF safely and make arrangements to get to Israel.

She sipped her tea, hyperaware of Gideon, who'd moved

in from the doorway and now hovered directly behind her. "Well," she started slowly, "I went in with the objective of heading straight to the Rose Tower, but, as I told you, I was kidnapped and ended up in the Black."

"In the Black?" Maddoc chortled. "You're using their lingo."

"Yes." She smiled shyly. "Stay there as long as I did and you would, too. Now, as I said, I was ambushed . . ."

She told them a much modified story. According to her revised version, it was a horrible Unseelie creature who'd attacked her in the Boundary Lands. She'd escaped with her life, barely. The queen had been so aggrieved at her situation that she'd set her up in excellent quarters and had offered her a monetary recompense for what had happened to her.

She told Maddoc and Gideon that since she'd developed this special relationship with the queen of the Unseelie Court, one she didn't have in the Rose, she'd decided to stay there and glean what information she could.

"And the piece?" Maddoc asked, leaning forward, his tea on his desk, now cold and long forgotten.

"They're unable to get to it, but you can."

"Where do they think it is?" asked Gideon, breathless. He'd sunk into the chair beside her. By Gideon's reaction to her story—hanging on her every word—she was now sure he didn't know her true identity. The jewelry comment had certainly put her on edge, but maybe it was nothing.

"I can even give you coordinates of its likely location, though much digging may be required. Much digging. The spot is in Wales." She paused and tried to look apologetic. "There's a large manure farm there right now. . . ."

"I think you're moving too fast with this woman," Calum said, watching David from across his suite.

"Thanks for your concern, Calum, but I know the real thing when I feel it."

"Dude." Calum paused. "I hate to point this out, I really do, but you're divorced. I think your track record where the 'real thing' is concerned is pretty skewed. I hope one day I don't have to say I told you so."

"Yeah, I know my marriage with Emmaline didn't work out. I don't need to be reminded. Anyway, it's not like I've asked Kiya to marry me."

"Not yet. Give it a couple weeks and I bet she'll have a ring on her finger."

David's irritation flared. He grabbed his coat from where it lay on the end of his bed and started toward the door. "I love her, man."

Calum stopped him before he could leave. "No. You still love Emmaline and everyone knows it. Kiya is beautiful and charming, but she's just a rebound for you. Consider what's best and fair to her, if not to yourself."

David looked Calum in the eye. "Don't worry about me or Kiya. I have no plans to jump into a rebound relationship and really have no plans to hurt Kiya. It took me a long time to get past my feelings for Emmaline, but I'm over her now. Really."

"You're lying to yourself." Calum sighed and held up his hand. Backing away he said, "Hell, you're also an adult. You don't need a relationship nanny."

"Especially not one as ugly as you." David grinned.

Calum laughed. "I think I'm just tense, you know—"

"Yeah," he answered quickly. "I know. But Emmaline will be here soon. She's alive and she's got the key. We can help her deal with whatever mess her head is in when she gets here."

David had been incredibly relieved to get the message from the HFF. Emmaline was out of Piefferburg—finally—and was in possession of the key. She'd be in Israel tomorrow. The HFF had also said she wasn't quite herself. Obviously something had happened when she was in Piefferburg. As usual, he wanted to jump right in and make the hurt go away.

This time, he reminded himself firmly, it would be strictly as a friend.

"Now can I please leave? You're blocking the door." David

added a friendly smile, but he was sure that Calum understood he wasn't happy about his friend's intervention.

Calum backed away. "Of course."

"What are you doing tonight?"

"Me? I was planning to get stinking drunk. There's a minibar, you know."

David took a moment to smirk at him as he opened the door. "Yeah. Don't act like you're surprised. You've gotten nice and cozy with the minibar every night this week."

He stroked his beard and nodded. "So I have. So I have."

David went crosstown in his rented car to Kiya's small two-bedroom apartment. He had a rather important question to ask her tonight and his palms were sweating that she might say no. It wasn't *the* question, of course. He hadn't lied to Calum about that, but it was a big question. Her answer would define where their relationship was going.

She let him in and he walked through a cloud of her subtle scent. "Ready to go?" she asked as she reached for a light wrap. It was a little chilly tonight.

"Uh. Can we sit down and talk first?"

"Sure. What's going on?" Her face took on a serious expression as she closed the door and went to sit on her dove gray couch. "You know we can always talk about anything."

He sank down next to her. "That's just the thing. I feel like you know me better than any other woman ever has and I feel I know you."

She reached out and poked him in the chest. "See? I told you my question game would be fun."

He grabbed her hand and pulled her toward him. "My time here will be over soon, Kiya—"

Confusion clouded her face and her smile faded. "It will? But I thought you said it was open-ended."

"We were waiting on something, a delivery. That delivery will be here tomorrow and we can commence our work. That work probably won't take long, so—"

She pulled back away from him, her eyebrows knit. "But I thought you said you were going to explore the ruins of Atlit

Yam and you wouldn't know how long it would take until you got down there."

God, he hated lying to her this way, but he still didn't feel comfortable telling her about his work with the HFF. She was sensitive to the plight of the fae; that had been one of the first things he'd found out about her. He just felt there needed to be a larger commitment on both sides of this almost relationship for him to reveal that kind of information.

He licked his lips, wanting more than anything to come clean with her. "Things have changed. I'll probably be leaving Israel within the week."

She wilted. "By the end of the week?"

"I don't want this to mean the end of us." Gathering strength, he took her hand, now limp, in his. "I hoped you might consider a trip to the States. Just a couple weeks. So we can see where this might be going." He paused, unhappy with the blank look on her face. "I wouldn't ask you to relocate or even to have a long-distance relationship. My job might allow me to move here."

She pulled her hand away and stood with her back to him. "Wow, this is all so sudden."

"I know. I'm sorry, Kiya. Our whole relationship has been a whirlwind, but I think there's something here, don't you?"

"It's a big decision to make." She sniffled.

He stood. "Right now, all I'm asking for is two more weeks with you. If you would prefer, I can go back to the States, take care of my business, and then come back. I—"

Kiya's hair melted.

Then her shoulders.

Her back.

Her legs.

Then it all rebuilt in another form. One that was not Kiya.

He stood arrested, watching it happen, his tongue suddenly several times too large for his mouth.

The strange woman turned with a sly, self-satisfied smirk. Her skin was milk white and pockmarked, marring what once might have been great beauty. Her thick, dark red hair tangled around her face and curled down her shoulders, framing the coldest set of pale green eyes he'd ever seen.

David stood staring, struck completely dumb. God, he'd been totally fooled and so had Calum. This woman was a fae, one with the same ability with glamour that Emmaline possessed.

Dread clutched his chest. His Kiya . . . didn't exist.

I know the real thing when I feel it. He was so blind.

Rage gripped him. He brought his fist forward fast, only to have the woman duck out of the way faster than his eyesight could track.

She backed away from him cautiously, though she still wore that irritating smirk. She clucked her tongue and said, "No, no, lover boy. Now, you wouldn't want to be hurtin' your lady, would you?" She spoke with a thick Irish accent.

"Who are you?" He seethed with anger, making his voice come out low and hard.

"Oh, I'll never be telling you my name, boyo. There's power in names. In the right magicked hands, a true name can cause a lot of damage. It's not Kiya, though, that's for bleeding certain."

"Did she ever actually exist?" Maybe his Kiya was still alive somewhere. The hope of it nearly made him dizzy.

"Sorry, lover. I killed her off and took her place the day you showed interest in her at the coffee shop." The fae looked thoughtful for a moment. "In a way, it's like you killed her."

David made a sound of complete rage and lunged toward the woman. She sidestepped away from him and smashed her fist into his back with surprising strength. He wobbled, off balance, and she pivoted on her right foot, bringing her other foot straight into his face. For a moment, the whole world became pain.

He grunted, staggering to the side, wiping blood from the corner of his mouth.

The woman bounced on the balls of her feet, like a boxer in the ring, full of energy and strength. "I have the same magick your Emmaline has, boyo. Very rare in the world of the fae. 'Cept I'm better than your precious because I have extra killing ability." She cocked her head to the side. "Sort of poetic, isn't it? The reason your buddy Calum couldn't tell I was fae is because of that, the nature of my glamour. Nice try, though."

He spit out a glob of blood. "You're with the Phaendir? A fucking *fae*?"

"The Phaendir?" She laughed. "No, I'm not with those amateurs."

"Then who?"

"Oh, lover, do you think I'm going to stand here and tell you my whole agenda? Like some villain in a cartoon?" She moved almost too fast for him to track and he had a foot in his face again. He fell backward, sprawling onto the couch, and the world went black.

He woke briefly to the bite of a needle in his arm. His vision grew blurry and his limbs became warm and heavy. The last thing he saw was the fae woman's fuzzy, smiling face. Triumphant.

TWENTY-ONE

MEGHANN stood from her work with the syringe in her hand. Her task here was done and she'd accomplished it admirably, in her opinion. Once David had revealed that the key had been made and was being delivered, she didn't need him anymore. She had more than enough information about the man to impersonate him properly. Emmaline wouldn't suspect a thing.

She studied David. It was a pity she'd have to kill him. He was good-looking, for a human.

Calum needed to go, too. By morning she needed to set that man's fae spirit to restlessly roaming the earth. The Netherworld, of course, would not be an option for him since the Wild Hunt was trapped in Piefferburg.

That was the nice thing about having escaped the Great Sweep and living beyond the walls of Piefferburg. She could kill as many fae as she liked and there were no consequences. The Wild Hunt's reach didn't extend this far.

She could get away with murder. And she did, quite often.

It was one of the many reasons she couldn't allow the warding around Piefferburg to come down. She'd be swept up by the Wild Hunt faster than she could say *bloody hell*.

She'd murder again once she had the piece. Little Miss Perfect, Emmaline Siobhan Keara Gallagher, would end up with a knife in her throat as soon as Meghann had her hands on the object of her desire.

It would be a pleasure.

Masquerading as Kiya, she'd had to plumb the depths of David and those depths were filled to the brim with Emmaline. She'd been working to find out as much about David as possible and in the meantime had learned more than she'd ever wanted to know about the Seelie Queen's former assassin.

Meghann really didn't give a shite that Emmaline had offed so many of her Unseelie brothers and sisters during the fae wars, but she was so fecking sick of just hearing about her so much from David that killing her would be a gift.

She dealt with David and then went into the bathroom to wash her hands. Concentrating on her reflected image in the mirror above the sink, she engulfed herself in magick, changing her visage to David's. She smiled as his face and body appeared without flaw in the reflection.

In just a few hours, she could return to David's hotel suite and have some real fun with Calum.

EMMALINE yanked her suitcase from the baggage carousel at the airport in Haifa and a strong hand gripped the handle and hauled it up for her. She looked up into the face of an old friend and smiled.

"Hey, nib."

"David! It's so good to see you." As soon as he set her suitcase down, she hugged him. "How have you been?"

He smiled ruefully, twisting his lips in that expression she knew so well. A pang of wistfulness went through her for the way she'd hurt him when she left. "I've been bored, nib. I bet you haven't, though."

She gave a laugh. "Yeah. Boredom really hasn't been a problem."

He hefted her suitcase. "Come on. I've got a rental car.

You can fill me in on the way to my hotel." He paused. "Where is it?"

"Somewhere safe."

He nodded, started to say something, but then shut his mouth and started walking toward the exit.

She already missed the weight of her crossbow. Not even her glamour could have gotten it past airport security, so she'd been forced to leave it back in the States.

They drove through the heart of Haifa to his hotel, where she checked in at the front desk. By the time he'd played bellman for her and got her suitcase up to the room, she'd filled him in on everything relevant.

Everything that wouldn't wound him even further.

She knew that he still had feelings for her. She was happy to see he'd taken off his wedding ring, though there was a thin white mark on his ring finger that told her that removal had been recent.

"I never would have pegged Gideon for a pervert," said David, walking into the foyer of her lovely, expensive hotel suite. "I mean, he's a lot of scary things, but I can't picture him breaking into your apartment to sniff your panties."

She shuddered as she unzipped her suitcase. "I don't know. When I got to my place the first thing I checked was the jewelry box. Everything seemed to be exactly where I left it. Nothing messed with, nothing missing."

"Yeah, but that doesn't mean anything."

She shrugged. "Maybe I'm just paranoid. I guess I have reason to be."

"No doubt."

"So, diving?" She turned to him. "When?" The key was burning a hole in her pocket—or bra, actually. She wanted to get the piece and get back to Aeric.

"Tomorrow. I have a boat and all the gear secured. Be ready to go early in the morning, okay?"

"Okay, great. I'm more than ready to do this, David. Where's Calum?"

He pushed a hand through his hair and sighed. "You know Calum."

"Ah. Right." Sleeping one off. She leaned up against the wall of the foyer and crossed her arms over her chest. "He never changes."

"He'd never admit it, but being away from the fae makes him suffer. Drinking is his way of coping."

She nodded. "I've often thought the same."

"So, can I see it?"

She frowned, then realized he meant the key. "Um, well, actually not right now." The last thing she wanted to do was dig around in her bra in front of David. "But I'll have it with me tomorrow, for sure. You can see it then."

They looked at each other for several long moments. She yawned. Pointedly.

"I'll let you get some sleep," he said. "You must be exhausted."

"I am. Thanks, David."

She followed him to the door of the suite. Right when she thought he was leaving, he turned and crowded her against the wall of the foyer. "Emmaline," he breathed. "I've missed you."

Oh, shit.

His mouth came so close to hers she could feel the heat of his breath on her lips.

"David?" She pushed him away. "Please."

"I can't get you out of my mind, Emmaline. Every woman I'm with I measure against you."

She closed her eyes. "David, we're divorced."

"I know that. I'm just saying that I still—"

"David. You need to know." She swallowed and chose her words carefully. "I'm in love with someone else."

His eyes instantly showed the emotional injury. His pain was like a blow to her stomach, but she needed to be up-front about this situation. She knew that David still had feelings for her, but this blatant display wasn't like him.

She swallowed hard and continued. "I'm sorry. I am. I wish things could be different. I wish . . . for many things, David. Not the least of which is your happiness."

His eyes went cold and he turned toward the doorway.

"I'll see you in the morning, bright and early."

"David?"

He half turned toward her. "It's okay, Emmaline. I knew that already, all right? I knew through our whole marriage that you were really stuck on someone else."

He left and she sagged against the wall. Guilt over emotions she had no control over weighed in her chest. The last thing she wanted to do was hurt him, but it seemed she couldn't avoid it.

It wasn't really David's style to be aggressive that way. Maybe something had happened to throw him off his feet.

It had definitely thrown her off her feet.

THE boat was small, sleek, and very white on the warm and blue waters of the Mediterranean Sea. The key was in a box and hung around her neck on a heavy chain. She wore a bikini and sat in the back while David navigated the boat out to the site.

This was far better than a manure farm in Wales.

All morning David had been quiet and efficient in his dealings with the boat and the diving equipment. Things between them had smoothed since their uncomfortable moment the night before. Mostly they were pretending it had never happened. She didn't know what to say. She just wished that he could move on and find someone worthy of him.

She wanted his happiness with all her heart. He would make a woman very happy, but she was not that woman. The sooner David could move on from that fantasy, the happier he'd be.

The boat's engine throttled down and came to a gentle stop. Together she and David threw the anchor over the side and started to don their wet suits.

She watched him as he silently worked himself into his suit. He was a good-looking man and always had been—with glossy hair that had a charming habit of falling across his forehead; deep, expressive brown eyes; and a lean, muscled body. Right now his beautiful brown eyes were clouded with pain.

"David? Are you okay?"

He flashed a fake smile at her. "I'm fine."

She stopped what she was doing. "Bullshit. I know you better than that. I was married to you, remember?"

He sat down on the bench with his wet suit half on and sighed. "I was here for almost a month all alone and it gave me a lot of time to assess my life." He looked up at her. "My feelings for you still run deep and they're interfering with my ability to have other relationships."

"Oh, David." She sank down on the bench.

He held up a hand. "It's okay. I know you don't feel that way about me anymore. This is mine to deal with." He gazed into the distance for a long moment while she struggled for something to say. "Come on, let's go get the piece." He stood and finished getting ready.

She studied him as he dressed, chewing her bottom lip. There was something he wasn't telling her. Something had happened. He just wasn't acting like himself. Something was *off*.

Her hands were steady as she finished suiting up, putting the box with the key just under the collar of her wet suit for easy access. Once done, her gaze scanned the horizon. So far, so good. No Phaendir in sight. Looked like they'd slipped past them from all angles. But she'd still be holding her breath until she got the piece out of that stupid magick box and back to Piefferburg.

"You ready?" asked David. He sat on the bench, watching her finish up.

She took a deep breath, staring at the surface of the water, where the gentle waves lapped at the side of the boat. The suit squeezed her body, making her feel awkward on land. As soon as she slid into the water, she'd feel as graceful as a selkie. "I'm ready."

Danu, she hoped that box wasn't booby-trapped in some way.

They turned their air on, put their mouthpieces in, and plunged into the water.

Falling in silence.

Above her the white bottom of the boat was visible amid the blue of the sun-drenched morning sky. It grew dimmer and dimmer the farther they went down.

She looked over at David and made the okay symbol with her hand. He grinned back at her and gave a thumbs-up.

What?

Under the water the thumbs-up signal unequivocally meant you wanted to return to the surface. It never meant okay.

She frowned at him, giving him a thumbs-up sign in return and pointing up toward the surface of the water with the index finger of her other hand. Was there a problem? Did he need to ascend? Yet he didn't seem to be in distress.

He waved his arms at her—*no*—and pointed downward, toward the box. Giving the thumbs-up again, he headed down, leading the way. After hesitating a moment, she followed. David was a master diver and he'd just made a rookie mistake. Worse, he'd done it twice and acted like he didn't even know he'd done something wrong.

There was definitely something going on with David. Something bad.

Frowning and on edge, she headed down farther and farther into the darkness, the white bottom of the boat growing smaller. The box was half buried in the sand, wedged between two rocks. Magick had kept it from being completely buried after thousands of years, as if whoever had hidden it had wished to conceal it enough to be very difficult to find, but not impossible.

As if they'd meant for only those who really needed the piece to have a shot at recovering it.

David hovered near her as she extracted the box and removed the key. Beside her, David looked tense. She took a deep breath and said a prayer to Danu that this would work. Then she slid the key into the lock. . . .

It turned.

No magickical explosions. No booby traps.

She closed her eyes for a moment in relief. Aeric had done his part of this well.

Slowly, still half anticipating magick blowing up in her face, she opened the lid. Inside, on material that looked like red velvet—velvet that had been produced the day before instead of thousands of years ago—lay the piece they were looking for. Odd, sharp angles; shining metal. Innocuous. Mesmerized, she lifted it, turning it in her hand to examine all the sides in awe. It was such a simple object, yet it meant so much to the fae.

Something yanked her by the air hose, ripping her mouthpiece away. Bubbles rose in her face, blinding her.

Then, ominously, the bubbles stopped.

She scrabbled at her air hose for a panicked moment. Bubbles still rose in the vicinity of her back. Her air hose had been cut. What the hell?

Confused beyond belief, she whirled, coming face-to-face with David, who held a sharp diving knife and a less than reassuring expression on his face. Malice danced in eyes she barely recognized.

Oh, sweet lady, have mercy. He'd done it. He'd cut her breathing tube.

He reached for the piece and she darted away from him, pushing upward toward the surface as hard as she could. But, Danu, she couldn't hold her breath for as long as it would take to get to the top.

He grabbed her ankle and pulled her down. She came eye to eye with him, her heart breaking and her mind whirling over possible reasons he would do this and coming up blank. All she knew was that it had something to do with the piece, so she dropped it. He dove after it, but she grabbed at him, trying to get his air hose from behind.

His knife flashed, swooping up toward her. She gripped his wrist and thrust with all her strength away from her. They struggled, rolling in the water. Her lungs were starting to burn. Time was not on her side. Pain ripped through her upper arm and she looked down to see her blood coloring the water. Her suit was cut and her skin neatly laid open.

She scrabbled at his face, yanking his mask and mouthpiece off. Bubbles rose from the freed mouthpiece, obscuring his vision. His eyes went wide with surprise and panic and his face flickered . . . shifted. . . .

Another fae. A fae with the same glamour magick she had.

Danu. She'd thought she was the only one.

The fae looked at her, eyes wide, realizing the slip—then the glamour dropped. It was a woman with pasty white skin, dark red hair, and a pockmarked face.

With that click of realization, "David's" strange behavior all made sense.

The strange fae's knife arched toward her again.

She grabbed her wrist and they battled, the edge of the blade coming closer and closer to Emmaline's throat. Gods, but the woman was strong, stronger than she should have been. Her injured arm screamed with pain and her chest burned from holding her breath. Time was quickly running out. If she couldn't get the upper hand quick, she was dead and the piece would be lost.

Giving it everything she had, her adrenaline surging, Emmaline gained control and forced the blade in the other direction. With one last burst of strength, she forced the tip to the fae's throat.

And pushed.

Blood floated out in a cloud. The light green eyes of the pockmarked fae woman showed only fear now. She knew death had her. The fae thrashed in the water, floating away and gurgling incoherently.

Emmaline let the knife drop and took up her own severed, yet still bubbling, air tube. Before all the air was gone, she took in as much as her lungs would hold. Then she dove through the murky blood-and-sand-swirled water to find the piece.

Precious moments passed as she frantically searched. Sharks would be attracted to the blood, which was a complication she didn't need. Worse, she wasn't sure she had enough air to get to the surface.

There! She grabbed the piece and shrugged off her tank. It fell to the ocean floor, making her lighter. It would help her ascend faster, and she needed *fast*. Luckily she wasn't so far down that she had to worry about the bends. She pushed off the sandy bottom and propelled herself toward the surface, clutching the piece close to her chest and breathing out slowly and steadily as she went.

Breaking the surface of the water she threw her head back and gulped in air, thanking Danu for being down there with her. She was still alive. Amazing.

Her mind was spinning, but she knew two things.

She'd found the piece.

Now she had to find the real David.

TWENTY-TWO

SHE went back to the only place she could think to look, the hotel.

Securing the piece in her backpack and with her wounded arm wrapped up tight under her shirt to stop the bleeding, she used the hotel room key she'd found in David's pack to enter his suite. There was a Do Not Disturb sign on the door.

The smell hit her as soon as she cleared the threshold—the metallic scent of blood.

She followed the scent through the suite and into one of the bedrooms. "Oh, Danu," she cried as soon as she glimpsed the slumped figure tied spread-eagle to the bed.

Calum's eyes were closed and his mouth gagged. His face was ashen and his limbs were sagging against the rope that bound them. Blood soaked the mattress and sheets from long, deep cuts to his stomach, thighs, and chest. It wasn't unlike what Lars liked to do to her, but on a much more violent scale. This was a scene straight out of a horror movie. The redheaded fae had tortured him slowly, until she'd bled him out.

"Calum," she sobbed, coming up to the side of the bed. "Oh, Calum."

She stood there, looking down at his body for several moments, in total shock. She'd seen dead bodies before, of course. She'd produced quite a few of them herself, but it had been a long time and this was a friend.

Another grief-drenched sob escaped her. She pressed her hand to her mouth and closed her eyes on a wave of anger and sadness welling up from somewhere deep inside.

"Hey," Calum croaked, "you can untie me whenever you want, okay? Sooner would be better than later, though. I need a drink."

Her eyes had opened at *hey*. Calum was still as ashen as death, but his eyes were opened into slits and a trace of a smile played over his mouth. She let out a tear-laced laugh and made quick work of the knots securing his wrists and ankles.

Then she reached for the phone. "I'm calling an ambulance."

"No. They'll figure out I'm fae and throw me in Piefferburg. Don't you dare." Calum blew out a careful breath and rolled his considerable, blood-drenched bulk over the side of the bed. There was a thump as he landed on the floor.

Putting the phone down, she ran around to help him.

He put a hand up. "I'm okay, I'm okay." He struggled to his feet and grinned. "Bitch didn't know part of my magick is healing. She cut me; I healed it." He winked at her. "You know the drill, right?"

Yes, she did, though her skill was not as pronounced.

"I pretended like she was really hurting me—which, of course, she was. Made the bitch think she'd killed me so she'd leave me alone."

"I didn't know you had healing ability of that magnitude."

He nodded. "I figured in my line of work this might happen one day. It was a good secret to keep. If the Irish cow had known I was healing up all her torture, she'd have tried harder to kill me instead of assuming she'd done me in."

"Irish?"

He glanced at her arm, which was bleeding through her shirt despite her efforts. "Didn't you meet her?"

"Yes, well, our meeting was underwater. I never heard her talk without glamour masking her voice. She pretended to be David and she was after the piece. That's all I know."

"God, I'm glad you're all right. What about the piece?"

"She's dead and the piece is safe."

"That's my girl." Relief had him sagging so much he had to sit down on the bed. He winced at the pain it caused him. "I don't know much about her other than she's—she *was*—free fae and came from Ireland. Still had a hell of an accent. Oh, and that she definitely didn't want the warding around Piefferburg broken."

"A free fae who didn't want the warding broken." Emmaline felt the expression on her face go hard. "What the hell?"

"Yeah," he said with a lift of his brows. "I don't know. Come on, let me wash up and change clothes so I don't scare the hotel guests. While I do that, you tell me what happened. Then we need to take a trip across town to try to find David." He started across the room at a halting, pain-filled gait.

"Across town?"

"Yeah, David met a woman here and was dating her. Turned out it was really the fae bitch. The woman she was impersonating had an apartment across town. I'm hoping he's there." He paused. "Hoping he's not dead."

They went into the bathroom, where Emmaline helped Calum clean and bandage his wounds. All but a few exceptionally deep slashes were already healed. Calum's healing ability beat hers to smithereens. As she worked, she told him everything that had happened since she'd landed at the airport.

As they left the room, he turned to look at the bloody bed. "The maid's gonna need therapy after cleaning that up," he said and then shut the door.

On the way to Kiya's apartment, Calum filled her in on what had been going on in Haifa. How they'd never known there was another fae—a free one, at that—with the same ability Emmaline had. It had masked her from Calum's ability to sniff out fae and Phaendir. He'd shaken her hand and never felt a thing.

Emmaline was so angry at the fae she'd killed that she wanted to do it all over again by the time they'd reached the apartment building—only this time, slower. Jaw clenched, she followed Calum up the stairs and kicked the white wooden door open before Calum could say a word.

Inside it looked as though there'd been a struggle. The coach cushions were on the floor, a chair was knocked over, and everything had been swept from the coffee table. There was no blood. That was a good thing.

Spotting something on the carpet in front of the coach, she knelt and picked it up.

"A syringe," said Calum. "Interesting. Either she drugged him up to keep him quiet, or she drugged him up so she could transport him easier." He paused. "Or maybe kill him easier."

A chill shivered down her spine. "Let's search the apartment." She hoped he was here.

She hoped he was still alive.

It didn't take long. The fae hadn't even bothered to hide him very well, that was how confident she'd been that her plan would work. Emmaline found David lying in the bathtub, still out from whatever drugs she'd given him.

"Hey," she said, kneeling beside the tub and slapping his cheeks. "Hey, David." No response. She stood up and turned the shower on full blast—cold, icy water.

David came awake with a shout and nearly leapt out of the tub.

Emmaline shut the water off and grinned down at him. "Hi, you."

Shaking his head, he groaned. After a second, he grinned up at her. "Hey, nib. I can't tell you how happy I am to see you."

"How about your loyal alcoholic sidekick?" asked Calum from the doorway. "Aren't you happy to see me?"

David ran his hand over his face, wiping water away. "Calum, I'm happier to see you than a whole room full of strippers."

"You know, David," said Calum, "I hate to say it, but . . . I told you so."

GIDEON'S palms were sweating. He rubbed them on his trousers, amazed that he was confident enough to try to overthrow the Phaendir, yet this woman could make him nervous. Taking a deep breath, he knocked on her door.

He heard Emily on the other side, peeking through the peephole. After only a second's hesitation, she opened it with a smile. "Brother Gideon, what a wonderful surprise!" She swept her hand toward her living room. "Come on in."

He beamed. "Thank you."

"Please, have a seat. Can I get you something? A cup of tea, maybe? I was just heating up water for some."

"That would be great. Thanks." He sat down on the couch.

She went into the kitchen and clanked around. Then she reappeared with two cups of steaming water, a tea bag in each. Smiling, she handed a cup to him and sat down in a chair. "So why have you stopped by?"

He played with his tea bag and tried not to feel anxious. "I was just following up on finding a way to repay you for going above and beyond the call of duty for the Phaendir."

"You really don't have to do that."

"I want to do it," he said quickly. "It's not on behalf of the Phaendir. It's . . . personal."

"Oh." She blushed and looked down into her tea with a small smile on her face.

"I asked you before about antique jewelry. Do you collect it?" *Please, say you do. Please, please, say that you do, Emily.*

She looked up. "I really don't."

Gideon's hand tightened on his cup. He was going to have to make that phone call after all. Something dark and sharp twisted in his gut. He'd been right to suspect her after all. Damn it. *Damn it!*

"But I did inherit some from my grandmother Martha, who liked to collect it." She smiled. "Some really valuable and unique pieces. Oh, it's beautiful stuff. I should probably put them in a safe-deposit box, come to think of it."

Gideon relaxed. *Thank you, Labrai.* "So, if jewelry isn't an option, how can I show you my thanks for all you've done?"

She took a sip of tea and appeared to sink deep into thought. "Well, I do love a nice red wine from the Côtes du Rhône. Maybe you could buy me a bottle—"

He laughed. "That's hardly enough to say thank—"

"—and you could come over and help me drink it one night?" She smiled.

Gideon snapped his suddenly dry mouth shut. "That would be wonderful."

She beamed at him and his heart skipped. "Great. We have that settled, then."

"Yes," he murmured into his teacup, totally pleased with himself. He wasn't quite sure how he'd bumbled his way into a date with Emily, but he wasn't complaining. "So, did you have a nice visit with your mother?"

"I did." She nodded. "Very rejuvenating after such a stressful few weeks in Piefferburg."

"I'm told you intend to reenter Piefferburg now that you've returned from your leave."

She looked at him, eyes sparkling. "Yes! It's so exciting! I figured, you know, since I already have an established place there, I'd go back and see what else I can uncover."

"Very admirable of you."

They finished their tea, making small talk, until Gideon decided it was time to leave. He practically floated back to headquarters, where he planned to catch up on some paperwork.

Still musing about the jewelry, he wondered where her grandmother Martha had managed to obtain such a rare piece as the pearl pendant. He wondered if Emmaline even knew she had a fae piece in her collection. It would be interesting if he could dig up some information about such pieces of jewelry and subtly bring it up while they drank wine together. He could impress her with his knowledge and she would remember the pearl pendant in her possession. She would run to get it from her bedroom . . . and he would follow.

Ah, and his imagination should stop there while he was at the office.

Had her grandmother come from Ireland, perhaps? Interesting question. Martha's maiden name might give him a clue.

It was late in the evening and he was one of the few people in the darkened building. There would be no one to hassle him if he went down to the records room and took a quick peek at Emmaline's personnel records.

He walked down to the office in the basement and flipped on the fluorescent overhead lights then headed to the proper filing cabinet. In some ways the Phaendir were still old-fashioned. They still kept paper records of all their employees.

Finding the right file, he flipped it open and turned the pages to the information on her family. The Phaendir did a more in-depth background check than most employers did, considering the sensitive nature of their business. Now, just to find . . .

"Huh."

Gideon frowned down at the paper that listed the names of her grandmothers. She had a Beatrice and a Caroline. No Martha. He frowned a little more. Beatrice and Caroline were not even close to Martha. Nor was Martha short for Beatrice or Caroline. Gideon replayed the conversation with Emmaline in his head again. Yes, she'd definitely said her grandmother's name was Martha.

Could the information be wrong?

Clutching the file, Gideon headed to his office and turned his computer on. A search with their resources online should clear this up. He would just have to delve a little deeper into her history to figure it out. He started tapping away.

Fifteen minutes later and he flopped back against his chair.

Beatrice and Caroline were correct. There was no Martha.

What was more, there was no mention of any Martha anywhere in her immediate family.

Gideon rubbed his chin, trying to come up with an explanation for why Emily didn't know her own grandmother's name.

He came up blank.

After several moments of dark glowering, he reached for the phone.

"ARE you certain you want to go back again?" Gideon watched her with his mild brown eyes that would have seemed innocuous in any other man's head.

She adjusted her pack, slung over one arm. It jostled her glamour-hidden bow. "I'm sure, Gideon, but thank you for your concern. I think I've found my calling with this kind of work. It's frightening but also exhilarating. And I love that I'm helping the Phaendir so significantly. Have you begun to follow the lead in Wales?"

"The manure farm? Yes, of course we have. The location is slightly . . . unfortunate."

"Yes." She tried to look grave. Once they figured out the manure farm was just a stinky dead end, Emily Millhouse was going to have to disappear forever.

Of course, that wouldn't be a problem. As soon as she stepped through those gates, Emily Millhouse *would* disappear forever. Emmaline Siobhan Keara Gallagher was going to disappear, too, at least from the human world.

She'd put the piece in her pocket and used glamour to conceal it—she could disguise anything touching her body, as she did her crossbow. Her pocket was by far the safest place for it . . . as long as they didn't decide to strip-search her.

Calum and David were already back home. They'd all left the day after the fireworks. She'd returned to Phaendir headquarters as soon as her appointed leave was up, still with many unanswered questions. They were no closer to finding out who the rogue fae woman was, why she'd done what she done, and whether she'd been working alone or with others.

The biggest question on all of their minds was how the rogue had found out about the piece to begin with. How had she known where to go? How had she known whom to target in her bid for the piece? They were certain she hadn't been aligned with the Phaendir, but that was all they knew. Clearly there were more players in the game than the HFF, the fae—or even the Phaendir—were aware of.

"And we are grateful for your help," Gideon finished with an oily smile.

"Thank you."

Gideon's eyes sparkled with sudden unexpected malice. "Would you mind if we searched your possessions?"

A little jolt of shock went through her. Her steady, bright smile slipped a little before she caught it. "Search my possessions going into Piefferburg? Is that some new regulation?"

"You could say that."

He was suspicious of her. Really, really suspicious. She'd thought she'd successfully navigated through all of that. She looked to the gates and cold dread fisted in her stomach. *Oh, Danu, no.* She hadn't gone through hell to get this piece just to have it taken from her five feet from the finish line.

"Where's Brother Maddoc?" she asked as sweetly as she could. "Shouldn't he be here, too?"

"He's on his way," Gideon answered in a diamond-hard voice. It sounded a bit like he was clenching his teeth. Also, she noted with unease, Emily's womanly powers of distraction and persuasion didn't seem to be working on him right now. How odd. What had happened to change that?

That cold fist in her stomach got a little tighter and a smidgen colder.

"So. Your bag?" Gideon held out a hand.

A smile flickered over her lips. "Of course, but I have to admit I'm a little offended to think you believe I'm bringing some kind of illegal contraband into Piefferburg. What could you possibly think I might have, by the way?"

"I'm afraid that's not information I'm at liberty to reveal," he replied, taking her bag. "And I'm sorry you're offended by our actions, but we can never be too careful." His gaze met hers and held. "We are talking about the very fate of the world, you know."

"Of course."

He set her backpack down on the ground, unzipped it, and began methodically laying the contents onto the grass. Her heart beat a little faster. Any normal person might check her belongings but not ask for a strip search. Gideon was not a normal person.

Just as he'd laid the last item onto the ground and had turned his attention to possible secret compartments in the bag itself, he said the words that chilled all the water in her body. "You have no grandmother named Martha."

"What?" She blinked and took a step backward. *Martha.* Yes, she'd mentioned her grandmother's name was Martha back at her apartment. Sweet Danu, had she gotten it wrong? Had Gideon checked?

Gideon looked up at her, his hands splayed on the objects of her pack spread out on the grass. His face was made of malevolence. "You heard me."

"I don't know what you're talking about. Of course my grandmother's name is Martha." She gave a laugh. "I would know the name of my own—"

He leapt up, grabbed her wrists, and gave her a sharp tug forward into his body. His face was an inch from hers. "*Stop lying.*"

Just then Brother Maddoc came striding down the path, gravel crunching under his boots. At the sound of his approach, Gideon immediately released her and took a step back. "Brother Gideon, what are you doing?"

"He's checking my bag for any contraband I might be carrying into Piefferburg," Emmaline answered for him.

"*You're what?*" Maddoc turned an interesting shade of purple. Oh, this was going to be fun.

Gideon stood with the empty bag in his hand. "Given recent events, I thought it best. We can't be too careful."

Brother Maddoc went from purple to scarlet. "Labrai

damn you and your half-baked conspiracy theories, Brother Gideon! You put her bag back together and apologize to her. If we can't trust someone like Emily, who can we trust?"

A regular person would not have noticed the white-knuckled grip on her backpack, the tense set of Gideon's shoulders, the subtle clench of his jaw, or the twitch in his left eye. They would only see the smooth, sheepish smile Gideon gave his superior along with the easy answer, "Of course, Brother Maddoc, I meant no offense to Emily. I am simply, as always, looking out for the best interests of the human race."

"Put. Her. Bag. Back. Together." Brother Maddoc turned toward her and began apologizing.

Her eyes still on Gideon, she glimpsed a moment of perfect, bone-chilling violent intention enter the Phaendir's eyes as he stared at Maddoc, tingeing his expression dark before he knelt and put all her things back into her pack.

Gideon rose and handed it to her. "Be well, Emily, and I wish you much luck uncovering more information. You've done a brilliant job so far."

"Thank you, Brother Gideon," she replied frostily. Then she leaned forward and pecked Brother Maddoc on the cheek. "You take care of yourself."

It was all calculated, of course, to drive Gideon insane. Plus, she was pretty sure this would be the last time she ever saw Maddoc alive.

There were dark and rocky times ahead for the fae.

She turned and walked toward the gates, allowing herself one small smile of victory. The second piece of the *bosca fadbh* would soon be in the hands of the fae.

In a few moments they would be one step closer to freedom. By the look in Gideon's eyes, it appeared it was coming none too soon.

GIDEON stood staring at the closing doors of the gates of Piefferburg with rage churning in his gut. Brother Maddoc had turned and walked away without another word as soon as

Emily had said good-bye. Disrespectful. But that was all right: Maddoc wouldn't matter soon.

All his instincts were screaming at him that something was not right. He'd been trying to stall her for as long as he could to find out if his intuition was correct.

His cell phone rang. He gritted his teeth. The gates had just locked. If Brother Maddoc hadn't interfered . . .

Flipping his phone open, he growled, "Yes?"

He listened for several moments, then closed the phone and clenched it in his hand so hard he heard the plastic casing crack. The doors were closed now. She was gone.

And she was fae.

A primal scream of rage and frustration tore at his throat, wanting to free itself. He tamped it down with effort—muscles straining, face reddening, veins popping, tendons in his neck tight.

A fucking fae. Undercover in the Phaendir for the last five years. Her real name was Emmaline. The manure farm was literally and figuratively a bunch of shit. She'd probably gone into Piefferburg for her own reasons, reasons that were very likely connected to the *bosca fadbh.*

And there was a chance he'd just sent her into Piefferburg with another piece of it.

If he had been in charge of the Phaendir this never would have happened. His plans to unseat Maddoc were now more urgent than ever. Whatever it took, Maddoc had *to go* and Gideon knew *he* needed to take his place. The fate of the world depended on it. Labrai willed it.

He wanted the bitch dead. He'd coveted that trash, *that fae.* Had chased her filthy skirt for the last two years. She'd been laughing at him the whole time. He felt dirty. He needed a hard scrub in a hot shower and then needed to whip his back into a bloody, meaty mess to make up for this colossal mistake. He needed to punish her. He needed—

And an idea burst into his head.

He was not without resources inside Piefferburg. Resources, of course, that Brother Maddoc didn't know about.

Brother Maddoc.

Telling him about this would almost make up for the rest. Maddoc had fucked up worse than any of them. That worked just fine for Gideon, considering the trap he had waiting for him. This moved his timetable up, in fact; he'd spring his trap earlier than he'd been intending because of it.

The fae could fucking *have* their two pieces of the *bosca fadbh*. He'd be in charge soon, so they'd never have a chance to obtain the third, not to mention use them.

Maybe all was not lost. Because of Emmaline he was closer than ever to the top of the Phaendir food chain; and Emmaline, well, that fae bitch was about to taste his vengeance.

A smile curling over his face for the fate he was about to settle on Emmaline's shoulders, he flipped his phone back open and dialed a number.

Little Red Riding Hood was about to meet the Big Bad Wolf.

TWENTY-THREE

THE doors shut behind her with a loud thump. This time the red cap gate attendants merely waved her through. She turned and looked at the gates, content to have them locked behind her. It was a marked difference from the first time she'd gone through them. The first time she'd had a moment of panicked claustrophobia followed by the sensation of being trapped.

Now all she wanted was to get back to Aeric.

God, she was so thankful that Maddoc had shown up. Danu had been with her on that one. If Maddoc hadn't shown when he did, she wasn't sure she'd be in Piefferburg right now. A light sensation in her chest had her closing her eyes and inhaling the fresh air.

Ah, she was home.

Blowing a strand of hair away from her face and shouldering her backpack more securely, she started off on the road that would bring her to Piefferburg City.

A little way down the road, she dropped her glamour. It felt good to do it, which was also a large change from last time. This time she wouldn't be meeting Aeric in the woods. He didn't know she'd returned. The magickal alarm system that had alerted him the first time had been deactivated when she'd broken it.

The upside was that so had the queen's. The Seelie Court Royal wouldn't have a clue that she was walking through the woods on her own right now, thank Danu. Unless, of course, she'd had another one put in place.

Her blood went cold.

She'd made it about halfway to Piefferburg City when she began to sense she was being watched. The hair at the nape of her neck rose and the pressure of a gaze seemed to follow at her back. She stopped on the road and peered all around her, feeling foolish, but considering her track record with being attacked within the borders of Piefferburg City, maybe she wasn't being so paranoid, after all.

Suddenly the weight of the crossbow on her back began to feel very reassuring.

Only green foliage and the gently curling tendrils of flowering plants met her gaze. All she could hear was the low twittering of birds in the trees and the rustle of leaves in the breeze. Maybe it was just nerves making her feel like she was being watched.

The wind was picking up and dark clouds were rolling in. She lifted her face to the sky and let the incoming storm buffet her hair around her face. Closing her eyes for a moment, she soaked in the sensation, in this place that was so saturated with magick. The magick of her people, the same that flowed in her veins. It felt so good.

Opening her eyes, she turned and walked on, faster now since the storm was approaching quickly. The sense she'd had of being watched could have been anything. In a world of fae magick even the trees had eyes sometimes.

Fat drops of rain began to come down, plopping onto her cheeks like tears and falling on her backpack. Soon the wind picked up, ripping at her clothes and whipping her rain-wet hair around her face. A peal of thunder sounded in the distance . . . and a dark figure stepped out from the woods ahead of her.

She stopped, staring at the person. Aeric? No, not Aeric. This man was smaller than he was, the shoulders narrower.

Unslinging her bow from her shoulder, she pulled a bolt from her quiver and nocked it into the bow's runner. Planting her feet slightly apart on the road, she ignored the rising storm and sighted at the figure.

The man hadn't moved and the rain was coming down hard now. The way he didn't move, just stood there staring at her, was unnerving. "Hey, whoever you are," she yelled. "Come closer so I can see you. Watch yourself while you do it. I'm capable with this weapon."

She blinked and he was gone. Damn it. This was getting more threatening by the moment. Turning in a wary circle, she sighted down her bow, trying to find him. Shooting a wet crossbow, even a magicked one, was not a fun thing. Her heart was thumping now. The rain obscured her vision. She could barely see the edge of the foliage.

Hands grabbed her roughly from behind. How the hell had he gotten behind her so quickly? With a strength she wouldn't have expected from a man with such a slender build, he ripped the bow from her fingers and flung it far away, onto the muddy road.

She brought her knee up fast and hard, catching the man in the gut. He grunted and fell back. Ah, flesh and bone, then. Something she could fight. Thank Danu.

Taking advantage of his pain, she lunged for her bow, but he was on her as soon as her fingers closed around the wood, knocking her to the ground.

She slammed her elbow back into his face. He grunted again, a low inhuman sound, but didn't let go of her. He rolled her to her back, pinning her body beneath his, and the hood of his jacket fell back, revealing his devastatingly handsome face in the half-light.

The Will o' the Wisp. Otherwise known as Will the Smith, a man so evil it was said that when he died, the Powers That Be expelled him from the Netherworld, giving him a second life.

Handsome and charismatic, he could win the trust of

almost anyone, but this man was like all the worst serial killers of the human world rolled into one and with magick added in.

This was not good.

"I've been sent for you," he said in a low, smooth voice. He still had a heavy English accent. She wondered how many unsuspecting women he'd managed to lure in and slaughter during his lifetime.

"Who?" she breathed.

He smiled, revealing perfect, straight teeth. "Gideon."

Terror jolted through her.

That meant Gideon knew the truth. She wondered if this meant Gideon knew she had the piece.

"He sent me to get the piece he thinks you're carrying."

Well, that answered her question.

"Where is it?" Will asked.

"Like I'm going to tell you, freak."

"Oh. You're going to fight me." He gave her a greasy smile. "Goody. This will be fun."

Yeah, fun for him. Her, not so much. Out of the corner of her eye, she spied her quiver, full of nice, sharp quarrels. Unfortunately, it was just out of reach.

His face hovering just above hers, she began to scream. Long, loud, piercing screams that echoed through the woods. Emmaline had learned over the years that it was better to seem weaker than you were in a fight. Scared. Vulnerable. It gave her an edge.

Will smiled and a trail of spittle trailed out of the corner of his mouth and down his chin. He threw back his head and laughed, a raw guttural sound that chilled her blood between her girly screams of terror.

Oh, that was not attractive at all.

He punched her and pain exploded in a shower of stars behind her eyes. It hurt, no doubt about that, but Lars had done far worse to her. She kept screaming.

The screaming made him think she was terrified out of her mind and paralyzed with panic, not looking for an opportunity to free her hand and hit him in the flat of his nose—

hard. He yelped and blood poured from his nostrils. He rolled to the ground, his hand to his face.

She took her chance. Lunging for the quiver, she snatched a quarrel and gripped it with the tip cupped in her palm and the shaft held tight along the inside of her arm.

Will grabbed her ankle and yanked her toward him. She slid on her stomach in the mud, her wet hair tangled over her face and rain streaming down into her eyes. Twisting to meet him head-on as he pulled her under his body, she brought her arm up and rammed the quarrel toward him with all her strength. At the last moment, he saw it and flinched away.

She missed the target of his throat, but managed to embed it deeply in his shoulder. Sharpened to a deadly point, it slid in like a knife into a thick, raw steak. Hot blood welled and coated her hand, mixing with the rain.

Will screamed and grabbed at the shaft of the quarrel, staring down at her with crazy, bulging eyes. He was no longer handsome and didn't even approach the realm of charming. Now he looked like the insane man he was.

And, boy, now he was really pissed.

She scrambled backward on her hands and feet, scrabbling in the mud for her quiver and crossbow. Clutching one in each hand, she rose and ran stumbling into the woods while Will screamed behind her, trying to break the shaft of the quarrel stuck so deeply in his shoulder.

Plunging through the tree line, she crashed through foliage and jumped over fallen logs as quickly as she could in the storm- and rain-darkened woods.

Behind her, roaring with perfect rage, Will followed. And, *Danu*, he was fast. Right now he was the hunter and she was the deer. She needed to change that around. Now.

Darting to the left, through a particularly thick area of the woods, she found a good tree with thick branches within arm's reach. Slinging the crossbow and the quiver onto her back, she swung herself up then hoisted herself upward on the rough, wet limbs, into the dripping leaves to conceal herself.

Will approached fast. Wrapping her arms and legs around

a heavy limb, she went as still and as silent as she could. The sound of the rain masked her labored breathing. Directly below her, he crashed through the foliage and went past. His face and shoulder both were covered with blood and he was making low grunting noises of pain and rage.

After he passed, she dropped down silently to the forest floor. Nocking a quarrel into her crossbow, she sighted along it as she followed behind him. Her fingers slipped on the weapon and she cursed inwardly. Rain was the worst enemy of an archer. It obscured the line of sight and made the string slippery.

She walked quietly, the steady sound of the rain masking the noise made by her passing. Still grunting, Will was doing nothing to conceal his location, yet she still couldn't see where he was—she could only hear him. Balancing the crossbow on her shoulder, she used her free hand to push aside the branches in her way.

The forest had suddenly gone quiet. Disturbingly so. Even Will's grunting had ceased.

The rain slowed and then stopped. Still she saw no sign of Will in front of her.

Something dark moved in the corner of her eye. She turned, finger ready to loose the quarrel, but there was nothing but trees. Her heart pounding, she backed up flush with a trunk and made a slow sweep of the area, looking for any sign that she was now the stalkee instead of the stalker.

Another slow sweep, emotion choked up tight in her throat.

There.

He stood behind a tree, only the bloody half of his body showing. Her stomach went leaden. He stared at her with total malice, his head tipped down and his pupils rolled to the top of his eye sockets. The broken shaft was still embedded in his shoulder.

He appeared absolutely insane. Every violent thing he wanted to do to her seemed to be broadcast in that horrific gaze.

Never mind. It didn't matter. No way was she going to let him intimidate her. This man was going down.

She sighted, cursing the rain, and loosed, aiming for his head. The quarrel stuck in the tree trunk level with his eye. He'd ducked behind the tree the moment she'd fired.

Silence.

Her breathing was coming in shallow pants. She swallowed, trying to get a grip. He'd disappeared again, probably standing behind the tree. That had to be it. To her knowledge, the Will o' the Wisp didn't have the magick to allow him to teleport.

For as scary as he was, he was still a man. He could be killed. She had to remember that.

She nocked another quarrel. Moving slowly and blinking so she could keep the tree in her view, she inched closer and closer.

A wet branch cracked beneath her shoe and she cursed inwardly. She'd given away her position.

Will leapt. Yelling out for her death in a guttural voice, he rushed her.

Sighting on his chest, she loosed. The quarrel arched through the air and Will tried to dodge it. No luck this time. With a wet crunch, it hit his chest and broke bones.

Eyes wide, he stumbled and went down into the wet leaves. Blood poured from his mouth. He rolled on his side, gurgling and pulling at the shaft with weak, blood-wet fingers.

Heart pounding and breath coming fast, she lowered the crossbow to her side and walked over to him. "So, you were sent to kill me." She looked down at him as he lay bleeding in the leaves. "Didn't Gideon tell you it wouldn't be that easy?"

His eyes widened a little, he gurgled, and then he died.

TWENTY-FOUR

AERIC felt her a moment before she walked in the door, as if they'd forged some kind of psychic link. "I have it," she said as soon as she'd cleared the threshold. Angry bruises marked her face and she was streaked with grime and blood. Her hair and clothes were damp and her boots were covered in mud. "I've got the piece in my backpack. We need to take it to Queen Aislinn."

"Hey, hold on a minute," he said, going to her. "I have a feeling you're skipping a few things." He drew her against him and held her for a moment. "What the hell happened to you?"

She melted into him and sagged against him bonelessly, her arms coming around his waist. "I don't even know where to start." She sounded exhausted.

He drew the crossbow and quiver off of her, then her pack. "Tell me everything."

She started from the time she left Piefferburg. As she spoke, he drew her into the bathroom, taking care to place the precious pack on a nearby table, and carefully stripped her clothing off. While he ran a bath for her, he cleaned up the cuts on her face and arms, then herded her into the warm water. As he did all this, she told him about David, Calum, and the strange fae who had the same magick she did. While she sat in the water and he washed her back and hair, she told him about Gideon's suspicion and then about Will.

The Will o' the Wisp. She'd fought him, *killed* the bastard.

All on her own.

After she'd finished he was silent for a while, content to have her safe in his apartment and pissed as hell she'd been in danger in the first place. Rage and relief, all at the same time.

He dropped the washcloth in the water and, swearing low, rose and turned away, his fists tight.

"Aeric?"

"I want to kill Gideon for what he did."

"You're not the only one."

"I feel so fucking helpless trapped in here." He leaned against the counter, emotions pulling him all over the place. He was coming to care very deeply about Emmaline and the thought that she'd been in danger and he hadn't been there to protect her made the caveman part of himself insane. He knew she was totally capable of taking care of herself. That had been shown amply by recent events, but he was a man and he'd claimed her as his—and a man protected what was his, no matter if she needed it or not.

She touched his shoulder. "Hey."

He turned and pulled her against him, uncaring that she was wet from the bath, and buried his nose in the place where her neck met her shoulder, breathing in the scent of her skin.

Her arms came around him. "I'm okay, Aeric."

"Yeah, I know." He didn't let go.

He slid his hand to the nape of her neck, angling her face up to his, and kissed her softly, aware of the cut on her lip where Will had hit her. He kissed the corner of her mouth on the side that wasn't hurt, her chin, her throat.

Her body went taut against him, her breathing becoming heavier. His, too.

"Do you want this right now?" he murmured against her throat.

She nodded and swallowed hard. "Make me feel something other than scared."

"And I need to feel you, Emmaline. Warm, breathing." He paused. "Mine."

She went very still and tense. After a moment, she looked at him. "Where is this going, Aeric?"

He studied her, his throat going tight. "Going? I'm already gone. I love you, Emmaline." He dipped his head and kissed her again very gently, then proceeded to try to kiss every remaining water droplet from her skin, starting at her throat and working his way down.

By the time he'd trailed his tongue to the junction of her legs, neither of them were capable of speech.

He pulled her forward by her hips and slid his tongue between her thighs, licking up stray droplets of water and finding her clit already blooming with need. It made his body tight with desire. She'd only been away from him for a couple weeks, but every day had felt like twenty. He lowered her to the plush carpet of the bathroom and gave it the much more thorough attention it was begging for.

She shuddered and came, moaning his name in that way that heated his blood. He moved up her body and she pulled his shirt over his head, then her fingers went to the button and zipper of his jeans as if she couldn't wait.

He covered her hand with his. "We have lots of time. Let's take this slow."

"Slow sounds good to me."

Once he was as bare as she was, he gently brushed his lips across her hurts and limned the bottom of her mouth with his tongue. Then he dipped down and gave the same attention to each of her nipples in turn, until they were hard and red, like little cherries.

Skating his hand down the gentle curve of her spine to her rear and then to the tender back of her knee, he lifted her and fit her against his groin. She positioned herself against him, the heat of her sex warming him as she moved to push him within.

Sliding deep inside her was like coming home. Her breath hissed out and he emitted a low groan of pleasure. He stayed like that, not moving, just looking down at her for a moment. Her lips were slightly parted, her eyes glazed with desire, her pain forgotten for the moment. She was beautiful.

Holding her gaze, he moved inside her with long, slow strokes. Their bare bodies brushed together like silk and her breath came faster, the look on her face more passionate with every passing moment. He loved watching her approach orgasm, how her body and face showed her heightening pleasure—he loved it even more when she came apart beneath him.

Knowing how she best liked him to move, he increased the pace and strength of his thrusts, turning long and slow to long and hard. Gentle to forceful and possessive. She moved her hips in time to his thrusts, until they achieved a perfect rhythm.

Her breathing caught and her muscles tensed in that way that was becoming familiar to him. Letting out a sigh and a long moan, her back arched as she came. The muscles of her sex spasmed around his length and she cried his name.

Pleasure rippled and pulsed in his balls, then exploded upward, engulfing him. He let out a low groan ending with her name as he released inside her. He collapsed on top of her and then rolled to the side, taking her with him and kissing her all over.

After they'd caught their breath, she rested her head on his chest and said, "God, that's one thing that's never going to get old with you."

"What do you mean?" *Goibhniu*, he hoped it meant what he thought it meant. "Does that mean you're staying with me? Here in Piefferburg?"

She raised her head. "Yes, and it's not because Gideon won't let me back out. I'd decided to stay here before that happened." She paused. "I want to be with you, Aeric. Stay here with you."

In the mess of the story she'd told him about what had happened with Brother Gideon, it hadn't occurred to him that she was now trapped in Piefferburg as a recognized fae. He leaned forward and kissed the uninjured part of her mouth. "I love you, Emmaline."

She held his gaze for a pregnant moment. "I love you, too, Aeric. I always have."

He set his forehead against hers and let out a long, slow breath of relief. *She was staying.*

"Are you okay?" she asked.

He stood and then scooped her into his arms, making her squeal. That was one of the advantages of having the build of a blacksmith. "I'm okay now. More than okay."

She laughed and then hit him. "Don't make me laugh. It hurts."

He carried her out of the bathroom and put her in his bed—a place he intended to keep her for a very long time to come. He came down over her body and kissed her while he eased his hand between her thighs. "Don't worry, *hurt* isn't what I plan to make you feel. Not ever, if I can help it."

She sighed and relaxed into the pillows. "I can never get enough of your hands on me."

"That's, good, because touching you is something I want to make a hobby." He lowered his head and gave some special attention to one nipple, then the other.

Soon they were making love again, this time softer and slower, while he murmured words of love to her, ones he'd thought he would never say to another woman again.

Afterward, sated and relaxed, they lay in an easy silence, their legs tangled together and with as much skin touching as possible. "Do you want to see it?" she asked.

It took him a moment to remember the piece. He'd been more concerned with her when she'd walked through the door.

Before he had a chance to answer, she'd slid from the bed and retrieved her backpack. Digging into the bottom, she popped a secret compartment and drew it forth. "I had it in my pocket when Will rushed me. After I got through that I thought it might be safer away from my attack-prone body for the rest of the walk into the city, so I put it in my pack."

He took it from her and examined it. It was small, curved on one side and jagged on the other. It fit, of course, the other piece that the Summer Queen had in her possession. One more piece and it would be whole. Then it would unlock the back of the Book of Bindings and the magick contained within those pages could be used to break the warding around Piefferburg. Copper colored and unassuming, it was something that could easily be lost in a pile of junk or at a thrift store.

The first piece had been locked in a government vault, freed by Ronan Quinn at the request of the Phaendir . . . and then stolen from them. The second piece had been buried at the bottom of the sea and protected with strong magick by an unknown party. There was no telling where the third piece was or if they'd ever locate it. One thing was certain—it was not within Piefferburg.

"We should bring it to the queen as soon as possible," she said. "There's no telling what Gideon might try now since his first plan failed."

Aeric grunted in acquiescence. "We're only missing one piece." He looked up at her. "The Phaendir will act soon. We're getting too close for them to remain passive."

She nodded. "But they'll do it covertly. No matter how they may believe they've got the fae under their thumbs, they fear us. They won't come pounding into Piefferburg with Phaendir foot soldiers. They'll do something like what Brother Gideon might do: use fae turncoats within Piefferburg to sabotage us from the inside."

Aeric gave the piece back to her. "The Phaendir might use the human military. Send in troops to get the pieces and the book back, along with Phaendir to bolster them with magick."

"Maybe. It wouldn't be pretty. It'd be bloody, in fact." She chewed her lip. "For them."

He studied her. "So, you're trapped in Piefferburg now."

She looked up at him, her eyes suddenly wet. She reached

out and cupped his cheek. "I'm not *trapped* in Piefferburg. I'm in love and happy to be here."

He met her halfway, lips meshing. The piece fell to the bed between them.

BROTHER Gideon pushed open Brother Maddoc's office door with a thump and walked in as though it was already his. In about five minutes, it would be. "Archdirector Maddoc, I'm afraid you've got quite a bit of explaining to do." Seven brothers followed him within. Two were Gideon's men. The rest were Phaendir that had always followed Maddoc.

No longer.

Maddoc looked up with a surprised expression on his face that quickly turned to anger. He rose. "Brother Gideon, why are you here? I haven't summoned you. Leave my office immediately."

"Oh, I don't think so." Gideon took the upper arm of a thin, pale-haired brother named Aloysius. "Brother Aloysius has revealed some very interesting information."

Maddoc's face clouded with rage. "What information? What are you saying? Kindly leave and let me—"

Gideon gave Aloysius a helpful push forward.

"They know," said Aloysius in a small voice, his hands fisted at his groin. He cast a quick, frightened glance at the other brothers in the office. "I just couldn't keep it to myself anymore. The guilt was too great."

"What guilt?" sputtered Maddoc. He scanned the thronged room. It was becoming more crowded with every raised syllable that emanated into the corridor. "I have never seen this brother in my life. I have no idea what he's talking about!"

"Murder," said Gideon. "That's what he's talking about. The murders of Brothers Cederick, Rhys, and Baeddan. Not to mention the attempt on my life."

"Murder!" Maddoc gave a strangled laugh. "That's insane."

"Aloysius helped you commit the heinous murders of

three of our dear brothers and aided in your attempted murder of me. He couldn't take the guilt and has confessed to Labrai."

Maddoc's face went taut and ashen.

Aloysius fell to his knees, keening. "I can stand it no longer. The blood has stained my hands. Labrai, I pray for your mercy. I helped Brother Maddoc in his misguided attempt to cull your flock. I have seen the error of my ways. Please forgive me."

"This is ridiculous!" Maddoc bellowed. "I would have no reason to kill Brothers Cederick, Rhys, and Baeddan!" Gideon noticed Maddoc left out his name. *Huh.* Maddoc pointed a finger at Gideon. "Him! *He* had a motive! Not me. Don't you see? He's setting me up!"

Gideon laughed. "Why would I do that?"

"Because you want to be Archdirector!" Maddoc gave a half-crazed laugh. "Everyone knows that!"

"My attempts to move up in the power structure are no secret, Brother Maddoc, but I obey Labrai in all things. I would never go against him." And he wasn't. Labrai sanctioned every move he made.

Brother Hugh, one of the oldest and most respected of the Phaendir, stepped forward. "And perhaps it's time that Brother Gideon did take your place as Archdirector."

Maddoc went perfectly still. Gideon gazed smugly at the sheen of absolute terror in his eyes. "What are you saying, Brother Hugh?"

Brother Hugh bowed his bald head and cupped his hands in front of him. "The council has conferred and is in agreement. You have failed, Brother Maddoc. The fae now have the Book of Bindings and two pieces of the *bosca fadbh.* Even without the very compelling murder allegations brought forth by Brother Aloysius, those facts remain. We have entered a critical time in our relations with the fae. At no other period in the history of Piefferburg have things been so dire. This happened under *your watch*, Brother Maddoc. I'm afraid we can no longer take the tack of mercy with the fae. It may be time for a stronger hand."

"No," sputtered Maddoc. "You cannot mean to turn the reins of the Phaendir over to—to *this monster*!"

"That is enough," said Brother Hugh. "I have spoken for the council. Our decision is final."

Maddoc just stood there, pale and staring. It was over and he knew it. He'd been outplayed.

"Aloysius?" Gideon prodded softly. "Didn't you have something you wanted to show the others?" He didn't need this last touch, but he'd gone to all the trouble of setting it up.

"Wait!" Aloysius piped up in his screeching voice. Maddoc flinched. "I have proof of Maddoc's attempted murder of Brother Gideon!"

Maddoc didn't even move a muscle as Aloysius walked over to a filing cabinet and opened the bottom door. He pulled out a box of rat poison. Then he opened the top of the box and showed it to Brother Hugh. "He had me cube it. See?"

The Phaendir in the room gave a collective gasp.

Maddoc dropped like a stone back into his chair.

Gideon smiled. That chair was now *his*.

TWENTY-FIVE

HER Majesty Aislinn Christiana Guinevere Finvarra, formerly of the Seelie Court and now Shadow Queen of the Black Tower, took three people with her when she went to deliver the second piece of the *bosca fadbh* to the Summer Queen: her husband and king of the Black Tower, Gabriel Cionaodh Marcus Mac Braire; the man who'd made the key that had unlocked the magicked box at the bottom of the sea, Aeric Killian Riordan O'Malley; and the woman who had sacrificed so much to retrieve that piece and bring it into the city, Emmaline Siobhan Keara Gallagher.

The four of them traveled across the square in full formal dress, accompanied by thirteen of the silver-and-black-bedecked Unseelie Shadow Guard.

Aislinn had dressed in a heavy, layered gown of red velvet and black silk with a heavy train that required four of her lady's maids to carry it. The décolletage plunged so far that Gabriel had tripped over his tongue when complimenting her. The sleeves were piped with thread of silver. She'd chosen her jewels carefully, rubies and diamonds to show off the wealth of the Unseelie. This was the game the royals played and the one she'd signed up for when she killed her biological father—after he'd tried to steal her soul—and gained the Shadow Throne by right of blood.

Her boots were the subtly kick-ass kind she favored, steel toed and laced up the front in a Victorian fashion. Not that, as queen, she got to kick very much ass on her own. She was expected to use her Shadow Guard for that, and, frequently, she did. Her captain walked beside her, the precious piece resting on a red and black satin pillow.

Her husband and Aeric both were dressed in head-to-toe suits of expensive black material, one man as dark as midnight and the other man like the sun.

She'd sent her servants to Emmaline with several dress choices and the Seelie fae had chosen the gray silk. It was an elegant gown, the flow of the garment accentuating the willowy build of her body and the color seeming to make her eyes an even deeper brown. Her hair was long, left natural—as opposed to the practiced upsweep Aislinn was required to wear—curling darkly over her narrow shoulders.

Aeric hadn't been able to take his eyes off her.

During the last year she'd come to know Aeric very well. She knew his history, knew about Aileen, the assassin, and how he felt about both of them. It was hard to believe he'd gone from hating the wraith who'd existed in his mind for so many years to appreciating and respecting the complex flesh-and-blood woman she actually was.

Aeric was deeply in love.

And Aislinn knew love when she saw it. Emmaline loved him back.

The fae in Piefferburg Square all paused and stilled to watch as they glimpsed the procession, whispered among themselves about the piece and about Emmaline, whose story had already begun to spread all over Piefferburg.

Emmaline hesitated at the heavy double doors of the Rose Tower. "This is wrong."

"This is necessary," Aislinn answered in a strong voice. "I

don't like it any more than you do, but when the Unseelie Court makes a promise, we keep it."

Two of the Rose Tower's Imperial Guard opened the doors. They entered and traveled down the necessary corridors to get them to the Rose Tower's throne room.

More whispering. The Seelie Court nobles were highly interested in the entourage from the Black. Especially interested in the Shadow Queen. Oh, yes, she was big gossip in the Rose Tower, of course. She'd been one of them for decades, secretly Unseelie in the Seelie Court—no less the biological daughter of the Shadow King himself.

They reached the throne room and the doors were opened for them. They entered to see the sneering Summer Queen on her rose quartz throne, dressed in shimmering rose and gold, like her guard, and ready to receive her "due."

Aislinn wanted to punch her in the mouth. That was her true due.

Judging by the way Aeric's body had gone tense, she wasn't the only one who wanted to commit violence on the Summer Queen, though she guessed that even more brutal fantasies were flitting through his head.

"You have the piece?" Caoilainn Elspeth Muirgheal always came right to the point.

"We do," answered Aislinn. She gestured for her captain to approach the throne with the piece on the pillow. "It is yours in good faith, as promised by Aeric Killian Riordan O'Malley, the Blacksmith, in return for Emmaline Siobhan Keara Gallagher's freedom."

"Excellent. And I accept it in good faith."

"Do you?" Aislinn's voice snapped out like the lash of a whip. It had taken her a while to understand she could talk to the Summer Queen that way without fear of repercussion since she was her equal. Now it came easily.

The Summer Queen was a bitch and a half.

The Seelie Royal appeared surprised. She halted in her examination of the piece, the copper shiny in her palm. "Of course I do. What are you speaking of, Aislinn?"

"When it comes time to join the pieces of the *bosca fadbh* and open the back of the Book of Bindings, will you hand yours over?"

She lowered the piece to her lap, a look of consternation creasing her perfectly beautiful face, suspended always in youth. "We do not yet have all the pieces."

"That was not my question, Caoilainn. My question was, When we *do* have all the pieces, will you hand your two pieces over to be joined with the third? Will you not impede the opening of the back of the Book of Bindings and the removal of the prison in which we now find ourselves? *That* was my question."

The Summer Queen studied her in icy silence for several moments before speaking. "I resent the implication. I would not impede the freedom my people so desire."

If only Aislinn could be sure that was the truth.

Aislinn did the only thing she could do; she inclined her head. "My lady queen, we leave you."

Her entourage backed away a few steps, as was proper, and then turned to leave the throne room.

"Wait. Our business is not yet finished," called the Summer Queen.

Aislinn, Gabriel, Aeric, and Emmaline all turned back to face her.

"What other business is there?" asked Gabriel with suspicion lacing his tone.

She motioned with her hand. A door to her left opened and out stepped Lars Elof Thorin Anderssen. Aislinn was familiar with him. He was a nature fae—not all of them were shiny, gentle, and good—who dealt in the realm of death in some capacity that she had never fully understood. Lars was somewhat like a vulture—a necessary and ugly part of the ecosystem. Lars had been the queen's right hand for her more unpleasant tasks over the centuries. What could any of this have to do with him?

Emmaline seemed to know.

Aislinn watched Emmaline take several steps backward,

grim realization dawning on her face. Aeric looked ready to explode.

Aislinn stepped forward. "I claim Emmaline Siobhan Keara Gallagher as a member of the Unseelie Court. She's mine, Caoilainn."

"You cannot claim her, Aislinn. She has no magick that draws blood on its own."

"Emmaline has drawn plenty of blood in her lifetime." She glanced over to see that Aeric was now holding Emmaline protectively.

The Summer Queen shook her head. "The law says the *magick* must be capable of drawing blood, not the fae."

"You know as well as I do that those ancient rules are rarely obeyed. I claim her for my court."

"She is mine." The Summer Queen's voice snapped like frozen branches. "The assassin was mine three hundred and sixty years ago and she remains mine now."

"We had a deal," Aeric shouted, stepping toward the throne. The Imperial Guard advanced on him, drawing their charmed iron swords. In Aeric's case, the charmed iron wouldn't take away his magick or cause him illness, but the blade would make him bleed well enough.

"We did have a deal," the Summer Queen answered with a smile of self-assurance. "I agreed to free Emmaline when you asked for her three and a half weeks ago. In return, you agreed to let me hold the second piece of the *bosca fadbh*. The deal was not that I could never take her back. I'm not breaking any promises I made."

"You coldhearted deceitful bitch."

Aeric always knew how to keep a civil tongue.

"Guards!" the Summer Queen barked.

All hell broke loose. Gabriel, Aeric, and Emmaline engaged the advancing Imperial Guard. Aislinn gave the order for her Shadow Guard to fight, while her lady's maids—not exactly the delicate flowers they appeared—drew sharp iron and stood in defensive positions around her with the intent to guard their queen.

But they were in the Rose Tower and had not anticipated a fight. The Imperial Guard outnumbered the Black entourage by at least one hundred to one.

Soon five of them were on Aeric, pressing him to the floor to incapacitate him, while he thrashed and shouted out obscenities. More wrestled Gabriel down and handcuffed him. More still overpowered Aislinn's thirteen guards and effectively quelled her lady's maids, until it was only Emmaline alone fighting in hand-to-hand combat with armored men twice her weight. Her crossbow, sadly, was back at the Black Tower, not a suitable accessory for an official envoy to the Seelie Court. Now Aislinn wished Emmaline had worn it and disguised it with glamour.

Holding her arm and bleeding from a cut in her cheek, Emmaline backed away warily from Lars, who had entered the throne room confident of the Summer Queen winning this fight. A thing, apparently, he had every right to be confident of.

Aislinn contemplated calling the sluagh into the throne room; as a necromancer, she commanded that army of unforgiven dead. But the Summer Queen was right: Emmaline was her subject, not a member of the Unseelie Court. By the laws they obeyed, Aislinn had no recourse here. She couldn't call the sluagh or the goblins, which she also commanded, without declaring an all-out war between the courts and that was something they couldn't afford right now.

Gods, sometimes she hated being Shadow Queen.

"We would not have that piece of the *bosca fadbh* if it weren't for the help this woman has given us," said Aislinn loudly. "This is no way to repay her for risking her life several times over."

The Summer Queen smiled. "And now her life is in Lars's hands. I cannot say what he will do with it."

"You bitch," Aeric yelled from the floor. "You fuck—mumpf!" One of the guards brutally smashed Aeric's head into the floor. His hands were handcuffed at his back and the five Imperial Guards still had to hold him down. He was as enraged as Aislinn had ever seen him and—Aeric was a hothead; she'd seen him that way often.

Lars approached Emmaline, who was retreating steadily toward the back of the throne room, an expression of pure terror on her face. Obviously just the sight of this man was enough to send her into shock.

Silently, Aislinn willed her to fight and fight hard.

"Why are you doing this?" Aislinn asked the Summer Queen, genuinely mystified.

"Lars has been a loyal servant to me for hundreds of years and he has always fancied Emmaline. I'm just giving him a little reward."

A little reward, like Emmaline was a treat for a rabid dog.

Aislinn guessed there was more to it than that, though. The Summer Queen had prided herself for so long on the effectiveness of her assassin, and then her assassin had run away from her. Had chosen certain poverty and destitution over life under her command. It must have been humiliating for her. This was personal revenge.

Lars laid hands on Emmaline, fouling her gorgeous gray silk dress, and Aeric went insane on the floor.

Emmaline didn't say a word. She looked like a small animal confronted by a wolf. Lars gave a low, dirty-sounding laugh . . . and, then, all of a sudden, she moved.

Like some graceful but deadly dancer, she brought her arm up to break his grip in a motion almost too fast for Aislinn to track. Then she brought her fist forward into his throat. He gurgled and staggered to the side. Pressing her advantage while he was stunned, she drove her opposite fist into his kidney. Giving a strangled yelp, he went down on one knee. Whirling on one foot, she gave him a solid roundhouse kick to the head and Lars collapsed, motionless. All of it seemed to happen in less than a second—in one smooth movement.

Emmaline bolted for the door, but the Summer Queen motioned to the Imperial Guard and they surrounded her immediately. She fought and kicked like an animal, but there were too many. A moment later she was handcuffed in charmed iron.

By that time Lars had recovered. Holding a hand to his injured back, he advanced on her. He wasn't laughing anymore. He took Emmaline by the upper arm and yanked her forward, dragging her out of the room.

Aeric made a noise of anguish and renewed his futile efforts at obtaining freedom until she was well out of sight and the door they'd disappeared through was shut.

The Summer Queen inclined her head. "Queen Aislinn, always a pleasure. Our business here is concluded. If the Blacksmith agrees to leave without fuss, I will not be required to keep him in my dungeon."

Aislinn said nothing. She only favored the Summer Queen with an icy glare and walked toward the door. Aeric and Gabriel stood with aid. Still handcuffed and pissed as hell, they were both a bloody mess.

"Aeric," Aislinn said softly as she paused, "don't do anything rash. You can't go after Emmaline if you're locked in a dungeon."

"Yeah, I know. Pity, though. I was thinking about some very creative ways to kill her," he murmured as they exited.

As soon as the Unseelie entourage was once again in Piefferburg Square, Aislinn drew Aeric to her. "Think about creative ways to kill *Lars*. I know two things about him. He's a nature fae woodcutter who lives in the Water Wastes and he loves to torture. So go, Aeric. Take whatever you need, whoever you need. My Shadow Guard is at your disposal. You have weapons enough or I'd offer those, too."

"I need to know where his lair is in the Water Wastes. It's a big place."

"That I don't know, but I know of someone who might. Go to the Piefferburg witch. You'll need to pay her and it won't be cheap."

"I'll pay anything."

"Then go. You don't have any time to lose if the stories about Lars Elof Thorin Anderssen are true, especially if he's off the Summer Queen's leash."

THE last thing Emmaline remembered was being pushed into the bed of a truck. That was when she'd blacked out, but she didn't think that Lars had done anything to cause it. He hadn't hit her or given her any drugs. She'd just . . . fainted. How embarrassing.

Though as Lars lifted her from the truck, hurting her shoulders because her hands were still cuffed behind her back, she really felt like passing out again. Maybe it was a good idea; it would be easier to endure what was to come.

He set her on her feet and she tried her best to stay aware, looking around to take stock of her location.

He'd driven her to a place where, instead of the majestic, ancient trees of the Boundary Lands, there was scrub and marshland, giving way to a brackish, swampy area. They had to be somewhere near the ocean, maybe the Water Wastes.

A small house stood not far away. It was built of wood and stone, with a thatched roof in the old style of the fae. It appeared ancient and hadn't adapted well to the passing of the centuries. Lars yanked her toward it and her feet squished into the mud.

"I killed the Will o' the Wisp, Lars. Did you know that?" Her voice promised him the same fate. She was proud that she sounded so confident. "Me, I did that. All by myself."

Lars laughed. "The Will was nothing to you but a thing from boogeyman stories." He grinned at her, baring his straight, white teeth. "I'm much more threatening because you and I have a past. To you, I'm a very real monster. That gives me more power over you than the Will ever had."

And he was right.

It hadn't been easy to kill the infamous Will o' the Wisp, but it would be a hundred times harder for her to fight Lars because of the psychological baggage that came with him. She had to get past her fear of this man and tap into her rage. Find the rage and she would find her courage and her strength.

"I have missed you, my sweet. Thought of you often," he murmured. "I'm excited to have this time with you now. When it's over I plan to keep you close to me forever, so I can always remember it."

She gave him a look of disgust. The man was insane. Half the time she couldn't even track his meaning.

Lars pushed her into the building and the sharp scent of chemicals mixed with the nauseating sick-sweet smell of death bit into her nose. She gagged and pressed her lips together, trying not to throw up.

The house was composed of one large room. A small kitchen stood in the corner, with a fireplace and cauldron instead of a stove. A narrow bed rested against one wall. The rest of the place was dedicated to Lars's occupation of taxidermy. Tools and bottles of chemicals rested all over the tables, along with half-finished "works" from which Emmaline quickly averted her eyes. The walls were "decorated" with all the different kinds of animals that she would rather cuddle than have stare at her with dead, glassy, fake eyes.

"Do you like my trophies?" Lars asked, staring around the walls.

"Lovely," Emmaline replied in a flat voice, curling her lips. "You're truly an artist."

"I am." He forced her down into a straight-backed chair. "And you will be my greatest creation."

Emmaline looked at the tables filled with chemicals and gore-coated knives, her mind fumbling drunkenly for a moment after his meaning. Her gorge rose and she lost her breakfast all over the floor.

TWENTY-SIX

THE Piefferburg witch lived in the shadow of the Black Tower, not far from the outer limits of Goblin Town. Her magick was not unlike that of Ronan and Niall Quinn's, though no one knew her origins. She was a strange mix of Seelie and Unseelie fae, the genetics of whom had produced a unique, powerful—and somewhat deceitful—woman of extraordinary power.

Aeric pulled his cycle up in the alleylike street where her shop was located, a narrow cobblestone passageway only big enough for the smallest of cars. He parked his bike out front and knocked on the door. The witch answered in the guise of a maiden, a lithe young woman with long chestnut-colored hair and big blue eyes. She appeared innocent in this of her three appearances, but her eyes showed her true nature.

She leaned up against the doorway and a sly expression came over her face. "Oh, Blacksmith," she growled, giving him a head-to-toe sweep. "You are very nice on the eyes, just like they say. If you've come on personal business, the answer is yes, a thousand times, yes."

Aeric was in no mood to flirt, and even if he wasn't in a race against the clock for the life of the woman he loved, he wouldn't flirt with Priss, the Piefferburg witch. He grabbed her firmly by the upper arm and guided her inside, letting her know he was not to be swayed from his purpose.

"I need to know the location of Lars Elof Thorin Anderssen's house in the Water Wastes."

She pushed her lower lip out in a pout and pulled her arm away from him. "Well, if you're all about business . . ." She transformed into the guise she wore most of the time—the crone. Holding out a wrinkled hand, she said in a broken voice, "That will require payment."

"How much?" He got out his billfold.

"For the life of the assassin?" She put a hand to her chin and pretended to think.

He paused with the billfold in his hand. "How do you know about that?"

She cackled. "Everyone underestimates me. I know much more about what goes on in Piefferburg than anyone thinks. You wish to save Emmaline Siobhan Keara Gallagher from the amorous violence of Lars Anderssen. I know that much. For the information you need, I require five hundred dollars."

Aeric opened his wallet and counted out a thousand. Pressing the bills into her hand, he said, "Here's double to ensure you're quick and accurate. If you give me the wrong location, I'll come back here with a charmed blade. Understand?"

She raised her hands in the air, money gripped in one gnarled claw. "I understand. I have no reason to steer you wrong."

Hmm. Yes. Except that the witch liked to make chaos for the sake of chaos. She was more a sociopath than a saint.

Still, he had no choice. He was going to have to trust her.

"Okay, then steer me," he replied. "And do it soon."

She clucked her tongue at him and turned into the cluttered room. Tables lined the walls of the large area, all filled with vials, boxes, and bowls. "The information doesn't come into my mind instantaneously. I have to work a spell to divine where this man resides. It would be helpful if you had something of his." She turned and gave him a toothless, hopeful smile. "Do you?"

Aeric gritted his teeth. "No."

She turned away, waving a hand at him. "Then it will take longer."

"Just move, woman. Do it."

EMMALINE was almost naked and kneeling on the cold, hard floor of the little house. Her mind kept threatening to shut down, flipping back to her adolescence and young adulthood, and she kept fighting it tooth and nail. She couldn't lose it now. To lose it now would mean her death.

Still, kneeling there shivering in front of the man she feared most in the world, it was very, very difficult not to escape into the recesses of her mind where she could find safety, as she had so many times before. When she was younger it had been the memory of her parents—warm and alive—who had occupied that safe corner of her mind. Now it was Aeric who resided there.

The material of the beautiful gray dress ripped a little more. Lars sighed in contentment, his boots shuffling on the floor as he moved around her. He was unwrapping her like a Christmas present, though one didn't normally cut into the flesh of the gift being revealed and watch in fascination as the blood welled and trickled down its bare skin.

Emmaline squeezed her eyes shut and was grateful for her loose hair shadowing her face. She needed courage now.

"Stand," he ordered roughly, yanking her up by the arm.

"I remember you," Lars said in a low voice. "When you were first given to me to shape according to the queen's request. You rested in my hand like the finest piece of wood, so smooth, so easily malleable. It was a pleasure to take my knife to your psyche and carve you to fit the curve of my palm."

Flashes of memory flooded her mind's eye, beat against her emotions. *Lars's face, greasy and dirt streaked, not far from hers while the queen looked on. . . . The feel of cold steel against her flesh when she was punished for disobeying.*

His fingers bit into her waist and she realized she was swaying on her feet, lost in some goddamned nightmare of recollection in her head. Her hands were freed from the cuffs and he was taking his time stripping the rest of the dress off her.

Now.

Her chance was now. If she didn't take it, all would be lost.

She whimpered deep in the back of her throat and Lars laughed, confident of his mastery over her. Unfortunately, unlike her screaming with Will, this whimper was no ruse.

She squeezed her eyes shut. *Strength.* She had to find it. *Where? Where was it?*

His fingers stroked her skin and she flinched away from him. No, she couldn't dwell in the past anymore, she couldn't hide from it, and she definitely couldn't *relive* it.

This needed to stop. It was time to break the chains. *Then break Lars.*

She whirled, bringing her foot up around hard and fast. Caught in the solar plexus, he flew backward into the wall, completely taken by surprise. She lunged for one of the tables, not seeing containers of chemicals, but weapons. Selecting one at random, and hoping it would injure, she turned and threw the contents directly into Lars's face.

Lars howled, scratching at his eyes while he sprawled on the floor. She ran for the door but found it locked and without a key. Frantic, she went for the window—same thing. Swearing under her breath, she grabbed a chair and threw it, breaking the glass. She was so desperate to get away from Lars, she didn't even care about having to climb over the jagged shards that remained around the edges.

Before she could hoist herself out, Lars grabbed her around the middle and hauled her backward.

And now he was pissed.

ARMING himself with a charmed iron hatchet, small enough to fit up the sleeve of his shirt, a pair of handcuffs, and several wickedly sharp blades, Aeric got on his motorcycle and headed out toward the Water Wastes.

He eschewed taking any Shadow Guard for two reasons. The first and primary reason was that he couldn't trust any of them. He wasn't sure who held a grudge against Emmaline and who didn't, and he couldn't trust them not to lie about it when he asked them. Pick the wrong ones and they could be more a hindrance than a help. The second reason was that a hundred boots tromping on the ground near Lars's house would make Lars flee. One pair of stealthily moving boots, wielding weapons meant to take off his head without warning. . . now *that* would be effective.

Given, of course, that the monster was taking his prize back to his lair to have his disgusting way with her. If he wasn't taking her there . . . Aeric stopped that line of thought. Piefferburg was a big place. Lots of room to hide.

The trees of the Boundary Lands began to whip past him as he reached the outer limits of Piefferburg City. Beyond that stretch of woods lay the great expanse of Piefferburg itself. It more resembled Europe of old than it did the United States, as far as Aeric could tell from what he saw on television. Dotted through with small villages filled with houses of varying sizes with curved clay shingled roofs, and fae places of worship, it was all connected by farmland, narrow roads, and even smaller hamlets. Clutches of particular types of fae lived in the hills, or near the ocean, depending on their nature. The Water Wastes were sparsely populated. That was near the edge of Piefferburg that gave over dominion to the sea fae—the selkie, the anjia, the sirens, and the rest.

Accelerating as fast as his bike would go, he settled in to attempting to make a three-hour drive a three-minute one.

It was almost full dark by the time Aeric reached the edge of the Water Wastes. The witch had played with various potions and powders in a vat in one of her back rooms until she'd come forth with an approximate area.

He prayed it was accurate. He was running out of time. His only hope was that Lars wouldn't do so much damage to Emmaline that he couldn't put her back together again.

As for Lars, he had every intention of taking him completely apart. Piece by agonizing piece.

He parked his bike where the land began to give way to marsh and swamp. From there he was forced to continue on foot. Moving by the light of the moon, his boots sticking in the mucky land, it took him a good hour to find the wood and ancient cottage that the witch had described.

The moon was full tonight and the sky was clear, the silvery light shining down and bathing the world in natural magic. On any other night, it would have been beautiful.

Light flickered from inside the building, the inconstant kind made by an oil lamp or a candle. His heart rate sped up. Thank Goibhniu the witch had directed him to the right place.

Armed with as much charmed iron as he could carry, he strode up to the front door and kicked it in, his stomach clenched with worry about what he would find inside.

The place was empty, but it probably hadn't been for long. There were signs of a struggle—broken furniture, spilled bottles of chemicals, a shattered window. Obviously Lars hadn't scared all the fight out of Emmaline.

Then he spied the strips of gray silk on the floor and his breath caught in his throat. He knelt and picked one up, seeing that it was streaked with blood. Strands of her long dark hair were mixed with the scraps of her dress.

Dropping the fabric, he whirled and ran out of the house, looking for any clue as to where she might be. There wasn't much light to see by, but outside the mud showed deep indentations, maybe made by someone running.

He followed the only clue he had into a scrubby wood where the light was even dimmer due to the cover of the trees. There he looked for broken branches—anything that could help him find her.

In the distance, someone screamed.

Emmaline.

TWENTY-SEVEN

HE raced toward the sound, jumping over obstacles in his path and allowing branches to pull at his clothing and scrape his face and arms.

As he neared the source of the scream, he heard sounds of a struggle. In a nearby clearing filled with silvery moonlight he found them. Emmaline knelt in the mud, her head bowed. Her loose hair hung tangled around her face and shoulders and her dress was in tatters, revealing large swathes of her creamy skin. Her chest seemed to be heaving, as though she'd been exerting herself and was now exhausted.

Lars stood near her, his chest also heaving. Ah, so Emmaline wasn't going down without a fight. Aeric had expected as much. She was fierce and he was proud of her. He knew she wasn't going down *at all*. Over his dead body.

He moved his wrist and the head of his hatchet fell into his cupped palm, the charmed iron cool against his immune skin. One more drop and he had the handle in his hand, the blade of the hatchet gleaming sharp and ready in the moonlight.

He stepped into the clearing in the same moment that Lars made a move for Emmaline. She gave an enraged battle cry, leapt to her feet, and spun on her heel, taking Lars in the throat. He gagged and fell backward into the mud.

"Emmaline!"

She turned from her defensive position in front of Lars, spotted Aeric, and gave a sound of deep relief. He stepped toward her and she started for him. That was when Lars—whom he'd thought incapacitated—moved.

"Watch out!" he yelled, but it was too late.

Lars took her from behind, putting her in a choke hold. She gagged and her hands flew to his imprisoning arm, scratching at him as she tried to get some air.

Lars leveled a stare at Aeric. "Come any closer and I'll break her—"

Aeric threw his hatchet. It hit Lars in the head with a wet thunk. Immediately he fell backward into the mud, freeing Emmaline, who went down on her knees, her hand to her throat.

Aeric raced to help her. She rose and collapsed into his arms. Dirty, bloody—but alive. "We've been fighting, Lars and I, for the last hour at least. He's strong. *Danu*, I miss my crossbow."

"You're safe now. It's all over. He's dead."

Her knees sagged and all the breath went out of her. "It's over," she whispered. She looked down at Lars's body. "It's really over. Finally." His unseeing eyes stared up at the moon, ax blade stuck in his head. "Get me out of here. Get me as far from this place as you can."

HE took her to the birch ladies, which was the place of safety closest to them. Emmaline was exhausted—physically and especially emotionally. She'd probably been too exhausted from her battle to ride on the back of the bike, but the only other available vehicle had been Lars's truck and she'd wanted no part of that other than expressing a desire to blow it up.

So he'd bundled her onto the back and hoped like hell she'd be all right for the long ride.

Aurora let them use one of the cottages in the Boundary Lands. Aeric laid Emmaline on the bed, where she immediately closed her eyes.

"Will she be all right?" Aurora's brow furrowed with concern.

Aeric gazed at Emmaline. She had her arm curled protectively over her abdomen and was turned slightly on her side, facing away from them. Mud and blood marked her all over. "She'll be fine now. I'm going to spend the rest of my life making sure of that."

"I know you will." She smiled at him and retreated, leaving him alone with her.

While Emmaline slept, he ran a bath for her and started a dinner from the contents of the cupboards and fridge.

"I've always wanted a man who could cook."

He turned to find her behind him, wrapped in a blanket from the bed. Her hair was tangled, blood marked her chin and cheek, and a bruise was blooming on her forehead. She looked beautiful to him all the same.

She looked like his future.

He pulled her to him and she melted against his chest. His arms tightened around her and he kissed the top of her head. "I will cook for you every night for the rest of your life if you want."

She laughed, a tired and rough sound against his chest. "Sounds good to me."

He held her away from him so he could look into her eyes. "Good, because I love you, Emmaline. I want you to stay with me."

"I love you, too, Aeric. I think a part of me has loved you for the last three centuries and change."

"That's a good thing for a man's ego, you know."

She laughed again. "And you don't need any help."

He pulled her to him and kissed her forehead. "No, all I need is you."

Dear readers,
Curious where Piefferburg is located?

Visit my website for an interactive map:

www.anyabast.com

GLOSSARY

Abastor The mystic black stallion that leads the Wild Hunt.

Alahambri Language the goblins speak.

Black Tower A large building on one end of Piefferburg Square that is constructed of black quartz. This houses the Unseelie Court.

Book of Bindings Book created when the Phaendir and the fae were allied. The most complete book of spells known. Contains the spell that can break the warding around Piefferburg.

bosca fadbh Puzzle box consisting of three interlocking pieces. Once was an object owned by both the Phaendir and the fae, back when they weren't enemies. When all three pieces are united, it forms a key to unlock part of the Book of Bindings.

Boundary Lands The area where the wilding fae live.

ceantar dubh Dark district. This is the neighborhood directly abutting the Black Tower.

ceantar láir Middle district. Fae "suburbia." Also borders a mostly commercial area of downtown Piefferburg where the troop live and work.

charmed iron Iron spelled to take away a fae's magick when it touches the skin. Used in prisons as handcuffs and by the Imperial and Shadow Guards, it's illegal for the general fae population to possess it. Charmed iron weapons were a major reason the fae lost in the war against the Milesians and Phaendir in ancient Ireland.

Danu The primary goddess of the Tuatha Dé Danann, both Seelie and Unseelie. Also followed by some other fae races. Danu is accompanied by a small pantheon of lesser gods.

Furious Host Those who follow the Lord of the Wild Hunt every night to collect the souls of the fae who have died and to help ferry them to the Netherworld.

Goblin Town The area of Piefferburg where the goblins live. The goblins are a fae race that has customs that differ greatly from the other types of fae.

Goibhniu (Go-ive-nu) Celtic god of blacksmiths, brewers, and weapon makers.

Great Sweep When the Phaendir, allied with the human race, hunted down, trapped, and imprisoned all known fae and contained them in Piefferburg.

Humans for the Freedom of the Fae (HFF) An organization of humans working for equal fae rights and the dismantling of Piefferburg.

iron sickness The illness, eventually fatal, that occurs when charmed iron is pressed against the flesh of a fae for an extended period of time.

Joining Vows Ancient, magick-laced vows that twine two souls together. Not often used in modern fae society because of the commitment involved.

Jules Piefferburg Original human architect of Piefferburg. The statue honoring him in Piefferburg Square is made of charmed iron and can't be taken down, so the fae constantly dishonor it in other ways, like dressing it up disrespectfully or throwing food at it.

Labrai The god the Phaendir follow.

Netherworld Where the fae go after they die.

Old Maejian The original tongue of the fae. It's a dead language to all except those who are serious about practicing magick.

Orna The primary goddess of the goblins. Accompanied by many lesser gods.

Phaendir ("Fane-dear") A race of druids whose origins remain murky. The common belief of the fae is that their genetic line sprang from them. The Phaendir believe they've always been a separate—superior—race. Once allied with the fae, they're now mortal enemies.

Piefferburg ("Fife-er-berg") Square Large cobblestone square with a statue of Jules Piefferburg in the center and the Rose and Black Towers on either end.

Rose Tower Made of rose quartz, this building sits at one end of Piefferburg Square and houses the Seelie Court.

Seelie ("Seal-ee") Highly selective, they allow only the Tuatha Dé Danann into their ranks. Members must have a direct bloodline to the original ruling Seelie of ancient Ireland and their magick must be light and pretty.

Shadow Amulet The one who wears the amulet holds the Shadow Throne, though the amulet might reject someone without the proper bloodline. It sinks into the wearer's body, imbuing him or her with power and immortality, leaving only a tattoo on the skin to mark its physical presence.

Shadow Royal Holder of the Unseelie Throne.

Sídhe ("Shee") Another name for the Tuatha Dé Danann (Irish) fae, both Seelie and Unseelie.

Summer Ring Like the Shadow Amulet of the Unseelie Royal, this piece of jewelry imbues the wearer with great power and immortality. It also sinks into the skin, leaving only a tattoo, and may reject the wearer at will. This ring determines who holds the Seelie Throne.

Summer Royal Holder of the Seelie Throne.

trooping fae Those fae who are not a part of either court and are not wilding or water fae.

Tuatha Dé Danann ("Thoo-a-haw Day Dah-nawn") The most ancient of all races on earth, the fae. They were evolved and sophisticated when humans still lived in caves. Came to Ireland in the ancient times and overthrew the native people. The Seelie Tuatha Dé ruled the other fae races. When the Milesians (a tribe of humans in ancient Ireland) allied with the Phaendir and defeated the fae, the fae had to agree to go underground. They disappeared from all human knowledge, becoming myth.

Twyleth Teg ("Till-eg Tay") Welsh faeries. They're rare and live across the social spectrum.

Unseelie ("UN-seal-ee") A fae ruling class, they'll take anyone who comes to them with dark magick, but the true definition of an Unseelie fae is one whose magick can draw blood or kill.

water fae Those fae who live in the large water areas of Piefferburg. They stay out of the city of Piefferburg and out of court politics and life.

Watt syndrome Illness that befell all the fae races during the height of the race wars. The sickness decimated the fae population, outed them to the humans, and ultimately caused their downfall, weakening them to the point that the Phaendir could gather and trap them in Piefferburg. Some think the syndrome was biological warfare perpetrated by the Phaendir.

Wild Hunt Comprising mystic horses, hounds, and a small group of fae known as the Furious Host, led by the Lord of the Wild Hunt, the hunt gathers the souls of all the fae who have died every night and ferries them to the Netherworld.

wilding fae Nature fae. Like the water fae, they stay away from Piefferburg proper, choosing to live in the Boundary Lands.

Worshipful Observers Steadfast human supporters of the work the Phaendir does to keep the fae races separate from the rest of the world.

HE made her want to be bad, and Charlotte Bennett was never bad.

She lay on her side in bed, eyes slowly coming open, the remnants of an amazing nocturnal adventure still clinging to her mind. In adulthood her dreams had a tendency toward monotone colors and were about as interesting as the act of folding towels. This dream had been real enough to make up for a lifetime of black-and-white snorefests.

Rolling onto her back, she stared at the ceiling fan over her bed and groaned. Apparently her body was trying to tell her something. She was still tingling in places that hadn't tingled in a very long time. Considering she hadn't had sex in nine months, the reason for the dream probably wasn't all that surprising.

That man! She'd never met anyone like him in real life. That was because men like the one in her dream didn't exist. Her subconscious had probably fashioned him from bits and pieces of the heroes she'd read about in romance novels, or characters she'd seen in movies. He'd been—

The phone rang.

She closed her eyes for a moment, cursing it inwardly. Just a few more minutes cuddled under the covers, immersed in her dream would have been nice. Reality was about to steal away the clinging vestiges of the luscious, sensual experience—and the delicious man who'd given it to her. Ah, well. It couldn't be helped.

She rolled over, grabbed the phone and gave a sleep-husky, "Hello." At the same time, she groped for her glasses and shoved them on.

Pause.

Charlotte sat up a little. "Hello?"

"Charlotte? Is that you?"

"Harvey?" She sat all the way up, clingy, dreamy deliciousness now completely eradicated. Panicked by the only reason her boss would be calling on a Monday morning, she glanced out the window—daylight-bright she now noticed—and then at the clock. Shock rippled through her.

"Are you all right, Charlotte? It's—"

She smacked her forehead with her open palm. "It's ten a.m., I'm not there, and I haven't called."

"Ah . . . yes."

She threw the blankets back and bolted from the bed, her bare feet going cold on the hardwood floor. "I don't know what happened. I'm so sorry! I guess my alarm never went off. You must think I'm a total incompetent." She stared accusingly at her alarm clock, which was set to play Tchaikovsky's *1812 Overture* every morning.

She frowned. Her alarm clock had never failed her before and she never forgot to set it.

"That's okay, Charlotte. This isn't like you at all. You've never even been late, not once since you started working for us. Remarkable, really." Harvey chuckled. "So we knew you hadn't suddenly gone crazy and were sleeping off a bender or anything." Chuckle. "Or that you'd had a hot date and were—"

Charlotte gave a forced laugh and tried not to grind her teeth. "Right, yes, of course. That would be crazy."

"Of course it would. No, we just wanted to make sure you were all right. So, you're coming in?"

"Absolutely." She'd missed only two days of work in the last five years. Flu. Hand washing was so important. "I'll be there within the hour."

"Great, Charlotte. You know we're lost without you."

She smiled, warmth from the compliment suffusing her.

It didn't take her long to get dressed, throw her hair up into a clip, and dash on a minimum of makeup. She grabbed her purse and headed out the door. It was now almost ten thirty. Her in-box would be growing more unmanageable by the moment. Stupid alarm clock.

Charlotte.

She stopped with her hand on the doorknob, the low, shivery voice blowing through her like a breeze. That had been the voice of her dream man and it had come from . . . *inside her house.*

Blinking rapidly, as she did when she was nervous, she scanned the kitchen to her left and the formal living room to her right. Then she peered up the stairs to the second floor. All was calm. All was silent. The house was empty.

She gave her head a shake. "Crazy," she muttered and headed out the door.

JUST as she'd presumed, the papers on her desk had multiplied like rabbits. The problem with being a capable employee was that your boss had lots of confidence in you and that was a double-edged sword.

She paused at the entrance of her cubicle and stared at the pile of work for a moment, sighing. Then she firmly reminded herself that this was why she'd obtained her MPA from the University of Illinois, cheating herself out of a personal life while she'd done it. It was true that her position at Yancy and Tate wasn't her ultimate dream, but it was a steppingstone to the career she really wanted. Everyone had to pay their dues and she was no exception.

"Charlotte?"

She jerked a little, startled, and turned to see Harvey behind her.

"Sorry." He grinned, transforming his plain face into something close to handsome. He studied her for a moment. "You're wearing glasses."

Glancing at him, she touched the frames, readjusting it on the bridge of her nose. "I didn't want to waste time with my contacts today."

"Ah, well, glad to see you made it in."

She entered her cubicle, setting her purse onto the only free space on her desk, and sank into her chair. "Glad to be here."

"Just stopped by to remind you that we have a client meeting at one thirty."

Panic shot through her veins as she remembered. "Tricities, Inc.?"

He nodded meaningfully.

She practically lunged at her desk. She'd totally forgotten and she had so much to do! "I'll be ready, Harvey."

He smiled at her. "I know you will. I have complete confidence in you."

She spent what was left of her morning cutting through the pile of work on her desk and then, instead of taking a lunch, preparing for the meeting with Tricities.

By the time early afternoon rolled around, she felt caught up and prepared to make the presentation. Knowing she must also *look* prepared, she headed into the bathroom with her makeup bag and examined her face in the mirror.

"Ugh." The sound echoed in the empty room.

Her face seemed sickly white and gaunt. She hadn't had much time to fuss with her hair that morning and it was decidedly "pillow-styled." She undid the clip, extracted her brush, and went to work. There wasn't much she could do with the thick mass other than straighten it up and put the clip back in. That accomplished, she set her glasses aside and freshened her makeup.

Then she stood back and took a critical appraisal of her clothing. She'd thrown on a white button-down shirt, a plaid cardigan, and a pair of black pants. Frowning, she saw the top two buttons of her shirt were undone. She corrected them, put her glasses back on, and gave herself a critical head-to-toe sweep. Marginally better.

She gave her shirt one last downward tug to settle it more smoothly in place and smiled at herself in the mirror to practice for the meeting. Her face was not deathly pale, her skin was good; her teeth were great; and although her glasses hid them somewhat today, she had very nice eyes. More important, she was intelligent.

Grabbing her makeup bag from the counter, she turned to leave the bathroom.

Charlotte.

She stopped short, her entire body going cold. The voice of her dream man again. At work. In the bathroom. Oh, hell, she was going insane.

Charlotte, come to me. Images flashed through her mind. An airplane ticket, destination Protection City, Carolina. A flash of heavy, tall gates—the gates of Piefferburg, if she wasn't mistaken. She'd only ever caught glimpses of *Faemous* on TV, but she thought she recognized the gates.

With the flashing images came a nearly irresistible compulsion to leave work *right now*. Drive to the airport *right now*. Buy a ticket to Protection City *right now*. All of a sudden she *had* to get to Piefferburg, no matter what. Dropping her makeup bag onto the floor since it no longer mattered—nothing except getting to Piefferburg mattered—she went for the bathroom door. If she hurried, she could make it to Protection City by evening.

"Wait a minute!" She stopped cold with her fingers wrapped around the door handle, and then yanked her hand away, scrubbing it on her pants as though she could wipe the germs off. Ugh, she never touched door handles.

What was she doing? She couldn't leave; she had a presentation to give. Anyway, she had no reason to drop everything and fly to Protection City, Carolina. Even less reason to go to Piefferburg.

The fae? *No way.*

She wanted no part of them. Dangerous, dirty creatures. They were right where they belonged and she had no wish to consort with them. She was quite happy to live all the way across the country from that zoo and nothing was going to force her there.

Still, the compulsion lingered. She gritted her teeth and furrowed her brow, fighting it. It eased a little and she sagged against the door. What was wrong with her? It had to be the dream she'd had. It must've jarred something loose in her subconscious that she hadn't known she needed to deal with. Find the root of the problem, address it, and she'd be able to continue with her job. She just needed a little time to sit down and think, analyze the situation. Unfortunately she wasn't going to get that, not right now.

Feeling suddenly sick, she backed away from the door and leaned down to pick up her makeup bag. Just then Erica, one of her colleagues, came into the bathroom.

"Oh, my gosh, Charlotte, are you all right?" Erica breathed, her blue eyes wide. "You look like you're about to vomit."

She glanced into the mirror. Her face had taken on a distinctly greenish hue and she was covered in a light coating of sweat. Lovely. She blinked rapidly, searching for a response.

Charlotte, you cannot ignore me. Come now.

Compulsion filled her once again. The only thing that kept her from bolting for the door was her willpower. She bowed her head, closed her eyes, and grabbed the edge of the bathroom counter to stop herself from complying with the mystery man's wishes.

"Charlotte? Should I call someone? Are you all right?"

Come now.

Charlotte forced her eyes open and returned Erica's panicked stare. "Did you hear that?"

"Hear what?" Erica's frown deepened and she shook her head. "You really don't look good. You should go home, Charlotte." She entered one of the stalls.

Go home? In the middle of the day? She'd never done that in her entire life, but maybe she really was sick. She touched her forehead and found it warm and feverish.

Charlotte.

Letting go of the counter and not bothering with her makeup bag, she lunged for the door and raced all the way back to her cubicle. Her watch showed it was exactly one-twenty. Past time to get to the conference room. Scooping her papers into her arms, she raced across the office toward her destination.

CHARLOTTE LILLIAN BENNETT, COME TO ME.

Strong compulsion filled her. She fought it, but this time nothing stemmed the tide of *must*. Ten times stronger than what she'd felt in the bathroom, there was no denying this. Right outside the double doors of the conference room, she dropped all her files.

Leave. Yes, that's exactly what she should do. Harvey could give the presentation solo. She needed to get to Piefferburg right now.

The heavy wooden doors of the conference room opened and Harvey stuck his head out, surveying the mess of paper on the floor and then looking up at her. "Charlotte?"

"I need to leave. I'm so sorry, Harvey." She turned and fled.

Stopping only long enough to grab her purse, she went to her car and drove immediately to the airport. In her head shouted the refrain, *What am I doing?* Yet she was completely unable to stop herself from handing over her credit card to the clerk at the Transnational Airlines service desk for a seat on the next flight to Protection City.

The lady behind the counter looked up at her with a bland smile on her face. "Do you have any luggage to check?"

She glanced down at her side as if a suitcase had magically appeared there. "No." She had nothing with her. No extra clothing, no toiletries. She'd even left her vitamins behind, drat it all. This was obviously fae magick of some kind. The prospect terrified her almost as much as it angered her. What if she'd had a critical prescription she needed to take? What if she'd had a pet at home? Or kids!

The lady gave her the boarding pass and soon Charlotte passed through security and reached her gate. She collapsed into a chair and stared at the waiting plane, every fiber of her being straining to get on it *now* so she could get to Piefferburg *now*.

Her father would kill her if he knew what she was doing. Whether or not she was under some magickal fae mind control, her father would skin her alive. Her family had a dark and sordid history with the fae and she'd been fed stories about their treachery since she was a child. "Never consort with the fae," her father had warned her. "Stay away from Piefferburg at all costs," he'd said. "Don't be seduced by the glittering images that *Faemous* feeds the public. The fae are bad. Evil."

"The only good fae is a dead fae" had been a familiar utterance in her home.

She glowered at the airplane. She had no idea what was going on here, but once she found out, there was going to be hell to pay. Of course, that was mostly the fear talking. She knew she lacked the ability to bring hell to a fae. The weakest one was twenty times more powerful than she was.

And this man was powerful indeed.

Her mind strayed back to the dream. At the time she'd thought it had been a lucid dream, harmless. She'd played out all her fantasies with that luscious man. Now it turned out . . .

Oh, hell. The realization slammed into her.

That had never been an innocent dream and the man she'd committed all those erotic acts with was probably real. He had to be the one holding her leash at the moment, the one he was yanking so forcefully.

Her hand drifted to the collar of her shirt. The things she'd done in that dream . . .

A man swathed in the traditional attire of the Phaendir sat down across from her. Many of the magickal sect of druids wore ordinary clothing: dark suits, dress pants, polo shirts. Usually you couldn't tell a Phaendir from an ordinary man, but this one wore the heavy brown robes of a monk.

Still holding the collar of her shirt, she gave him a tentative smile, which he returned with a stern look. Almost as if to say he knew what she'd done last night.

She slid down into her chair and looked away from him.

The Phaendir were always male and most of them were big and imposing. And don't forget the powerful magick. Magick enough to keep all the fae of the world imprisoned. They deserved everyone's utmost respect and were not to be trifled with.

Except she was about to both disrespect and trifle with them.

How was she supposed to get permission to be admitted into Piefferburg? It used to be that any human could enter at their own risk, but now that Gideon Amberdoyle had become Archdirector, every human needed to be approved.

Lie.

She blinked several times. "Excuse me?"

The Phaendir looked at her sharply, his eyes narrowing. The action reminded her of a hawk that had just caught sight of a juicy mouse.

Don't say anything out loud. Speak to me in your head.

Her mind whirled for a moment. She chewed her lip. Finally, she tried it. *You're real?*

As real as you are.

Oh, God. *You're fae?*

Pause.

Do you know any human capable of long-range telepathy and dream invasion?

She went silent for a minute, processing everything and trying very hard not to freak out in front of the brother.

When you arrive in Protection City it will be very late. Stop at a store and buy a suitcase, clothes, and toiletries. Find a hotel and stay there for the night. In the morning, go to Phaendir Headquarters and ask for entry into Piefferburg.

What will I tell them?

Tell them your company is doing some work for the Piefferburg Business Council and you're coming in at their request. They need help with their accounting system and a few other issues. Tell them you'll be there for an extended period of time, two weeks at a minimum, to complete the project.

She forced herself not to react physically to his words. *Two weeks? I can't be gone from my job for two weeks. Anyway, the Phaendir will check my story and discover I'm lying.*

We've got you covered.

What was that supposed to mean? *What's going on?*

Pause.

Are you going to hurt me? There was no reply for several moments.

We have no plans to hurt you. That was not exactly a comforting answer.

I hate you with all that I am. Even in her mind, her voice shook with emotion.

Silence.

BROTHER Gideon Amberdoyle stared across his desk at Charlotte with his watery brown eyes. Slight of build and average in height, Mr. Amberdoyle was hardly the imposing figure his position might lead someone to believe him to be. In fact, he was far slighter in physical stature than the majority of his Phaendir brethren. With his thinning hair and cheap gray suit, he put Charlotte more in the mind of a car salesman than the leader of the Phaendir, the most powerful group of individuals in the world.

Still, just being in the same room with him choked her up. It was better than meeting the president. "I can't even tell you what an honor it is to meet you," she gushed at him for the third time since she'd sat down.

He smiled a little, but it was cold and his eyes flashed for a moment when he did it. Her smile went flat. Ah, so there was strength behind the unassuming visage. "You seem to be an awfully big fan of the Phaendir, Miss Bennett."

"I am. My whole family is very grateful to the Phaendir. I'm not sure my father's line would have survived if the Phaendir hadn't stepped in during the fifteen hundreds and created Piefferburg. In fact, I might not even be sitting here if you hadn't imprisoned the fae."

"Yes." He glanced at a file on his desk. "Your family has had intimate dealings with the fae throughout the centuries, not all of them very pleasant."

"None of them pleasant, according to my father and grandfather." She shuddered and looked down into her lap. "Believe me when I say I'm not looking forward to spending time among them." She hadn't lied yet, but it was coming.

The magickal compulsion lay as heavily on her will as it had since yesterday.

Brother Gideon smiled his hard little smile again and leaned toward her from behind his desk. "That's why I find your request so odd. Why would someone with a history like yours take an assignment that put her in Piefferburg City for two whole weeks? Why didn't you request that your accounting firm send someone in your place?"

The wave of compulsion was so strong that when she opened her mouth to tell Gideon the absolute truth, no words came out, only little puffs of air.

Brother Gideon's eyes narrowed.

"Sorry, I'm a little overwhelmed." She blinked a few times and smiled. "I don't like it, but it's my job and I'm looking to be promoted. I couldn't turn this assignment down, not at this point in my career. You can call my boss if you're suspicious of my intentions." She opened her purse, extracted one of her business cards and handed it to him over the desk.

She hoped he called. Her boss would tell him the truth—he had never assigned her any such special project—and she could get out of this mess somehow. Even if it meant she went to jail or the loony bin, anything was better than Piefferburg.

He took the card, stared at it for a moment and set it aside. As he moved, she noticed the thick, white mottled skin peeking from his cuffs. Scar tissue, it looked like. Charlotte knew that the most pious of the Phaendir self-flagellated. Apparently this man was really into it.

Licking his thin lips, he steepled his fingers on his desk and raised his gaze to hers. "I can see no possible ulterior motive for your entrance into Piefferburg, Miss Bennett. I'm satisfied after performing a very thorough background check that you have no sympathies with the HFF."

She gasped in genuine shock. "No, I most certainly do not."

He smiled. "That said, you must understand we need to be very careful these days. My predecessor, Brother Maddoc, allowed the fae to recover several magickal artifacts, ones that might be of use to them. It's why we checked your luggage and purse when you arrived this morning."

"Yes, I know. I read all about it in the paper. There's a possibility the fae could break the walls and run loose." A shiver went up her spine at the thought. She wasn't alone. After the news had broken there had been a run on survival supplies and weapons that could be used against the fae. The media had, of course, shamelessly hyped the hysteria.

Brother Gideon's face went hard. "No, Miss Bennett, there's no possibility that such a thing might occur. Not on my watch."

She nodded. "I believe you."

"But in order to keep it from happening, we need to analyze every entrant into Piefferburg. My predecessor's methods were too lax and people got in who shouldn't have. Our processes are not meant to offend."

"I'm not at all offended. I'm happy to see such strong controls in place."

He smiled at her and picked up the business card. "I'm glad you understand." Then he reached for the phone.

Oh, thank God.

Say this, As Labrai wills, so shall it be.

Charlotte jerked at the abrupt intrusion of her puppet master's creepy psychic link. His words were accompanied by a compulsion so strong that the phrase tumbled from her lips before she could even think about uttering them. Smiling serenely, she said, "As Labrai wills, so shall it be."

Brother Gideon paused with the phone halfway to his ear. She could hear it ringing on the other end. Her office was in Oregon, three hours behind Protection City, and had just opened. Brother Gideon almost set the receiver back into the cradle. Instead, he lifted it all the way to his ear.

Ha! Take that, puppet master. She received no reply. The magick man was probably shaking in his boots right now.

She smiled smugly as Brother Gideon connected with one of her superiors and attempted to verify her story. Any moment now and the jig would be up. Brother Gideon would—

He hung up the phone and gave her a wide smile. "Everything checks out. I hope your project in Piefferburg City is successful, Miss Bennett."

Her smile faltered.

Still under the magickal mojo, she stood smoothly and offered her hand across the desk. "Thank you very much, Mr. Amberdoyle. It was truly a pleasure to meet you."

He stood and shook her hand. "I'll walk you to the gates. Shall I order a car to meet you once you're inside? You're not dressed for a hike through the Boundary Lands and I don't advise it. It's very dangerous."

"Nor would I ever want to take one. Yes, a car to Piefferburg Square would be lovely."

They made their way out of the office, headed toward the exit. Her hands were shaking as she picked up her suitcase, packed with clothes and other items she'd bought as soon as she'd reached Protection City, and followed him. In a mere matter of minutes she would be in the one place on earth she'd never wanted to go.

"I understand you're going to the Piefferburg Mercantile Exchange, among other locales," Brother Gideon said mildly as he led her to the gates.

"Yes. They're having trouble with their accounting system and need me to consult."

"Yours is not the first company to be doing business in Piefferburg City, of course. Piefferburg has done well in creating an economy." Brother Gideon's teeth barely kept from gnashing. "And the government allows them to do it."

"Of course. Business is business, I guess, though I agree the morality is a little murky."

"Indeed."

Gravel crunched under her shoes and the wheels of her suitcase as they walked in silence for a moment. Outwardly, it was likely she appeared calm. Inwardly, she seethed. As soon as she met this man pulling her strings as if she was some marionette, she was going to let him have it. Now she understood that expression about blood boiling with rage.

The huge gates, they were already opening as Gideon and

Charlotte reached them. The hinges made a low moaning sound, a little like what she imagined the gates of hell might sound like. Her stomach churned.

Brother Gideon turned toward her and bowed a little. "Safe travels. May Labrai always be at your side."

She bowed in response, a little stiffly. "And also at yours."

"Call the front gates when you're ready to leave. Your name will be on the list of approved exiters. They'll send a car for you if you ask them."

"Thank you." She stood staring at him for a long moment. Stalling. The compulsion was pushing her toward the gates and she was resisting, but her ability to do so flagged more with every second.

Brother Gideon fidgeted, motioning at the entrance. "You're free to enter now."

She closed her eyes briefly. "So I am." The compulsion forced her to turn and walk through the gates, leaving her world behind her. The gates closed with a thump that made her jerk.

The other side of the gates looked much the same, though the trees and foliage around her seemed to have extra color—like she'd stepped into a painting in which the artist had used slightly unreal hues. She stood on a paved area with a dark brown gravel road beginning not far away that led off into what appeared to be an enchanted forest.

All she could see past the paved area, other than the road stretching away to what had to be Piefferburg City, were trees. Huge, towering, ancient trees. She'd never seen the California redwoods, but this is what she imagined they must look like. She felt dwarfed by them, and they seemed almost sentient. As though they were watching her, judging her, and found her . . . wanting.

"Miss Bennett?"

She turned to meet her first fae. Wanting nothing more than to scream and run away, she froze, staring. It was a red cap, of all things. She knew what they were because every human did. No human hadn't been told horrific campfire stories about these creatures or wondered if they lurked under beds in the dead of night when they'd been a child.

He was a hulking monster of a humanoid fae with a dark red "cap" of skin on his otherwise bald head. A swirl of black tattoos marked his massive face, swarming down one side of his neck. If she could see inside his mouth, she would see viciously pointed teeth—all the better to tear the flesh from the bones of his enemies.

Red caps needed to kill periodically to survive—luckily periodically was every few hundred years. It was also lucky that they kept their restorative murdering to their own kind in elaborate gladiator-like tournaments that all the fae turned out to see. *Faemous* was always trying to get permission from the FCC to air the tournaments and, lucky for all, the FCC always denied them.

"Please don't eat me." She snapped her mouth shut. Her sudden fear had just pushed the words she'd been thinking right out there.

The red cap guard leered at her and smiled. Oh, yes, there were the teeth. Suddenly she felt a little woozy. "You're not to my taste."

Another guard motioned with an excessively long arm toward a classy black sedan waiting at the curb. "Your car."

"Th-thank you." She walked to it and opened the back door. Peering in, she hoped nothing would make her want to pee her pants.

A man with artfully tousled, thick dark hair and a face fit for a men's magazine cover grinned charmingly at her from behind the wheel. He had dimples, a trait that gave him an innocent air that was immediately offset by the mischievous—maybe even dangerous—glint in his eyes. He was devastatingly handsome. He was not, however, the man from her dream. "I'm Niall Daegan Riordan Quinn. Get in and I'll take you where you need to be."

She paused, leaning into the car with one hand on the handle of her suitcase and the other on the door. "I'm nowhere close to where I need to be." Her voice shook with badly controlled rage. "Tell your friend to let me go back to my life."

His eyebrows rose. "You have more guts than your looks imply."

"Gee, thanks for the compliment."

He grinned again. This time it was far more irritating than it was charming. "Get in already, would you? You've got no choice but to go to Kieran and you know it."

Kieran? "Is that his name?"

"Get in and I'll tell you more."

She hesitated a moment longer, then pushed her suitcase onto the backseat and climbed in after it. No way was she sitting in front with this guy.

Once she'd closed the door, he pulled away from the curb. "Normally the goblins drive the cars to and from the gates, but we figured getting into a vehicle with one of them behind the wheel might be a little too much for you."

She shifted impatiently. "So Kieran is the"—she struggled to find the right word. She never swore, but the urge to do so now was nearly overwhelming—"jerk who did this me?"

"Whoa, nelly. That's some strong language there, girlie." Sarcasm dripped from every syllable. He chuckled . . . irritatingly. She was really starting to hate this fae.

"*Fine*. Bastard! Asshole! Dick!" she yelled at him. Her cheeks heated.

"Ah. Now that's more like what I'd expect from a woman whose had all her free will taken away." He gave a genuine laugh this time. "Still, take a tip from me. I wouldn't be calling Kieran Aindréas Cairbre Aimhrea an asshole or a dick to his face. He's got somewhat of a bad temper. Calling him a bastard is okay since he is one in the literal sense of the word." He paused as if thinking. "In the figurative sense, too."

"Will he hurt me?"

"Kieran's got a bad temper, but I've never known him to harm a woman. Still, he's holding your leash, so to speak, so it's probably wiser to keep him happy."

"What does he want from me?"

"All will be revealed once we reach the Unseelie Court."

Her spine snapped to attention and she gripped the seat in front of her, leaning toward Niall. "The *Unseelie* Court?"

He cast a look of disbelief over his shoulder. "Did you think we were going to the Rose, the tower of sunshine, lollipops, and unicorns that poop rainbows? No fae with juice dark enough to bind and compel a human all the way across the country is going to be Seelie, woman.

ALSO FROM NATIONAL BESTSELLING AUTHOR

ANYA BAST

"Sizzling suspense and sexy magic are sure to propel this hot new series onto the charts."

—*Romantic Times*

THE ELEMENTAL WITCHES SERIES

WITCH FIRE

WITCH BLOOD

WITCH HEART

WITCH FURY

PRAISE FOR THE AUTHOR

"Deliciously sexy and intriguingly original."

—*New York Times* bestselling author Angela Knight

"Fast-paced, edgy suspense."

—*ParaNormal Romance Reviews*

"Anya Bast tells a really passionate story and leaves you wanting more."

—*The Romance Readers Connection*